Some plans are best laid in secret

"There may be no good time for such things," Victoria's father said. "I'm afraid I have terrible news, Victoria. It's about your wedding."

"What's happened, Father? I do hope Wilfred is well."

"My dear, that word can have many meanings," he said, his mouth and eyebrows deepening into a scowl that lifted Victoria's heart. "He is well finished with polite society. That means he's well finished with any daughter of mine."

"Is there no hope?" her mother said, tears standing in her eyes. "No salvation?"

"None. An inspector will likely be round to ask whether we have anything to contribute to the investigation. I told him we had no secrets of Mr. Abernathy's or our own to keep. I am sorry, Victoria. Other suitable arrangements will be made, I can assure you of that."

"Yes, Father," Victoria said, her voice and face reflecting her mother's heartbreak perfectly. "I'll speak to the inspector if it will help. I trust it will all work out for the best in the end."

Victoria stood, holding her napkin to her face to hide her smile, and walked quickly out of the room.

Independent by Means of Magic

The Odd Society

Copyright © 2020 by Kari A. Kilgore

All rights reserved

Published 2020 by Spiral Publishing, Ltd.
www.SpiralPublishing.net

Book and cover design copyright © 2020 by Spiral Publishing, Ltd.

Cover art copyright © 2020 by BigAlBaloo | depositphotos.com

ISBN-13: 978-1-948890-65-6
Digital ISBN-13: 978-1-63992-049-5
Large Print ISBN-13: 978-1-948890-66-3
Hardcover ISBN-13: 978-1-948890-67-0

*For the deity of writing who put the words
Clockwork Voodoo into my head one night while I slept.*

Thank you!

INDEPENDENT BY MEANS OF MAGIC

THE ODD SOCIETY

KARI KILGORE

SPIRAL PUBLISHING, LTD.

CHAPTER 1

Victoria Jade Haversham, a perfect vision of a proper English girl who took care to appear so, sat in the highest room in her father's house. Sweat trickled down her neck even with her thick brunette curls piled carelessly on top of her head.

Most people in London would consider the third floor dreadfully hot this time of year, and Victoria admitted it was unusually warm even for summer in such a dreary place. She preferred the heat, though, and the quiet and solitude suited her far better than the cooler lower levels.

The wavy, leaded glass windows were both open, and the breeze helped. In frigid February, the light, spring-green tea gown Victoria wore would be intolerable even with a heavy overcoat.

Not so many years ago in this supposedly forward-thinking city, she would have been obligated to drape and obscure herself in layers of silk and absurd sleeves that puffed up to her ears and cinched at her wrist.

In the heat of August, the delicate, airy layers of a modern tea dress worn without a crushing corset freed her from one of the burdens of womanhood in a still burdensome life.

The small room was made even smaller by a false wall a few feet behind the girl, one that she and Jaji, her beloved nanny, had put in years before. Neither Victoria, her mother, nor Jaji had been in favor of the trip from Mr. Haversham's Caribbean plantation back to England.

His business interests—and his simple authority, uncontested at the time—overrode all with not so much as a discussion.

The privacy screen Jaji required in her room now suited Victoria's own needs perfectly. Anyone passing by in the hallway would see the same textured and tasteful wallpaper that covered the rest of this level. Magic older than words took care of troublesome memories or suspicions.

In a sharp contrast to the tidy bedroom on the far side—much smaller than her own bedroom on the second floor below—the space Victoria occupied whenever she could was a crowded workspace. If she'd only had more room, things wouldn't look so jammed in and chaotic.

The truth was Victoria knew where every single thing was and what it was for. She'd created nothing less than a miniature factory for herself, one only she knew about.

The walls held several shelves sitting in front of that same flowery wallpaper, most of them full of tiny clockwork figures. Teapots that appeared to pour themselves into cups that in turn waddled forward to deliver the tea without help. Common and exotic animals, from cats to giraffes to birds to ornamental carp with legs to lions that roared in miniature.

Small men and women who could dance together, fight with each other. Pretend to murder one another, or strike altogether shocking and scandalous poses.

Victoria didn't build these herself, though she certainly could have. This part of her operation was best left to an anonymous factory. It simply would not do to have her handiwork traced back to this house. She ordered the ordinary little toys from cramped and hideous factories in London, same as everyone else did.

By the time the clockwork trinkets left her workshop and found their way to their intended owners, they were anything but ordinary.

Victoria adjusted her magnifying glasses, an incredibly helpful gift from a watchmaker her father knew, and pushed a long metal pick into the exaggerated bowtie that matched the black tuxedo on a clearly male penguin. With just the right amount of pressure, the head popped up, and Victoria caught it before it could fall.

Trying to repair or conceal nicks in the paint was far too much trouble when she was in a hurry. Her velvet jewelers cloth over the rough wooden table helped, but if the pieces fell onto the uncarpeted floor, the damage would be unavoidable.

She angled the pick inside, toward the back of the penguin, shifting until she felt a click. A bit of downward pressure had the entire toy in pieces in her hand. The front and back of the body fell away, the wings slipped to the side, and the exposed gears glinted in the bright sunlight.

Victoria smiled. Plenty of open space inside of this one. Just what she needed.

A different sized gear here, a small adjustment there, and

the penguin suited her purposes. The original designer likely wouldn't notice the difference, and neither would the horrible man Victoria's father had promised her to.

Skill, careful planning, and a bit of old, dark magic would do the rest.

Several small, irregular pottery jars, brought carefully padded on the long return voyage from the Caribbean several years ago when Victoria was just thirteen, lined two of the shelves just to her left. Nothing in the entire house full of treasures from England and abroad, nothing in the entire world meant as much to Victoria as these jars and what they held.

She pulled out the primitive cork stopper on the orange and green and brown streaked vessel closest to her. Larger than the rest, the size and weight of a small melon, the middle curved inward to perfectly fit into Victoria's hands. She'd carefully formed and fired it for this purpose, her own salty tears creating streaks and smudges in the rings of color, the resulting imperfection sealing their beauty and power.

"Jaji," she whispered, "Hear me now. My love is deep, and my need is strong."

Victoria used a tiny silver spoon, smaller than her smallest fingernail, to scoop out a bit of the gray, irregular ashes in the jar. That amount fit perfectly into a dainty tan muslin bag, small enough that pulling one thread closed it. She picked up the penguin, reassembled except for the head, and hung the bag inside. A practiced twist and snap set everything right.

For the last most powerful touch, Victoria held the toy to her lips for a few seconds, delicate brow wrinkled in concentration.

"Go out from here and do my bidding."

She set to work on an identical penguin, this one with long, painted black hair and a girlish flowered dress.

CHAPTER 2

THREE DAYS LATER, in a grand, countryside estate house a few miles away, a portly, middle-aged man collected the post from his private courier. He had taken this duty upon himself as a newly married man nearly twenty-five years ago. He saw no reason to change with adult children and a young fiancé soon to join him.

A man's business was a man's business, no matter who passed into and out of his life.

Wilfred Abernathy carefully placed the armful of letters, bundles, and packages on his gleaming mahogany desk. The huge desk sat in the middle of his study, surrounded by floor to ceiling shelves, some open, some locked and fronted with glass. Hundreds of books and dozens of treasures from home and abroad were tastefully arranged throughout the room.

He unbuttoned his restrictive top coat as he sat, swallowed his customary afternoon snifter full of fine apple brandy, and smoothed his fringe of gray hair.

The estate had been missing a woman's touch for far too long now. Servants kept the grounds and house immaculate, of course, but only a lady of the manor could fulfill certain duties. Women delighted in dinner parties and social engagements, and even more in arranging beautiful things around the home. His first wife Maria had excelled at all of those things.

Another thing Maria had excelled at was producing strong, healthy children.

Three lovely daughters and four sturdy boys. Sadly for all of them, and for Wilfred too, of course, Maria had not survived her last pregnancy. Neither had the baby. Several highly recommended nannies had been unable to fill the void left by her passing, not the way a new wife would.

He hoped this young Victoria would be able to take so many things on, and as successfully.

Wilfred shook his head, realizing he'd been staring out the window, daydreaming of more sons to carry on his legacy. And of the most pleasant marital activity required to make them. He turned his attention to the package on top of the pile.

The light blue box, small enough to fit in the palm of his hand, came from an address he didn't recognize. *G. Smith, London.* The pink ribbons parted under Wilfred's post knife, and a card slipped out onto his desk. *Warmest congratulations on your engagement. G.*

Puzzled but more intrigued than he wanted to admit, he pulled the rest of the paper away and slid the knife under the top of the box. A tiny clockwork penguin stared back at him. Wilfred grunted and tipped it into his hand. He sat it on the desk for a moment, turning it from one side to the other. The means of operation was unclear, but he was certain it was supposed to do something.

He was about to call in his second son, fourteen years old and obsessed with all things clockwork, when he spotted a tiny switch hidden under the penguin's left wing. He used the tip of the knife to depress the switch, then put the penguin down on his desk.

At first nothing seemed to happen, but before Wilfred could pick up the toy and start over, it hitched and shuddered into life. The wings flapped at its side, and the comical yellow feet moved it forward. The toy walked to and fro across the desk, moving in an odd, spiral pattern Wilfred felt he was almost able to grasp.

This mystery gift was charming no matter who had sent it.

Smiling, he leaned in closer to get a better look.

The penguin turned to face the man, and a tiny burst of steam floated out. Wilfred sat back in his chair and folded his hands across his middle.

Anyone watching would have seen his eyes roll back to white and wondered why he was muttering under his breath.

The clockwork toy was still the whole time, but it seemed to be staring at Wilfred. Something in the tiny, painted black eyes had transformed since he started it up. It never crossed his mind to make an effort to find out what.

In fact, Wilfred's mind was incapable of being crossed.

After several minutes, the toy gradually bent forward, hinging at the division between its belly and legs. Finally it settled back and sat on the desktop, appearing for all the world to be in desperate need of a nap. Wilfred stared at it, then got to his feet. He called sharply to his head butler as he walked through to the front door of the house.

Cheryl Mallory.

He *had* to see Cheryl, the second nanny who'd tried to work with him and his children. She hadn't left because of incompetence or theft or any of the other reasons that had turned this estate into a revolving door for help. Cheryl had been called back to care for her own elderly grandmother up in Highgate, London.

Wilfred had been fond of Cheryl, but only as fond as of his own sister.

He didn't feel that way anymore.

Seeing her wavy blonde hair and soft green eyes was an imperative now, one he could not resist or deny. Seeing her young, fertile body sprawled across his bed, her skin flushed with pleasure, was suddenly more important to Wilfred than drawing his next breath.

The face of his fiancé, her name, and her father's name had entirely left his mind, obliterated by the mad heat of his desire.

When he did remember them in a few weeks, the recollection would not be kind.

IN A RESPECTABLE, long-established home in Mayfair, far removed from the smoke and soot and foul smells of the lesser parts of London, a young, beautiful woman named Cheryl opened a tiny pale blue package.

A clockwork penguin peered up at her.

CHAPTER 3

Metropolitan Police Inspector Rob McDuff stood in the middle of a crowded, overly-decorated teenaged girl's room, far larger than his own humble home and half that of his family's house far to the north in Scotland. Not familiar space or circumstances to him at all.

That was a good thing, though.

If he had to look at everything, he would miss nothing.

The late afternoon sun flooded the space with light, giving him a perfect opportunity to examine every curio, overstuffed pillow, and overly expensive painting on the walls.

McDuff had rather impolitely closed the door on Mr. and Mrs. Mallory several minutes ago. He could hear them stalking up and down the obscenely expensive carpet in the hall outside, no doubt wringing their hands and debating whether they should knock or not.

No doubt horribly distressed at his cheap black jacket, vest, and trousers, built for durability and easy cleaning rather than the excesses of fashion. Nothing but sackcloth compared to the Mallorys' perfectly tailored and generously decorated attire, soon to be discarded for even more fussy and elaborate dinner clothing.

Besides needing a break from the trappings of wealth, self-righteous chatter, and amateur theorizing, McDuff had to remove himself before he backhanded one or both of them.

Mr. Mallory with his reeking pipe and aggressive mustache was full of suggestions about how to punish a man for a crime he had not yet been convicted of. Even if the case could be proven, McDuff thought charging someone with destroying the virtue of a willing participant was the height of absurdity.

Real crimes, serious crimes, happened every minute of every day all around them, and he was stuck wasting time with this.

Mrs. Mallory, on the other hand, seemed to believe her daughter may as well have been a victim of one of those serious crimes. She'd stopped just short of saying that would definitely be less scandalous and far less disappointing for the entire Mallory family.

McDuff grimaced at a stab of memory: his younger brother lying bleeding and beaten in a jail cell.

That was what real trouble looked like. The damage of too many bad choices.

He was sure this girl's mother—with her bejeweled fingers and elaborately arranged hair that towered over everyone else—would honestly prefer to see her daughter half-dead from a beating rather than in such disgrace. Half-dead in hospital, poisoned by unknown means, didn't satisfy the woman's need for revenge.

That way Mrs. Mallory would never have to accept that the girl might have enjoyed herself before everything went wrong.

McDuff walked along the edges of the room, gathering his initial impressions. She had more books than he did, not that such a feat was terribly hard to accomplish. He lived the life of a monk when he wasn't working, though monks likely had better accommodations.

Cheryl didn't have childish story books, though. She had weighty volumes about philosophy, religion, history, even natural science.

This young woman was too smart and too well-educated to have fallen for old Mr. Abernathy and his dubious charms. The prospect of marriage wasn't even certain, with him engaged to another young girl.

McDuff made a mental note to interview the fiancé as soon as he could.

A dainty wooden desk sat in front of the window, with a pink skirt that matched the pink pillow embroidered with yellow flowers on the chair. He didn't hesitate to open the drawers and look around. In the back of the smallest waited a forever half-finished correspondence with Mr. Abernathy. McDuff slipped it into his case, but he didn't bother reading it. His assistant could wade through the lovesick ramblings of a seventeen-year-old.

His brother had been fifteen when he went down the first time, nineteen the last. Excuses of the age hadn't changed in the years since.

He stopped in the center of the room and turned in a slow circle, eyes half closed. A meticulous catalog of the whole space, what some of his colleagues who'd been formally trained for police work would have wanted, was just as much a waste of time here as in every other crime scene.

McDuff had been at this long enough to know it was what you overlooked, what you assumed didn't matter, that proved essential. He hadn't needed years of expensive training to understand that.

The investigative engine between his ears understood without being told.

He stopped, scowling at the desk again. This girl had several expensive trinkets scattered about the room, but what sat in front of a little blue box didn't fit in with all the others. Frills and hearts did not naturally lead to a tiny clockwork penguin, even one with a skirt.

That had to have come from somewhere else.

McDuff turned the box over, but found only the address of the house he was standing in. He nearly missed the blue card, small enough to be dwarfed by the palm of his hand. A generic *London* and name, *J. Smith,* in oddly made but textbook-neat handwriting. That could lead anywhere, or more likely nowhere.

He slipped the note into his case, not sure why, but not about to ignore that familiar flutter of warmth in his gut. He had no doubt the box would be in his care within moments.

He slowly walked across the room and opened the door.

"What have you found?" Mrs. Mallory said in a whispery voice, nearly drowned out by her husband's bluff and bluster about closing a door against him in his own home as he charged through.

"Either of you know where your daughter might have got that clockwork penguin?" McDuff said, his eyes and attention on the notes he was writing.

"I… No, never saw it until just this second," Mr. Mallory said, hands on his hips and chest thrust out. "Where did you find it?"

McDuff waved his hand toward the desk.

"Where it sits."

He didn't have the time to waste on coddling or discussion. He had to get to Cheryl Mallory's hospital before night fell and she slept. If he left right now, he had a good chance of being able to visit Mr. Abernathy, her disgraced former lover, along the way.

Mrs. Mallory sank down onto the narrow bed, one hand covering her eyes. Her husband followed close on McDuff's heels, the blue box clutched in his hand.

"I trust you're going to trace this thing back to where it came from?" he said, plump cheeks glowing. "And take it out of here if it came from that murdering bastard. I'm not paying you bloody good money above and beyond whatever the city pays to leave evidence scattered around my house."

"It most likely came from a factory in London," McDuff said, lifting his coat from a hook by the door. He took the box and dropped it into his case. "Just like hundreds of them do every day. The question may be who sent it to her. And why. If you have any information about that, get in touch right away. Good day."

He closed the door and stood for a second, half hoping the

man would charge into the evening after him. The only thing he despised more than cases like this—with promise of an off-the-books bounty far too rich to pass up—was the man rich enough to offer it.

When no such pleasures pursued him, Rob McDuff walked away.

CHAPTER 4

A month later, Victoria sat waiting for her father to make his appearance for dinner. Her mother sat across from her at the long, mostly empty table set with the necessary silverware, embroidered napkins, and required crystal glassware for fifteen. Several ornate vases made of engraved silver or fine painted china held sweet-scented pink and red and yellow flowers from the greenhouse, presented for guests who wouldn't be in attendance.

Each and every piece would be inspected daily, cleaned if necessary, and rearranged. None of it would be removed to the expertly crafted heavy oak cabinets that lined the walls, all far too cumbersome to have made the trip to the colonies before Victoria was born.

After years of waiting in this echoing room, abandoned and unused, they now waited, perpetually missing much of their contents for no good reason.

Victoria had never understood why this peculiar pointless

ritual of keeping the table set for no one brought her mother comfort, since she'd never insisted on such nonsense before returning to London.

No more than she understood her mother's need to regale her with a vivid, detailed description of her day.

The shopping she'd done with the cook that morning, the intricate preparations for the meal they'd be enjoying soon, the lovely things she'd bought but hadn't had a chance to display yet, even the correspondence she'd spent her entire afternoon catching up.

Judging by the elaborate loops and curls of her mother's dark blonde hair, piled high all over the top of her head, she'd insisted on having it restyled after wandering the markets wearing the expected broad hat for modesty. Same with the close-fitting sunshine yellow gown covered with sky blue accents. Even with barely-puffed sleeves covering her shoulder and halfway down her arm rather than too-youthful bare skin, she would have never been out shopping in such an outfit.

Victoria half-listened to the enthusiastic retelling, nodding, thinking all over again that she'd never manage the life her mother led. No matter how many times it was carefully described to her.

Certainly not if it involved Wilfred Abernathy and carrying his vile children one after the other as long as she lived.

The thought of the procedure involved in making those children, with him at least, twisted her entire body into knots. She didn't wonder why his first wife hadn't survived long.

In conscious contrast to her mother, Victoria wore another pleasantly modern tea gown, the same brilliant blue one she'd put on that morning. The fragile fabric didn't suit her nearly as well as the sturdy cotton she'd lived in before they left the Caribbean, when she never would have considered anything as restrictive as even the small corset she knew her mother wore. But she cherished her ability to breathe freely and move as much as possible within the confines of English society.

"There you are, dear," her mother said, stopping her ceaseless monologue and brightening immediately. Victoria's father strode into the dining room, cheeks flushed and thick hair a mess. "What have you gotten yourself into?"

"I don't believe it's suitable dinner conversation," he said, sitting down and blotting his face with a spotless white cloth napkin. He'd loosened his knotted ascot tie and shed his jacket, leaving only a dark gray vest over his white shirt. "Time enough for unpleasant things later. How are my two favorite girls today?"

While her mother launched into a replay of her activities, adjusted for manly interests, Victoria took care to hide her excitement. The timing was just about right if things had gone according to her plan, and she couldn't imagine why they wouldn't have.

She'd never failed, not when she followed Jaji's teaching and used her own considerable intelligence and planning.

She pretended interest again, managing not to grit her teeth in frustration at having to wait. At last, after five courses and coffee with pudding, her father folded his napkin and leaned back in his chair.

"After dinner may be no better than before," he said, his voice low and somber. "There may be no good time for such things. I'm afraid I have terrible news, Victoria. It's about your wedding."

Her mother's hand flew to her heart, and she stared at her daughter with wide eyes. Victoria took a deep, slow breath, settling her mind and nerves for her performance.

"What's happened, Father? I do hope Wilfred is well."

"My dear, that word can have many meanings," he said, his mouth and eyebrows deepening into a scowl that lifted Victoria's heart. "He is well finished with polite society. That means he's well finished with any daughter of mine."

"Is there no hope?" her mother said, tears standing in her eyes. "No salvation?"

"None." Her father nodded once, then pushed his chair back and stood. End of conversation, and no more questions asked or answered. "An inspector will likely be round to ask whether we have anything to contribute to the investigation. I told him we had no secrets of Mr. Abernathy's or our own to keep. I am sorry, Victoria. Other suitable arrangements will be made, I can assure you of that."

"Yes, Father," Victoria said, her voice and face reflecting her mother's heartbreak perfectly. "I will speak to the inspector if it will help. I trust it will all work out for the best in the end."

Victoria stood, holding her napkin to her face to hide her smile, and walked quickly out of the room. Before she turned the corner to the dark wooden staircase, she heard her father trying to comfort her sobbing mother.

"Shouldn't have let him barter me off to the highest bidder, Mother," she said under her breath. "And you should *never* have let him bring us back to this awful place."

She climbed the stairs, feet silent on flowery carpet trapped under brass bars. Her face and arms started to sweat before she made it halfway up the second flight of stairs, but Victoria took comfort in the warmth, so rare throughout most of the year.

Her mind and body had grown and grown up for weather far away from here, in the land of her birth. She had no wish to ever adapt to this dank island.

Victoria had no reason to suspect anyone had been in her private chamber, but she inspected the space out of habit. The small flower vase on a shelf outside the door held a touch of Jaji's magic along with that of her beloved Caribbean island home of Enceleas. The huge pink dahlia seemed like a perfect touch to reflect her elation. Just inside the room, several small containers on shelves close to the window not blocked by the false wall held the same protective charms.

Just as when Jaji still lived in this room, anyone passing by would feel profoundly disinterested. That was a potion and spell Victoria could set in her sleep.

She often wondered if she did inadvertently send out magic in her unconscious state. Perhaps her problems with Wilfred Abernathy could have been solved while she slumbered by his side.

Cheered by that prospect, even at such a high cost of intimacy with a man she found repulsive, she moved a floor-to-ceiling bookshelf aside. The perfectly balanced bearings helped, as did the hollowed-out books.

With her latest crisis averted, Victoria needed to take a long-overdue inventory. Having her supplies run low with her father scheming anew on her pre-meditated marital bliss would not do. She retrieved a pad of paper from a high shelf, sat at her desk, and twisted her hair into a loose bun. If she couldn't cut the horrid mop, she could at least keep it off of her neck when she was alone.

The most important thing, Jaji's ashes, was the one item she didn't have to weigh or measure. Such a treasure was constantly in Victoria's mind, and every tiny pinch she used mentally recorded. She noted the use for those last two clockwork toys in her careful, neat handwriting.

For less potent spells, she could use the sacred soil of the ancestors Jaji had brought with her on that long and terrible voyage. For now, she had enough for years of more potent work should she need it.

Victoria smiled, remembering her wonder as her beloved nanny told her what was in those jars, years ago when she was a far happier child still living on her father's vast and beautiful plantation.

She hadn't been able to get her mind around all those people, all those bones.

She might never have learned what all she could get her mind around if her father hadn't forced all of them to leave and return here.

She counted the various toys on her shelves, making sure she didn't have too many of the same kind. Victoria doubted anyone on this whole blasted island would understand what to even look for, but arousing suspicion by being careless was a risk she would not take.

She'd learned that by watching her father in his business and personal dealings, and even more as Jaji started Victoria's true education once they were settled in this drafty old house.

Victoria at first thought her nanny—grey-haired and slow-moving after being forced away from her own home and family

—was only pretending when she told the young girl about the magic and spells she'd brought with her from Enceleas. She understood now better than she'd ever wanted to about having no say over her own life.

If Jaji was powerless to stop it when Mr. Haversham decreed she was to live in this world so far away from her home, she'd damn sure control the bits that she could. And she'd damn sure teach Victoria to do the same.

Victoria carefully arranged the tiny tools of her secretive trade, making sure every one was in good repair. Both she and Jaji learned from Mrs. Haversham's example of how powerless and weak women could be in the great advanced and enlightened and ever-so-superior English society.

Her mother had wept and begged to stay in the Caribbean, to raise their daughter and eventually grandchildren in the open, healthy air of the Enceleas plantation, not in the smog and congestion of London. Victoria hadn't inherited her mother's weak lungs and various breathing problems, but Mrs. Haversham still seemed to live in terror that she would.

Her own health was far more sturdy and vibrant in the warmer, cleaner air, and she was certain her daughter's would be as well.

A particularly emotional quarrel Victoria still regretted overhearing concerned the fact that Mrs. Haversham had only been able to endure carrying one precious child to term, and that only far from the damp, chilly environs of London. Surely leaving the land of that miracle behind would prove dangerous to them all.

Mr. Haversham would have none of it, and by the end he no longer made any attempt to soften the blow with kind and gentle words, or fanciful promises of their future lives in the north.

His business interests required his return to England. He required his family to return with him.

Therefore they would, and the matter was settled.

He'd shown no more compassion for far more measured requests and later quiet pleading from Victoria's Jaji and her large, extended family. Mrs. Haversham's health deteriorated noticeably as the date for their return grew ever nearer. She was obviously in no condition to raise a wild young girl and train her in the ways of polite society on her own.

The nanny's services were required. Therefore she would leave her home so she could continue to perform them.

Victoria's hands paused in her inventory and note taking, her eyes on the curved form of the jar of ashes worth more to her than all the treasure in all the world.

She caught a tear before it could fall and mar her neat handwriting, then touched the glistening drop to the cork stopper. The moisture disappeared. Absorbed and mingled with the magic within.

Thus connected to her beloved nanny—the true parent to the young woman she'd become—Victoria continued with plans for a future of her own making.

CHAPTER 5

The Park Lane neighborhood wasn't nearly as opulent as the Mallorys' in Mayfair, but Mr. Haversham's study was nearly a mirror image. McDuff wondered if he was keeping his disdain to himself as he mentally catalogued the shelves packed full of exotic souvenirs and keepsakes from the man's world travels. The unfortunate Cheryl Mallory with her girlish fluff and clutter had a far more serious collection of books than this adult man.

Nothing in the collection or the carved wooden desk or the thick-cushioned leather chairs or even an incongruous little brass vase with a spray of sweet-scented blue flowers that cut through the air of tobacco and wealth had anything to offer McDuff's investigation.

He doubted the man who enjoyed spending time here would add anything of value. This entire detour would likely bring him only time wasted that could have been spent on useful pursuits.

Haversham even kept silly clockwork toys too modern to have been from his or even his daughter's childhood. So much money wasted on baubles. Money that could have done so much good to help real, suffering people.

"Please, Inspector, do have a seat," Mr. Haversham said, walking in and bustling about like a nervous hen. "What will you have to drink?"

"I'm fine, thank you, unless you're getting something for yourself."

Mr. Haversham stopped, hands on the dark wood and elaborately carved back of his desk chair. His brown hair lay smooth where it remained on his head, but McDuff had the distinct impression he wanted very much to run his fingers though it.

"I'll tell you the truth, Inspector," he said, then sighed heavily. "I was thinking of rum myself, even before you arrived. This has been a difficult business. Terribly upsetting to all of us."

"In that case, I'll join you," McDuff said, allowing himself a small smile.

He watched as the older man visibly relaxed, calmed by his own routine of fetching sparkling glasses with deep, twisting grooves and a cut glass bottle filled with dark amber liquid.

For the first time, McDuff hoped one of the people involved in this whole mess spared no expense.

"Here you go. Our own brand. I hope you'll find the time and attention to detail as worthwhile as I do." Mr. Haversham handed the glass over with a quick nod. He walked back around the desk, unbuttoned his black jacket to reveal a blue paisley-patterned vest, and sat heavily before he held up the glass. "To swift resolution of an unpleasant situation."

"Indeed," McDuff said, then sipped his drink.

His estimation of the soft, overly pampered man across from him rose a good bit. Fine, expensive alcohol freely shared had that effect on him. The rum was rich and surprisingly smooth, with a lingering touch of sweet molasses.

"Now, how can I help, Inspector? I'm ashamed to admit I didn't know the man particularly well, and apparently I misjudged him quite badly as a suitable match for my daughter."

"Such things are challenging at the best of times. How did you meet Mr. Abernathy?"

"We did business together a few times, before I went to the Caribbean and after I returned. He always seemed a decent sort."

McDuff knew something so common knowledge as to be boring among people like this could give him the essential clue. He had little to no knowledge or understanding of the colonies, or expectation that colonial matters would ever affect his small life in London.

But hesitating to ask obvious questions had never done him any favors.

"What took you to the Caribbean?"

Mr. Haversham shrugged. "I own a plantation island there, one that needed direct oversight to get it through challenging times with the local population well enough to trust to a manager. Sugar, a bit of tobacco for personal use. Our rum distillery as a most pleasant added bonus. We lived there for almost twenty-five years, finally making use of the grand manor house that had been in my family for generations but useless to me for too long. I rather think my wife and daughter preferred it to this place, but duty called."

"Anyone there or here want to do your family harm? Likely to want to stir up trouble this bad?"

Mr. Haversham put his elbow on the desk, head in his hand.

"I'm certain there are, Inspector. That seems to go along with the territory in this line of work, especially with unrest in the older colonies that I prefer to keep my family away from. I can't imagine why one of them would go after my daughter's fiancé in such a cowardly manner."

"Still, it might help if I had their information available," McDuff said. "If I make a connection between Mr. Abernathy and one of your other colleagues, that could give us the pieces we're missing. And possibly warn of who to keep your daughter and wife away from."

Mr. Haversham leaned over and pulled out a floor-level desk drawer. When he sat back he had a thick stack of white calling cards clutched in his hand.

"I'm glad to cooperate in every possible manner if I can help bring this nightmare to an end."

McDuff took the stack and flipped through them. He'd heard the absurd rules and customs about these things, but he'd never seen reason to worry about it for himself. Most as large as playing cards, some smaller, all nothing more than stiff white paper with names on them. Several had writing on the back or a certain corner turned down.

The clever little markers of more games for people with too much time to waste.

He recognized many of the names, and some of them hadn't ever been suspected of a crime. They were merely men who moved in Mr. Haversham's circle, far too wealthy to ever stop fighting to earn more. A festering drain on society to be sure—despite their imported goods—but one that would come in handy in trying to track down whoever did this.

"May I keep these long enough to copy?" McDuff said.

"Certainly. I have notes on the cards, but I can tell you anything you need to know about every person."

"Thank you, I'll let you know," McDuff said, dropping the cards into his scuffed brown leather case. "I'll return them by courier as soon as possible."

Several minutes later, McDuff knew the cards were by far the most useful thing he'd get from Mr. Haversham. His family's acquaintance with Mr. Abernathy had been brief, and designed to serve the simple purpose of marrying off and marrying well.

Mr. Haversham simply didn't know what had happened to his disgraced near-son-in-law, nor why.

Mr. Abernathy in his unusually posh jail cell had been no better, too shocked and frightened to speak much. McDuff would have almost bet that man didn't understand what had happened himself, as if someone had borrowed his brain and body for a few weeks.

Long enough to get a young girl who was not his fiancé pregnant, anyway.

McDuff stood as Mr. Haversham continued prattling on about his other wealthy colleagues, walking around the study, watching for details much like he had in that unfortunate girl's room. He didn't have much else to go on, so it was worth taking every chance he had to learn more.

"I'd like to speak to your daughter if that's acceptable to you," he said. "She may remember something strange from her own limited time with Mr. Abernathy."

"Certainly." Haversham got slowly to his feet. "Victoria is a remarkably sensible and mature young woman. We made certain she received a top-rate education here in London, right through college. Sometimes I suspect she may be more intelligent than I. I've already spoken with her to let her know to expect you."

"I'm sure that will be a great help to me, Mr. Haversham," McDuff said, the fake smile on his face hiding his true feelings.

The great fool had likely ruined any chance he had of getting honest information out of the girl with his ill-advised warning. No matter.

Despite Mr. Haversham's carrying on about his daughter's great intelligence, McDuff doubted anyone in this house knew much that went on outside their own expensive wallpaper.

CHAPTER 6

McDuff followed a brooding Mr. Haversham down the hall, his eyes constantly moving over the paintings, furniture, and collections that covered every space in the huge house. These weren't people he understood, and on a basic level, he had no desire to.

He just wanted to get this over with so he could get out and breathe some fresh air not quite so tainted with money and the desperate, endless pursuit of it.

Before they turned the last corner, he smelled something even more enticing than the clean, Scottish air he'd been craving. Sweet, but clear and natural, not a heavy artificial perfume that too many women and men alike wore these days.

A young woman waited for them in the shadows at the entry hall. The purple and red nosegay attached to her collar seemed too small to account for such a lovely aroma, but nothing else made sense.

"Inspector McDuff, this is my daughter, Victoria Haversham," Mr. Haversham said, pride obvious in his voice. "She's been such a wonderful help to me over the past couple of years with the business. I know she'll be able to answer your questions."

"Mr. McDuff, such a pleasure to meet you," Victoria said, offering McDuff her hand.

Her grip was surprisingly strong for a small woman who stood not much taller than his shoulder, even more so than her father's. Mr. Haversham already turned back toward his sitting room, ponderous steps carrying him away from a situation he clearly loathed dealing with.

"Good day to you, Miss Haversham. I'm Inspector Rob McDuff with the Metropolitan Police. Sorry to have interrupted your day for such an unpleasant business."

He wasn't quite sure what he'd been expecting beyond the typical empty-headed useless child of wealth. But when Victoria stepped forward into better light, he saw she had none of that air about her. She seemed more studious than frivolous.

Her heavy, dark brown hair fell well past her waist, and her skin was clear and perfect. She wore a pale yellow gown that was well-made, but far more classic than stylish. Fitted to the curves of her body rather than hanging loose in the modern style, but not corseted or tight enough to raise a scandal.

Her dark blue eyes met his gaze with no hesitation or shyness, as if she didn't have a thing on God's green earth to hide. He somehow felt in that brief instant that she gained more knowledge of him than he ever would of her.

"Please, you may call me Victoria. Won't you join me for tea while we have our talk?" she said, holding out one long, graceful arm and hand.

He glanced that way into a charming round breakfast nook with views out to the neatly kept gardens and a sparking greenhouse, cozy table already set with a full high tea.

"Of course, I'd be glad to," he said without thinking.

He couldn't quite bring himself to use her given name, certainly not while he was supposed to be conducting an investigation. Having a drink with her father was bad enough, and here he was having a meal with the bereaved young fiancé.

As soon as they arranged themselves, a local boy of about fourteen appeared from out of nowhere. When he reached for the kettle, Victoria shook her head and touched his arm.

"No, thank you, Charlie. I'll be happy to serve Inspector McDuff and myself."

The boy bowed his head, not quite hiding his dark red cheeks, and retreated. McDuff stood to pour the hot fragrant tea through the strainers and into the waiting cups before she could.

"Thank you, Inspector. I know the servants mean a lot to my parents, but I never have liked the whole idea of it. I heard more than enough grumbling about the demise of slavery in the colonies to turn me against such things for life. I'm quite capable of taking care of myself. Did you grow up with such nonsense?"

"I… No, not at all. I'm as working class as they come."

"Milk or sugar?" She pushed both containers, made of a sturdy sky blue pottery in a style he'd never seen before, over to his side of the table. "Am I guessing correctly that you come from Glasgow or thereabouts, Inspector McDuff? What brought you to London?"

"I grew up there, but I've been in London for years now. I moved for work. Family matters as well, I suppose."

He'd caught himself on the verge of asking her to call him Rob. He rarely even thought of himself that way. And he'd nearly shared the joyful news of having a brother in Fodelson Prison chaining him to this wretched city. He proceeded to add too much milk and sugar, which only increased his discomfort.

What had addled his thick head this afternoon? One drink, even of such fine rum, would have done no such thing, but he was dangerously close to acting like a pure idiot.

"I've never been so far north as Glasgow," Victoria said, staring out the window as she stirred her tea, the spoon never touching the side of the cup. A trick Rob never seemed to manage. "I'd love to visit, but I fear it would be more cold and dreary than here."

"It, ah, the climate there can be a bit challenging. I'm sorry to be so dreadfully rude, but may I ask you a few questions about your fiancé?"

She closed her eyes and pursed her lips for a second, and McDuff held his breath. Miss Haversham wasn't being investigated for anything. She would be perfectly within her rights to get up and leave, and to throw him out on his ear as well.

He hoped she wouldn't.

Mostly for official reasons.

"*Former* fiancé, please," she finally said, looking into his eyes. "I've only heard a small bit about what's happened, but that was more than enough."

"I'm sorry to upset you, Ms. Haversham. If it's too difficult—"

"I want to help if I can, of course. That poor, poor child.

The sooner I can end my association with Mr. Abernathy, the better."

"Very well," McDuff said. "Please let me know if the questions get too uncomfortable."

She nodded, dropping her gaze. McDuff took a deep breath, sternly reminding himself to focus on why he was here. A young girl's life had nearly ended over the same man who'd made this young woman in front of him miserable. That man could still easily be tried for murder if the girl's condition worsened, and a charge of attempted murder was a near certainty.

That was the only reason McDuff was here, no matter what his racing heart and warmer parts of his body tried to tell him.

By the time they finished the tea and all of the cakes and cookies, McDuff was no closer to finding the answers, or even the starting point. Despite her outward independence and professed abilities to take care of herself, which he did not doubt for an instant, the entire relationship with Abernathy seemed to be sadly typical.

Victoria had hardly spent any time with the man she was supposed to have married in a few short weeks. Her father had found a suitable match—for appearances and business and financial interests, everything except matters of love—and that was intended to be that.

And yet...

Something about Victoria Haversham, besides that intoxicating scent, her lovely eyes, and her clear intelligence, kept McDuff a bit on edge. Something that felt just a bit out of place, like a crumb caught between his teeth.

There was no reason to suspect anything here, but McDuff

knew how his own mind worked once he caught a trail. He'd worry at it like his tongue after that bit of food.

He didn't know whether it was that nearly irresistible scent or the sunlight glinting through Victoria's mass of curls, but McDuff wasn't quite ready to leave after he'd exhausted his supply of relevant questions.

"I understand you spent time in the Caribbean."

"Most of my childhood. The best part of it, anyway. When I wasn't being shipped off here for one purpose or another, of course. I suppose my college years formed and shaped my adult mind, almost as much as my youth in the colonies."

"You preferred the Caribbean to England, then?"

"I know I'm supposed to be proud and patriotic," she said, staring at her hands. "But yes. Many times I've wished we'd never left Enceleas. I hope to return someday."

McDuff was startled at the way his mind seized on how she pronounced the word.

Lilting, like a caress.

In-seh-LAY-us.

Time to get himself away from such heady surroundings and back to familiar ground.

"Well, when things calm down a bit, perhaps you'll be able to," McDuff said as he pulled out his watch. "I'm so sorry, Ms. Haversham. I've taken up far too much of your time with this difficult matter."

She smiled, the first one he'd seen, and McDuff caught himself hoping her flush had something to do with him.

"I thought it was a rather pleasant tea myself," she said in a way that he didn't feel mocked at all.

"You have a point," he said, getting to his feet. "The

company has been lovely, even if the topic of conversation has not. Thank you for your time."

"You're quite welcome, Inspector." She stood before he could get around to pull her chair back. He was quite sure she'd noticed his intention. Victoria seemed far more pleased than annoyed. "I do hope you're able to get to the bottom of all of this."

"I'll certainly do my best. For now, please do your best to keep him off your mind."

"I'm finding that easier with each passing day," she said. "Do you remember the way out?"

"Certainly. Thank you for your time, Victoria."

She smiled again, and McDuff turned and walked out as quickly as he politely could.

That smile hadn't been sneering or mocking, but he couldn't pretend she didn't look satisfied with herself. Pleased over something, maybe his saying her name in such a familiar manner.

Best to make a quick escape before he made even more of a fool of himself.

Rob McDuff stood outside the closed door, breathing deeply though he could smell the soot and smog from London even so far out. He couldn't quite get the aroma of those delicate flowers out of his nose.

Or maybe that was his mind wishing to hold on to it.

"Victoria," he said under his breath.

He shook his head and walked away.

CHAPTER 7

THE STRANGE AND untrustworthy afterglow from McDuff's conversation with Victoria Haversham only lasted until he walked down his own Paddington street, far from those posh, sprawling mansions around Mayfair.

If these creaky old dumps had ever been grand, it had been years before he was born. The clusters of boarding houses were hardly as dire as the tenements and slums in London or any other city, but McDuff didn't bother trying to ignore how shabby and run down everything he saw truly was.

The house itself may have been a pleasant enough tan color in days gone by, or perhaps green. Now the dingy paint was more peeling than in place, and the square, blocky building wouldn't have been graceful or elegant in its prime. Twelve rooms, more or less clean, rented out to fifteen or so men who weren't anyone's idea of a dream match.

Many, like McDuff knew himself to be, would be lucky to marry at all, much less marry well.

He walked onto the stoop, avoiding the loose third step out of years of habit. The front sitting room, with decades-outdated but clean furniture and a threadbare rug, was blessedly empty. McDuff passed through quickly, not wanting to give over-attentive Mrs. Richards a chance to chat about his long, sad day.

She was pleasant enough, he supposed, and the meals he took in her dining room were generous if not particularly flavorful. She and his brother Michael had been friendly with each other. Besides not wanting to speak to one more person after a day full of unpleasant conversation, McDuff had no desire to reminisce about his brother today.

They'd rented out the room on the third floor—the freshly arrived McDuff brothers—nine years before. He still paid the extra rather than moving to a single room. Jamming all of Michael's clothing and shoes and various assorted junk into an even smaller space would help no one.

And leaving that room they'd found when they were both full of the hope and optimism of a new start would hurt too much.

McDuff lifted the doorknob and shoved with his shoulder just like Mrs. Richards showed them that first day. The air in the room was thick and miserable with heat from two south-facing windows overtaking the breeze from one on the north side. Those same sunny windows helped a bit with the cold in winter, but the drafts nearly canceled them out.

The wardrobe on his side of the room stood open from that morning, the mirror on the door mottled and cracked. His dark blue policeman's uniform hung inside, untouched for the last two years he'd been given clearance to work in ordinary clothes. When asked, he repeated the lines about witnesses and even suspects being far more willing to talk to him, and more honest, when he knocked on the door looking like them.

All of that was certainly true, but he suspected his own comfort simply made him a better investigator.

McDuff hung his jacket, trousers, and shirt on a string in front of the window instead of putting them away. The evening breeze should dry everything out and let him avoid paying Mrs. Richards for a wash for a few more days. His worn and scuffed brown shoes on the windowsill did nothing to help the stale aroma of the room, but they needed the airing out even more than his clothes did.

He sat on a creaky wooden chair in front of a tiny, battered desk in his shorts and undershirt, stocking feet up on Michael's bed. McDuff never slept or even sat on that bed, still covered with a scratchy brown blanket from the last morning his brother left here a free man six years ago.

Even after so much time, and with no hope of sharing the room again, the habit persisted.

Files and notes from the investigation waited, tucked into the case beside the desk. The hour was early yet on a Friday evening.

McDuff could dig into the mess and try to find any connections.

And no one would be willing to talk to him for the next two days, even if he could track them down away from work. The only things sitting on the desk at the moment were a nearly full bottle of whiskey and a relatively clean glass that fit perfectly into his hand. What McDuff could afford on his salary, or more because he was loathe to spend the money, would pale in comparison to the fine rum Mr. Haversham had shared.

McDuff knew from long experience that what he had on hand would do the job just fine.

He poured himself two fingers of light brown liquid, unable to stop himself from comparing all of it to Haversham's fancy cut glass and far superior libation. McDuff held his version up in the general direction of his brother's closed wardrobe.

"May this find you well, brother."

McDuff's first swallow found him well enough.

That girl, Cheryl Mallory.

That poor girl.

From all accounts, she'd been bright, curious, full of excitement about her life. Seventeen years old and all of it thrown away whether she managed to keep the baby or not. No one yet knew how the poison Cheryl had nearly killed herself with would affect her pregnancy.

McDuff privately thought a child so deeply unwanted might be better off never drawing a breath.

His brother had been that same age. Not nearly so bright or curious, but always full of excitement, believing things would work out for him in the end. Believing his big brother Robbie would set it all to rights, even before McDuff had turned to policing for a living. He hadn't been able to save Michael any more than he was going to be able to save Cheryl.

McDuff was again left with no choice but to do all he could to stop it from happening to anyone else.

With full knowledge that he would fail far more than he managed to succeed.

Warmth spread from his throat and stomach through the rest of his weary body. McDuff was already far less concerned about working this evening, or during the weekend. This time he poured three fingers and didn't bother with the toast.

When his mood turned so dark and melancholy, he wasn't even suited for talking to himself.

Everything he'd done for Michael had only made things worse. Getting him out of those original arrests, right back onto the street and deeper into the gangs. Dragging both of them hours away from home into a strange city. Too slow to understand what was happening when Michael suddenly had new friends with connections back to Glasgow.

Those so-called friends pushed McDuff's little brother into far worse trouble than he ever would have found on his own.

If he'd never gotten Michael out of trouble that last time back home, he might have served his time and found some other way. McDuff finished his whiskey and poured a third to keep in reserve.

After a long hot day and on a mostly empty stomach, the spirit was hitting him like a sledgehammer. His feet felt impossibly far away on Michael's bed, his head floated a bit on his neck. Every ache in his body had faded away.

The aches in his heart only grew deeper.

If he hadn't been so determined to arrange Michael's life for him, maybe they'd both be in Glasgow still. Instead he beat his body and mind against the river of crime in this wretched city, as deep and never-ending as the Thames. And his brother rotted in Fodelson Prison.

McDuff finished the third drink after all.

CHAPTER 8

Ten years ago:

McDuff followed Station Chief Edwards through the dank, mildewy gray stone passageway, wondering how long since this reeking Glaswegian hell had been cleaned out. Most nights, he didn't give a damn.

People were in for a reason, and it wasn't up to him or anyone else on the outside to make sure they had a comfortable little vacation at the city's expense.

He supposed this one was in for a reason.

Well, he knew this one was, more than most.

Reasons didn't always matter when it was his baby brother thrown in the pit.

"He's in bad shape, Rob," Edwards said. "Might have to move him to hospital before day breaks. Or the lunatic asylum. It's not like Bedlam any more, not here. They might be able to—"

"No asylum," McDuff said. "They'd break whatever mind he has left. Did he come in that way? Or did it happen here?"

Their shoes echoed for ten steps before Edwards answered. The man was easily thirty years McDuff's senior, hair pure white, gait slow and stiff. Edwards had probably arrested their father more than once before the bastard who spawned them got himself taken out of the world permanently.

"I'll not lie to you. Most of it was his own doing, before we ever picked him up. The worst of it, even. I wasn't back here when the fight broke out."

McDuff shook his head, not sure if he was denying what Edwards said or trying to stop him from continuing.

"My brother hardly inspires careful treatment when he's into this," he said. "Long as you say it was mostly outside, I believe you."

"I say that's the truth."

The wall to their left opened up to a long row of heavy metal bars interrupted by thin layers of stone. Most of the cells were occupied right now with the gang riots escalating all over the city. McDuff knew his brother wouldn't be in any of these group holding pens after he'd already been at the center of some kind of riot.

Michael was too much trouble in any crowd, to himself and everyone around him.

They were heading toward the smaller, solitary cell blocks at the end of the row.

Downstairs, in the true pit.

"What are the charges?" McDuff said. "How long is he in for this time?"

"I'm sorry, son. They should have told you when it happened. He's not getting out any time soon. Even if he manages that, as long as he stays in Glasgow he'll get picked up again. Too many of these bloody thugs know he's an easy mark. I've known Michael as long as I've known you. I don't think he quite understands what he gets himself into, but that only means no one can stop him"

McDuff didn't speak again until they were at the end of the hall, right before they went down the stairs into the purest hell of the solitary wing. He touched Edwards' shoulder and stopped.

"I know his past, more than I want to. Who's the judge on this one? I can take him out of here, down to London when I go. That's one reason I put in for this bloody transfer, Edwards."

The chief looked up, his eyes moving from side to side. McDuff saw the hard lines of his jaw flexing.

"These gangs aren't only in Glasgow, Rob. They fight this disease in Manchester, London, Liverpool. New York and Baltimore in America are crawling with this vermin. A cousin of mine tells me it's got all the way to Australia. You up for keeping him out of trouble no matter where you go, for the rest of your life and his?"

"I can't let him rot here," McDuff said through clenched teeth. "I won't. Just tell me the judge. I swore to our mother before she died, you know that."

"It's McChafee. And you know what a hard arse he is. I don't want to interfere in your family business, Rob, but you may not want to get into this with Michael. Sometimes guys like this, they never find their way out. He's been nothing but heartache to your mother. What makes you think he'll be anything less to you?"

"I don't know what else I can do." MacDuff's stomach churned with sickening reality, and the near certainty that Edwards was right. "Leave him here to rot? Let him get himself killed on the street next time like our bastard of a father did?"

Edwards nodded. "And you feel like you let him down, not raising him right. He's not your son, Rob. He's your brother."

"I had even less choice there than I do now. Look, the man got himself killed when we and our mother needed him most. I can't change that, and I'll never replace him. But I should have been able to keep Michael from following in his wasted footsteps."

"Sometimes we do all we can and it's never enough," Edwards said, starting down the uneven stone stairs. A few electric lights barely touched the dark down there. "Work in a jail long enough and you learn that lesson more than any other. You did your best. You made something more of your own life. Maybe he *can't* do better. Maybe this is all he's got."

McDuff followed, trying to keep the images away.

Michael as a wee baby, one of his own earliest memories. Michael always seemed to smile, even when his troubles started as a teenager.

Michael sobbing at their father's funeral, their mother too far in shock to help. McDuff's first adult failure, when he couldn't get anyone's tears to stop.

Michael laughing when he got kicked out of school, not understanding he was heading right into the seething nightmare that took their father.

"Maybe it is all he's got," McDuff finally said right before they reached the first cell. "And maybe all I've got is to do the best I can by him. I'll talk to McChafee, see if I can get him to listen. He might be willing to get him out of town if nothing else."

"I wish you the best," Edwards said, his words slow and sad. "I hope this doesn't eat your own life the way it is his."

McDuff followed him past three cells, two occupied with fierce-eyed men who stood at the bars and stared. A new arrival kept everyone on edge, especially one dragged in bloody.

At the fourth Edwards pulled out his keyring big as his hand. He flipped the correct key into his fingers without even looking.

"Ready?"

McDuff closed his eyes for a second. "No. Let me see him anyway."

The lock clanked when the key turned, and Edwards had to push with both hands to get the door open. The hinges squealed, the harsh noise echoing through the jail and into McDuff's bones. The cell was so narrow that he couldn't see anything until he stepped in front of the open door.

Michael sprawled belly down on the filthy bunk, head over the edge, one arm hanging down with it. A pool of blood glistened on the nearly black floor. His pale wool trousers stained and ripped, and his long-sleeved shirt only had small patches of white showing through the blood and muck.

McDuff stepped forward, his guts twisting inside him. Seeing thugs in worse shape on patrol nearly every day didn't make seeing his brother easier.

"Michael? Mike? It's Rob."

The man on the bunk jerked and groaned. He pushed himself up, but his head hung close to his chest. When he finally looked up, McDuff wished he hadn't.

CHAPTER 9

THE MAN in the cell was barely recognizable as human, much less as McDuff's little brother. One eye barely open, the other a bruised, lumpy mass. His lips were nearly as swollen, his nose twisted to the side.

McDuff had no idea whether the blood caked on his chin and throat came from his nose, his mouth, or any number of cuts and scrapes on his face. Michael looked like he had more blood on the outside than the inside.

That along with his rattling breath made it clear he needed to go to hospital sooner rather than later.

He managed to follow McDuff's progress as he walked into the cell and squatted in front of the bunk. Michael's head swayed on his shoulders, though. He struggled to focus with his one open eye.

"Come to take me home then, Robbie?" he said, his voice raspy and harsh. McDuff never would have understood the words if he hadn't heard them many times before.

"Not just yet. What have you got into this time?"

"Nothing I haven't got into before." Michael tried to move back against the wall, but he groaned again when he tried to push against the bunk. "Out with me mates, got out of hand."

McDuff stood. "Yeah, nothing new there at all. Those loyal lads told you to sneak into one of the bloody Irish gangs, and they beat the shite out of you. What did your scum of the Earth mates offer you this time? Whiskey? Money? Women?"

"Let's just say all three and be done with it," Michael said, shaking his head slowly. "I'm not stupid, Rob. All worth it if it worked."

"No, you're not stupid. You trust the wrong people and you trust too much. Then you expect me to clean it all up for you."

Michael tried to grunt, but a fresh gout of blood flowed from his nose.

"You here to take me home or not?"

"No," McDuff said. The promises he'd made their mother, over and over again the day she drew her last breath, ripped through his mind. "I'm not taking you anywhere. You're off to hospital from the looks of you, but after that you're here until you're in front of the judge."

"Leaving me after all." Michael tried to get up, but he fell back, banging his head against the stone wall. "What you wanted all along."

"Yes, Michael. That's what I've wanted all along. That's why I took you in, took you on. That's why I've done everything I could to keep you out of places like this, to get you job after bloody job that you managed to lose. That's why I've risked my own job more times than I can count. Because I wanted you in jail all along."

"Just in time for you to run off to London. Knew *that* was coming." Michael slumped down onto the bunk again, shifting until he was in the same face-down position with his head over the edge. "I was trying to build up enough to get you set up down there, so you won't live like a rotten beggar fresh off the street."

"Right. Don't do me any favors. If you wanted to help me, you would have kept any of the jobs I got you so you could take care of yourself for a change. I'll see you for the trial. *If* I can get the time off work. That's what men have to do. Work."

McDuff walked out of the cell, and Edwards swung the door closed. Before they could walk away, Michael cried out.

"Robbie! Don't leave me in here."

He was propped up on his arms, but they were shaking so badly McDuff was afraid he would tumble off onto the floor.

"I don't mean to cause trouble for you," he said, tears squeezing out of his swollen eyes. "Can't seem to find the right thing anymore."

Edwards walked down the hall and waited with his back turned. McDuff stepped up to the bars.

"Listen, Mike, listen to me. I'm telling the truth. I can't take you out of here. You've been picked up too many times. They're not letting you loose like before, not even with me. I need you to let Edwards take you to hospital, okay? You'll stay there while you heal up."

Michael shook his head again and drooped forward.

"Not gonna make it without you," he said, his words running together. "No reason to try if you go."

"Just hold yourself together for now." McDuff stepped back until he felt the cold stone digging into his flesh, then he tried to step back more. "You have to get better before we can do anything. Let them help you get better."

McDuff turned and walked away, but he didn't move fast enough. The ragged, pathetic, and somehow infuriating sound of his grown baby brother crying followed him down the hall and back up the steps.

Michael choking, struggling to draw air into his lungs, then wailing again.

McDuff nearly crashed into Edwards waiting at the top of the stairway.

"I'll get him looked over," Edwards said. "Probably send him to hospital in the next hour or so. I know you don't want to hear it, but you've done all you can. Go to London, Rob. Now. Start your own life."

CHAPTER 10

Now:

Victoria stood by the open window in her third-floor room, breathing in the fresh, cool air of an afternoon rain. Much as she disliked England, these soft showers pleased her senses and her mind.

She sipped her lukewarm tea, a bit sweeter than she usually took it, and wondered if Inspector McDuff had made it indoors before the rain started.

A gust of wind brought the scent of her nosegay to her attention, and she removed it carefully. The tiny embossed silver vase, made to hold a small reservoir of water to keep dainty flowers fresh, had been a gift from her mother when they returned to England.

Jaji had taught Victoria how to put it to far better use.

She pulled the tiny blooms out and absently dropped them into a larger vase that held various flowers to choose from. Her mother maintained a lush garden and greenhouse behind their ostentatious home, or at least she claimed to while she paid local girls from lesser families to do the grubby work for her.

Victoria participated as much as her mother would tolerate, desperate for the feel of her hands in warm soil to remind her of Enceleas. Her own special projects, both outdoors under the faint northern sun and inside the glass confines, held every minuscule variety of flower she could obtain, along with many species she'd never seen outside of the Caribbean.

Underneath the few drops of water inside her wearable vase was the most important cargo: a tiny muslin bundle.

She'd made this one less than a week ago, so no need to discard it just yet. Victoria settled the bundle into a glass beaker, barely as large as her pinky finger and filled with dark purple liquid, and slipped a bit of cork into the top.

The crumbled herbs and more exotic flowers—imported at terrible expense from her longed-for garden on her father's plantation or grown in her own greenhouse—magnified and gave her secret dust far more power. The addition of her intentions and magic created a stunning potency in such a minuscule package. Several more waited on the shelf beside the beaker, ready to be activated and used when this one lost its power.

Inspector McDuff never had a chance, any more than her father or any other man did when Victoria wore her perfectly unremarkable nosegay. That strong desire to please her never failed.

The effect didn't seem to be as strong on women, but she was certain she could make adjustments if needed. The relentlessly masculine power structure in London hadn't yet given her reason to do so.

Victoria walked over to the one space in her room not covered with shelves. A painting of her father's plantation house hung there, one that always brought tears to her eyes.

The house was low and painted white, with huge windows and long eaves to capture every possible breeze. A massive porch surrounded it, screened in against the mosquitoes for use at night. A smooth expanse of dark green grass contrasted with the wild varieties of tree and flower and vine sprawling close behind the whole thing.

She pushed her nostalgia into the background and swung the painting aside to reveal a large wall safe. Her father had given her the combination several years ago, saying one of his uncles had installed it when the house was built.

Victoria made certain he forgot all about it shortly thereafter.

The painting itself was more than enough protection for what she had inside, and she regularly freshened the small dishes on the shelves around it. She also enjoyed the crude, mechanical action of entering her combination and pulling the door open.

Three deep shelves held her collection of expensive jewelry (some of the finest from Mr. Abernathy), enough pounds Sterling to cover several years of income for even a wealthy family, Jaji's most powerful tools and ingredients, and her notes and records.

One notebook was full of the recipes and procedures she'd long ago committed to memory, but wrote out from time to time to test herself. Another held her ongoing records of her activities and their success or failure.

She pulled the second out and sat at her desk.

Victoria was a huge believer in the power of lists, and she had more than she'd ever bothered to count. This notebook alone was more than halfway full, and most of those were crossed out as accomplished.

She drew a line through *Break the Engagement*, smiling.

A serious detriment to plans for her future now receded into her past.

She scanned up the list with items going back five years. Attending college, gaining influence as her father's business partner, turning her need for the clockwork toys into a tidy income stream by selling them overseas, and building her own network of powerful businessmen and politicians through enchanted correspondence, Victoria was enjoying faster progress than she'd expected.

Now that the threat of a husband was behind her, along with Mr. McDuff's annoying investigation, she turned her attention to the next step in her overall plan. She needed to secure a far-less expensive shipping partnership, one she could adjust to her needs.

Victoria flipped through her copy of her father's business contacts, pondering which would be best to next approach in her own special way. Many of those contacts had helped her more than they could possibly know and in ways they never would have imagined. And of course, none of them had any idea who they were dealing with, or often that another person was involved at all.

The deep and urgent desire to invest in a new venture or advocate for a new law was hard to argue when a man couldn't see the source.

She took a deep breath as Jaji had taught her, catching the faintest whiff of her potion lingering in the tiny flowers.

Inspector McDuff's intelligent brown eyes moved through her mind, staring into hers more openly than most men did. As did his handsome face, shining brown hair, and broad, strong shoulders. Not to mention his only being a reasonable amount taller rather than towering over her, forcing her into awkward contortions to see his face.

All of that combining nicely with the air of a man who clearly never entertained the faintest suspicion that he was the least bit attractive.

Those soft and easy questions had only been part of why tea was such a pleasure.

No matter, he was likely out of her life, and she had work to focus upon.

Time enough for such frivolous pursuits later, if she chose.

She pulled out the card of a man she'd never met, but who'd been making innovations in shipping around the world for quite some time.

Victoria glanced at the title of this particular list.

Return to Enceleas, under my own power.

She set to work.

CHAPTER 11

A week after his unusual meeting with Victoria Haversham, McDuff waited in an office that didn't leave him nearly so uncomfortable. The space was cramped and dusty, the desk and chairs old and scarred, the street outside noisy and smelly. He didn't fool himself that the manager of a global import company lived in the same way at home, but he didn't feel like he was going to break everything by taking a breath at the wrong moment.

For some reason, he appreciated the absence of the useless little clockwork toys everyone else he'd interviewed lately seemed to have.

Besides being silly, the things were oddly disturbing.

"So sorry about that," Mr. Smith said, closing the door behind him. The owner of Global Endeavors was a small, wiry man with thick red hair he smoothed down constantly. "Hate to keep you waiting, Inspector."

"That's quite all right. I'm sure I've taken up enough of

your time already." McDuff glanced down at his notebook to make sure he hadn't missed anything. He had pitifully little to go on with only the contact lists from Mr. Abernathy and Mr. Haversham to draw from. "If you think of anything or if anything strange comes up, I'd appreciate it if you could let me know."

"Well, talking to you is easy enough," Mr. Smith said. "Certainly compared with that mess just now. Half of London's gone crazy."

"Oh?" McDuff said, his mind mostly on the next person on his list.

"Bloody partner's decided to eliminate his routes to India and Africa and concentrate on the Caribbean instead. Idiot."

McDuff sat back in his seat, no longer thinking of the rest of his day. He'd never been one to believe in coincidence.

Certainly not during an investigation.

"The Caribbean, did you say? That does seem an odd choice these days. I've recently heard the colonies are in decline."

"Odd is a very polite word for it," Mr. Smith said, then he ran his hands over his face. "That was well and good ten years ago, and certainly fifty years ago, but the market for sugar has shifted. Not to mention constant trouble with the native types. Have to shift with the tides rather than against them to survive, so to speak. Damn fool's forcing me to find new partners when shipments have already been promised. No warning, no good reason."

"I hope you won't think me too intrusive. But I do have a few shipping men to interview. Mind telling me his name?"

"Of course I don't mind. I'm not the one making an ass of

myself and dragging everyone down with me. It's Steven Winston."

McDuff closed his eyes and raised his eyebrows. Mr. Winston was indeed on his list, one of several far more closely associated with the Havershams than Mr. Abernathy. Each of his interviews with people more strongly in one orbit than the other, clearly circling around Mr. Haversham, had seemed…off somehow.

As if the man didn't quite understand what he was being asked about, or he couldn't quite remember his own business. That sort of memory loss did not suit these cutthroat types at all.

"He's on my list, yes," McDuff said, getting to his feet. "I appreciate the warning that he's acting a bit strangely."

"Best of luck with him," Mr. Smith said as he walked over and opened the door. The din of the huge shipping warehouse hit McDuff like a physical force. "I think you missed your chance to interview a rational man."

"I'll see if I can make arrangements to visit with him this afternoon."

"Hang on." Mr. Smith rubbed his stubbled chin. "If you don't mind waiting in my office for a bit, I'll wager I can get my son to take you right over there. That will be sure to get you in the door, and he may yet talk sense to you."

McDuff nodded, glad for any introduction he could get. He couldn't imagine why his mind was racing, looking for more connections between the Havershams, that plantation in the Caribbean, and Mr. Abernathy's strange behavior. Almost everyone he'd spoken to said they were shocked by what had happened, and Abernathy himself had been the most surprised and distressed of all.

He'd heard rumors of strange diseases, strange fevers that could make a man think and behave in an outlandish manner. Certainly in those who lived in or had business with the colonies. Rumors he'd never paid much attention to before. No need.

McDuff wasn't sure what he'd do if something like that were at work here, but he knew he wouldn't stop until he understood the truth.

"All set then," Mr. Smith said, striding back into the cluttered room. "He'll take you right now."

Though the younger Mr. Smith was eerily similar in build and feature, he had none of his father's talkativeness. He and McDuff barely exchanged any words on the quick walk from the warehouses to the docks.

He was uncomfortably settled in a far more impressive waiting room less than ten minutes after leaving the cluttered office. Much like the homes he'd been visiting for the past couple of weeks, the fine furnishings, rugs, and collections in this one room easily exceeded his yearly salary.

Another harried young man showed him into Mr. Winston's office, promising a short wait and apologizing profusely. McDuff had the clear impression the man, barely more than a boy, had been apologizing for his boss all day long.

Before anyone else walked in, and before McDuff finished his customary glance around any new space, he froze.

Sitting on top of a wooden file cabinet were two clockwork pink flamingos.

Nothing else like that was in the entire office.

No trace of a toy or anything even as frivolous as a book that didn't focus on ocean navigation or ship engineering.

McDuff rubbed his temples with his thumb and fingers, trying to catch the images flashing through his mind.

Every one.

Every single one of the strange interviews, the ones that kept him on edge.

Each office or sitting room—or bedroom for the girl this all started with—held one of those ridiculous toys.

Just like the close associations with Mr. Haversham, this didn't make the slightest bit of sense. And just like that, once McDuff saw the pattern, he could not un-see it. He was sorely tempted to get up and walk out.

He knew exactly how this interview would go.

The confused, blank stares, the round-about answers, the failed attempt to hide how little the subject did know. He hated to sit through that again, but trying to work out a reason why he'd disappeared would be challenging at best.

While the impressively tall and excitable Mr. Winston talked—just as uselessly and indeed Caribbean-obsessed as expected—McDuff pretended to take notes. He was really drawing in his notebook, two large circles with names in the middle of each.

Haversham. Abernathy.

He wrote in the names of all the strange interviews, the ones like this one that simply did not make sense, inside the circle they were most closely associated with.

Every single one fit into one circle.

Haversham.

One more glance around the office as Mr. Winston finished his incoherent musings told McDuff where to go next.

CHAPTER 12

MCDUFF PACED UP and down the sidewalk outside the Catholic Church closest to the docks, strangely unable to convince himself to go in. He'd been raised Protestant, but he was hardly a man of faith himself.

Not after what had happened to his brother. Religion was a pastime for those who knew less of the world.

But if anyone could help with such odd events, or at least tell him where to look, that person would surely be inside the imposing building.

His brother's sad path to prison had brought McDuff here, as it had brought him to so many places he'd rather not be. After hesitantly asking several other clergy members all afternoon, and trying not to cringe at the looks they gave him, he'd finally visited a Presbyterian church he'd been to before. The only one in London he'd set foot inside before, in fact.

The last place Michael had gone in his own erratic attempts to keep himself out of trouble.

The grandfatherly minister hadn't fought back laughter or glared suspiciously at the toy and McDuff's questions. He'd looked a bit sheepish himself when he suggested the church McDuff paced in front of now. A challenging young priest, and a decidedly odd visiting scholar, supposedly lurked within.

The Presbyterian laughed and shook his head when he said it, but apparently these two inspired enough rumors to cross all the lines of faith across the vast city.

A man in a black gown with a white collar opened the arched door of the Catholic church and walked slowly down the broad steps. McDuff nearly walked away, but he didn't want to appear as uncomfortable as he felt.

Perhaps this was the renegade clergyman he was seeking.

"You're certainly welcome to continue your tour of the sidewalk," the priest said as he descended the last few steps. "If you're hesitant to come inside for some reason, let me reassure you. All are welcome here."

"I didn't want to intrude," McDuff said, horrified at the words out of his own mouth. Lapsed Protestant or not, lying to a priest in front of a church had to be a bad idea. "I'm sorry, that's not true. Yes, I'm hesitant."

The priest was a few years younger than McDuff, probably in his late twenties. He had fine blond hair and delicate features that made him look even younger. When he smiled, though, McDuff couldn't help smiling back.

"Well then," the priest said, "if you're seeking someone to talk to, I'll walk with you. If you're seeking solitude, I'll leave you in peace."

"Now there's a sensible offer," McDuff said, shrugging. "I'll go inside, but I don't know the procedures and rules and such."

"No, no rules today." The priest swept his arm toward the door. "Only us two sinners in attendance."

"At least I know I'll fit in," McDuff said, following the priest up the steps. "I'm Inspector… Never mind that. I'm Rob McDuff."

"Good to meet you, Rob. I'm Father William Hall."

The cathedral was both more grand and more humble than McDuff expected. The glorious, colorful stained glass windows soared over two stories high, making brilliant patches on the plain wooden floor. The pews looked hard and uncomfortable, as if they'd been hand made to those specifications.

They weren't terribly different from the benches at police headquarters where families of the accused had to wait.

The only other major signs of religion sat on the stage, raised a few feet above the benches. A grand tapestry of Biblical scenes hung behind the pulpit, and thick candlesticks as tall as McDuff stood in a row.

"I have an office back here if you'd be more comfortable," Father Hall said. "Or we can talk out here. Don't worry, I won't make you use the confessional."

McDuff laughed, glancing uneasily at the mysterious brown booths along the wall to his left.

"Out here is fine, Father."

The two men sat in the front row, Father Hall leaning back with one arm along the back of the pew. McDuff reached into his case.

"I was wondering if you could take a look at this."

Father Hall turned the clockwork penguin over in his hands. It was the one from Mr. Abernathy's house, a gift he claimed he'd been surprised to receive and relieved to get rid of.

After his experience of the past few weeks, the man had been eager to hand it over.

"And what am I looking at, Rob?"

"That's nothing more than an ordinary clockwork toy as far as I can tell. Made all over the place, including right here in London. But the behavior of people I've met over the past several days who have these things hasn't quite been so ordinary."

"You honestly believe these toys are involved somehow?"

Father Hall wasn't smirking, but he did look worried.

McDuff wasn't sure which was worse.

"I honestly don't know. But a young girl's in hospital after trying to kill herself, or maybe someone poisoned her. She had one of them as well. Several men stare at me as if they've been drugged, with no idea of what they've done or why. Even if their strange behavior has changed the course of their business. This is a long shot, but at the moment I have nothing more to go on. I couldn't think of anywhere else to bring such a strange idea but into a church."

Father Hall held the toy cupped inside his hands, staring up at one of the sparkling windows.

"I have to ask if someone sent you my way. You'll understand why in a second."

"Actually, yes. I visited several other churches before this one. The last minister suggested you. He said you and a scholar staying here created enough gossip to pass right through the battle lines of faith."

The priest laughed, the echoes through the vast empty space lifting McDuff's tension for the first time all week.

"I'm not sure whether to be mortified or flattered. Now, I

can't say for certain. And I can't make any promises. But you may have come to the right place. We do have a visiting scholar here who's spent time overseas. She recently returned from time in Jamaica and other islands in the Caribbean."

Chills raced over McDuff's flesh, and he stared at the priest. As the coincidences got bigger, his ability to doubt them got smaller.

This one was gigantic.

"Think she'd be willing to take a look at this thing for me?" he said, not sure if he wanted to be right or wrong. "See if she has any ideas?"

"We can only ask. She's in the rectory across the street if you want to check with her now."

"Lead the way."

CHAPTER 13

The priest's residence was made of the same dark gray stone, but was far less grand than the church proper. The windows were few and made of plain glass, covered with white curtains.

"I'm sorry, I'm no expert in church matters," McDuff said before they got to the plain wooden door. "Not much about any church, really. Did you say this is a woman?"

"I did. You're in luck, Rob. Dr. Marchér happens to be an expert in...I'll just say things that have been said to cause odd behavior."

The priest opened the door before McDuff could ask any questions. A small, surprisingly bright sitting room was just inside, filled with several dark leather chairs and a bright floral sofa that looked far more comfortable than the pews. Several open books were scattered on the wide table in the middle, various slips of paper covered with notes on top of them.

A tall, slender person with close-cropped black hair stood,

hands on hips, staring at one of the crowded bookshelves that lined the walls. McDuff had only the priest's word that this was a woman. Black trousers and a white shirt much like his own revealed nothing of the slender frame.

"Dr. Marchér," Father Hall said, his voice soft and respectful. He pronounced her name in the French manner, mar-*shay*. "I'm sorry to disturb you, but we have something here you might like to examine."

She shook her head, the loose curls shifting.

"No, thank you," she said, her voice deep and her accent indeed French. "And you've known better than to call me *doctor* for years now, William. I'm quite busy here."

"This is Inspector McDuff," the priest said, winking. "He has an object here that may be having a strange effect on people's behavior."

Dr. Marchér turned her head, then her entire body, looking over her round glasses at the men. She had pale skin and a square jaw, and McDuff saw the bright green of her eyes from across the room.

"What sort of an object?"

"It's…ah, well, it's a toy, ma'am," McDuff said, wondering why he suddenly felt nervous as a schoolboy. "I've found several like it during my investigations over the past couple of weeks."

He held out the toy in a sweating hand. Dr. Marchér closed the distance in a few quick strides and leaned over, peering at the penguin from only a couple of inches away.

"You're welcome to examine it." McDuff took a step back before he could stop himself. He was quite sure Father Hall's cough was to cover a laugh. "Several others have already with no ill effect that I can observe."

Dr. Marchér watched him for a second, then took the penguin and sat down at a small table by the window in one motion. McDuff glanced at the priest, but all he did was jerk his chin toward the other chair.

"What sort of investigation?" She said without looking up as she turned the toy over in her hands.

"Pardon me?" McDuff's head was so addled by this change of roles that he took a few seconds to realize what she'd asked. He immediately wished she hadn't. "Oh, I'm sorry, Dr. Marchér. It's rather unpleasant. A man, an engaged man, he had, well. He had relations with a younger woman."

"See what you've done, William? Now he's taken up with this *doctor* nonsense. I take it this woman was not his fiancé?" She looked at McDuff over the top of her glasses again.

"No, ma'am. The wedding was called off."

Dr.…Miss Marchér carefully put the toy in the sun coming through the window and sat back, crossing her arms.

"I should certainly hope the wedding was called off. Why do you think this toy has anything strange about it, Inspector?"

"I'm not certain," McDuff said, trying not to stammer. "Several people who've been acting strangely had these close by. Everyone I've spoken with, including the man who had this, didn't seem to remember what they did, much less why."

McDuff was relieved when she turned that intense gaze toward the priest.

"You were thinking of the charms we discussed earlier." She waited until Father Hall nodded. "That's possible, yes. Well, this is your opportunity to see what I've learned in action, if you like."

She stood and strode across the room again, then rummaged in a large back bag, like a doctor's bag, on one of the chairs. McDuff knew his confusion showed on his face when he saw the priest's broad smile.

"Where shall we set up, Miss Marchér?" the priest said with a wink at McDuff.

"William, I've told you and *told* you to call me Jean," she said, still digging through the bag. She again used the French manner: *Zhon.* "Yes, I'm perfectly aware that is considered a masculine name. My parents didn't protest when I left Jeanne behind, so no one else has standing to do so. That table where we were is just fine, William."

"The table it is," Father Hall said, pulling up another chair.

Before McDuff could ask what was happening, Miss Marchér returned. He wasn't sure he'd ever manage to call her Jean or Jeanne or anything else without feeling intimidated.

"These things can be dangerous," she said, "especially if the practitioner does not wish to be found."

She put a small brown candle, a rough bowl about the size of her palm with three legs underneath, and an odd pottery jar on the table. McDuff knew he'd seen pottery like that somewhere recently, but he couldn't bring it to mind.

"I have the matches," Father Hall said, placing a small open box beside the candle with red-tipped matchsticks inside.

"Since you're investigating," she said, "odds are quite good we have someone who'd rather stay hidden." She sat, moving the clockwork penguin into the middle of the other three objects. "We'll just use a bit of a protection spell and a totem to keep the three of us safe."

"Safe from what?" McDuff blurted out before he could stop himself.

"Safe from whoever made this, of course," Miss Marchér said.

She poured a bit of water from a pale blue pitcher into the bowl as Father Hall lit the candle. She lifted the lid from the jar, and a strong smell of earth and flowers wafted out even before she dropped a few pinches into the water.

MacDuff tried to keep his puzzlement from showing when she picked up one of the matches and dragged it along a rough strip on the side of the box. She frowned at him as she lit the candle.

"I won't allow the white lucifer match in my presence, Inspector. The ease of striking a light anywhere rather than using this perfectly simple method is not worth the pain and suffering of so many women laboring to manufacture them."

Father Hall nodded, his eyes sad. McDuff added to the list of things he'd never heard much about until today, certain that would continue to increase. When Miss Marchér moved the candle underneath the bowl, the fragrance intensified enough to drive curiosity about matches from McDuff's mind.

The smell brought the pottery more clearly into focus, but he still couldn't catch it.

"What do you need us to do, Jean?" Father Hall said.

"Concentrate on keeping any power this may still hold directed toward that holy water." She placed a small dark red cemetery rose on the table beside the penguin. McDuff struggled not to laugh at the bizarre tableau. "This flower should capture it, but there's no use taking any chances. Inspector McDuff, do you need this intact for your investigation?"

"No, not really," he said, unsure what else he possibly could have said. "There are several more in different places all across the city."

"Then I'll begin."

CHAPTER 14

Miss Marchér muttered under her breath for several seconds, then placed several small tools on the table, one by one. McDuff didn't recognize any of them, though he thought they might come in handy for thieves and lock-pickers.

She slipped the point of a tiny knife blade along the neck of the penguin and pushed inward.

The head popped off and rolled onto the floor, making a sharp clatter on the bare wood. Neither man moved to pick it up. A tiny puff of steam floated out of the penguin's body and dissipated within a few seconds.

"Did you..." McDuff whispered.

She ignored him, and Father Hall only nodded.

She shifted the toy toward the sunlight, then peered into the body. She raised her dark eyebrows before tilting it over. A tiny bundle of white fabric, no bigger than a pea, landed beside the candle.

Miss Marchér picked it up with a set of tweezers and

dropped it onto a white handkerchief. Quick twists of the knife had the bundle open in a few seconds, and a bit of brown dust filtered out.

"Most interesting," she said, barely loud enough to hear. "That would be the source of power."

"Power, Miss Marchér?" McDuff said, quite sure he'd misunderstood. "What power?"

"Did you not see that steam, Inspector?" she said, holding a magnifying glass over the dust. "As soon as I opened this? And have I not asked you to please call me Jean?"

"I saw something, Jean. I'm not ready to give it magical abilities just yet."

"No?" Jean poked the rose in the middle of the table. "Remember what I said this was for?"

McDuff's jaw dropped, and he had a hard time catching his breath. The delicate red flower, soft and vibrant just a few seconds before, was now a brown, dry husk. He heard the crunch when the tweezers touched it.

He reached for it, but Father Hall put a hand on his wrist.

"I'm out of my element here," he said. "But I don't think you should touch that bare-handed. Jean said it was there to absorb any spells."

"Exactly so, William," she said. "My guess is that was a memory spell, placed there so anyone who was prying around wouldn't have a clue what was inside a few minutes later."

"You can't be serious," McDuff said. "That or you're trying to make me look a fool."

"I know you don't really know me," Father Hall said. "But I'm not the sort to make a fool of anyone. Certainly not an inspector, and not in front of a well-known scholar."

"Listen, that's something I didn't ask about earlier," McDuff said, leaning as far back from the table as he could without getting up. Every single aspect of this made him uncomfortable. "What exactly are you a scholar of, Jean?"

"I started out studying how cultures move from one place to the other," she said, slipping the knife down inside the toy. "I first went from your Scotland to Wales and Ireland, then followed that path to the United States. What I found there changed my focus, you might say."

The body of the toy fell into pieces, and she pushed them around with her tweezers. A couple of the miniature gears were brighter than the rest.

"I found not just culture there, in the South even after that terrible war. I found *rituals*. Spells. Magic. All of it changed, but much clearly descended from those Celtic roots. Once I learned more of the native culture there, the Red Indians who had their own ways of working with the elements, I knew I'd found my life's study."

McDuff got out his own handkerchief and leaned over to pick up the penguin's head, partly to give himself a break from this insane conversation. A brief space where he could let his face relax into disbelief.

She continued, still examining the remains of the toy.

"Then I heard of a most rich and vibrant part of the American South, where the rituals of slaves brought from Africa were alive and well. Not quite in their original form, but in some ways even more strange and potent. Many of the people I spoke to had much more recent origins from the islands of the Caribbean." She paused in her examination and gazed toward McDuff, and he knew she didn't see him at all.

"But it was said those island traditions blended with still others," she went on, "brought along with indentured servants after the end of the even more barbaric practices of slavery. From India, from China, all mixed with native beliefs and those from South America. Even some of your own Celtic traditions, brought along for their long colonial residence. From New Orleans, I journeyed there to trace those origins. I hope to make the trip to Africa someday to learn more."

"This is not quite what I was expecting," McDuff said, dropping the penguin head on the table and pushing back his chair. "Spells and potions, like in a children's book?"

"No, not at all, Inspector," Miss Marchér said. She put her tools down and sat back, watching McDuff with her head tilted. Her gaze bored into him. "This is no child you're dealing with here. This is a woman, and a talented and well-trained one at that."

"A woman," McDuff whispered, closing his eyes.

That was what he'd been trying to remember.

The pottery.

The clear, strong scent of the flowers.

Those lovely dark blue eyes. Intelligent eyes.

Victoria Haversham.

CHAPTER 15

"How can you tell this came from a woman?" Father Hall said.

He didn't seem as upset and confused as McDuff was feeling. The priest only seemed curious. Jean Marchér took her glasses off and polished them with the front of her shirt.

"Women's magic is different than men's," she said as she resettled them on her nose. "Even in these so-called enlightened times, most women must be subtle. They must suggest. Give ideas. Use a gentle push, not a solid blow."

"I wouldn't say dragging a poor girl through all this nightmare is exactly subtle," McDuff said, clenching his fists on his thighs. To hell with keeping secrets. "She tried to kill herself when she found out she was pregnant by the man who had this damn thing. Or else he tried to kill her. She's been poisoned nearly to death either way."

"And did she have one of these toys as well?" Jean said.

McDuff blinked, jarred right out of his anger.

"She did have one," he said. "A match for this one, but more feminine."

"In that case, what we have is a push from both directions. I'd bet you found both were willing participants. Possibly until she realized how neatly she was trapped by her pregnancy."

McDuff could find no words for her easy understanding of the situation. That was exactly what had happened, despite what Mr. and Mrs. Abernathy were desperate to prove. All he could do was nod.

"I hope you've interviewed the former fiancé, Inspector," Miss Marchér said. "There may be some question as to whether she found out about this little tryst or caused it herself. But there is no doubt she must now be your primary suspect."

"I've interviewed her, yes." The words sounded pathetic to his own ears. "Neither she nor her family seemed to be involved."

"I'm terribly sorry, Rob," Father Hall said. "But you did say a girl's life is at stake here, and an unborn infant. I promised I wouldn't make you use the confessional, but I don't need it to know you're lying about something right now."

McDuff stared at his hands on the table for a few seconds, then looked up at the two people he'd only met less than an hour before. His years of reading people, watching for clues large and small, left him certain neither of them were lying to him.

Of course he'd thought the same of Victoria Haversham, hadn't he?

No, not quite.

He'd felt something odd, something off. McDuff may not

have been expecting all of this, but he wasn't completely taken by surprise, either.

"I don't believe her parents are involved," he said. "She seemed charming enough, but I can't say she seemed entirely innocent."

"Very good," Jean said, a tiny smile curving her full lips. "She most likely had you under her influence, especially in her own house. We have no way to know what abilities she might have, learning her craft in such a fertile magical land. If you were able to catch even a hint of something, you're not as unaware as most."

"I'm unaware of what the hell I'm going to do now," McDuff said, then he remembered where he was. "My apologies, Father Hall. I shouldn't be talking that way in here."

"I assure you I'm not going to expire from the shock of hearing a policeman swear," Father Hall said, patting McDuff on the back. "You're going to report her now, aren't you?"

McDuff rubbed the back of his neck. "I might if I had any idea who to report her to. I'm not convinced my superiors will take this accusation seriously."

"No. All joking aside, that's not going to work," Jean said, tapping her short fingernails on the table. "But she's causing harm to too many people to be left alone."

"Can you help him, Jean?" Father Hall said. "Protect him somehow?"

"I'm nowhere near strong or trained enough to go up against someone like this," she said, picking up the toy again. "She had at least two very strong charms activated in this tiny thing. And that's only what we've detected. None of us would likely remember a bit of it if I hadn't set up this meager protection spell."

"That, then," McDuff said. "Can you give me something to keep me safe? Keep me from falling under her influence, as you say?"

Both men drew back when Jean shove her chair away and walked toward the table littered with books and papers. By the time they glanced at each other and toward her, she was coming back with a notebook bulging with papers.

"I believe I can do that, certainly," she said. "I may be able to protect more than you, though, if we can draw her out. How does she spread these clever little toys around the city? Or the world?"

"As far as I know, she sends them through the post," McDuff said, frowning. "You can't protect the whole of the postal network in London."

"Not the way you're thinking, no," she said, turning to a page covered with looping handwriting about halfway through the notebook. "But if this woman is a creature of habit, as most humans are, I may be able to protect her way into it. Can you place some small objects near the house?"

"I don't see why not," McDuff said. "What did you mean, draw her out? How can that protect anything?"

"You'll be far safer if you confront her outside of her house, Inspector. I expect she has quite a store of items there, probably charms and spells all over the place. Much as I admire a woman this strong and determined, and even more how I'd dearly love to learn from someone so powerful, letting someone continue to harm others this way isn't how I'm made."

CHAPTER 16

A MONTH LATER, Victoria stood in the entryway of her father's house, weak sunlight coming through the narrow windows beside the door barely lighting the space. For the first time in years—since returning to live in London—she hadn't been bothering to collect the post herself.

A familiar pale blue box sat on top of the letters and cards stacked in a silver tray on a high cabinet.

She nearly dropped the box directly in the waste with all the rubbish advertisements or crushed it under her heel rather than acknowledging it.

The past few weeks had been the most frustrating of her life.

She carried it up to her safe room before she opened it, not wanting any more unpleasant surprises. Jaji had taught her ways to eliminate magic from objects, a skill she'd never needed until now.

Victoria had wondered for years if anyone else on this

dank, miserable island had any knowledge like what she possessed. The Havershams were far from the only family who'd lived in the Caribbean and returned over the past decades. For education or to live, or simply to visit.

Having every charm she sent out from home fail, day after day, week after week, already had her halfway convinced she'd been found out before she'd received this especially unwelcome intrusion.

She'd carefully inspected their seldom-used brass letter slot in the front door: the normal post delivery route her father had years ago deemed unacceptable with Victoria's quiet encouragement. She then turned her attention to the rather grand post box he'd had built in the narrow front garden: a shoulder high tower made of rough-edged tan and black stones brought back from the Caribbean.

Victoria had quite happily played a role in selecting each stone, claiming to inspect it carefully for flaws and beauty, all while imbuing them with her and Jaji's magic. Ever since the private postbox had been completed—with a slot for receiving in front and a keyed box for outgoing in the back—everything she sent out from here had performed as she expected.

Until now.

She generally sent out more delicate work from a nearby public postbox, of course, including all of the pale blue boxes containing her special clockwork toys.

Why she'd received one back at this address at all was as big a mystery as why her special post lost all of its effectiveness as soon as it entered her own magically enhanced and protected dispatch system.

She lit five candles as much to light her work room against

the heavy rain as to create a neutral circle. She sprinkled a nearly invisible line of dust and salt from Jaji's stores in a ring around the candles before putting the tiny blue package in the middle.

"Please keep me safe, Jaji," she whispered, then used her knife blade to flip the lid open.

Victoria jerked back so hard her chair creaked, her body burning hot, then freezing cold.

The clockwork penguin, the one she'd sent to Mr. Abernathy.

In pieces inside the box, but unmistakable in more than appearance.

The toy *felt* like her magic.

She tipped the box over with her blade and watched the contents shift onto the table. Everything seemed to be there, including her tiny bundle of herbs, flowers, and dust. The packet had been cut open, the contents scattered inside the box. The original small blue notecard was still there, along with a new one with her name written on one side.

She hated to see it, and she wouldn't admit it even to herself later, but Victoria's hands trembled when she picked up the new note.

For the first time in all the years since Jaji started teaching her these ancient and incredibly powerful rituals, she was frightened of the unknown.

We have vital matters to discuss. Please meet my companion and me on Wednesday at 15:00 to discuss adjusting the limits to your influence.

An address she didn't recognize was written below. Victoria

stared out at the gray clouds low overhead, considering her options.

As much progress as she'd made in the past few years, she was nowhere near being able to return to Enceleas safely. Her father would never permit it, and one of his employees would undoubtedly tell him if she went in secret. If it were even possible in her society to travel alone, without anyone along to protect her supposedly weak and delicate person.

She might chafe at his control, but it was still reality.

He'd only redoubled his efforts to get her suitably married off after Mr. Abernathy faded into disgraceful oblivion. Victoria wanted no marriage at all, not before she achieved her goals. Even then, she would only accept a choice of her own making.

And still, for reasons she could not discern, all of her efforts to shift her circumstances were meeting with failure. Fresh herbs, new materials, even a recently opened container of Jaji's priceless ashes made no difference.

Victoria was left with the meager tools of a woman in a society built to suppress and ignore.

It wasn't enough.

Try as she might, she couldn't find another way to move out of her trap. She had to meet with this mysterious person who'd eluded her best memory charm and recognized her handiwork.

But she would not meet them unprepared.

CHAPTER 17

McDuff paced up and down the narrow lawn, trying to avoid the brown spots from the heat. A row of listless, drooping oak trees lined the boundary just beyond the grass. The sun right overhead offered no shade from the unseasonable and unpleasant weather.

A handful of wooden tables under a wrought iron shelter waited on the other side, but he couldn't imagine sitting calmly.

He was too busy fighting the urge to start running and not stop until he couldn't breathe any more.

He could run for a very long time, but that might not be far enough.

Jean sat at one of those tables, watching people walk through the broad, open park further on and writing in her notebook. This was nothing more than a simple research trip for her. Tracking down an oddity she hadn't expected to find in modern day London.

She'd even gone to the trouble of wearing an ordinary—if a bit old-fashioned—light blue dress rather than her usual trousers for the occasion. Her addition of a matching parasol to block the sun left McDuff wishing for his own version of the same.

Jean caught him staring at her and smiled before she went back to her notes.

McDuff decided he didn't want to know what she wrote about him.

He couldn't understand how Victoria Haversham had gotten under his skin so badly in one afternoon meeting. Even before talking to the priest and the scholar, he'd been thinking of the supposedly bereaved fiancé far too often.

Jean said he may have already fallen under Victoria's influence. That much was true, unknown magic or not.

McDuff walked a few feet into the oaks and sipped out of his own flask. Not nearly as fine as the rum Mr. Haversham kept in his study, but it would do.

The hell of it was he'd been thinking of his now-primary suspect even more after learning of what she might be able to do.

McDuff understood the hard push. The punch.

Physical force wasn't his first choice when it came to his work, and he'd seen first hand what it could lead to with his brother. And the scum he'd gotten mixed up with were nearly impossible to rat out that way, much less stop.

A subtle push, though, that was a different matter.

A suggestion could very well get McDuff right into the middle of the real criminals he'd been chasing for years, not just these cutthroat business types he'd been dealing with for weeks now. If he could do that, he could make a real difference in this city that groaned and twisted under the weight of their wicked games.

A subtle push might have let McDuff stop his brother before any of Michael's dreadful troubles began.

And maybe, just maybe, armed with whatever delicate weapon Victoria wielded so successfully, MacDuff could still manage to save him.

"Rob," Jean said, her voice low but demanding.

Victoria walked toward them, her head high and confident while her eyes tried to watch everywhere at once. Her dress was just as fine and stylish as when he'd last seen her, made of a lightweight dark blue silk that matched her eyes, and her hair was caught in a thick braid. She carried her own lacy parasol against the fierce sun.

She'd clearly added a typical corset to the more formal clothing as opposed to the loose fabric she'd worn when they first met. McDuff was of the opinion that she looked unnaturally…*contained* today.

Her figure and form were uncommonly appealing to his eyes without the restriction.

McDuff walked forward to meet her, making sure he was outside the salted circle Miss Marchér had cast to try to keep them both safe.

His job was simple and terrifying.

Keep his distance, but notice if anything changed once they passed inside.

Victoria's small purse and parasol didn't seemed like they could be threatening, but neither had a blasted clockwork penguin. Or a tiny nosegay brooch.

She wore it again, filled with tiny white flowers. He caught her irresistible aroma from several feet away.

"Inspector McDuff," Victoria said, glancing at Jean. "I'm surprised to see you today."

"Miss Haversham. Thank you for joining us. This is Dr. Jean Marchér. She's been consulting with me."

Victoria turned to face Jean, then walked toward her.

As soon as she stepped over the salt boundary, the scent from her flowers disappeared completely.

McDuff's fascination with her did not.

"Consulting," Victoria said. "May I ask what your consulting could possibly have to do with me, Dr. Marchér?"

"No, *please* don't call me that," Miss Marchér said, and her face actually turned a bit red. "Makes me feel too grand and old and distant. All I do is travel, learn, and write about it. Occasionally I teach. That hardly merits such an imposing title."

"Merit or not," Victoria said. "I presume you've earned the right to be called so, Jean."

Victoria pronounced the masculine form of the name perfectly without so much as raising her eyebrows. She sat across from Jean, leaving McDuff wondering which side to choose.

"I did my study and published my work, yes," she said with another broad smile. "Mainly because some of my teachers didn't believe a woman could, therefore they didn't try to stop me until it was too late. The title opens doors from time to time, so I'm glad of it."

Victoria inclined her head. "Though I was lucky enough that my parents allowed me to attend college here in London,

I've encountered similar limiting beliefs in my own life. Well done. I'll ask again, what has any of this to do with me?"

"From what I can tell, Miss Haversham," Jean said, leaning forward with that same smile, "you're far more accomplished than I in getting what you want."

"I don't know what you're getting at, but I'm afraid you'll be disappointed." Victoria's calm expression never changed. "Perhaps you have me mixed up with my father. He's the one obsessed with control. He's quite good at it."

"Outwardly, to be sure," McDuff said, taking his turn. "But I suspect you hold your own quite well when you must."

CHAPTER 18

McDuff pulled a small blue box out of his case and put it on the table in front of Victoria. The one he'd retrieved from the unfortunate Cheryl Mallory's desk.

Victoria leaned forward to glance at the open top, and her composure finally slipped. She closed her eyes for a few too many seconds, then folded her hands on the table.

"If you believe you know so much about me," she said, "why am I sitting here rather than being taken into custody?"

"That's the problem, though," Jean said. "We know almost nothing about what you're doing. Or why you're doing it."

"I'm quite sure Inspector McDuff knows a great deal about what I'm doing," Victoria said, smiling at him with no trace of warmth. "You won't have stopped at putting these two together."

"No," McDuff said. "What I'm afraid of is *you* won't stop at putting the two of them together."

"That little trick served its purpose," Victoria said. "I hadn't used it before, and I have no need to use it again. You'll find everything else I do is far harder to trace. Even if you had someone you could actually report it to."

"You have a point," McDuff said, his inspector's nature finally awake and in full control. "The businessmen you're turned to your own desires wouldn't be pleased with your interference, but they'd be as much at a loss about what to do as I am. On the other hand, we have your former fiancé and the young girl."

"Were you aware the girl tried to kill herself, Miss Haversham?" Jean said, leaning forward.

Victoria drew back, her brow wrinkling for an instant.

"My father didn't share that with me, no," she said in a low voice.

"That's how I came to be involved, you see," McDuff said. "Her parents were understandably distraught. They hired me to find out whether Mr. Abernathy was the one to poison her. Despite her family's suspicion, and my own, it turns out she did that herself once she realized she was with child."

"Wilfred never did learn how to keep that from happening," Victoria said. She blinked, as if surprised she'd said that out loud. "I am sorry to hear that about the girl. I was obviously wrong to use her that way. You, however, still haven't told me what you want of me. If I get up and walk away, you know as well as I do this matter would come to an end."

McDuff shook his head slowly, exactly the same way he did when questioning a murder suspect.

He wondered if he should be asking exactly the same questions.

"As far as the laws of the land," he said, "I'm sure you're

right. What I can do, though, is let Mr. Abernathy in on the secret. And Cheryl's parents would be most interested. I can assure you, they will take action."

Victoria stared at her hands, then looked into McDuff's eyes.

Hers showed no sign of fear.

"I have no interest in a partner, much less two. My father has yet to take the hint when it comes to marital *bliss,* but the two of you have far more information than he does."

"What is it you do want, Miss Haversham?" Jean said. "Besides not having an arranged marriage, which I wholeheartedly agree with."

"And if I tell you?" Victoria said, her head held high.

Mysterious broken spell or not, her hold over McDuff grew deeper in her defiant stare.

"Much as I would love to learn from you, this sort of interference cannot continue," Jean said, the regret in her voice clear. "If what you want is reasonable, might that be a fair trade for putting an end to your practice?"

"You've just stumbled onto the heart of it, Dr. Marchér," Victoria said. "This isn't only about control or interference. This is not some whim or way to fill my spare time while I wait for my father and future husband to provide my true destiny. This practice, as you accurately call it, is the focus of that destiny. Stopping is not so simple as you may think."

The answer flared into McDuff's mind as it often did during moments like this. Unlike at almost any other time, he hesitated. If his idea was correct, and in his gut he knew it was, this might be the best way to never see Victoria again.

"You want to return to the Caribbean," he said, forcing the words out. "To Enceleas."

"Inspector McDuff, you *have* been paying attention," she said, a half smile on her face. "You've even pronounced it correctly, when so many here can't manage. I didn't want to come to London in the first place, and I do not intend to live my days out in such a crowded, stinking, dank city. I will *not* live under someone else's control."

"What do you require to reach such a lofty goal?" Jean said. She turned her notebook to a fresh page. "I do have several contacts in that part of the world after my own explorations and studies. If I can be of assistance, I will."

Victoria scowled, then stared at the children running across the grass.

"I require my own power," she said, sounding angry for the first time. "Not what is grudgingly allowed by my father, nor you, nor some dreadful husband. I require not being dragged from one continent to another at someone else's bloody whim."

"I can arrange passage for you," Jean said, nodding to herself. "And I'm sure Inspector McDuff can make this troublesome investigation go away."

"Can he now?" Victoria said, eyebrows raised. She turned to McDuff. "And what would the price be for such generosity?"

"You'd have to stop your activities in London," Jean said. "Returning here wouldn't be acceptable, of course."

"Just ship me off and be done with me," Victoria said, getting to her feet. "As long as I'm a good little girl and stop this nonsense of controlling my own life, I get to be out of sight, out of mind. Out of the question."

"I can't… *We* can't let these things go on," McDuff said. He hoped neither woman noticed his distress.

"Well, even in oh so enlightened England, Inspector McDuff, Dr. Marchér, I don't have to have permission from either of you. Thank you so much for your concern."

McDuff grabbed her arm, horrified at his own action.

"I can't just ignore this, Victoria. Cheryl Mallory is still in hospital."

"Let go of me," she said in a terribly cold voice he couldn't force himself to ignore. "I won't interfere with Miss Mallory or Mr. Abernathy again. You have my word on that."

"I can't accept that," Jean said, standing herself. "Too much damage has already been done."

"Then do what you will," Victoria said over her shoulder as she walked away.

CHAPTER 19

McDuff sat in the residence across from the church again, staring at the clean table and orderly shelves. Two massive steamer trunks and a few smaller bags were piled up by the door. Not a trace of Jean remained in the austere space besides the woman sitting across from him.

She wore her usual white shirt and black trousers, but a black dress more akin to a riding habit waited tossed over a chair.

"Just wait until we get this straightened out," he said for at least the third time. "It *has* to be her."

"We're right back where we started weeks ago, my dear Inspector," she said with a sad smile, her French accent stronger than usual today. "Rob. Who can we complain to? Father Hall has no choice but to follow the orders from the bishop."

"And terminate your year of study after only a few months?" McDuff said. "We can't just give up this easily, Jean!"

"No? What exactly are you going to do about the reprimand you received a few days ago?"

McDuff sighed, rubbing the bridge of his nose.

He'd had his moment of rage and fury, followed immediately by enough whiskey poured down his gullet to forget his troubles for a little while. It had done him no good whatsoever.

What he was going to do now was put his head down, keep his mouth shut, and hope he could make everyone forget. Vicious lies about drinking on the job, far more than an ill-advised rum with Mr. Haversham, could follow him the rest of his career.

"She's found some way to work around your boundaries," he said.

"Evidently," Jean said, laughing softly. "That doesn't mean I have a clue what to do about that. If you do, by all means please speak up."

A key rattled in the door, and Father Hall walked in. His normally open face was downcast and sad, and he had dark, swollen circles under his eyes.

"I'm terribly sorry about all of this, Jean. The Bishop won't take another meeting with me, and no one in Rome has an interest in this tiny, poor parish. The biggest thing we have to recommend us is this collection of books and records. The Vatican is hardly impressed with our collection compared to theirs."

"It's quite all right, William," Jean said. "I always manage to land right side up."

"No, none of this is all right!" McDuff flinched at the harsh sound of his voice and the way the other two drew back from him. "We can't let her grow even more bold with every single thing she gets away with."

"Our only other option would be to find out what she wants," Jean said. "That or make good on your promise to tell people what she's done."

McDuff sat back, wishing he did have a large supply of spirit fine or cheap right that minute.

"Cheryl Mallory is finally out of hospital," he said. "But she's hardly recovered. I can't just drop a bomb like this in the middle of their family. Certainly not when I already had to report back to them that she nearly succeeded in killing herself with no help from the father of her child. And Mr. Abernathy's fortunes have soured to the point that I doubt he could influence anyone to act, even if they believed him."

"That again leaves us with finding out what she wants," Father Hall said. "We don't necessarily have to act on it, you know. Just find out and decide if it's worth the cost."

"She already tried to get to you, Father," McDuff said, glancing at an ornate white metal cross on the windowsill. "You think encouraging her to do more is wise?"

Thankfully the priest had brought it to Jean as soon as he received it in the post. They still had no idea what the dust and flowers in the tiny compartment in the base were meant to do before she disabled the whole thing.

"She's already managed to get to the Bishop anyway," Father Hall said, shaking his head. "Listen, she already knows where all of us live and breathe. Bring her here, Jean, where you're able to do whatever you can for our protection. Then we see what she has to say."

"You've seen more of her handiwork than we have, Rob," Jean said. "What do you think?"

"I think we're all vulnerable. Here or anywhere else. You managed to stop her for a while. She found a way around that, then attacked each of us directly for our troubles. We can't fool ourselves into thinking we're stronger than she is."

"No, we're not stronger," Jean said, "nor are we better trained. We'll just have to make certain we're more clever."

McDuff doubted very much that was true.

He didn't have the heart to say it out loud once he saw the looks on their faces.

They doubted it, too.

CHAPTER 20

Victoria lingered over her tea, in the same round room she'd shared with Inspector McDuff. Back when she hadn't expected anyone to be able to interfere with her in such a way. She stirred her cooled drink, staring into the cloudy cup without seeing it.

The frustrating man with his maddening questions hadn't simply intruded into her life. She was having trouble keeping him off of her mind.

"Victoria," her mother called from the entry. "You have a letter by courier!"

She sighed, wondering if she could manage to sneak past her mother without being seen. Probably nothing more than another lovesick missive from her father's latest idea of the perfect son-in-law, a loathsome man nearly twice Victoria's age. Bertrand wasn't the least bit put off by her best efforts at a disgusting aroma and repulsion charm.

Both her parents had adapted to this new savior for their

nearing-spinsterhood daughter with alarming speed and enthusiasm.

"I'll be right there, Mother."

Victoria got slowly to her feet, wondering for the thousandth time why she couldn't manage to influence or stop her father's matchmaking. She thought she had him slowed down after the end of Mr. Abernathy's threat, but the reprieve hadn't lasted. Whatever that Marchér woman had done to kill Victoria's power let her father get back to full strength.

The current preferred future son-in-law was even worse than the previous ones.

Her mother waited by the door, smiling, but not beaming the way she did when a suitor came calling. Victoria nearly tripped when she saw a nun in full black habit, surely not yet twenty years old, waiting just inside the front door.

She hadn't expected her special gifts to the bishop and Father Hall to go unnoticed, but this wasn't a response she'd imagined.

"I tried to explain to this young woman that it must be a mistake," her mother said, more curious than upset. "We're not Catholic, and I don't know why you'd have a message from a nun. She had your name and the house address, but she won't give me the letter."

"Thank you, Mother. I'll see what she wants."

When they were alone, the girl opened the small black bag she carried.

"I'm sorry to have upset your mother, ma'am," she said. "I'm Sister Amelia Taylor. I had clear instructions from Father Hall to give this to no one but you."

"She's not upset," Victoria said, opening the small white

envelope and pulling out a folded sheet of heavy paper. "Unless it's because she didn't get to read this."

We hope you'll join us to discuss all of our plans going forward and how we can assist one another.

Jean Marchér

"And what are you supposed to do now?" Victoria said, handing the note back to the nun. "Force me to go back with you?"

"No ma'am, of course not," Amelia said, her eyes wide. "Father Hall was hoping you'd specify him an hour to be expecting you. Dr. Marchér has been called away unexpectedly and will be leaving within the next few days, so time may be short."

Victoria managed not to say she was surprised the doctor was still there at all. At least the Bishop wasn't immune to her charms when she sent them in the correct manner. He simply operated more slowly than she expected.

"I'm free this afternoon if you think that will be acceptable," Victoria said.

"Oh yes, they'll be most pleased," the girl said, wiping sweat from her brow under the white cloth around her face. Victoria didn't want to imagine the heat collecting under the many layers of black fabric. "I'll let them know right away."

"If you can wait a few minutes, I'll have the carriage brought round and we can both ride back. I do hope the surprise won't be distressing to them."

Victoria watched the young nun thinking it through, shifting from one foot to the other.

"I believe they'll be too pleased to be distressed, ma'am.

And I would surely appreciate the passage. Warmer than usual today again."

"Come inside while I prepare myself, have some tea if you will," Victoria said. "Or some cool water. I'll let my mother know I'll be out this evening."

Back in her workroom, Victoria took the time to attach her nosegay to her dark green gown on the off chance Dr. Marchér wouldn't have time to set up whatever protection she was using.

She retrieved her gaudy new engagement ring from the small, rubbery bag Bertrand had ordered her to store it in. Victoria had listened to his condescending lecture about keeping the opal stone from drying out. She'd wondered how that could possibly happen in such a damp climate, but she was all too happy to comply with his pompous, detailed instructions.

He hadn't specified the liquid she should use for the moisture, after all.

Going out the back to the carriage house would solve another problem as well. Whatever the scholar had done to block her magic seemed to focus only on the front of the house. Any charms Victoria carried out this way and either entrusted with a courier or dropped in the public postbox weren't affected.

If this conflict continued, she expected the block would extend to every door of the house and possibly beyond. That would have been her next step if the positions were reversed.

Interference in her life and in her plans had gone on long enough, from her father or from this policeman and his priest.

Victoria had no intention of tolerating it any longer, whatever the cost turned out to be.

CHAPTER 21

McDuff walked as fast as he could without breaking into a run in the unusual afternoon heat. He was convinced the yellow and red brick buildings reflected the sun back on these narrow streets, leaving no hope of relief until nightfall. A nearly shoulder-to-shoulder crowd stretched as far as he could see in every direction.

If only the fancy new underground trains came out this far, he would retreat from the pandemonium at once.

An overturned delivery wagon full of chickens had turned this whole side of London into a nightmare of stopped carriages, trapped horses, and shouting drivers, so escaping into a hansom cab was impossible. McDuff felt a true and brotherly sympathy for the policemen struggling to force order onto the chaos. But not enough that he offered to stop and help them.

He armed sweat out of his eyes and spotted the church tower a few blocks away.

The blasted woman—witch, sorcerer, whatever she was—

waited for McDuff in Father Hall's office at the church. No word, no warning, and the advantage of surprise completely on her side. All McDuff could do was keep pushing his way through the gawking crowds reeking of sweat and too much perfume, and hope Jean was there to set up the guards against whatever spells Victoria Haversham surely brought with her.

Despite his lack of interest in helping clear the mess, for the first time in years he wished for his old patrol uniform and something as simple as a whistle to force his way through the staring hordes of people.

By the time he finally made it to the church steps and past a dozen more staring idiots, McDuff's hands itched for the coarse comfort and utility of his wooden truncheon.

The stark, quiet contrast of the cool and dark sanctuary hit like that club, leaving McDuff's head and eyes pounding. He kept walking, down the central aisle, past the vacant confessionals and empty benches. A splash of light from Father Hall's open door cut across the dull stone floor behind the ornate rugs on the stage.

McDuff's ears strained for Jean's soft, European accent even as his nose and other parts of him searched for Victoria's seductive presence.

Only Victoria, glorious in a dark green gown, and Father Hall were in the office. McDuff's heart pounded more from fear than from his mad dash through the streets.

What had the man been thinking, sitting alone with a woman they knew to be a dangerous manipulator?

"Inspector McDuff," Victoria said, smiling at him, her skin somehow looking cool and radiant. Her matching parasol could only explain part of the effect. "You look like you ran all the way from Glasgow."

"Almost," he said, resisting the urge to wipe at his sweaty brow again. "I was surprised to hear you'd dropped by to visit Father Hall unannounced."

"It's quite all right, Rob," Father Hall said. "We've only been talking. I haven't signed or agreed to anything."

McDuff sat beside Victoria, watching them intently. Both seemed calm and relaxed, as if they'd known each other for years with no difficulties to sort out. He hoped the rich, floral scent from her nosegay drowned out any aromas he'd brought with him from the street or from his armpits.

"Will Dr. Marchér be joining us?" McDuff said.

"She'll be here any minute." Father Hall glanced at a black slate mantel clock, lurking like a huge humped eye above the huge fireplace. "She's been visiting with the Westminster Diocese, hoping to view a few items in their collection before she has to leave."

Victoria turned to McDuff, then dropped her gaze to the floor.

"I was disappointed to hear of her transfer."

"I'm sure you were completely surprised by that," McDuff said, his voice sharp.

"I wasn't surprised, no," Victoria said. Her eyes and voice at least seemed honest. "I know the two of us could learn a lot from each other. I hope suitable arrangements can be worked out between us."

The solid thump of the closing door in the silent church followed by quick, tapping footsteps kept McDuff from responding with more anger. Jean swept in a few seconds later, looking far more put together after her hurried trip than he felt. She wore a light blue cotton dress, long in skirt and sleeve but nearly as scandalous in the thin fabric as her usual trousers would have been.

"I do hope all is well here," she said. "I arrived as quickly as I could."

"We're fine, Jean," Father Hall said. "Thank you for cutting your visit short."

When Jean caught his gaze, McDuff shrugged.

"I haven't set any spells or charms," Victoria said. "If that's what your concern is, please put your minds at ease."

"Do you mean to tell me that unusual aroma I smell is innocent?" Jean said. She lingered by the door, spinning the tip of her closed parasol against the floor, and McDuff finally noticed she held her black doctor's bag in the other hand.

"It may not be innocent, but all of you have seen it before." Victoria slipped the tiny silver vase full of purple and yellow flowers away from its place above the swell of her breasts and placed it on the desk. "Feel free to set whatever sort of containment you wish. You'll find I have nothing else to defend myself with."

Jean stared at her for several seconds, and Victoria looked back without flinching. The scholar took a deep breath, deposited her parasol beside Victoria's, then set her bag on the desk as well. She pulled out the same brown candle, rough three-legged bowl, and primitive pottery McDuff had seen her use several times.

The same sort of rough pottery he'd seen at Victoria's house at tea, in another lifetime.

"I'll set a basic charm, then," Jean said. "Enough so we can speak honestly. Father, you may want to bring whatever powers you have to bear as well."

Father Hall drew back, then nodded. McDuff only stared as the priest bowed his head and muttered under his breath and Jean did nearly the same. Victoria watched McDuff instead, her dark blue eyes more curious than afraid.

Her confidence and willingness to cooperate made McDuff far more uneasy than her earlier defiance.

When Jean finished, she, McDuff, and Victoria watched Father Hall in silence, none of them willing to interrupt whatever elaborate prayer he was sending up.

He didn't quite hold his hands together like McDuff remembered seeing in church as a small boy. The priest's hands moved in a tight, shifting grip, one on top, then the other, the skin turning pale under his fingertips. His face shifted in much the same way, his eyes, forehead, and lips clenching and wrinkling as the low stream of words continued.

To McDuff's eyes, so long practiced in observing people in distress, Father Hall didn't look like he was making a request or having a conversation with his God.

The man was begging, desperation clear in every bit of the constant motion.

Father Hall finally took a deep breath and sighed.

"Shall we begin?" he said.

"We've already begun," Victoria said, waving her hand at the arrangement on the desk, her tiny vase surrounded by Jean's charms. McDuff realized he could no longer smell the flowers or whatever else the container held. "You've disarmed me. Now please tell me why you've called me here."

"You called yourself here," McDuff said, falling back on his normal interrogation routine in the least normal situation he could imagine. "When you arranged to have Jean's residency terminated, got me reported for drinking I didn't actually do, and sent only you know what to Father Hall."

"If you were trying to get our attention," Jean said, "you succeeded."

"Now you must tell us what you want," Father Hall said. He leaned back in his chair and laced his fingers together over his black robe. "Once we get past you getting back at us for interfering, of course."

"I will agree to nothing if you continue to interfere with my plans." Victoria's voice was calm, but McDuff didn't miss the flash in her eyes. "I'm sure that will come at some cost to me."

"You say you want to leave London," Jean said. "I'm sympathetic to how difficult something as ordinary as travel can be for a young woman in these times. When do you hope to depart?"

"Within a year. Assuming I can manage to undo the damage this little delay has caused."

"And when you go," McDuff said, "your activities in London will cease?"

Victoria stared at him for several seconds before she answered. Something in her gaze—a heat altogether different from the misery outside—made McDuff's heart pound without his permission.

"I may need to attend to my father's business affairs from time to time. As long as he allows me to support myself in the Caribbean, I don't foresee the need for more overtly criminal activities."

"You think he'll let you go?" Jean said. "Just like that? I'm quite sure I saw the announcement of your new engagement a few weeks ago."

Victoria held up her left hand, the flash of an engagement ring clearly visible. McDuff thought the huge, oval stone was a fiery red opal surrounded by smaller red stones.

He didn't have to ask to know that bauble Victoria was obviously disgusted by cost more than he earned in a year. Probably two.

"One of the results of your meddling," Victoria said. "Bertrand isn't quite as virile as my father's first choice, with only three children. Every horrid one of them older than me. This latest vile match made it clear he expects me to add to that total, and quickly."

McDuff's stomach turned at the thought of a grizzled old man pawing all over such a beautiful, if dangerous, young woman. Her lack of interest only made the image more disturbing. Father Hall's features were as clenched and drawn as they had been in prayer. Jean scowled, her full lips turned down.

"This part I'm truly sorry for," Jean said. "No woman should have to endure such arrangements against her will."

Victoria leaned forward, both fists tight in her lap.

"Then let me fix it! If this nightmare doesn't go much further, I won't have to take the drastic action I did before. I acted selfishly, and in desperation for myself. I truly did not want that girl to suffer so."

McDuff watched her, his eyes narrowed. He hadn't spent enough time with her to know for certain whether she was lying or not. If she was, Victoria was as accomplished as any actress on the stage. He supposed the stakes were far higher than for the largest theatre in London.

"Won't your father find another?" he said. Once the words had escaped, McDuff couldn't find any way to retreat. "If you dispatch this new fiancé, will your father resume the search?"

"He will want to," Victoria said. "If I don't find a suitable match for myself. One my father *and* I can live with."

"And where will you find such a man?" Jean said. Her eyes met McDuff's for the briefest instant, and his heart again lurched against his ribs. "He seems to prefer you with men at least twice your age. I assume that is not your preference."

Victoria turned away and stared at the floor.

"My preference is to avoid such nonsense," she said. "At least until I'm settled back at home. If we're to keep my father from searching the obituaries for recently widowed wealthy men, I'm afraid a cooperative match must be found."

"*Cooperative?*" Father Hall said. He leaned forward and tapped his fingers on the dull, scarred wooden desk. "How do you mean that?"

"I simply mean a man who doesn't disgust me on sight." Victoria glanced at the priest, then she stared into McDuff's eyes. "One who will let me pursue my own interests, even if that means leaving England. A man who will impress my father, with my assistance, even though he's not ancient and focused on nothing but money. Even if he has a passion all his own that consumes much of his own life. A passion one might even call noble."

CHAPTER 22

MCDUFF OPENED HIS MOUTH, but his brain could go no further. Had he not daydreamed, and nightdreamed, about Victoria since he first shook her hand in her father's house weeks ago? He certainly didn't have the brightest prospects when it came to making a match for himself as a glorified policeman with the anchor of his brother round his neck.

No.

Nothing romantic or even practical was on the table here. No matter how attractive this woman was, how intelligent, how beautiful, how powerful, he'd be nothing more than a pawn.

A useful plaything with no chance of ever knowing the rules of the game.

"I do not like the way this is going," Jean said. She glared at McDuff, but his brain remained useless and frozen. "We all agree that enforced matchmaking for women is horrible. What would be the difference if the same happened to a man?"

"No one is enforcing anything," Victoria said. "That is the difference. *Choice* is the difference. A man in this situation would be free to decide for himself. I would never have that simple freedom with my father's parade of suitable old men. I'd be nothing more than a pretty little brood mare with a babe at each teat, year after year, until I join the nameless, forgotten first or second or third wife in the grave."

McDuff shook his head, finally jarring his mind into motion again.

"Are you saying Mr. Abernathy freely made the decision to ruin his life?" he said. "To ruin the life of that young girl? The same way your father's business partners decided to make questionable changes in their work that happened to suit you?"

"Or that your father freely decided to turn so many aspects of his business over to you?" Father Hall said. "Even though you're his only child and quite gifted at such things, he remains a man who wants to marry you off to the best prospect."

Victoria shook her head. "No, I'm not saying those men decided, though I can only work with their desires in some way. That's the hard limit of my power, you see. But a man who joined forces with me in a true partnership would know what I can do. That alone will help keep him free of mind."

"He'd be nothing more than a piece on your chessboard," McDuff said, more loudly than he'd intended. "The same way so many men rotting in prison are, all around this bloody country."

"I understand your feelings about your brother, Inspector McDuff," Victoria said. "Please allow me to point out that someone with my abilities, or with Dr. Marchér's, may have been able to help him before he ended up in such dire straits."

Cold deeper than the stone of the church sank into McDuff's bones. Of course she knew about Michael, how could it have been otherwise?

Victoria knew the secretive inner workings among many of London's most prominent businessmen. His brother's arrests and imprisonment were hardly secret.

The last thing he needed was more temptation to agree to an insane offer that had not yet been made.

But what if she truly could help his brother, succeed where McDuff had repeatedly failed?

"You can't change a man's nature like that," McDuff said, rubbing his face. "Not if your power is limited to their natural desires as you say. If you know about my brother, you know he's had this trouble all his life."

"Can't I bend someone's nature, though?" Victoria said, tilting her head. "Or at least their actions? Someone unaware of what I'm doing? You mention Mr. Abernathy and Cheryl Mallory to me at every turn. Do you believe their behavior was not at all influenced by me?"

"I wouldn't go so far as to call that a dramatic change," McDuff said. "From your accounting, Mr. Abernathy lusted after you as nothing more than a young woman suitable for producing more children for him. Cheryl Mallory would have proven far more pliable, and she's clearly able to serve his purpose. And what teenaged girl with overbearing parents wouldn't be flattered by such attention, the promise of a life of ease and luxury in a home all her own?"

"If you are indeed limited in this way," Jean said, "the matter of your father still trying to marry you off despite your best efforts will remain devilish to solve. Otherwise you wouldn't need an ally to shift him against his own desires."

"You're not suggesting using Rob as some kind of pretend suitor," Father Hall said, his face nearly as pale as his hair. "Nothing more than a way to bend your father against his will and toward your own. None of us can allow that. Not at all, and certainly not with the fate of your previous fiancé."

"No one has mentioned doing any such thing, Father," Victoria said. "But I must say the only one who could allow or not allow the arrangement would be Inspector McDuff himself."

"No." Jean's face was stony and nearly as sharp as her voice. "He would never know his own mind, his own desires. For all we know, you're influencing all of us right now, Miss Haversham."

"Wait, just wait!" McDuff said. This time he wasn't upset by his rising voice, nor by his thick Glaswegian rolled Rs and clipped words reasserting themselves. "I am right here. I can hear you. I'm a grown man, not some simpleton who must be guarded and cared for."

"You're also the one who worked all of this out," Victoria said. "No one else has ever suspected me or my abilities before. No one else in all of England would be safer from my influence than you."

"This is madness!" Jean shouted, her French origins as clear as McDuff's Scottish. "You may have seen her pattern, Rob, but it was outside of you. In other people. How could you ever know what's been laid against you by someone so skilled in magic you don't understand?"

"Skilled in manipulation as well," Father Hall said. "I'm

young by the Bishop's standards, as he's made quite clear over the past few days. But I've heard more than enough confessions full of justifications, endless explanations. All the reasons on God's green Earth that the confessor was right in what he or she did, and I'm simply not able to understand. Spells or not, Miss Haversham, we can't trust a word you say."

"That's another choice you have," Victoria said. She twisted the opal ring, staring at the brilliant play of colors across the stone. "You've managed to thwart me, at least a little. You also understand I still have ample powers and influence to wield as I will."

McDuff rubbed at his temples with one hand, wishing he could make everyone stop long enough for him to think. Wishing for one of Victoria's spells to freeze time, or at least freeze people, so he could take his time and understand the currents and clashes all around him.

"I am not agreeing to anything," he said without uncovering his eyes. "All I want to know is what you think you could do for my brother."

"Rob, *no*," Jean said, touching his arm. "This is—"

"I know that, Jean" McDuff said. "This is madness. My whole life has been taken over by my brother and whatever his own madness is. If there's a chance I can get him out instead of leaving him there to rot, I at least want to know what that chance is."

CHAPTER 23

McDuff counted five of his own breaths before he opened his eyes. Victoria watched him, hands folded in her lap, the perfect image of calm. He nodded.

"I'd first have to arrange for his transfer," she said. "Out of Fodelson Prison into an asylum."

Father Hall leaned forward, his pale eyebrows drawn together.

"Please, Father," McDuff said. "Let her speak."

"An asylum where I could influence his treatment," Victoria continued. "He won't be left to experiments and torture. He also won't be in danger of being picked up on the street or falling into worse company than he kept before. He's your brother, he must hold you in some sort of esteem. I hope he can be made to trust you more than these street thugs, or any of us if you like. You can see how he does, Inspector. All of you can. I hope you do. That will let me know more about what works and what doesn't in a case like this."

"And then?" Father Hall said. "If you sway him to turn toward us rather than toward more trouble?"

"If he recovers sufficiently, it should be fairly simple to arrange for his release. If my treatments work, he would return not to his former habit of only getting arrested again, but to a chance to live safely among peaceful society. You could keep him from drifting back to the ones who used him and let him end up in prison."

"How long would this treatment last?" McDuff said. "Would my brother be living out his entire life under your control?"

For the first time, he was sure he saw a flash of sympathy in her eyes.

"Most likely, yes," she said. "Mine or yours. All of yours if you like."

"I would feel better if it were all of us," Jean said.

McDuff couldn't think of any reason to argue.

"As you wish," Victoria said. "No spell or enchantment lasts forever, and they're not as powerful as I'd like. My father appears to have convinced himself sharing his business with me makes sense, despite the fact that he wants me to be a breeding slave in another man's home. If I were to withdraw all of my pressure, his ideas would probably change. Would a life under another's guidance be preferable to prison or gangs in this case, Inspector?"

McDuff stared at her for several seconds, while a dim, slow rolling tide started up in his belly. A hope too faint and fragile to trust, especially when so many hopes for Michael had caused him nothing but pain over the years.

Jean rescued him from an answer he couldn't yet give.

"And if this guidance works?" she said. "What's your price, Miss Haversham? What debt would we all carry to keep us in line?"

"We return to choice, Dr. Marchér," Victoria said. "Right now I'd accept removal of whatever blocks you've placed. That would make it possible for me to help Michael McDuff and make my own arrangements. And I ask for consideration of an alliance against my father's interference in the future. I'd hear your terms, please, Father Hall. Dr. Marchér."

"Stop Jean's transfer," Father Hall said at once. "She stays out her year here, longer if she wishes."

"Agreed," Victoria said. "I'm sorry to tell you your Bishop is most easily suggestible. If we could find a way to trust each other, Dr. Marchér, we may learn a great deal from each other in the future."

"That remains to be seen," Jean said, her voice and eyes cold. "If you're able to help Michael McDuff, will you consider helping others? Treatment methods have improved, but too many souls remain trapped in those barbaric places, here and overseas."

"I can make no promises until I understand how this will work," Victoria said. "I hope Inspector McDuff can guide me in how to best help his brother. The minds of strangers, especially those who are already ill, may prove far harder to soothe. If I find success, perhaps I can teach you what worked, Dr. Marchér."

"This is all wonderful and exciting," McDuff said. "I'm truly sorry to interrupt with a bit of reality. What makes you think you can get my brother transferred, Miss Haversham? If you know about him, you know how serious his convictions were this last time."

Jean and Father Hall stared at McDuff, and guilt joined the other emotions roiling inside of him. He'd never spoken a word of Michael's troubles to either of them. Despite Michael's convictions standing as public record, he doubted any of his acquaintances in London outside the police knew what initially brought the two of them here.

"The charges say he was involved in a bombing," Victoria said. "Not as the mastermind, but Michael placed the device. Far more serious than the trouble he got into in Glasgow. That bomb was found before it detonated, correct?"

All the air left McDuff's body, leaving him light-headed. She said it so matter-of-factly, as if she'd simply read about a stranger in the news that morning.

"If it had detonated…" McDuff said. He had to stop and force a deep breath into his lungs. "If that bomb had gone off, he'd have hard labor or worse. As it is now, he's inside for life."

Victoria shrugged. "Were you aware that one of the men who attempted to kill Queen Victoria was ruled insane? He was sent to Broadmoor for treatment rather than to prison."

"That was decades ago," Father Hall said. "Has your brother ever had that sort of trouble, Rob?"

"Michael is not insane," McDuff said. "I don't know what causes him to do these things, no. He's far more suggestible than he should be. More innocent, almost simple sometimes. I've seen true madness closer than I ever wanted to. I've never seen it in him."

"That doesn't mean others won't see it," Victoria said. "I've persuaded people of less reasonable things than a career criminal having mental problems. I don't yet know how you've managed to block me so successfully. If this doesn't work, I'd expect you to put whatever it is back in place."

"If your brother is not insane, what happened to him?" Jean said. Her voice was soft, her eyes kind, but McDuff still felt as pinned to the spot as any suspect under questioning. "What is his weakness that leads to such problems?"

He stared at his hands, knotted together in his lap as tightly as Father Hall's had been in prayer. Michael was an adult, and as so many had pointed out over the years.

His brother. Not his son.

He still felt keenly responsible for where his brother had ended up.

"Michael will promise you Heaven and Earth," he said, still focused on his hands. "And I believe he means it when he does. Then he'll walk away from you and talk to another person he wants to please. He'll promise that person the same, no matter if he told you the opposite. The person he's with at the moment controls what he thinks. And what he does."

He tried and failed to rotate the stress out of his shoulders, tried to rub the tension of memory out of his neck. He knew from too much experience that he'd never get his brother's choking sob and screams out of his mind.

"Michael always seems to remember that I'm supposed to help him, though. He never forgets that, no matter what he's done. What an impossible place he's put me in. I suppose he never fails to depend on me, even when he believes I've let him down yet again."

"I'm so sorry, Rob," Father Hall said before he turned to

Victoria. "If Rob agrees, is this a weakness you believe you can help with, Miss Haversham?"

"Again, I won't know until the spell is cast," she said. "Odds are high I can persuade him to keep his focus on you, Inspector, and not fall victim to criminal minds."

McDuff kept his feelings about Victoria's criminal mind to himself for the moment. His stomach twisted at what he was about to say, to suggest, but he had no other option if they were to even consider this thing.

"It won't be as simple as that," he said. "Michael isn't the only one we have to worry about. There were several successful bombs that day that he had nothing to do with. That doesn't mean anyone involved has forgotten what he tried to do."

"What are you suggesting, Rob?" Jean said. "Do you think this won't work?"

He held his breath, trying to force his thoughts into some other shape and form. By the time his head pounded and nothing changed, McDuff understood what he was about to put into action and why. And how horrible it would be for his brother, and for him, if they succeeded.

"I think the only way it could possibly work is if he believes it," he said. "Michael is not the sort to be able to fool the guards or doctors, even if he understands why. To get him transferred, you'd have to make him and everyone around him believe he actually has gone insane. Him most of all."

Jean winced and looked away, and Father Hall stared at his fingers, slowly moving a rosary from one bead to the next. Only Victoria met McDuff's gaze.

"Are you able to do that, Miss Haversham?" he said. "Make

my brother believe he's insane, make him act that way, when he isn't?"

"Many would argue she has already done this to two others," Jean said, the corners of her mouth turning up just a little. "That's what brought all of us together."

"I won't deny what you already know," Victoria said. She looked up at the white plastered ceiling, her red lips pursed, the first time McDuff had seen discomfort from her. "He's been there for six years, I believe?"

McDuff nodded, certain where the conversation was about to turn and determined not to force it there. Victoria needed the leverage over his brother. He still wasn't about to give it to her without trying to resist.

Jean scowled. "Would the guards and administrators accept such a change in him, then? Even with your impressive knowledge and best efforts, I cannot believe you could convince the entire prison system."

"This is where the supposedly model prison does much of the work for us," Father Hall said. "An alarming number of previously stable inmates have deteriorated and been transferred to asylums since Britain adopted this new constant isolation system. Sadly many in the clergy were advocates in the beginning."

"Michael tells me he never sees or speaks to anyone besides the guards," McDuff said. "And the chaplain. They don't even exercise with other prisoners." He leaned forward and looked into Victoria's blue eyes. "Yes, I believe you can do this after seeing your previous work. What you must ask yourself, all of you, is if you can live with the results. I'll be asking myself the same question. I have been for years when it comes to my brother."

"I'm afraid I've spent more time than you might imagine with that same question," Victoria said. Her words were slow, her eyes again sympathetic. "Sometimes my actions have unintended results, so asking doesn't always prepare me. It didn't with Cheryl Mallory. I ask all of you to consider the chance of the same thing happening with your brother."

"Can you promise not to work your charms on any of us?" McDuff said. "Jean will help us take precautions, but that's not enough. You must prove your cooperation, if not your trustworthiness."

Victoria stared at the priest, the doctor, and finally back at McDuff.

Even knowing they'd have to put his brother through such hell, the potentially damaging hope had worked its way into his chest and his throat, warming him nearly as much as too much whiskey did.

"I promise to direct all of my efforts toward helping Michael McDuff," she said without looking away. "I give you my word."

McDuff could only hope they weren't making a terrible mistake.

CHAPTER 24

VICTORIA STARED at the long mirror in the residence across from Father Hall's church, trying to recognize herself. Sister Amelia, the same young nun who'd brought her to the strange, intense meeting at that church two weeks ago had helped her get dressed. Even as an acolyte not yet in her twenties, Amelia knew the order and procedure for each garment to perfection.

London society hardly allowed simple clothing for women, but Victoria never would have managed the complicated layers without help.

A band of white cotton cut across her forehead right above her eyebrows, in front of her ears, and under her chin. With her unruly waves of hair invisible, her eyes looked huge and vividly blue. The white didn't do her pale complexion after years spent in England any favors. Bare of any cosmetics or embellishments, Victoria's flesh was closer to washed out milk rather than the porcelain tones her father praised so highly to anyone who would listen. A matching collar curved down to just below her breasts.

Above her face's strict confinement, a heavy black drape fell from across the top of her head to nearly the tips of her fingers. More soft woolen fabric made into a robe with a full skirt and wide sleeves completed the display. Victoria's features floated like a disembodied marble sculpture.

She wore no jewelry, perfume, or any other decoration under or over the heavy clothing. Only a long strand of dark red garnet and silver beads at her waist broke up the monotony. Father Hall had provided the rosary a week ago from the church's collection, and Sister Amelia attached it to the robe.

The crucifix hanging close to her right hip was beautifully made with an elaborate brass cross, nearly two inches long, and a finely detailed silver figure of Jesus displayed in eternal pain. Father Hall said it was from far to the east in Europe, nearly to the Black Sea.

The most important feature for Victoria's purposes was the cleverly hidden latch on the thicker than normal cross. And the compartment inside.

Thankfully the cool, rainy day reflected the season's turn toward autumn, leaving the windowless room chilly and damp rather than stifling and hot. For the first time in her life, she was grateful for typical England weather. She turned at a knock on the varnished dark wooden door, by far the most interesting thing in this empty beige bedroom.

Only the bright green flash of Jean Marchér's eyes were recognizable in the tall Frenchwoman's face. Every trace of her energetic black curls had been contained. Victoria had to admit Jean looked far more uncomfortable in the long, flowing gown than she felt. She'd only rarely seen the scholar wearing anything but dark trousers.

"I'm still not convinced this is entirely necessary," Jean said. "But since we're nearly identical and unrecognizable, I suppose it's worth it."

"I doubt my own mother would know me if I knocked at her door," Victoria said. "At least there's no need for a corset."

Jean watched Victoria for several seconds.

"I can ask our young Sister Amelia for confirmation," Jean said, "but I'm asking you. Have you hidden any spells aimed at Father Hall, Inspector McDuff, or myself in all these yards of fabric?"

Victoria held out both hands and looked down at herself. Her flat black shoes barely peeked out under the skirt.

"I'm defenseless. No jewelry or charms of any kind except for this rosary. The charms I did bring in case we run into trouble are all downstairs in my bag. All of you know what they are and what they do."

After another level gaze, Jean nodded. "I am also without any protection. Today is about Michael, and I didn't want to block your work. Still, I appreciate your trust."

For the first time since Jaji died, Victoria was being completely honest with another person.

And Jean was right. Her continued enchantment on her companions, especially Rob McDuff, would wait for another day.

"And the rosary is ready?" Jean said.

"Everything fit inside perfectly." Victoria caught the heavy crucifix in her hand, carefully avoiding the triggers at the top and bottom. "I had more room to work with than I often do with the clockwork toys. I just need to get close enough to him."

"That part we must leave up to Rob," Jean said. Victoria followed her out into the hall, dimly lit with gas wall fixtures. "He will have the hardest job of all knowing what's to come for his brother. Have you ever been inside a prison, Victoria?"

"Thankfully I've never had need to. I doubt the visits will be any easier once they transfer him to the asylum."

"The only one that would be easier on is Michael if all of this works."

The steep stairs going down to the library were easier to navigate with the sensible flat shoes rather than the heeled boots she'd worn on the way up. Victoria recognized the voices of Father Hall and Inspector McDuff.

She corrected herself silently. If her plan was to move forward, she had to get used to calling him Rob. At least inside her mind, for now.

"Sister Amelia outdid herself," Father Hall said, getting to his feet with a smile. "I wouldn't have recognized either of you."

"We're a matched set," Jean said. She turned in a slow circle, the skirt flaring out a tiny bit. "Inspector McDuff, you look far more respectable than usual."

Rob stood on the opposite side of the room, his face bright red. Victoria had to admit Jean again spoke true. The dark blue long coat and pants suited him whether he looked comfortable or not. The row of big silver buttons down the front gleamed, and he carried his rounded top hat with its own metallic embellishments under one arm.

He was obviously trying to keep himself from staring at

Victoria in her acolyte's garb. She took that as clear evidence that her previous efforts with him were working.

"Yes, thank you, Jean," he said, looking at the floor. "Haven't worn this thing in a while now. Can't say I've missed it."

"I'm sorry all of you are out of your element," Father Hall said, no longer smiling. "A bit of discomfort may help keep everyone focused on the difficult job at hand. Are your things ready, Victoria?"

"Everything I could think of." Victoria opened her plain brown leather satchel, smaller and far less noticeable than Jean's black doctor's case or Rob's brown inspector case. She lifted the false bottom under the stack of religious texts and white fabric squares. "Another of the charms for Michael, memory charms in case the guards suspect. Jean prepared these handkerchiefs to protect us from what I have to use. Everything we agreed to is here."

Rob stood beside her, peering at the small, opaque green jars hidden inside. Victoria knew the different shapes and sizes by touch, and she'd shown everyone what they were that last time they'd met two days ago. She suspected he committed details to memory every bit as well as she did and needed no reminders.

She was more gratified than she wanted to admit at the way his arm brushed against hers. Absent evidence of the overwhelming stink of the city in warmer weather, his clean, masculine scent appealed to her more than any of her suitors and their heavy perfumes.

Sister Amelia stepped through the front door, and her face lit up with a broad smile when she saw them.

"Oh, the two of you look wonderful," she said. "I'll admit I had my doubts this morning, but I'm well pleased. Your coach is waiting out front."

"Thank you for all of your help, Sister," Father Hall said. "This may all seem a bit strange, but this gives our errand of mercy the best chance of success."

CHAPTER 25

The coach was small and plain, less than half the size of the one Victoria's family owned, and painted a dull black. The bright red and green Haversham coach was designed for accommodating full hoop skirts and tall hairdos, with plenty of room for attendants to ride inside and out. This church-owned vehicle barely held four adults on benches not far removed from the hard wooden pews inside the sanctuary.

Father Hall sat with Rob McDuff on one side, leaving Victoria and Jean struggling to arrange piles of black fabric on the other. While the priest and the doctor talked quietly about the work ahead, Rob pretended not to stare at Victoria.

She didn't bother pretending not to watch him fidget. Adjusting his stiff, high collar, gazing out the small un-curtained window, feigning interest in the soft conversation he was not part of.

All while glancing at Victoria and looking away just as fast.

So much of her time and energy over the past year had been wasted doing her best to ward off male attention, mainly from her father's horrifying ideas of a perfect husband. Now Victoria tried to drag up her mother's advice for responding positively to a suitor.

Jaji's training on how to bend those suitors to her will was already proving effective.

Rob could not possibly trust her, not after learning exactly how she planned to control his brother and everyone around him. Even as young and inexperienced as she truly was in such matters, Victoria didn't need her mother or anyone else to tell her his desire was winning the battle with distrust, at least for the moment.

She did hold Rob's warm hand a second longer than was necessary when he helped her down from the coach, before she turned all of her considerable attention to the job ahead.

Fodelson Prison just outside the established area of London wasn't as frightening as she'd expected, at least not from the outside. The hulking gray stone facade held an intimidating soaring arched entryway and almost no windows, but it seemed more like a hospital or school than a permanent home for hundreds of dangerous criminals.

Once the harried and anxious guard dressed almost the same as McDuff saw their clothing, he barely glanced at their letter authorizing the visit. The only thing that mattered was his fingertips touching the heavy spell-infused paper. He and anyone else who handled the letter would quickly forget what they'd seen or read.

The guard's brief peek into her bag and McDuff's case

convinced Victoria she could have carried everything out in the open with a pistol on top and he never would have noticed.

Any impression the entry created of a place for people to heal or learn vanished when they passed through a gate with bars nearly as thick as Victoria's wrist.

The smell inside wasn't nearly as horrific as everyone had warned her. Rather than filth and human excrement, she only caught stale sweat and a harsh cleaner of some kind that made the back of her throat ache.

No warning could have prepared Victoria for walking through a huge, round three-story room opening out to four long hallways of the same height, each lined top to bottom with solitary cells as far as she could see.

The windowed glass dome and archways created a space that was surprisingly bright and airy. Victoria still felt smaller than a rat scurrying through a sewer.

She didn't want to contemplate the horrible crimes the men in those tiny rooms had committed. The thought of spending years locked up in a sunny but still decidedly un-gilded cage was nearly as bad.

Thankfully they followed McDuff to a small room instead of down one of those nightmare halls. A small, scarred table surrounded by six spindly wooden chairs took up the entire dim, stuffy space. Before they had a chance to work out who would sit where, someone rapped on the thick metal door.

Another guard, this one looking more sullen than harried, still held the slender club he must have used to make so much noise in one hand. He held the arm of a man who cowered but did not try to pull away in the other.

"S'posed to leave this thing here," the guard said, his voice a low growl. "Supervise these visits most of the time."

Rob moved quickly to shake the guard's hand and give him another copy of the memory-charmed letter. Father Hall folded his hands together and nodded.

"And we deeply appreciate your kindness and trust," he said. "We come to offer solace and comfort to this troubled young man's difficult journey. Peace be with you."

The guard snorted, jammed the letter into his pocket, then shoved the man none too gently into one of the chairs.

"Don't give a rip about solace 'n comfort, not in this place. Just keep 'im quiet so I don't have to."

He left the door open, just like Rob had said he would, but at least he walked out of the room. Their expectation of being overheard, and planning for it, was paying off already.

Different as they looked in the moment, Victoria would have known Rob McDuff's brother passing on the street, much less with the two of them only a few feet apart. The shape and form of their faces were near identical.

But Michael's dull brown hair was cropped close enough that his scalp showed through, with evidence that clipper had been wielded none too gently. Despite knowing he was a few years younger, Victoria wouldn't have been surprised to find out he was ten years the senior.

His cheekbones stood out sharp in the gaunt skull, and lines ringed his dark brown eyes. The drab gray uniform hung on his frame, showing no trace of Rob's strong arms and shoulders.

"Michael," Rob said, sitting beside his brother. "Mike, it's Rob."

The younger man seemed confused, then looked up at all of them.

"Who are all these people, Robbie?" His voice was a ghostly echo of his brother's, hoarse and slow with the words a bit slurred. Victoria wasn't sure if that came from screaming or never talking, or which would be worse.

"These are friends of mine," Rob said, nodding to them to sit. When they were all settled, with Victoria on Michael's other side, he went on. "They just want to talk to you about ways they may be able to help."

Michael looked around and smiled in a sweet, innocent way that broke Victoria's heart. He looked no older than fifteen and overjoyed at any kind of attention.

Rob's claims that he never quite understood what he got himself into suddenly made a lot more sense.

"Not gonna argue what gets me out of that room trapped all by myself," Michael said. "Come to pray for me, have you?"

Jean reached over and touched his arm. Michael patted her hand.

"My name is Jean, Michael. Have you been drugged? Did that guard drug you?"

"Wish they'd bring me drugs," Michael said with a slow wink. "Gibson'd sooner crack me on the skull as help me that much. I'm getting better as fast as I can."

Rob shook his head. "He's usually not drugged. This happened the last time he was arrested." He put his arm around his brother for a second. "When they brought him in none too gently after the bomb. I'd hoped it would fade over time."

Victoria gritted her teeth, trying to fight off her tears and surge of compassion for Rob and for Michael. She had no siblings of her own—and had grown up with constant reminders of how miraculous and difficult her mother's carriage of her had been—but she'd grown quite close to Jaji's children and grandchildren on Enceleas.

The grandchildren's sobbing when her father firmly called a halt to the extended goodbyes had been one of the most agonizing parts of that horrible day.

"Michael, my name is Victoria." She held out her hand and he took it in both of his. "We can pray for you if you'd like."

"Never understood how the Catholic prayers worked," he said, shaking his head. "Regular prayers either, not really. Too long to follow along or memorize, even when my mind was more clear."

"Many people don't memorize them," Father Hall said. He pulled out his own rosary, with plain wooden beads worn smooth from frequent use. He seemed calm enough, but his eyes were red. Victoria wasn't the only one having trouble staying with their plan. "Don't worry about that. I'll lead and the rest of you will follow."

"Is it okay, Robbie?" Michael said, turning to his brother. He let go of Victoria's hand and folded his on the table. "Will you pray, too?"

"I'll pray too," Rob said.

He smiled at his brother and folded his own hands. When Rob looked at Victoria, what she thought of as the solid iron shield around her heart cracked, so deeply she would have sworn she heard it.

She saw his years of pain and worry, his terrible fear and

heartbreak. The way he'd pinned more hopes than he knew was wise on whatever she was able to do.

Victoria would have to repair that damage before too much of her own heart was exposed and vulnerable, and certainly before she moved forward with her plans for Rob McDuff.

But right now, she had to do the best she possibly could for his brother.

CHAPTER 26

SHE PULLED the handkerchiefs out with shaking hands and passed them to Jean, Father Hall, and Rob, keeping one for herself. Michael watched with a puzzled smile on his face until his gaze was captured by the glittering red rosary Victoria pulled from her robe.

"We'll just follow where Father Hall leads," Victoria said, running her fingers over the garnet and silver. The beads were cool under her fingertips. "I'll help you. Okay?"

Michael nodded, his eyes still on the glinting red stones. Victoria saw the exaggerated sparkle and fire thrown off by the garnets against the walls, ceiling, and table, though she and the others were immune to the effect.

The enchantment held Michael's attention and that was all that mattered.

Father Hall crossed himself, and Victoria noticed Jean and Rob did the same. She was no more religious than either of them were, but she followed suit. A beat later, Michael copied her.

"I believe in God, the Father Almighty, Creator of heaven and earth," Father Hall began. They'd all agreed he would speak loudly enough to be heard outside the door, but Victoria wasn't the only one who jumped.

Her heart beat hard, the noise in her ears making it hard to concentrate.

All the spells and enchantments she'd cast over the years. Many of them deliberately harmful, like what she'd done to her former fiancé and an innocent girl.

None of them had affected her like this.

Maybe being face to face with her target, close enough to hear him breathing, smell the faint undercurrent of sweat on his skin, had been her own terrible mistake.

Father Hall ended the creed with a much softer "Amen."

The next part she knew well enough to say on her own, and Michael did as well. He spoke a second ahead of the priest's raised voice without ever looking across the table.

"Our Father, who art in Heaven…"

She shifted the stones again, watching Michael McDuff closely.

Rob was right about the younger man not truly being simple. Michael's months and years of confinement with nothing but the same walls showed, though, in his quick attention to the flashes of crimson light.

Victoria held the heavy crucifix carefully, the slightest twitch away from triggering the magic within.

Father Hall ended with another amen, his grip on his own rosary shifting to the cluster of three dark wooden beads just above the crucifix. They'd all agreed the repetition of the short prayer was when the guard would likely stop listening, Catholic or not.

Victoria risked a glance at the others' faces. Father Hall had his eyes closed, his entire body paused with his thoughts. Jean watched the priest, her own green and blue rosary puddled in her upturned hand.

Rob stared at Victoria, tears standing in his brown eyes.

When he nodded, those tears spilled over.

Father Hall spoke again. "Hail Mary, full of grace! The Lord is with…"

"Michael," Victoria said in a low voice. "I need you to listen to me now."

His gaze locked onto hers.

"I have something to show you. Something for your sight alone."

Michael narrowed his eyes until she held up the crucifix. Victoria turned it so the silver reflected across his face.

Between the near chanting of the other three and her manipulation of the rosary, he was half hypnotized already. What Victoria had to do next would be absurdly easy.

That was surely what made it so hard.

"…Amen. Hail Mary, full of grace! The Lord…"

"Watch the light," Victoria said.

She raised the handkerchief to her nose, trusting the others to do the same. The amount of steam would be small, but amazingly potent.

"…pray for us sinners now…"

"The light?" Michael said. He leaned closer to the crucifix.

Victoria squeezed the nearly smooth buttons on the top and

bottom of the cross. Tiny gears whirred into life, far too quiet to be heard even without the ongoing prayer in the background.

A puff of faint white mist floated out of the hollow pinpoint of Jesus' navel.

Michael leaned closer and inhaled. Victoria breathed in the spicy aromas of basil and anise soaked into the white fabric, called upon the power of bloodroot and Jaji's ashes for protection and power.

"...and at the hour of our death. Amen. Glory be to the Father, and to the Son..."

The man beside her wrinkled his brow for a second, then sat back. His change from confused to curious was clear in the smallest shift of his eyebrows.

"Michael, you must listen to me," Victoria said, dropping the handkerchief and the crucifix in her lap. Both had served their purposes. "The only four people you trust are in this room. No one else. Do you understand?"

He looked at Father Hall, Jean, Rob, and back at Victoria.

"...Thy will be done..."

"I understand," Michael said.

"The next few weeks will be confusing," Victoria said. "You will say and do many frightening things, and worse may happen all around you. Just stay calm. Everything will change soon, but it will all be good for you. Can you do that?"

"I can do that," he said. "Are they going to hurt me?"

Victoria grasped the crucifix, focusing on the cool, sharp edges against her flesh.

"If one of the guards raises his club," she said, "or threatens to beat you, you must stop whatever you're doing. You'll be upset and surprised at your own actions. That's exactly what you'll tell the chaplain and doctor, too. You don't understand what's happened. Do you understand?"

"No," Michael said at once. He nodded, though, as she knew he would. "I'll do what you want, though, if you tell me why."

Victoria drew back, surprised at his words.

"…as we forgive those who trespass against us…"

"This is best for you," Rob said, leaning closer. "And for me. Things will be hard, but they'll change for the better. I promise. You can trust Victoria as much as you trust me, Mike."

Victoria closed her eyes for a second, struggling not to read too much into the words.

"It is for the best, Michael," she said. She touched his shoulder. "That's all any of us want for you."

Rob stared at her a few seconds longer before he closed his eyes and rejoined the prayers.

"I trust only the four of you," Michael said. Rather than sounding dazed or asleep, he seemed more alert, more aware. His words were clear and strong. "No one else."

"…Blessed art thou among women…"

"Then listen to me now," Victoria said.

She leaned close to Michael's ear.

Trying to convince herself she was breaking her promise to bind him to all four of them equally for an altruistic reason was a fool's errand she did not wish to pursue. Victoria's sense of self-preservation led her to take hold and press her advantage, as it always would.

Her guilt tempered the degree and strength of the spell, but not the reality.

Michael would listen to his brother, the doctor, and the priest, certainly.

And he would hold Victoria's wishes most dear and close to his heart.

She whispered the sing-song phrases Jaji taught her years ago, the strongest magic Victoria possessed. The sound rose and fell with the chanting all around them. The rhythm and music of voices joined in a common purpose built and flowed through her, deep and true.

Both channels of holy words combined into an overwhelming river of power, washing over her, the man beside her, and everyone else in the room.

"…save us from the fires of hell, lead all souls to heaven, especially those most in need of Your mercy."

By the time Victoria sat back and joined the prayer to hail Mary, her own tears were falling.

"…Is now and ever shall be. World without end. Amen."

CHAPTER 27

For the first three days after his visit with his brother and the clergy, all was normal for Michael McDuff. He went about his quiet life in Fodelson Prison doing everything asked of him, keeping his head down and avoiding attention.

Attention from the guards was never a good thing.

On the morning of the fourth day, the fractures began to show.

When Michael McDuff woke that morning, he knew his usual daily workload was expected of him. After all, he'd been one of the best examples of the model prisoner since his arrival.

Calm and relatively happy, cooperative with guards or chaplains or doctors.

Always doing his duty to repay the debt he owed for the terrible crime he'd tried to commit.

The crime he still didn't quite understand.

That day, Michael only sat on his hammock and stared at the loom filling the far end of his cell.

He knew what was expected of him. He always did.

And he always did the work, whether with a loom or treadmill or hand crank, without question or complaint.

He didn't question or complain on that day either.

Michael simply did not do what was expected of him.

The evening guard asked him about the abrupt change of behavior. The prisoner was calm and polite, as always, as he explained how the voices from his ventilation shaft made it clear he was not to do the work today. If he did the work today, Michael McDuff said, he and everyone on his third floor wing of the prison would be severely punished.

The guard warned Michael that he would be the one severely punished, and only him, if the work went undone the next day.

The next day, Michael McDuff did work, but only at half his usual speed and efficiency. Repeated threats from the guard were met with renewed claims of the voices commanding him. And a terrible conflict of not knowing whether to obey the guards or the voices.

He was scheduled for a full medical examination the next day.

That night, the model prisoner who always slept deeply and quietly started screaming as soon as the lights went out. He didn't stop until a guard came into his cell with his baton raised.

Then the prisoner broke down in sobbing moans.

The guard would later report he would have bet his month's salary that Michael had no idea what he was doing the second before the cell door opened.

As soon as the guard closed the door and walked away, Michael screamed again.

When he, the guards, and the other prisoners finally calmed down, Michael told the overnight infirmary doctor that the same voices started whispering in his ear the second the lights went out.

Even with medication, increased visits from the chaplain, and more than one complete examination of his physical and mental health, Michael continued to deteriorate.

He progressed from refusing to work to dismantling the loom, from screaming at night to screaming at random times during the day.

Clearly the intense isolation was simply claiming another victim.

The only choice that remained, for Michael McDuff's well-being and for calm and order in the model prison, was making arrangements for a transfer to a mental health facility.

Upon discovering that none of the prisoner's family members or anyone else had visited for quite some time, administration arranged to inform his brother immediately.

CHAPTER 28

McDuff sat on a plain, uncomfortable iron bench outside Fodelson Prison, trying to keep his eyes away from the towering gray stones and heavy bars on the windows.

Even the administration wing of this place was secured and guarded at all times. After all, the most dangerous criminals in all of London, and certainly some of the worst in all of England, were behind those thick walls.

The past few weeks of waiting had more than halfway convinced him the walls were there to protect the inmates, not the general public.

Surely even the most diabolical mind inside didn't deserve the blatant manipulation his brother had been subjected to.

He shifted against the cold metal, trying to find a less bruised section of his back to lean against. McDuff had arrived nearly half an hour early, ahead of both his appointed time and Father Hall's arrival. He doubted anyone would let him in before the transfer started, even if he had the heart to walk into that place by himself.

The telegram had been awful, and the hurried conversation with an anxious nurse about Michael's condition far worse.

Sudden, rapid deterioration, most unexpected in a prisoner who had no trouble before then. Not unprecedented, though, by no means.

The poor man had struggled to convince McDuff that no one from the guards to the doctors to the clergy could possibly be to blame.

Sometimes the men inside just broke.

Whatever held them together slipped away.

McDuff thought the nurse was truly upset by Michael's new difficulties. He even felt bad for the young man, trying to explain all of this to a police officer of all things. He didn't feel nearly bad enough to admit he'd been the cause of his brother's mental rotting.

A flash of black off to the side, vivid against the gray stone and the matching skies overhead, caught McDuff's eye. The cramped black coach, the same one they'd all ridden out here in last time he'd seen his brother, had just turned onto the street several blocks away.

A much larger coach, one that had a reinforced cage inside, already waited for the next leg of this nightmare journey.

He'd lived out this eternal moment of waiting—the dreadful journey to come attended by demons and devils and the gibbering ghosts of both his parents—more times than he could count over the last week. Every single night when he closed his eyes. No amount of exhausting himself during the day or drinking himself senseless at night made any difference in the horrors taking place inside his mind at all.

Penance, he supposed.

Lack of religion or not, he'd been putting himself through one form of penance or another for most of his life over Michael. The past few weeks had been strangely calm on that front when he was awake, strangely devoid of his normal undercurrent of guilt.

Everything he'd tried for so many long years had either failed or made things even worse.

Whether it was for a good reason or only his mind's desperate need to stop the mental flogging, once he'd walked out of here on that awful day with Victoria, Jean, and Father Hall, he'd felt only relief.

Until the news that their plan was working, at least. Then the guilt, backed up behind some kind of idealistic damworks in his head, rushed back in to reclaim lost territory.

And make up for all that lost time.

The coach jangled to a stop right in front of McDuff's bench, and he stood with a grimace. This damp, cold air sank deeper into his bones every time autumn gained a foothold over summer.

"Hope you haven't been waiting too long," Father Hall said. The coach was off the second the priest's feet touched the ground. "We'll send word ahead from the asylum so the driver can meet us back here when this horrible business is done."

"I haven't quite been here long enough. Still not ready to go in there and face this."

Father Hall nodded, closing his eyes. McDuff would have

sworn the priest had new lines around his eyes and mouth, perhaps even touches of grey in his blond hair.

This ordeal hadn't been easy on any of them. Not even Victoria.

Least of all his brother, from the sound of it.

"I question myself every day," Father Hall said, his fingers brushing the crucifix hanging over his breastbone. "I never find an alternative, a different way we could have acted. And yet the questions never cease."

"I hate to have dragged you into this." McDuff finally looked up at the square guard towers soaring four stories over his head. "You'll never step outside to talk to some poor wandering soul again after this."

Father Hall smiled a little, but it was enough to lift the age from his face.

"If it brings a good man like you into my life, I'll do so every chance I get. All of us only do the best we can, Rob. No better, no worse. Unless we belong in this model prison to begin with."

The two men walked slowly up the steps. McDuff's gut churned more every time he raised his foot.

"How's Jean holding up?" he said.

"She's fretting, wishing she could be here to help. We all knew Fodelson administration would not likely want women involved in this, even church women supposedly experienced in such things. She made me promise to ask if you'd brought the charms just in case."

McDuff grunted, then lifted his brown leather case.

"Won't do us a bloody bit of good if we're searched, but I've got 'em. Letters with memory charms, handkerchiefs full of calm for whoever needs it. Even that tin of candies that Victoria claims will put someone out like snuffing a candle. I'm sure I'd use that one on myself accidentally if I kept them for long, but they're here."

"She's waiting with Jean," Father Hall said.

"Who, Victoria? You must be joking."

"No. She arrived about half an hour before I left." They stopped in front of the heavy iron door, at the threshold of facing whatever demonic work they'd done together. "She said waiting at home was going to be the death of her, especially if her mother kept asking what was wrong."

"I hope Jean took precautions," McDuff said. He forced his hand forward to pull the door open. "We never know what Victoria's reasons are."

"No, we don't." Father Hall lowered his voice as they walked, shoes echoing on the polished tile floor. "And Jean did, at Victoria's insistence. In this case, though, I truly think she's concerned. For whatever that's worth."

McDuff was relieved to reach the medical director's door before he'd be forced to respond.

His mind was too distracted, his heart too shattered with worry over his brother, to contemplate anything about Victoria Haversham.

CHAPTER 29

An anxious young guard opened the door before Rob or Father Hall had a chance to. Bright red splotches marked his pale cheeks, and sweat beaded on his brow.

His grip was weak and clammy when he shook McDuff's hand.

"Inspector," he said in a breathless voice. "Father. Glad you're both here, truly sorry about all the rush. The warden sent me to tell you he'd be delayed, but he wants to be certain you're informed and taken care of."

"The warden." McDuff tried to ignore it, but his heart thumped in his throat. "Has something else happened?"

The guard shook his head so hard his shiny black hat shifted to the side.

"I can't say. I'm sorry. The head doctor's right through here."

His face was red as a brick now, the color seeping down

past his tight uniform collar. Father Hall touched McDuff's shoulder.

"Thank you, young man," he said. He somehow managed to sound older than the guard though he didn't look it. "Peace be with you."

McDuff followed the guard's gaze, trying to remember if he'd ever walked through the door in front of him. The bright wood gleamed, the brass handle even more so.

No, not even at the worst of Michael's troubles over the past few weeks.

The doctors and nurses had always met McDuff out in that same cramped room where they'd worked whatever foul magic was finally having its effect.

Michael's troubles always seemed to get worse all by themselves. Interference had only ever sent him spiraling further than McDuff ever could have imagined.

"Inspector?" Father Hall said, holding his hand out toward that door.

McDuff nodded at the guard, then forced his feet to carry his body forward.

One step, then another, each like ripping his foot loose from the flesh and bones that held him in one piece.

The guard darted ahead, rapped the door with his knuckles, then opened it. He didn't meet either of their eyes as they passed through.

A great tank of a man shoved to his feet behind a vast desk before McDuff could say a word. He had to be close to seven feet tall, with shoulders nearly as broad as the door itself. He looked like he should be the head of security rather than any sort of doctor.

"Inspector McDuff," he said in a deep, booming voice, leaning across the desk with his huge hand outstretched. "Thank you for coming down this morning. So many families don't want to see what's happening. Can't say that I blame them."

McDuff's hand was swallowed, not by a shaky, sweaty grip like the guard's, but by a dry, hard, firmer than necessary hand that may as well have been made of solid rock. The director shook hard enough to make McDuff's shoulder ache, then reached toward Father Hall.

"Father, always good to have the Lord's support and attention with these matters. We do all we can do, and so often that's not enough."

"I only hope I can bring comfort to Inspector McDuff as well as his brother, sir." Father Hall sat, and a beat later, McDuff joined him in another angular wooden chair. "And comfort to you as well, of course. Doctor?"

The huge man shook his head and shoulders before he settled into his chair with a great sigh.

"Upton, Dr. Upton. Sorry about that, Father. Sad business, even for a place like this."

McDuff's entire body vibrated now, muscles and nerves twitching to do something. Anything, no matter how hard, had to be better than sitting here wasting time chatting.

He hoped that would be true, anyway.

"What's happened, Dr. Upton? I only had word that Michael was to be transferred?"

"He is, yes. This is the soonest we could arrange it. He needs a change in his care, more than I can provide. I'm afraid we've had to sedate him for the journey. I didn't want you to be alarmed when you see him."

McDuff's empty stomach lurched, and he was thankful all over again for the priest's presence beside him.

"And exactly why would the Inspector be alarmed?" Father Hall's voice was as sharp as McDuff had ever heard it. The doctor ran a hand through his short brown hair.

"This is why we're moving him today instead of in a couple of weeks when we'd planned. Michael McDuff has declined, as you know. His mental state has. Over the last two days, he's started harming himself."

McDuff groaned before he could stop himself.

The doctor's eyes widened and he leaned forward, making his chair squeak.

"This sometimes happens, Inspector. He will recover fully once he has the right care. I assure you, I've seen this before."

Father Hall leaned forward as well, his knuckles white with his grip on the chair arm.

"And yet you continue to run this prison the way you have while men lose their minds."

A brief rap on the door nearly stopped McDuff's heart, but the other two men continued to glare at each other. His body refused his brain's commands to turn around when he heard the door open behind him.

What had they done?

What had they driven Michael to do to himself?

"Doctor Upton," a gravely voice said, somehow releasing McDuff's paralysis. "Father. Inspector. We have everything arranged for the transfer."

The doctor let out a gusty, sour breath and nodded.

McDuff turned to see Warden Higgins' stiff, imperious figure in the doorway. He'd only glimpsed the man a couple of times, and that only in passing. The young guard was nowhere to be seen.

"Thank you, Warden," the doctor said. "I've warned the Inspector that the prisoner's condition has changed."

"Yes, well." The warden brushed at some imagined speck on his impeccable blue uniform jacket. "He'll be where he can recover by this afternoon."

McDuff closed his eyes, trying to catch and avoid the images in his head at the same time.

Michael running across the open grass in Glasgow Green, arms flung wide, laughing as only a wee boy of five could do. Their father and mother laughing together. An unusually clear day in the city, and an even more rare memory of their whole family together.

Michael may have gotten worse with their interference, but keeping him locked up in a cage here or one on the other side of the city had passed beyond torture.

It was slow homicide.

"We'll see him now," McDuff said, pushing himself to his feet. "And we'll see him on his way."

McDuff took a few steps toward the meeting room before he noticed the warden had turned the other way. He met Father Hall's worried gaze before they both followed. None of them said a word until they were back outside the prison.

"He's already out here?" McDuff said a beat before he realized how absurd it sounded. Nothing else made sense, but then nothing else about this day did either.

"Standard procedure, I'm afraid," Warden Higgins said. "In

cases like this, if the prisoner sees family members on the way out, they become even more agitated. They're not usually sedated, of course, but this does tend to keep everyone calmer."

McDuff shook his head, clenching and relaxing his fists.

Nothing about this, including the warden's presence, had him the least bit calm.

"Families don't usually ride along for a transfer, either." The warden stood neatly at attention beside the hulking black wagon, but his fingers twitched. "Or our busy prison surgeons. We're making an exception on both counts since you're with the police, Inspector McDuff."

"Generous of you," McDuff said. "I expect everything will be in order on the *other* side of our journey."

The warden's ruddy face paled, and all of his fidgeting stopped. McDuff smelled his acrid sweat even in the cool wind.

"I personally assure you everything has always been in order on both sides, Inspector."

"Thank you for all of your time and attention with Michael McDuff," Father Hall said, his hand on McDuff's shoulder. "We won't forget that."

Warden Higgins stared for a few seconds, clearly not sure how to take such words from a priest. He nodded once, then turned on his heel and strode back inside.

"That bastard is trying to cover up whatever's happened," McDuff said under his breath. "Whatever was bad enough for Michael to need a bloody surgeon in attendance to make it from here to there. He's afraid I'll report them, and I just bloody well might."

"Now isn't the time, Rob. Let's get Michael seen to."

CHAPTER 30

A DRIVER MCDUFF hadn't noticed jumped down before he or Father Hall made a move toward the coach.

He was dressed like the guards on the inside, but he had to be at least twice the age of most of them. More like three times, McDuff realized when they got closer, with a fluff of white hair showing under his hat, and his face lined and wrinkled.

Thin enough that a stiff breeze surely threatened to blow him over, but his pale eyes were harder than the cobbles beneath their feet.

McDuff stepped aside as the driver scrambled up the three steps and jerked the solid black door open. A chain rattled against the side of the coach as it slipped through rusty loops on either side.

Years of policing experience, chilly and razor-sharp though the chaotic mess inside his head, steadied McDuff at last.

"Planning to lock us in, are you?" McDuff's voice was colder than the wind.

"Only if you give me reason to," the driver said. He squinted up at the two men, head tilted, thin lips slipping from side to side over his teeth. "Don't look like trouble. Not yet."

"As long as my brother is well, everything else will be."

The driver smirked.

"No worse than when he came to us, I'll wager. Keep yourselves calm as he is, then, and we'll get along just fine."

Father Hall stepped into the coach, then froze halfway through the cramped opening. McDuff watched his shoulders slowly rise and fall before he moved forward.

"We need to get moving, Rob," he said from inside.

McDuff raised his head and looked down at the driver, willing his face not to give him away.

No one needed to know how his guts had turned to hot liquid, his knees to trembling jelly. The driver snorted as he slammed the door shut behind McDuff.

Father Hall's pale, grim face caught his attention first, glowing in the flickering lanterns inside the windowless coach. An equally grim-looking middle aged man sat on the opposite bench, dressed in dark street clothes with none of the air of the prison about him. A bag not unlike Jean's sat between his booted feet.

McDuff was only relieved the surgeon had left the usual blood-crusted apron behind for this particular duty. He doubted he could have stood that, when thinking about it was enough to make his insides quiver.

Michael wasn't chained or handcuffed, not like when he'd first arrived here years ago. No one had expected him to ever leave a free man, and he would not be doing that today.

He'd been tossed on the filthy wooden floor like a sack of grain, wrapped tight in a dingy white jacket.

Dark red spots marked where his hands would be under the fabric, and matching grooves lined his cheeks. Patches of his scalp glared swollen and bare through the close-cropped stubble. Where he'd somehow managed to yank bits of his hair out despite it being so short.

McDuff fell onto the hard bench when the coach lurched into motion.

"Who did this?"

"Did this to himself," the surgeon said. "Started day before yesterday and kept getting worse."

Father Hall touched Michael's forehead, but he didn't stir.

"And his hands?"

"Guards told me he gnawed the nails more or less off. That or dragged them off on the walls. Don't know for sure. All we usually get is the result, not the reason. Said he started on his hair, then his face, then got round to the fingers late last night."

"This is normal?" McDuff said.

"Nothing normal about any prison, is there?" The surgeon shrugged as if they were discussing the state of the air over London. "Much less Fodelson. Asylum, either. I just do the best I can for the poor sods and move on."

A jolt in the roadway rolled Michael's head toward McDuff. Bruises shading from black to brown to pale yellow were visible in the brighter light. He also saw the gouges were deeper than he'd thought.

Not mere streaks or scratches, the wounds were deep enough to have shadows.

McDuff gritted his teeth, fighting to get his gorge under control before he spoke.

"And I'm to believe he bruised himself as well?"

The surgeon stared at McDuff for several moments, then raised his eyebrows and looked away.

"Just be glad he's out of that hellhole, that's what I say. That and pray the years are kinder to him going forward."

CHAPTER 31

JEAN'S STUDY in the residence across from Father Hall's church was surely the same size it ever had been. Victoria understood that in her mind, in her weary and overworked brain.

Her feet took the same number of steps as she paced, every time. Twelve steps if she walked from window to window. Fourteen from door to stairs.

Jean even sat in the same place as she always did, the great dark brown leather chair that threatened to swallow her from tip to tail. Victoria herself hated that chair, the way her feet dangled off the floor and her legs slipped and slid underneath her. Maybe if she were brave enough to wear trousers like Jean did, she'd be able to manage that lovely tucked leg posture herself.

Even with so many things the same as they'd been for the past several weeks, Victoria felt as though the solid brick walls were trying to swallow her alive. As if the books on the shelves only waited for her to turn her back long enough so they could swarm and attack and drown her forever.

Still, she paced, unable to stop herself. And Jean only watched.

Unwilling, or unable, to stop Victoria.

She did manage not to look at the mantle clock as she passed by. She didn't have to, not with her heels clicking out the time. Rob and Father Hall had to be at the prison by now. Probably on the way to the asylum, in fact, with Michael McDuff secured and sedated.

Victoria hoped Michael was sedated, at least. Drowsy and half asleep, even if he were confused and upset, had to be better than strapped screaming into a straightjacket.

She smoothed her own sturdy blue cotton dress, one perfectly suited for the volunteer work her mother continued to accept as an excuse. Even her father approved of Victoria's bustling activities outside his house. With her assistance, of course.

She made sure he believed she was finally taking an interest in her life in London.

Getting ready to be a responsible wife and mother at last, a proper angel to those in need.

Her fiancé showed signs of impatience, though, with Victoria's reluctance to set a date for her own imprisonment.

"We should have gone with them," she said, stopping beside Jean's leather fortress. "Something must have happened."

Jean sipped her tea, the steam curling up past her sharp eyes. Her gaze never wavered from Victoria's.

"You know this is men's work," she said, "as well as you know how badly it pains me to say that. They won't be finished moving him across the city yet, much less getting him settled in."

Victoria shook her head. She chewed her lip, wondering if she could resist both the urge to argue with Jean and the urge to continue her pacing. Her feet ached nearly as much as her head, though, and the long day was barely begun.

She walked slowly to the sofa, covered in floral silk and far more suited to her stature, but still she didn't sit. Her own tea had long since gone cold.

The stubborn resistance and need to keep moving persisted, at least until Jean spoke again.

"Which McDuff brother are you more concerned about, I wonder?" Jean's voice was gentle, but the words robbed all the strength from Victoria's legs. She finally sank into the over-stuffed cushions. "Rob or Michael?"

Victoria grabbed the tea cup to hide her shaking hands, managing not to grimace as the chilled liquid traced from her mouth, down her throat, and into her knotted stomach. She closed her eyes, wishing she could pretend the other woman hadn't spoken at all.

The hell of it was she had no idea who she was truly concerned about, any more than she knew what to do either way.

Jaji had taught her how to contain her feelings, how to protect herself. How to focus and concentrate and keep her eyes and mind on her own goals, even if that sometimes meant nothing more than avoiding the goals of her father.

None of that training, nor the experience of living in a society where her feelings didn't matter, had prepared Victoria for the deep well of compassion she'd felt for Michael when they set this day into motion.

He was as trapped as she was here in London, and she feared they'd only made his bars stronger.

His cell smaller.

And still, her feelings for Rob McDuff were far more confusing and difficult to sort out.

Jean waited silently, and every second that dragged on made the next harder for Victoria.

"Today I'm more concerned for Michael," she said, glancing quickly at the older woman. "I'd hate for him to be more confused and afraid than he already was."

Jean gave an odd sideways nod, but her face didn't betray any other response.

"Rob has the calming draughts you prepared," she said. "One for himself, one for Father Hall, and one for his brother. Perhaps we should have made a special one for *you*, Victoria."

Heat flared in Victoria's chest, pushing the bitter tea aside. Working with the scholar for several weeks hadn't soothed all of Victoria's suspicions and fears. That was another of Jaji's lessons, one she never failed to heed.

Watch out for yourself above all else. You can never know the motives of another.

"It is a delicate matter," Victoria said, looking into Jean's eyes. "Controlling the will and destiny of another. One none of us should take lightly."

"Indeed not." Jean unwrapped her legs and stood in one smooth motion, then poured more tea for herself and for Victoria. "Even in trying to do good, we can do more harm than we imagine."

Instead of retreating to the massive leather chair, Jean sat beside Victoria on the sofa.

"We both know what's at stake here, Victoria. Both for these men and for ourselves. Will you answer my question as truthfully as you can?"

The heat spread through Victoria's whole body now, but her mind finally settled into calm and steady focus. She had a far easier time recognizing and responding to a threat than to unaccustomed emotions.

"I will answer as truthfully as I'm able."

Jean nodded, her full lips compressed. "Do you still carry a protective charm against me?"

Victoria couldn't stop the sigh of relief, though she did keep her laughter from escaping.

"I carry a protective charm against everyone, Jean. There cannot possibly be many practitioners in London, but the two of us somehow managed to cross paths in such a teeming mass of humanity. With those odds, neither of us can take chances. And you?"

Jean held her right hand on her bosom, still visible despite her loose-fitting dark red man's shirt. She tapped her index finger against her chest, tapping an object invisible under fabric.

"I'm not as suspicious as you, though I probably should be. I still protect myself when we're together, yes."

Victoria managed a small smile, and she managed not to twist or even look down at her engagement ring. She'd dutifully stored the opal in liquid overnight, just as Bertrand still reminded her to nearly every time she saw him.

The fire in the red stone hadn't diminished since the day he'd presented her with it.

Neither had the potency of the spells it carried.

"Assuming all goes as well as possible with Michael," Jean said, "your end of this diabolical bargain will be complete. I also assume we'll learn more about what you expect of us."

"There's plenty of time for that. We won't even know if Michael's treatment is working for at least several days."

Victoria hoped she hid how Jean's words unnerved her. She knew the woman was maddeningly observant, but that felt far too close to actually reading her private thoughts.

"We won't know if the *next* part works," Jean said. "We already know the first part has. You've kept up your agreement as far as I can tell. I can't speak for Rob, of course, but we should at least do our best to keep up ours."

Michael's face, scarred but horribly trusting and innocent, lingered in Victoria's mind. She couldn't tolerate waiting and wondering and questioning her own motives, much less having someone as insightful as Jean questioning them.

"Please, Jean, let's wait. Once we know what's happening, how he's doing, we'll know more about the rest. Perhaps we can work out spells to help others in the asylum to better pass the time."

When Inspector McDuff and Father Hall returned nearly three hours later, their grim faces told Victoria all she needed to know.

CHAPTER 32

THE SILENCE when Rob and Father Hall stopped speaking threatened to pull all of Victoria's nerves screaming out of her body, one inch at a time. Both men were pale and shaky, staring at the floor and speaking in near monotones.

She wanted to cry when Jean pulled a well-used shiny metal flask out of her travel bag.

"Medicinal purposes, Father Hall," Jean said, pouring a generous amount into their four empty teacups. "This has not been an easy day all around."

Father Hall swallowed his whiskey before anyone else moved.

"Once yours is gone, Jean, I'll bring out my own."

Victoria watched Rob as she picked up her own teacup. He still stared at the floor, eyes glassy and face slack.

If he were a stranger off the street, she would have assumed he'd already been drinking heavily.

The dark amber liquid was thicker than she expected,

coating the sides of the white china when she swirled it. Victoria had never tasted anything stronger than champagne or sloe gin, despite all the rum her father kept and consumed. Her nose burned when she breathed in the almost earthy vapors collected in the small cup.

A tiny sip had her eyes watering at smoky fire filling her mouth before it went numb. The heat chasing away the lingering chill of her earlier cold tea convinced her to swallow a bit more.

Rob finally picked up his cup, staring into it as Victoria had. She felt her face and even her neck flush when his eyes met hers.

She almost convinced herself the whiskey was the cause.

"His body was worse than his face." Rob downed his cupful and looked at Jean, eyebrows raised. She refilled all four. "None of the gangs back in Glasgow beat him as thoroughly as those blasted guards. I suspect they've had far more practice at it."

"I truly am sorry," Victoria said. The second cupful didn't burn nearly as bad as the first. "I'd hoped we could protect him from that sort of treatment."

"Protecting him isn't possible in a place like that," Father Hall said. "We would have had to set a spell on every one of the guards as well."

Rob's gaze found Victoria again, this time fully focused and alert. The nerves and their strange, unsettling sensations that she'd wanted to abandon her a few short minutes ago were firmly in place, tingling in anticipation.

Inspector McDuff already knew what the next steps needed to be.

And he knew he needed Victoria to make that happen.

"From everything we can tell," Jean said, "he'll be treated far better in this asylum than he was in Fodelson. Victoria and I have a good start on how to make that more certain for him and the other lost souls held there."

"And none of that can start this evening," McDuff said. He still stared at Victoria, but the others didn't seem to notice. "We all have ordinary lives to lead in the middle of this madness. I know I'll need time to recover before tomorrow."

Victoria stood, her legs responding before her mind had a chance to.

"I'll go as well. My parents will only believe so much charity of me."

McDuff nodded, the movement so slight she wondered if the strong spirit had affected her vision. The warmth spread throughout her whole body now, and her feet felt strangely detached from the wooden floor.

But the intensity of his eyes meeting hers was unmistakable.

"Both of you will take the coach, of course," Father Hall said. He stood and caught Rob, then Victoria in a brief hug. "We can all rest a bit easier knowing Michael is in a better place tonight than he was last night. Just the same, I'll fetch that refill for your flask, Jean."

Jean stood as he left the room, and now she was the one pinning Victoria with her stare.

"Take care, both of you. None of us need a difficult day turned worse."

"That we do not." McDuff returned the Frenchwoman's embrace, then followed the priest out the door.

Victoria forced herself not to look away when Jean held

both of her shoulders. She may as well have been standing there fully unclothed.

"Be mindful of your protections, Victoria. And of Rob's."

"As always."

An unaccustomed euphoria flowed through Victoria's limbs as she walked down the steps to the waiting coach. Perhaps stronger drink than she'd ever had, and more of it, was affecting more than the floating sensation in her limbs.

A part of her wanted more, to see how much further that feeling of detachment could take her away from this increasingly complex situation.

A part of her mind, though, anticipated what offers and even proposals Rob McDuff might have for her on the ride home. Jaji taught her years ago that her talents and skills were no laughing matter, no parlor tricks or silly games used simply for amusement.

That had never been more true in Victoria's life than it was at that moment.

Rob walked around the back of the coach, speaking in a low voice with Father Hall. The priest nodded as he passed by holding a clearly bottle-shaped bag. She took Rob's offered hand and stepped up into the narrow space.

His knees weren't quite touching hers, but Victoria was certain she felt heat from his body, building up in the already warm coach. Now she was sure more than the whiskey was affecting her senses.

"What did you keep from us, Inspector? About what happened with Michael?"

He looked out the small window for several seconds before

answering. She had to strain to hear him over the horse's hooves and the creaking walls and floor.

"No matter how bad things got for him, he never hurt himself like that. Not physically, anyway. Not when our father died, not when he was in jail, not when he was sent to Fodelson Prison. Most of his fingernails…"

Strange and hard as his eyes were, Victoria was relieved when he stopped speaking to stare at her.

She didn't want to know. Not anymore.

"We'll have more control now," Victoria said. "We can keep him and at least some of the ones around him calmer. And we can eventually get him out of there."

Rob nodded and shrugged at the same time.

"Perhaps we will. I do know his mind is rotting away locked up inside one cage or another. And as has always been the case, the ones leading him deeper into hell go free with no consequences."

Sharp, painful chills raced over Victoria's flesh, but she could not stop her words.

"What consequences would you have for them?"

"I would have them suffer as he has," Rob said, leaning forward, close enough that she could smell that alcohol on his breath. "Not only to be beaten, but to never once understand why. Have those they consider friends turn on them, again and again and again. Have them lose their fathers when they were too young to understand what death meant, then have the meaning driven home when they lost their mothers not long after."

He sat back, closing his eyes for a few seconds.

"Have them utterly dependent on a brother too young for

the job, who only knew how to make things worse. No matter how hard he tried to do the right thing."

"I haven't known you for long, Inspector McDuff." Victoria took a deep breath. "Rob. But I know you've done the best you could."

His harsh laugh scraped through Victoria's mind.

"I would gladly give my own life if that were true. Tell me, Miss Haversham." He lowered his chin but didn't look away from her. "Victoria. What consequences would *you* have for them?"

"I don't… You mean the guards at Fodelson?"

He smiled, and she wished he would scream at her instead.

"The guards would be an effective start, don't you think?"

Whispers surged inside Victoria's head, harsh and precise and persistent. She could pretend she didn't know what he meant, or that she didn't know how to do such a thing.

Her pretense would not make it true.

Nor would her pretense, even to herself, make her less eager to do exactly as the man across from her was suggesting.

McDuff nodded, crossing his arms.

"The guards who were directly involved with beating Michael should be easy enough to target for someone as experienced as you. And while I may not have the same abilities with manipulating people that you do, I know at least a bit about reading people. You want to do this as badly as I do."

Victoria's desire for revenge—on Michael's behalf and on Rob's—struggled with her need to keep herself safe.

"Suppose that's true, about my wanting revenge. This is a bit more serious than one prisoner acting strangely. You're suggesting an attack on several men who work *inside* of a prison, Rob."

"You're right. I know exactly how serious this is. I've sent more men than I care to count, and a few women, into prisons. I'm convinced most of them deserved exactly what they got in the end. I'm convinced these men would as well, because I know for certain Michael did not deserve any of this. He's always been bumbling and too trusting, but he was never evil. Or cruel."

"Have you spoken to Father Hall or Jean about this new plan of yours?"

He scowled, only a brief flash of compressed brow and mouth, but impossible to hide.

"I don't want to drag one more person into this sort of nightmare. They've had enough risk and enough guilt as it is. You and I are at the center of the storm, Victoria. The ones who understood exactly what we were putting into motion. I believe you and I should be the ones to see it through."

Victoria tried and failed to hide her shiver at his words and the way he delivered them into the crackling air between them.

"Those guards didn't act on their own, though," she said. "They shouldn't treat anyone that way, of course, and they probably deserve punishment for more than your brother." Victoria hesitated, wondering if she was about to cross a line neither of them could turn back from. "It seemed to me he was getting along well enough there before we interfered. If anyone deserves punishment for what's happened to Michael, should it be anyone besides you and I?"

Rob held one hand up, and Victoria almost saw a much larger glass of whiskey in his grasp.

She had no doubt he wished that were so.

"You've hit upon the heart of it, my dear Victoria. We hold the greatest guilt. Father Hall and Jean will eventually walk away. They should walk far and fast away, before one more day passes. You and I, though, we're tied up in this thing. And if we follow through with my plans, and yours, we'll carry it with us the rest of our lives."

"Do you honestly think continuing to interfere will make that better? For any of us?"

Rob scrubbed at his face, then squeezed his temples with both hands.

"I don't think anything will make this better. Not for me. But I'll do what I must to keep it from getting worse for Michael. Only you can decide how much risk of long consequences you're willing to take on for yourself. Now, tell me if you have the ability to do what I need. We can discuss whether you're willing to do it later. Tomorrow if you like."

The whispers returned in Victoria's mind, this time louder than before. Slower. Easier to follow.

Of course she could do what Rob was asking. Perhaps even what he needed.

It would be a challenge, and a strain to Victoria and anyone else involved.

But she had no doubt she could.

And worse, and stronger, no doubt that she *wanted* to, for her own reasons.

A deep, moaning voice cut through everything else whirling through her head. The voice of Jaji. The voice of warning.

The voice Jean had been trying to sound.

Yes, this was a terrible idea. Far more risky than anything she'd done on her own. With far more ties and complications to a man she didn't know all that well.

A man she'd only been trying to use for her own purposes, with terrible results.

The warning could not have been more clear or strong.

She raised her head and looked into Rob McDuff's eyes.

Heat entirely unrelated to the whiskey settled into her belly.

"I'll speak to you tomorrow, Rob. I want to help Michael if I can."

He rose smoothly when the coach stopped, opening the door and holding out his hand in one motion. Victoria let him help her to the ground in front of her father's house.

She held his hand for a moment, meeting his gaze as he spoke in a low, rough voice.

"I want to help you, too, Victoria. I still hope we can help each other."

CHAPTER 33

Victoria's mother met her just inside the front door, pale cheeks flushed, hands fluttering over her lace covered bosom. The matron of the house wore an elaborate emerald green gown, her hair piled high and her face carefully embellished.

The contrast between the two women was even more stark than usual, with the younger in her sturdy work dress and plainly put together.

"At last, we've been holding everything until you arrived! Did you forget your dinner with your fiancé this evening, Victoria?"

Victoria managed not to say she'd forgotten quite on purpose, but it was a near thing.

Her awareness of this impending chore, firmly in her mind when she'd left that morning, had faded away long before she'd learned of Michael's deterioration.

"I'm sorry, Mother. We had more to do today than I expected."

"Charity is well and good, of course. But you must see to your social obligations without fail." She stepped back and looked Victoria up and down, rouged lips pursed. "You don't have time for a proper bath, I'm afraid. You can run upstairs and change into a more suitable dress, though."

Victoria scowled, shaking her head. The last thing she wanted after the day she'd had was struggling into the expected elaborate clothing to impress a man she'd just as soon never see again.

"No, young lady," her mother said in a harsh whisper. "That's quite enough. None of your scandalous tea dresses, not tonight. We've indulged your sudden interest in charity work, generously I might add. Your father and I knew this would help you through your disappointment after that unpleasant business with Mr. Abernathy. But you've had more than sufficient time to recover. And you have a perfectly wonderful future husband you simply must spend more time with."

Victoria tried to speak, but her lungs refused to cooperate.

Something had changed while she wasn't paying close enough attention here at home.

Even with Jean's blocks to her power removed, she may not be able to get out in front of this disaster fast enough.

"Yes, Mother. I'll need help getting dressed if you can spare someone."

Mrs. Haversham nodded, one brisk jerk of her head.

"I'll send one of the girls up in a few minutes. But you must hurry. He's been waiting for over an hour now."

She turned in a rustle of fabric and rush of perfume and was gone.

Victoria leaned against the wall with her eyes closed. She

contemplated dashing right back out the door, maybe trying to flag Father Hall's coach down.

As upsetting and disorienting as her day had been, even the strangest parts made more sense than what she faced now.

The most common, mundane aspects of life in London confused and frustrated her more than the most intricate and challenging spells and rituals. The ones she was already putting together in her mind for Rob, for example.

If she'd spent the same amount of time laying spells to fend off her fiancé and her parents—even half the time—this situation would never have gotten so far out of her control.

Victoria forced herself to move, to walk slowly up the steps and into her hidden workroom. If she had no choice but to deal with Bertrand and her parents, she'd make certain she was as well defended as she possibly could be.

By the time her mother's favorite maid joined Victoria in her bedroom, all giggles and questions and unwanted advice, her mind was again clear.

Fresh tiny orange blossoms waited in her nosegay, their aroma as intense and strong as the influence spells in the water underneath. She forced herself not to wince as Mavvie yanked her despised corset tighter.

"What sort of excitement does Mother have planned?" Victoria said when she could draw a breath.

"Oh, as if you didn't already know, miss. Only the most excitement of your whole life!"

"I appreciate the warning."

Victoria gritted her teeth through the girl's chattering and giggling, forcing herself to focus on what she could do to derail her mother's ambitions.

Even if she did decide to help Rob McDuff with his worthy ideas of revenge, she had to get her own life under control first.

When she walked into the dining room, Victoria realized control might already be irretrievably far out of her grasp.

Bertrand stood quickly, as he always did, his dark suit better fitted than usual. He was a tiny bit closer to Victoria's age than her father's first choice. Barely thirty years older rather than nearly forty. He towered over her to the point that her neck hurt when she tried to speak to him, almost as her mind hurt from trying to converse about nothing of substance. He did the best he could with thinning iron grey hair and a paunch he couldn't quite hide.

When she did try, Victoria couldn't imagine his rough hands moving over her flesh. His thin lips against her own.

She didn't want to imagine more.

And his condescending manner and patronizing way of speaking as if she were a small child were worse than Mr. Abernathy.

Tonight, though, his manner and the barely concealed sneer put Victoria on edge before anyone spoke.

The power in this game had shifted too far out of her hands.

"Victoria, my dear," he said, pulling out the chair beside him with a flourish. The insipid smile was worse than the sneer. "You look absolutely beautiful. What a joy and relief to have you by my side at last."

"Bertrand. I apologize for my late arrival. Thank you for holding dinner for me."

Trying to ignore his hot, heavy hand on her shoulder, Victoria sat. She had to assess the damage here, and fast.

"I was telling *Mr. Robbins* how you were busier with the children today than you expected to be." Victoria's mother glared, clearly not happy with her daughter's familiar use of her future husband's first name.

"Yes, teaching the poor crippled girls and boys to better care for themselves," Bertrand said. "Even to read and write a little. Such a noble effort. And admirable that you care so much for children not even your own."

This time he was positively leering, setting Victoria's flesh crawling. Her parents only beamed, no doubt excited at the prospect of having grandchildren at last.

Her tiny nosegay would not be enough to slow this disaster.

Victoria felt arrangements and agreements settling around her like steel traps.

"There will be plenty of time for all of that," she said. "No need to rush."

"And on the other hand," her father said, "why delay happiness when there's no good reason to? Bertrand has managed to clear his terribly busy schedule for three weeks of celebratory travel."

"We couldn't wait any longer to tell you the good news!" Victoria's mother clasped her hands together under her chin. "You're to be wed in a month's time!"

"A month?" Victoria struggled to breathe through the corset that continued to tighten its iron grip round her ribs. "I can't even begin to plan a proper wedding—"

"No need to worry." Now her mother dabbed carefully at her eyes, not wanting to spoil her powders and tints. "I know how busy you've been, and how much you care for your work helping others. I've made most of the plans and arrangements already."

"Have you?" Victoria said, her voice barely above a whisper. "How very generous of you."

"All you need to do is carve out time for your fittings," her mother said. "And help me choose the flowers and such if you'd like. You have such an eye for the sweet blooms you always wear and keep in your rooms. We can fill the greenhouse full in plenty of time. It will be such a lovely affair, Victoria. The one we've always dreamed of."

Victoria could only nod.

It was all she could do to keep breathing, in and out, forcing the air through her throat as it constricted to match her lungs. She'd never dreamed of any kind of a wedding, and certainly not arranged by other people.

And never with a man like this.

She took a deep breath through the crushing vise around her body, praying to Jaji that her trembling didn't show. Her mother wasn't fooled, though she reliably misunderstood the reason for her daughter's upset.

"Victoria, you've gone pale as a ghost. This certainly is a great deal to take in after a long and busy day. Perhaps you've been working too hard for your poor dear children. This is a perfect time to stay closer to home now, and prepare to run your new household. Let us all have our dinner and give the overjoyed bride-to-be a chance to adjust."

CHAPTER 34

McDuff sat motionless, ignoring the stiff wooden chair digging into his ribs and back. The room was dingy and too small for the eleven men who crowded into it. The smells of wet wool and sweaty bodies only intensified his sensation of being penned up like livestock.

Chief Inspector Wells and his ever-present pipe, even in such an enclosed space, made the dark ceiling seem nearly as cloudy as the skies outside.

Towering stacks of paperwork threatened to drown all of them, piled up on wooden cabinets and sagging tables. On a gloomy day like this, he suspected he wasn't the only one who'd be relieved at the excitement of digging themselves out of the suffocating space.

A change in numbing routine at last from all these endless meetings.

These discussions with the other plainclothes inspectors

had never been his favorite part of policing, not even when they meant something.

Today McDuff only counted out time, pretending to listen to the same reports on the same endless investigations that had been going on for weeks now.

He'd already doled out the last of his interviews over the case that turned his life into such a fever dream. The truth was poor Cheryl Mallory had eventually recovered enough to return home, though McDuff thought that was surely cold comfort to her and her parents.

The baby on the way was likely what kept them insisting on his continued attention to the case.

He wasn't sure whether to be impressed with his own detective work or disgusted with everyone around him. He'd gathered up enough material and evidence in a few days time to keep up the appearance of an ongoing investigation for weeks now.

Victoria's clever little clockwork toys—one aspect of the case he'd never mentioned inside this building—had given him more of an unfair advantage than he cared to admit.

Her toys' effects on Mr. Abernathy and Miss Mallory had been far more than unfair. Whether written laws applied or not, Victoria long ago crossed into criminal behavior. And yet partly because of his decision not to do his job, she still walked free.

McDuff wondered if that condemned her more or himself.

Beyond getting revenge for an already tragic situation, he still didn't know what would satisfy the Mallorys. He doubted they did, either.

After all the upheaval in his life that first interview at the grand Mayfair home led to, McDuff was more determined than ever to collect the bounty they'd offered him. Under the table and off the department books or not, he knew he'd damn sure earned it.

A beat after everyone around him, he realized the meeting was finally over. He stood, gathering his own damp wool raincoat.

Waiting his turn to head back out into his self-made hell of worry and confusion, with the constant stream of crime only an unpleasant, never-ending backdrop.

McDuff had no idea what he'd claim to have spent his time on next time he was due to report, but he was too wrecked over his brother to think about that.

"McDuff. A moment, please."

He turned, expecting to see his chief bearing down with several of Victoria's targets lined up behind him, all demanding more progress than he could offer.

Chief Wells was indeed striding toward him, but besides his smoldering pipe, he only held a crisp white envelope.

"Came for you this morning," he said, holding the rectangle up for McDuff to see. "Didn't have a chance to give it to you earlier."

McDuff recognized Victoria's neat writing, his name on the front and a Park Lane postal mark. He forced his features to stay as cool and neutral as during the endless meeting.

"Thanks for that, sir."

"About that Mallory investigation, is it?"

McDuff watched Chief Wells for a few seconds, wondering if he'd imagined the warning note in the man's voice. The scarred and deeply lined face looked the same, the deep-set blue eyes steady as always. The chief's only movement was drawing the flickering match down toward the pipe's bowl, puffing out thick smoke.

Unease prickled along McDuff's neck more deeply than before.

"Looks to be, sir. I only have the one case that close to Mayfair at the moment."

"The Mallorys have been most generous with this department, Inspector. I don't doubt they will be with you if this is resolved quickly. That would be best for everyone."

Wells shifted his stance, rising to his full height several inches taller than McDuff. That alone wasn't intimidating, not with many men he worked with every day standing taller. Father Hall for one.

What had McDuff forcing himself not to step back to protect himself ran deeper.

All his instincts, far more than his policing experience, rang out a warning.

"I'll continue to give it my full attention, sir."

Chief Wells looked into McDuff's eyes for another long moment before dropping the envelope into his hand. When he turned the corner without looking back, McDuff slipped it into his case.

Reading anything from Victoria with other officers close by was likely risky.

Staying inside the building full of policemen after that encounter even more so.

By the time he stepped back out into late morning drizzle, he was half convinced the fine paper would shine like a beacon, exposing the oddness of his life for the world to see.

McDuff sheltered in the first empty doorway he found to read.

Inspector McDuff.

I fear the situation has escalated. Please meet me in the park at the usual hour.

I pray this dreadful weather does not delay you.

Yours.

McDuff dropped the letter back in his case, then leaned against the wall.

On top of a near reprimand from his chief, now he was contemplating talking to Victoria without any protection. Without Jean and her own safety charms or Father Hall and his whispered prayers. In a location Victoria had chosen, and therefore one she could arrange to her satisfaction.

He stared at the scudding gray clouds, low in the sky above the row of brick buildings across from him. They carried a clear promise of heavier rain throughout the afternoon.

He could take that out she'd offered, say the weather had indeed delayed him. Their normal meeting hour in Jean's study of eleven was nearly upon him.

But then he'd never know what Victoria wanted, or needed.

What she was willing to give.

He might lose whatever slim chance he had of helping his brother at last. Or of helping himself shed the lifetime of guilt he carried over Michael's situation.

Perhaps more.

McDuff almost convinced himself that it was his chief's unusual attention combined with worry about Michael that got his feet moving at last. He couldn't ignore either one of those, no matter what sort of threat he was walking into.

He couldn't afford to lose his job, even as it ground the life out of him day after day, year after year.

And he couldn't tolerate leaving his brother in an even more uncertain situation than he'd had in prison.

The last word kept floating up into his mind, robbing him of the single-minded focus that normally kept him moving until the day was through.

Yours.

Even his rising curiosity wouldn't allow McDuff to wonder what she was offering him. If she spoke the words plainly to his face, he doubted he could ever believe her.

But he did wonder what she expected of him.

Your plaything?

Your puppet?

Your useful tool, to be discarded once it was broken?

Your suspected collaborator in any number of future crimes was most likely.

He continued his slow walk toward Victoria in the increasingly heavy rain.

CHAPTER 35

Victoria wished her words to Rob McDuff hadn't been so prophetic.

She was dry enough under the same wrought iron shelter where they'd met when the sun was high and hot.

Weeks ago, when she'd still believed she could limit the interference in her plans.

This morning, only one of her father's oilcloth umbrellas had protected her from heavy, awful, autumn rain pouring from a dark grey sky.

She'd never expected in all her imaginings to be so caught up with a rebellious French scholar, a young and idealistic priest, and a Glaswegian police inspector of all things. The inspector who'd recognized her activities least of all, and now she hoped he would turn out to be central to her revised course of action.

The damp wooden benches seemed to drink in the moisture in the air, and puddles formed between the stones under

Victoria's booted feet. The water seeped into everything on this wretched island, but rain continued when the land was overflowing.

In her beloved Enceleas, a horribly cold rain that lasted for days like this would have been unusual enough to be shocking. Most likely considered a curse or bad omen of some kind, and with perfectly good reason as far as she was concerned. Approached as something that could be lifted with the proper ritual or appeasement.

In London, people complained, put their heads down, hunched under their umbrellas, and scurried from shelter to shelter. They endured, rather than endeavoring to do anything about it.

A lone figure turned off the sidewalk and cut across the grass toward her shelter. Rob didn't bother with an umbrella or even a hat. His stride remained slow and steady, as if he were walking in bright spring sunshine.

When he drew closer, Victoria saw his face didn't reflect such ease and light.

He stopped just under the edge of the shelter, brushing sheets of water from his hair and shaking off his thick wool greatcoat.

"Miss Haversham. Victoria."

"Thank you for coming, Rob. I wasn't sure whether to expect you."

He sat on the bench beside her, draping the dark blue coat between them. Victoria knew he didn't smoke, but he'd been around someone who did. Rich aromas of tobacco rose up with the earthy scent of wet wool.

"Seems time is of the essence for both of us now," he said. "Want to tell me why I'm here?"

Victoria watched him, trying to imagine him under the relentless Caribbean sun.

He surely wouldn't stay so pale, though some British natives never did seem to adapt. They burned, suffered, and burned again.

She'd turned as pale as everyone around her over the past few years, but she was more certain than ever that she'd never adapt to England.

"Jean always says women aren't well served by playing games and being coy," she said. "My mother always complains that I'm not good at them anyway. What I need from you is very simple, Rob. I need someone to help me distract my father from trying to marry me off."

"You said as much once, a long time ago," he said, nodding. "And you've kept your promises to me so far. Here's the thing. I know how easily you manipulate men, and probably women as well. If I decide to play along with this little game, how would I know where the choices are, where they came from? Yours or mine?"

"I've shown all of you everything I've done so far. You've heard Jean asking me endless questions, making enough notes to write textbooks if she wanted. The three of you know more about me and what I can accomplish than anyone else alive. If we work out the plan now, between the two of us, you'll know if things change."

"What I won't know is if *I* change. It's one thing to be aware that you're a puppet, willing or not. Quite another to never see the strings."

Victoria smiled despite his resistance, reassured that he wasn't falling into place too easily.

Someone reluctant to trust, trained to be suspicious, could be exactly what she needed to help her resist her father.

And more importantly as things were turning out, her mother. Underestimating and ignoring a woman who'd always seemed so weak and passive was not a mistake Victoria would make twice.

"I think Jean suspects the nature of my magic," she said, "but I haven't told anyone the truth. There's a reason I haven't been able to stop my father from his matchmaking altogether, Rob. I can only do so much. My wishes when it comes to his business success are the same as his. He's cooperative with his own desires, though his focus remains stubbornly on London."

She shook her head and stared out into the downpour, more uncomfortable than she expected when admitting her weakness.

"And so, when it comes to finding what my father believes is a suitable husband for me, he can be swayed, but not stopped. If you truly do not wish to be involved with me, we'll only be playing a part. Acting. Nothing more."

He surprised her by laughing.

"Well, that's not as reassuring to me as you may have hoped. You're right that I know a lot about you. About what you can do if nothing else. I know you don't want to marry, at least not the men your parents think are appropriate. Before we continue this conversation or make any arrangements between us, you need to know more about who *you're* dealing with. Let me tell you a little bit about me."

Rob pulled out a neatly folded handkerchief and wiped the

rain from his face. He focused on his scuffed brown shoes, rippling a muddy puddle with one toe.

"I don't have much experience with women. My mother's long dead, only the one brother. Nearly all men in my work, too. I never have expected to marry, not really. Too many marks against me. I'm not wealthy, nor tall and handsome, nor particularly well-educated. Not even English, much less from London."

He took in a huge, slow breath and looked into Victoria's eyes.

"As if all of that weren't enough to make me a lifelong bachelor, I find far too many people tiresome, women as well as men. I'm no one's idea of a prize myself, and I see most others the same way. This time I've spent with Father Hall and Jean, and you, is the closest I've had to friendship since I was a boy. I would have grown weary or bored with most anyone else long before now."

Rob leaned closer, and now Victoria smelled coffee on his breath.

It almost managed to cover up the whiskey.

"You, though. You I have yet to get tired of. I'm certain you're smarter than me, enough so that I know I'll never be able to keep up with you. If what you've just said about your magic working with desire is true, I'll be even easier to manipulate. I'd never know my own mind when it comes to these little games. I won't know when they start or when they stop. And even if I did, I doubt very much I'd be able to react in my own best interests."

Victoria stopped herself from pointing out that he was

smarter than most if he understood that much. She doubted any other target of hers had ever even suspected.

They'd certainly never questioned.

She twisted her engagement ring, wondering if the heavy air stopped its potency.

"Just hear me out, Rob. You're the first to recognize me and my abilities. I don't plan to do anything behind your back, certainly not if you agree to work with me and we plan together. But we could always arrange to have an end date. Once I'm safely back on Enceleas, perhaps. A date when you know to expect a change, not be surprised by one. We could tell the others so they can help get you out of my grasp if that's what you want."

Victoria took her own cool, humid breath. Now she was getting too close to her own desires, nearly secret even to herself.

"I'm not in the habit of being so truthful, either, with anyone. But I find you more interesting than most people, certainly more than the vast majority of men. My mother would faint if she knew I were being so forward. Acting out this charade with you would likely be a pleasure."

He blew out through his nose, shaking his head.

"And if we carry this charade far enough to depart these dank shores for the Caribbean, what becomes of my brother? Does he stay in his new cage until he rots there?"

"I'm as concerned for Michael as I am for Jean or Father Hall. Or you. I thought he might make a fine hand at my father's plantation. The work is hard but good, and there are no gangs down there. He might find satisfaction, and I could help keep his mind calm. He trusts me."

"Then when this end date you propose comes round, when we conclude our business, you expect me to leave my little brother to your tender mercies and flee back to London."

"That is one of your choices." Victoria turned and looked into his eyes. "You may find satisfaction there, too, Rob."

He closed his eyes for a second, holding up one hand toward her.

"Stop. Neither of us are overly impulsive, but we're talking far ahead of what's going on around us. What of our plans for the guards from just last night? That isn't something I'm willing to let go this time."

"No, neither of us are impulsive. And I'm not willing to overlook what happened to your brother. Such men do not deserve to walk free with no consequence. I'll need your help, but I believe I know how we can affect all of them. One links to another, and so on until we have them all. Tell me what you would have me do to them, and I'll make that happen."

"On what condition, Victoria? I know you're capable, and I believe you're willing. What I don't believe is that you'll continue to work so hard on my brother's behalf without getting anything in return."

Victoria nodded and tilted her head toward him. With none of her usual charms and defenses—only an enhancement of her desirability and his desire—Rob was leading the way along the path she'd chosen.

"Before I have any chance of returning to Enceleas, I must disentangle myself from my father's plans. He won't rest until I'm successfully married off. His choices so far leave me worse than cold. What I need from you now is help in changing his course."

Rob laughed again, harsh and despairing.

"I've just told you why I'm not exactly a sought-after prize among London's high society women. What on earth makes you believe their fathers, *your* father, would feel any differently?"

"I'll not lie to you, not when you're being honest with me. That's going to be the hardest part. My father's desires for me are based on how he sees success. What he sees as security for me, as his one and only treasured offspring. A rich, older man, settled and established in the same sort of work he does. It only makes sense from his perspective."

"Someone who can protect you as well as he does." For the first time since yesterday, when he'd returned so shocked and upset from seeing Michael, Victoria saw the light of curiosity in Rob's eyes. The spark of a fine, sharp intelligence even he didn't recognize in himself. "He knows you have to go at some point, so he wants you to have the same thing you always had. The same kind of life."

"Exactly so. But there is another way that he's not seeing yet." Victoria hesitated, wondering if she was again moving too fast for him. She touched his cold hand anyway. "My father gave me a life before that I loved, years ago on Enceleas. Safe on our own island paradise, away from the crowds and crime in London, far away from the smoke and filth."

"And did he have hard men there? Men to protect you from whatever managed to threaten you in such a wild land?"

He laced his fingers through hers, a faint smile curving his lips. Despite the chill of his skin, Victoria's flesh warmed to his touch.

"He did indeed," she said. "Whatever my father's narrow-minded views about what it takes to keep me safe and happy, he does have that need deep in the heart of him. For me and my mother. He wants to protect us. *That's* the desire we can work with here."

Victoria didn't have to imagine or ask if Rob understood what she meant. She'd seen it in his eyes when he sat beside his brother in Fodelson Prison, when he'd allowed Victoria to influence the person he cared most about in the world.

And she saw a flash in his gaze right now.

"Fair enough, and enough for me to work with." He squeezed her hand gently, then got to his feet. "What I desire right now is to get in out of this bloody rain. Tell me the safest, warmest place you know, where we can plot and scheme in comfort. We'll go there now. And we'll learn what each of us is capable of."

CHAPTER 36

THE COOL, clear weather the next day let McDuff enjoy being outside again, with the air in the city almost clean for the first time in longer than he could remember. The fresh interlude would be short, with countless coal and wood fires starting up against the oncoming cold.

More people walking than usual obviously agreed with him that they all had to enjoy the fresh air while it lasted.

He slowed as he approached Father Hall's church, wondering at how it ever could have looked threatening to him. He couldn't imagine dropping by for a Sunday service by any means, but the towering gray stone walls seemed more secure than menacing now.

The smaller building across the street, the meeting place for their odd club of spell casters, felt more like home than his own boarding house did. He knew which chair suited him best, where the books were on the shelves, even which pub close by made for the best lunch or dinner.

McDuff had spent more time here than in his own place for the past several weeks. The generally threadbare and somewhat depressing state of his bachelor room was only part of the reason for that. Even knowing Victoria wouldn't be there today, it was no wonder the residence felt like home to him.

He slowed again, wondering if he would be better off turning around no matter how much he'd been looking forward to time spent with his friends after a couple of days away. A chance to get his mind off of worry over Michael, though from all appearances things did seem calmer for his brother. For the moment.

The questions about his brother and more would be inevitable, and pointed. From Jean for certain. And much as McDuff disliked lies, once attention moved away from his brother, he wouldn't be telling the truth about much of anything today.

He couldn't explain that Victoria was staying home today to focus on plans for the two of them. Plans that did not involve Jean or Father Hall.

He wouldn't tell them about the carriage ride with her after the torment of getting Michael transferred, nor meeting her in the park yesterday morning.

Definitely not about a long lunch in a quiet pub that turned into a longer dinner at an intimate, posh restaurant only a few blocks away that he never would have gone to on his own.

He wasn't even telling himself the truth about how his feelings had changed overnight, after so much time spent alone with Victoria.

McDuff knew he was still more guarded and cautious than

just about any other man would be with such a beautiful and wealthy young woman showing interest.

He was still in deeper than he felt comfortable with.

God help him, he wanted more.

He was afraid he'd passed the point of no return, with no way of knowing how true his feelings were. Or where those feelings were about to lead him. Not with a woman who could manipulate emotions and even actions as easily as she breathed.

And still, he could not pretend inside his own half-addled head that he wasn't anxious to see her again not even twelve hours later.

McDuff stopped a few feet away from the steps to Jean's adopted parlor, ready to turn away after all. Certain his resolve to keep arrangements between Victoria and himself *to* himself would fail under the slightest pressure.

As if he'd heard the unaccustomed thoughts about God from his friend the sinner, Father Hall opened the church doors just then. He crossed the street with a spring in his step, obviously enjoying the brisk day as much as Rob was.

"Good morning, Inspector McDuff. Our strange society meets again."

The priest shook his hand, and Rob couldn't stop himself from returning the younger man's broad smile.

"Remarkable that such things are allowed in modern times, Father. And so close to a house of worship."

"You'll find that's where the strangest of societies thrive, I'm afraid. Any word from Victoria?"

McDuff turned away to walk up the steps, shaking his head.

"Not since I saw her home, when I last saw you."

Jean strode forward when the two men walked in, her hair as rumpled as her usual men's clothing.

"Is Victoria with you?" she said, agitation plain in her voice.

"No, just the two of us," Father Hall said. "Have you heard from her? I do hope all is well."

"That depends on how you define your terms." Jean held out a page from the newspaper, folded so the top section showed. "I would guess she feels decidedly unwell."

Just under the headline *Engagements*, McDuff saw in cold, hard print what Victoria had confided in him the night before.

A plain but unmistakable announcement of Miss Victoria Jade Haversham to wed Mr. Bertrand Robbins, with a date barely a month away.

She either hadn't known this dreadfully public announcement was coming, or she hadn't wanted to accept it.

He closed his eyes, her words from the night before ringing in his ears. Dismay at her mother's plans, disgust at herself for letting the true architect of this disaster work unobserved and uninfluenced.

Longing for a land far away from here that McDuff could barely imagine.

He didn't have to imagine the warmth of her cheek, the scent of her hair when he'd kissed her goodnight.

"She hadn't said a word about any of this," Father Hall said. His eyes and mouth compressed as he read. "Not since the first day we all met in my office."

"I don't think she would have expected an announcement to the world," McDuff said, his eyes on the newsprint. "Or at least to London. Not this soon."

Jean crawled into her miniature leather throne, tucking her feet underneath her.

"Right or wrong, this makes matters so much harder for her. Wrong, I say, but that doesn't make it any less true. Anyone who knows her family, or his, will now have the matter settled and resolved in their minds. Another young woman tucked away onto the proper shelf."

McDuff sat across from her, his legs slipping a bit on the floral sofa until he got himself settled. His heart pounded, then seemed to fall through the floor at the thought of Victoria forced into a situation so distasteful to her.

Well, if he were going to at the very least be honest inside his own head, dismay at her being with any man besides himself drove the reaction even more.

He'd fallen right into Jean and Victoria's often discussed male habit of ownership.

Possession.

Being aware didn't weaken his impulses in the slightest.

"I fear we may be failing her when she's done everything she promised for us." Father Hall dropped the paper onto Jean's cluttered table and walked over the window. "Have you any word of Michael, Rob?"

"He's improving. Healing. Seems to be calm so far. They offered to let him have visitors sometime next week."

Father Hall turned back toward the room, arms crossed.

"We'll need to go as soon as we can, make sure they're used to seeing us. That was Victoria's plan, anyway. Take in the spells ourselves as often as we can."

"I'm sorry to sound so dramatic here," Jean said, "and possibly so cruel. Is it possible Michael may wait for a few days? I remember very well why all of us are reluctant to trust Victoria, but she has done every single thing she promised. Perhaps we need to help her now if we possibly can."

McDuff studied his shoes, wishing Jean would bring out her flask even though he'd had far too much over the last few days. Neither he nor Victoria planned for this announcement, but they had made detailed plans for both his troubles and hers last night.

The delightful twists of her mind fit perfectly with the darkest turns of his own.

Since he'd left her side, he'd alternated between horrified and aroused by how quickly and easily they worked together.

None of their plans involved the two friends he had to deceive right now.

"My brother will be fine for the moment. His body and mind need time to recover, and he'll get that where he is. The company of the insane will likely suit him better than the company of criminals."

"We can't exactly show up at Victoria's front door in any case," Father Hall said. "They're not Catholic, and I'm sure she doesn't want her parents to know of our association." He half-smiled at McDuff. "Our society. Jean, you're likely the least suspicious among us. Do you feel comfortable getting in contact with her?"

"I'll do my best," Jean said. "I can offer to take her shopping for her trousseau or some other such nonsense. If I may have her address, Rob, perhaps I will go tomorrow."

McDuff hoped the sharp-witted Frenchwoman didn't catch his hesitation before he answered. If she did, she gave no sign.

He was spending far too much time with people quicker

and more intelligent than he was, rather than working to bring down the criminals who'd earned their fates.

Instead, he and Victoria would be joining their ranks, perhaps sooner than expected with the wedding announcement. McDuff could not allow his two friends to get caught up in the unpleasant—and pleasurable—business they'd conjured the night before.

"There's still an investigation of sorts she could be part of," he said. "About what happened with her previous fiancé. Still under my charge so far, but sometimes these things have ripples."

"That decides the matter, then." Jean picked up her teacup, wrapping her long fingers around the porcelain. "I'll let you know when I'm going, and you let me know if you hear anything. We'll watch out for each other to make sure no one else suspects us. Not quite the sort of business you usually expect from a visiting scholar, Father Hall?"

The priest laughed, then crossed the room to sit beside McDuff.

"Only a little bit more unusual than your general presence, Jean. You know more than enough to get started. Let's do what we can to figure out where to go from here. Whatever Victoria's sins, we can at least help her avoid this fate not of her choosing."

"I couldn't agree more," McDuff said, relieved to speak with complete honesty for the first time all morning.

CHAPTER 37

Victoria lingered in the bright breakfast nook, pretending to listen to her mother's wedding chatter. The sun in the garden just outside the windows could almost convince her she was already in a warmer climate, one she would enjoy all year round instead of for a couple of brief months.

All she had to do was hold her hand closer to the rippled glass for the chill to break the delicate illusion.

She picked at her cold porridge instead, trying to nod when her mother expected it, smile when the time seemed right.

The mind-numbing litany of invitations and colors and attendants was preferable to the harsh shouting and icy silence between them the night before. Victoria wasn't quite sure how it was possible, but her father didn't seem to know about her long day and late night away from home.

Her mother did know, and she did not approve. She hadn't

questioned her daughter's explanation of a pageant for the poor, unfortunate children, at least not yet.

If she'd known all those many hours had been spent in the company of a man—and a lowly police inspector rather than her fiancé at that—Victoria had no doubt the reaction would have been swift and severe. Being old enough to be engaged and even married wouldn't matter if that little bit of information came out.

She'd be locked up and punished like a wayward child, and quite possibly spanked on top of it all.

Victoria nodded again, then schooled her features into appropriate amazement at her mother's choice of musicians for the blessed event.

If anyone besides herself or Rob McDuff knew what had really been going on all that time, that person would have been eager to believe they'd been engaged in ordinary sinful behavior instead.

Fornication was mild indeed compared to orchestrating and inciting violence.

Despite her calming spell before coming downstairs barely an hour ago, Victoria's cheeks heated at the thought of fornication, and at her own mind's use of such an old-fashioned word.

Jean would have scolded her for not saying sexual intercourse or lovemaking, right before immediately assuming Rob was the subject of those thoughts.

Mavvie bustled into the cozy room, all smiles and giggles, carrying the morning post.

Victoria hoped whatever the girl was so excited about would distract her mother long enough to let her escape to her workroom. She was eager to get started on the spells she and

Rob had discussed yesterday, the ones that would settle more than one need for revenge.

And she wanted time alone to get her feelings for Inspector McDuff into some kind of order. Or at least under control.

"Oh, Victoria!" Her mother was nearly grinning, most unladylike, and tears brimmed in her eyes. "This is just the thing to lift your spirits and set things to rights between us."

She held out the newspaper, but not folded to the business section that Victoria and her father often read and discussed together. This was one of the gossip columns turned to the wedding engagements.

Victoria's entire body ran colder than ice.

"I sent a note yesterday," her mother said, the words sounding almost one letter at a time through the roaring noise in Victoria's ears. "After the lovely dinner with Mr. Robbins. They hadn't yet gone to press, so I knew you'd be relieved to have one less thing to add to your list."

Victoria managed to tear her gaze away from the horrible words, words shared far and wide and completely out of her control. Her mother was openly crying now, her joy leaving her no room to recognize her daughter's dismay.

"You certainly have been busy, Mother. I don't know how I'll ever be able to repay you."

"You can never repay me, dearest," the older woman said, blotting at her eyes. "And I would never want you to try. The best gift any mother can have is to see her child in a happy and joyful life of her own."

"Then that's exactly what I intend to do." Victoria stood, holding the edge of the table until she caught her balance. "If you'll excuse me, I'll go upstairs and get ready for the day."

She accepted her mother's tearful hug, then Mavvie's, distantly wondering how neither of them noticed how dry her own eyes were.

Everyone knew.

Everyone who mattered for such things, anyway.

Her father and mother's friends, Bertrand's friends, all of their families. Victoria's visions of ending this engagement with less fuss and bother than her first evaporated in the time it took to read a tiny story in the useless rag of a paper.

She made it up the stairs before her stomach soured and clenched, trying to bring up the breakfast she'd managed to force down. Victoria tasted wine and whiskey from the night before in the undignified belches, but she managed to keep all of it in place.

She stood outside her workroom door until she was certain the danger had passed.

Of all the betrayals and traps her parents had put in her path, this had to be the worst. Trying to force an arranged marriage in an era when such things were firmly out of favor wasn't bad enough. Nor was choosing yet another distasteful man old enough to be her father, and all of it without considering Victoria's feelings for even one second.

Now her mother had made sure everyone she could reach knew, setting the date and the identity of the prospective groom in social stone.

Victoria wiped away furious tears, forcing herself to enter the workroom slowly and deliberately. This was not the time for making mistakes, nor for letting her concentration wander.

Not to her fury at her mother.

And not to the sweet memory and anticipation of more time spent alone with Rob.

The shelf full of clockwork toys had no place in this situation. Too strange, and as Inspector McDuff had proven, too easily recognized.

No, more subtle and appropriate materials were necessary here.

Victoria pulled down a dark green glass sphere with a flat bottom, no bigger than the palm of her hand. Elaborate copper filigree covered much of the perfume bottle, and a black fabric bulb protruded from the top.

Victoria had received the perfume for Christmas three years ago. Her mother had received an identical one, both from her father. Both filled with light, everyday fragrance of bergamot and lemon, with a tiny undercurrent of musk.

She'd never had use for hers until now, preferring her own mixtures created with far more care and purpose.

Victoria set to work.

CHAPTER 38

McDuff pushed the edges of the scratchy wool blanket against the window in his room, holding his hand a few inches away to catch any lingering drafts. He thought the fabric had been green a long time ago. Countless washes may have faded the color to an unpleasant dull brown, but the prickly irritation against his skin remained strong as ever.

Satisfied with his crude insulation efforts, he arranged his shoes along the ledge to hold everything in place.

Heat from downstairs rooms would soon reduce him to wanting to claw the makeshift curtains down in search of relief, but so early in the season his fingers were numb from the chill.

For some reason he didn't feel strange about wearing Michael's clothing anymore. A heavy, long-sleeved shirt and sturdy work pants that were only one size too big dampened the cold considerably.

He settled back onto his bed, contemplating whether to read one of the books he'd borrowed from Jean, make notes for a new case he actually was investigating, or chuck it all and go to bed early. The case was easy enough to ignore on a Saturday evening, and going to sleep at seven seemed too pathetic to contemplate.

He picked up the thick volume about magic and rituals of the ancient Celts instead.

No matter which section he flipped to, from his native Scotland to Ireland to far to the west in England, his mind wouldn't let him concentrate.

Did that poor girl up in Highgate still find comfort in her volumes of history and natural science?

Did she find comfort in anything?

Jean had long wondered if Victoria kept a secret journal or any sort of notes she could study, though Victoria denied all of it. She said her teacher insisted on learning by rote, by heart, to make sure the flesh and bones understood the magic as well as the mind did.

McDuff wondered if Victoria's heart understood magic as well as her warm eyes and her blushing cheeks seemed to when they were together.

He wondered how much Victoria's magic controlled his own feelings.

He wondered how much his weary flesh could learn from hers.

He shook his head, shifted on the bed, and tried to read again.

Strange round stone foundations and mysteries about their purpose just about had his attention when someone knocked on the door. McDuff scowled, halfway convinced to ignore it and keep reading.

No one of consequence could be up here this time of night, not without busybody Mrs. Richards knowing all about it. She kept prostitutes from roaming the halls all hours of the day and night, at least not without her own admission fee from the client to insure good behavior.

McDuff had always thought the relative peace and quiet was worth the observation and interference.

The knock sounded again, louder this time.

"Come on, McDuff. I can see your light under the door."

McDuff sighed as he recognized his neighbor from across the hall. O'Bana was a decent sort most of the time. Kept to himself and let McDuff do the same. Still, he wouldn't have bothered knocking without a good reason.

Rather than bundled up for a lonely evening at home, O'Bana wore a nicer jacket than McDuff had ever owned. The grey suited his dark red hair quite well, and that hair was as carefully arranged as a groom on the way to the altar.

"Visitor downstairs," O'Bana said. "Mrs. Richards caught me on the way out, insisted I come tell you. Now I'm about to be late."

"Visitor? At this hour?"

"Yeah, a woman, or else Richards wouldn't have stopped her. Go on, see for yourself."

McDuff's heart sped up, and he knew his own cheeks were flushed now. He spoke to O'Bana's retreating back.

"English or French?"

O'Bana stopped, shaking his head, hands on his hips. He turned slowly, trying not to laugh.

"All these years you live here. Never have one visitor that I know of. No sign of woman either, courted or paid. Finally one shows up, and you're worried about where she came from? Just get *down* there, man!"

McDuff nodded and waved his hand toward the stairs.

"Right, errand accomplished. Go on about your evening. I'm on the way."

He grabbed his shoes, growling when the blanket slipped off the ledge with a burst of cool, damp air.

Making whoever it was wait for him to change clothes didn't make a hell of a lot of sense. He'd never claimed or pretended to exhibit the heights of fashion. He did take a minute to try to smooth down his rumpled hair.

McDuff let out a long-held breath when he saw Jean.

She stood with her arms crossed, staring into the roaring fireplace in the common room. He was first surprised that she wore an unremarkable dark blue dress, perfectly acceptable anywhere in the city.

Relief that she wasn't wearing the same sort of pants and shirt that he did followed close behind. The handful of men gathered around the fire's warmth and pretending not to stare was bad enough without such shocking attire.

Mrs. Richards clattered up beside McDuff before he made it to the bottom of the stairs.

"Mr. McDuff, you have a visitor!" Her bright eyes and smile conveyed excitement he did not share.

Why on earth was Jean here?

"Thank you, Mrs. Richards. Mr. O'Bana accomplished his errand in letting me know."

Jean turned at the sound of his voice, and her shoulders sagged. McDuff hoped it was with relief. She crossed the distance in a flash.

"Rob! I'm sorry to bother you at home. Thank you for coming down." She turned to the owner of the boarding house hovering over McDuff's shoulder. "And thank you for sending word to him, madam."

Mrs. Richards fluttered one hand over her ample bosom, then turned away. Not before she winked at McDuff.

"What's happened, Jean? Did you see Victoria tonight?"

She stepped close to him, near enough so he saw the gallery of pathetic souls in the great room leer and grin out the corner of his vision.

"I'm sure your home is perfectly lovely, Rob. But I hope you won't mind if we go somewhere without such an audience. I saw a pub a few doors down from here."

"It's not lovely in the least, and neither is the audience. Terrible food and drink at that pub, but it is quiet."

She nodded, then turned and was out the door before McDuff could move. He ignored the laughter that followed him out into the evening.

By the time he opened the scarred wooden door of the pub to the smells of stale smoke, spilled beer, and dubious cooking, Jean was already at a table.

"Has something happened to Victoria?" McDuff sat across from Jean, realizing too late how distressed he sounded. She was far too smart to miss that.

"As far as I can gather, Victoria is perfectly fine."

McDuff breathed deliberately, forcing his imagination and his words to slow down.

"As far as you can gather? Did you go to her house?"

"I went there, but the doctors wouldn't let me go inside.

Nor would they let Victoria go out. It seems her mother has fallen mysteriously ill, Rob. They suspect typhoid."

McDuff gasped before he could stop himself.

Neither Victoria nor her family lived the sort of life that usually lead to that dread fever, insulated by their wealth and relatively clean houses. But no one in London was immune.

Certainly no one who ate in places as unreliable as the one they were sitting in.

"Is anyone else ill?" he said.

"Well, this is why *I* suspect they're wrong about what's causing the fever. No one else is ill at all. Not Victoria or her father, and none of the young women who work for them. One of them was most talkative after I used the trust charm Victoria taught me. That one's helped with a number of academics who didn't want share their materials."

McDuff paused long enough to order beer for each of them, newly afraid to trust the water or the food.

"Yeah, I've been wanting to try that one with a suspect or two. What did the girl say?"

"It seems Mrs. Haversham was fine this morning, though she and Victoria were up late last night. Some sort of loud discussion about being out all hours. Then right after the post arrived this morning, the lady of the house went upstairs to prepare for her day."

McDuff nodded, afraid to open his mouth. A fight over Victoria being out with him, then her first look at that wedding announcement.

He did not like where his mind was going.

The reality would likely be even worse.

"A while later, before lunchtime, Mrs. Haversham felt

poorly. Terrible stomach pains, brutal headache. Before she could even take to her bad for a rest, she was burning up with fever. Aches so awful she could barely stand the bedclothes against her skin. Only the slightest signs of the typhoid rash." Jean sipped her dark beer before going on. "Odd that the rash is only where she might have sprayed a bit of perfume rather than around the middle of her body."

"You think Victoria did this," McDuff said. He squeezed the bridge of his nose, trying to force his brain to stop. "That she poisoned her mother."

"Oh no, I doubt she'd bother with poison, Rob. Not with such an exquisite command of far more delicate means. The girl I spoke to, Mavvie was her name, was worried that Victoria may have brought it home from the poor unfortunate children she's been teaching to read and write all these weeks."

McDuff snorted, smiling despite his worry.

"And let me guess," he said. "Not a single child has taken ill."

"Of course not, according to Victoria herself. She could convince the doctors of whatever she wants with no effort whatsoever, couldn't she? Seems they're even teaching sanitation to the little dears at this wondrous charity. That's a place I'd love to see."

"As would I."

McDuff drained a good bit of the surprisingly agreeable beer while Jean watched him. He knew her next words would not be easy.

"Has she said anything to you about things like this to you, Rob? About making people fall ill?"

"Not like this, no. I don't doubt she knows how, though."

"And has she said anything to you about how to rid herself of her current fiancé? Some method that does not involve family members being dangerously sick?"

"Are you trying Victoria's trust charm on me, Jean?"

The scholar laughed, the huge, unrestrained sound surprising in the dingy pub. A few people looked around, but only for a second.

"I was not, Inspector. Are you telling me I should be?"

"We probably should all be using it," he said. "The deeper we get into this business, who can know where the truth lies any more?"

Jean tilted her head to the side.

"I believe you do know, at least about this. What I wonder is if we must be on guard against her attacking us in such a way? I suspect you've considered helping her. While you're a grown man capable of making your own choices, with a person like this, you can never be certain when your mind is not your own."

"That's true more often than not, isn't it?" McDuff said. "Most of us are weak-minded at best. Most of us are not scholars or as independent as you are."

Jean scowled, shaking her head.

"Oh come now. I haven't known you for all that long, but you never give yourself enough credit. Even in a case like this, you won't get taken in entirely against your own will, Rob McDuff. That's not how this magic works. Just be certain you stand willing to face the consequences."

Much as he wanted to fight it, Rob knew very well when he'd been caught. He'd been on the other side of that event far too many times to pretend.

"All right, Jean. Neither Victoria nor I wanted you and Father Hall to risk more than you already have, not with this. We have discussed actions we may take, but only in a general way. Victoria isn't happy with what happened to the innocent girl last time she tried to escape one of her father's choices. She doesn't want to involve anyone like that if she can possibly avoid it."

Now McDuff knew Jean wasn't using the charm that had gotten the Haversham's maid talking.

The truth that he was most unwilling to share remained locked safely inside his own head.

Neither Jean, Father Hall, nor anyone else besides him and Victoria needed to know their developing plans for the prison guards and Victoria's fiancé.

Or the feverish possibility of something so much more between them.

Jean smiled sadly and patted McDuff's arm.

"I suppose that feels honorable, not wanting anyone else to get involved. That's also a good way to try to keep your plans to yourselves. Father Hall may not recognize what's happening. What's already happened. He's likely never been in love. I have no doubt what I see between the two of you, my friend."

McDuff opened his mouth to protest his innocence, but Jean shook her head.

"Normally I would be delighted for you both. You're suited to each other, God help you, and I care for each of you. As much as I dislike seeing women caught in a situation with no power or control, I dislike it every bit as much for men. I'm worried for you, Rob. Being used is unpleasant for anyone."

McDuff finished his beer and gestured with two fingers to

the barkeep, using the excuse to avoid Jean's gaze. Much as he doubted the cleanliness of the place compared to many others around the city, he was here enough that the man knew just what he wanted.

Two small glasses and a bottle of Highlands whisky replaced the empty beer glasses.

"Well, Jean, sometimes being used can be better than being nothing at all. Both of you constantly tell me I'm smarter than I give myself credit for. Have you ever considered that I may be using Victoria, not the other way round? Maybe you're the ones not giving me credit."

He drained his glass, hissing air over his burning tongue, and poured himself another.

"Look around this place. You've seen how I live. You've seen the sort of prison I send men and even women to, day after day, year after year, because they can't be trusted even in a pit like London. Who wouldn't fancy a trip to a warmer climate with a beautiful, rich, young woman instead of this? And if she gets my little brother out of that hellhole or the next with a chance of living a worthwhile life? I'm not seeing a good reason to turn that down."

He wasn't sure if he was more angry at Jean making assumptions about his feelings and motivations, or for seeing right through him as easily as if he were a small child. Either way, McDuff knew he'd already said too much.

He wasn't exactly making himself sound better to a strong woman, nor to a friend who was trying to warn him. Not by claiming to take advantage of Victoria as surely as her lecherous fiancés planned to.

Jean let him twist in his own awareness, her expression

carefully neutral, until McDuff was struggling to keep his hands still and his mouth shut.

"I'm quite certain you're not aware of this," Jean said, "but you sound very much like many young women do when justifying loveless marriages. And more than a few men nowadays. For what it's worth, I believe you do care for each other. Or at least you're drawn to each other, for reasons only the two of you know. That puts you ahead of most."

"Maybe they have it all figured out, Jean. Those women and men. Maybe improving their lot in life is the best decision they can make for themselves. While the rest of us work ourselves to the bone and gain nothing at all."

This time she reached across the table and took McDuff's hand, squeezing and looking into his eyes.

"Take care then, Rob. Of yourself, and of Victoria if you can. Don't forget you have me and Father Hall on your side. Victoria is so young, and she carries the impulsiveness of youth in full measure. If we're all on her side together, perhaps this may all work out for the best. We can start by helping her end this attack on her mother before it all turns for the worse."

CHAPTER 39

Constant attendance by physicians and nurses was more than enough reason to wish for life in the Haversham household to return to normal. Victoria firmly believed this when faced with yet another visit, and she made plans to do just that every time they took her temperature, examined her skin, and asked after her bowel habits. No member of the household was spared the repeated indignity and frequent intrusions.

Her resolve to bring the entire frustrating episode to a close usually lasted until she returned to her workroom to fetch the antidote for the illness spell.

As soon as she slid the bookshelf aside, she invariably remembered the mortifying dinner with her fiancé and her parents. All of them chatting about how Victoria would soon be setting up housekeeping in another house. In *Bertrand's* house, molding herself to the choices and habits of a woman now rotting in her grave.

How she'd leave even this precious bit of control and

privacy behind in an unknown and undesired new life. After all, she'd soon be far too busy planning for the joyous arrival of new children to bother with all her own childish and stubborn ways.

And if that wasn't bad enough, she couldn't put the blasted newspaper announcement out of her mind for more than a few minutes at a time, even when she slept.

Concern for her mother's mental state made the delays increasingly tense and painful, and Victoria knew she'd remove the sickness soon no matter what kept surging up in her memory. Her mother did her best not to complain out loud, bringing out great pride in Victoria's father and encouragement from the barrage of doctors.

Anyone with a shred of compassion could see how miserable the woman was. A dreadful headache, discomfort when anything touched her skin. Aches in her arms and legs, and an itchy rash that defied all attempts to relieve it.

Victoria's own compassion for her mother slowly but surely eroded her anger as the days passed.

This was the first time Victoria had used this sort of specific and deadly serious magic. She didn't want to take the chance of the awful effects getting worse or lingering more than she expected. The guilt of not being able to remove symptoms of the horrid disease wasn't something she wanted to try to live with any more than she wanted to live with Bertrand.

On the fifth day of the family's medical confinement, she rushed to answer a knock at the door before Mavvie or anyone else could. Something different, any change in the routine, had to be an improvement over her own conflicts and anxieties.

She bit back a sob, at the expense of her lower lip, when she saw Jean and Father Hall.

"Miss Haversham, such a relief to see you in good health," the priest said. He winked, then turned to Jean. The French-woman wore a black dress that coordinated nicely with Father Hall's cassock. Not a nun herself in this performance, but at least someone who worked with them.

"We've been so concerned for you and your family at the orphanage," Jean said, playing up her French accent. "We do hope a visit is acceptable?"

"Yes, *more* than acceptable," Victoria said. She opened the door wide and stepped back. "Please, please come inside."

Mavvie fretted just behind Victoria, humming softly to herself, clearly not sure if anyone should be going in or out. She wrung her hands on her white apron over and over again.

"I'm so pleased to see you again," Jean said, nodding to the girl. "Mavvie, isn't it? I'm Jean Appréndia. She was most kind to me when I visited before, Miss Haversham. Mavvie, this is Father Sean Michaels. He does the hard work of running the charity Miss Victoria and I volunteer with."

The maid's face lit up as she smiled, and Victoria smiled herself when Mavvie dropped a perfect curtsy.

"Thank you, Miss Appréndia, I'm glad to see you again, too. I made certain to tell Miss Victoria whenever you dropped by." She curtsied again, flushing a bit this time. "Pleased to meet you, Father Michaels. You all surely do God's work for so many needy children."

He beamed and took Mavvie's hand in both of his, making her blush even deeper. His boyish, blond good looks served him well when the occasion called for it.

"Wonderful to meet you, Mavvie. We couldn't do anywhere near the good we manage without our generous benefactors and volunteers."

Victoria nodded, patting Mavvie's shoulder.

"We do as much as we possibly can," she said. "It smells a bit medicinal in here with all the doctor visits. Would you like to go out to the greenhouse to talk?"

Jean's eyes widened, enough that Victoria worried her enthusiasm would get the best of her.

"I'd *dearly* love to see your garden. I have a passion for gardening myself, especially when it comes to the miraculous medicinal herbs and plants. May we please, if it wouldn't be too much trouble?"

After a quiet but intense discussion with Mavvie—with Victoria forbidding her in no uncertain terms to disturb her mother, or to tell any of the physicians or nurses lest they all be quarantined longer—she, Jean, and Father Hall escaped the sick house into the garden beyond.

Victoria breathed deep of the garden air, full of soil and growing things, still pleasant so late in the season. Even the undercurrent of decomposition as summer slipped into autumn was a huge improvement over the camphor and vinegar inside.

The brisk chill cut the overheated, clinging atmosphere of convalescence out of her senses in an instant.

Rows of food crops, almost all cleared for the winter by now, were interspersed with roses and dahlias and other flowering plants. Only several rectangles full of cabbages, leeks, carrots, and other hardy winter greens and root vegetables remained green and neatly cared for.

Little remained of the usual screen of everything tall, flowering, and fragrant that blocked out the common foodstuff, as if gardening for sustenance was an activity to cause embarrassment.

Victoria couldn't quite dismiss the more common flowers she used so often as only for show, especially anything with a scent to carry her spells to their target.

"This is certainly a balm for the body and soul," Father Hall said. "Too many people in the city don't have space for more than a flowerpot."

"I've always thought the vegetables were lovely," Victoria said. "Mother does her best to hide anything edible with something she believes is only for show."

Jean didn't try to hide her excitement now that they were unobserved. She dashed ahead, nearly skipping like a schoolgirl, heading straight for the sprawling greenhouse. Panels of square, round, and triangular glass surrounded by bronze supports made up a fanciful building nearly as large as many houses, the corners and edges rounded and graceful.

"May I go inside?" Jean called. She already had her hand on the brass doorknob, made to look like an elaborate knot.

"Be my guest," Victoria said.

"And may I ask you a difficult question?" Father Hall didn't look angry, not exactly. He didn't look as calm as he usually did, either, with his brow knotted and his lips pressed thin.

"You may, but I'll guess at what it is. I am responsible for my mother's illness. It's not permanent, and I plan to restore her health very soon. I realize now I acted impulsively, and in anger. It was quite immature of me. You may have trouble believing this, but my childish response causes me no small amount of shame."

He nodded, remaining silent for several steps.

"That would be something to reflect upon if it grieves you. Do you believe this will accomplish your purpose?"

"It will delay her in arranging my life for me, or throwing absurd engagement parties for a wedding I refuse to participate in. The physicians are talking about at least two weeks of rest, possibly more. They're lifting the restrictions on the rest of us, but Mother isn't to be around great crowds of people for a while. They don't want her to fall ill again, or to spread whatever she has since it doesn't act as typhus normally does. Honestly, I believe she's secretly pleased to confound their treatments."

"So the wedding date may be pushed back. That's something for your efforts, I suppose."

Before Victoria could respond, he followed Jean into the greenhouse. That was probably for the best with the harsh words that demanded release.

Pushing the wedding date *back* only delayed her misery. Her efforts over the past few years had been to chart the course of her own life, not simply delay her inevitable capture.

She stood with her hand on the finely textured doorknob, waiting for her anger to die down a bit. She relied upon the glorious air inside the greenhouse to dissipate the rest.

Compared to the windy chill outside, the space was positively balmy. Even on an overcast day, the glass and the plants themselves added several degrees. The boiler would add a much-needed boost when winter settled in.

Victoria felt the skin on her cheeks and forehead, contracted and abraded by wind and constant medicinal scrubbing, relax and luxuriate in the humidity.

The scent of green and healthy plants rose to a symphony, with her many blooming plants the highest notes.

Jean hurried from row to row, brushing her fingertips over shining leaves and vivid blossoms in the high beds. Refraining from touching others. She stopped from time to time for a closer look before muttering to herself and moving on. Victoria could almost see her longing for a notebook and pen.

"This is glorious," she said, turning in a slow circle. "How can you stand to step outside and breathe the smoke and soot?"

Victoria sat on her normal bench at the gardener's table, long and low with a cool slate surface. She often worked here herself, with pots and seeds and her own special enhancements to the already rich soil.

With so much time spent away with these two lately, and with Rob, the table was clean and empty.

"Most of the time I leave because my mother decides I've spent quite enough time out here. She doesn't understand why I need to feel the soil against my fingers."

"And she doesn't understand what most of these plants are for." Now Jean stood in front of a box full of bright, colorful herbs most cooks in England wouldn't have heard of, much less know how to use. She wisely didn't touch any of them. "How is she feeling today, Victoria?"

She and Father Hall joined Victoria at the table, folding their hands on the smooth surface and waiting. They'd probably worked out every word before they knocked at the door.

Victoria wondered if Rob had been in on the planning, like he had been with her.

"She has a lower fever than yesterday, *Miss Appréndia*. Still has stomach pain and a headache, though. I'll start her cure this afternoon. *Father Michaels* here spoke the truth. This thoughtless action of mine has served its purpose."

"I'm glad to hear that," Jean said. "Is this what you have planned for your fiancé as well? Perhaps with the symptoms of cholera instead?"

"No, nothing so harsh as that." Victoria rubbed her hands together, enjoying how her flesh didn't feel so dry and constricted as only a few moments before. "I acted more impulsively than I normally do with Mother, or anyone else. I'm not often taken so completely by surprise, to be honest."

"I'm glad to hear this isn't normal for you," Father Hall said. "I'd hate to be the subject of one of these spells."

"No, that won't happen, Father. To you or to Jean. I haven't been paying enough attention to what my mother was doing. How far she'd gone in her arrangements, all for my own good whether I agreed or not. Things got out of hand while I wasn't watching."

"And do your plans with Rob include such spells?" Jean said. "With him, or maybe I should say *for* him?"

Victoria smiled, the expression at odds with the agitation churning in her gut. She hadn't expected a cross-examination from her friends, though perhaps she should have. At least they understood what her interests were, far more than her parents seemed to.

"Rob knows as much about our plans as I do. He had

nothing to do with my mother falling ill. I doubt he likes the idea any more than you do."

Jean shook her head, the corners of her mouth turning down.

"He seemed a bit surprised, but perhaps not as worried as I expected. Is that something he will regret, Victoria?"

"I can't speak for him, Jean. And I'm not about to try to predict the future. Right now, I have no desire to hurt him. We're far better off working together than in opposition."

Father Hall drummed his fingers on the table, staring at Victoria.

"I know this seems like we're ganging up on you. I'm sorry about that. I'm also worried for both of you. I hope you'll let us continue to help."

"Of course," Victoria said. "I can't possibly do this alone. Though you have already done so much. Getting Rob's brother through the next few weeks won't be an easy task even with all of us."

"And with your fiancé?" Jean said. As usual, she could be counted on for the most pointed, difficult questions. "Will you be needing us for that task?"

"I'm not sure what to do about that yet. Rob and I have discussed a few ideas, but nothing is certain. If you've spoken with him, I'm sure he told you we're both worried about putting you at risk."

"Risk that we've taken on knowingly," Father Hall said, "and willingly. If we can help, we stand ready to."

Victoria didn't have to ask how many things were unsaid, not after several weeks of working so closely with these two. Their omissions spoke volumes.

She had to make sure her own didn't do the same.

"I appreciate the support, as always. And the friendship. I'll know more once I see how Mother recovers, or more how the doctors respond to that recovery. Come walk with me, and I'll show you more of the greenhouse. We'll gather what I need to bring her back to full health before the sun rises."

CHAPTER 40

McDuff's mind kept wanting to push him into a disorienting double vision, one difficult day in the past layered atop the one he was trying to live through. He sat with Victoria, Jean, and Father Hall in a plain but clean reception room, more pleasant than standing in Fodelson's processing line.

A friendly young nurse dressed all in white sat with them after they signed in, rather than a glowering guard determined to figure out what they'd all done wrong.

And yet the odd spectacle of Victoria and especially Jean wearing the black and white nun's habits kept forcing McDuff to scramble for orientation in time. He again wore his own unaccustomed uniform, the stiff collar like a solid noose around his neck.

Jean and Father Hall ran their rosaries through their fingers, one bead at a time, though only Father Hall murmured words under his breath. Victoria wore one just as she had before, but she didn't touch it. She only sat with her eyes closed, wrapped in the disguise making her almost unrecognizable.

Unlike their last visit with Michael, Victoria wouldn't be using any of the tools of Catholicism today. With far more serious, and more difficult, work at hand, she'd returned to her most familiar means of control.

That was another disorientation for McDuff. The enchanted clockwork toys were the trigger that brought these people into his life.

Along with the continuing disorder he lived and breathed every day.

McDuff fell into his own routine of organizing what they needed to learn from this interview, meeting, whatever they wanted to call it. His mind and heart recoiled from interrogation, but it was closest to the truth. This wasn't a crime Michael had committed or gotten caught up in.

For once in his life, Rob McDuff's little brother Mike had a chance to give the punishment rather than receiving it.

The nurse turned to speak to another young woman dressed in white, then turned back to McDuff.

"Inspector? They're ready for you. Just follow Nurse Smith."

After a few seconds, McDuff realized they were waiting for him to move first.

He wanted to protest that he wasn't ready. Not for this. The last time they'd all tried to help Michael, he'd been beaten so badly he needed surgeons several times.

He'd wounded himself even worse.

McDuff pushed himself upright, wishing he had time to stop and talk to Father Hall, even for a second. He'd never been much of a praying man, but anyone who could help him right now would be more than welcome.

The nurse who'd waited with them touched his arm when he passed beside her.

"Your brother is a sweet man, Inspector. And so are you for bringing these good people to comfort him."

McDuff covered her hand with his and nodded, afraid to speak.

Michael waited in a small white room, not a dark, oppressive space like in the prison. This had a much smaller table and room to walk around, and a window that looked out over an open field surrounded by trees in the distance.

Michael looked a thousand times better than on McDuff's first visit a couple of weeks ago, too. All his hair had been gently cropped close to hide the regrowing patches that he'd yanked out, and the bruises on his face were all finally gone. Even his fingernails, or the nailbeds left behind, were less red and raw.

The younger man jumped up as soon as they all walked in.

"Robbie! Glad you're here. Doing better now, I am."

"You sure are, Mike." McDuff hugged his brother, trying to avoid the ribs he knew were still healing. "You remember Father Hall, and Victoria and Jean?"

Michael looked at each of the three of them in turn, but his eyes didn't really focus until he saw Victoria. McDuff thought he understood why.

He felt the same way, more so with every day that passed.

"Remember you," Michael said, nodding. He held out both hands, and Victoria held them carefully. "You were all there, at Fodelson. Before I had…had my trouble there."

"We were indeed, Michael." Father Hall smiled as if he were in his own church on an ordinary Sunday. "We hope to bring you comfort and peace."

McDuff jumped when Nurse Smith spoke. He'd forgotten she was there.

"If you've all worked with him before, I'll leave you alone. If you need help, just ring that bell there by the door. One of us will be right in."

She touched a small metal handle, attached to the wall inside a larger metal box. A wire ran up and disappeared into the ceiling.

"I know you'll do wonderfully, Michael," she said, smiling at him, before she closed the door.

"I know you will, too" McDuff said. "Did you have to help her along just then, Victoria?"

She walked around the small white table, watching for the best light from the window.

"No, that was all her. Just as well. I need all my energy for this. We all do. Can you sit here please, Michael?"

She stood behind one of the chairs right under the window. Michael glanced at McDuff, but he was already moving.

"Okay, Robbie?"

"That's right, Michael. I'll sit right here beside you."

Victoria moved around the table to sit opposite Michael. She waited for Jean to bring out her black medical bag, smiling at Michael the whole time.

"Will you pray for me again, Father? Don't want trouble like before."

"I'd be glad to pray for you, Michael. Sister Victoria has something important she'd like to show you first."

Michael's gaze darted to the tiny ballerina Victoria placed on the middle of the table, struck every bit as Rob had been by his first sight of it.

Of all the toys he'd see in fancy offices and overly decorated homes that led him back to this woman, McDuff had never seen one so delicate and lovely. The dancer's arms and legs were in perfect proportions to her slender waist, and her white, lacy dress was made of real fabric. The toy looked much too dainty and fine to be moveable, much less hold gears or cogs.

McDuff knew the mechanism was in the mirrored base. Victoria had showed him how the whole thing worked the day before. How the tiny glass segments moved and shifted, how all the movement of the dancer came from inside.

But when the toy girl rose up on one pointed foot, her other tucked against her knee, and began to twirl, his breath stopped as surely as Michael's did.

McDuff hadn't seen what Victoria intended to do with the toy, but she'd warned all of them it went far beyond anything the designers or factory workers who put it together could have imagined.

"I brought this toy especially for you," Victoria said, her voice low and soothing. She passed handkerchiefs to the three of them, just as she had before, soaked in herbs and potions to block the magic's effects. "Watch the way she moves, Michael. Watch the light."

Just then, the base rose up, barely an inch, and the segments shifted apart. The moving mirror started to rotate in the opposite direction from the ballerina, and the reflected sunlight sparkled against the white walls.

Michael's jaw dropped, his smile lighting his whole face.

The dancer raised both arms above her head and lowered her leg, spinning faster. McDuff knew this was their cue to cover their noses, but he was sorely tempted to let the magic affect him as it did his brother.

He was already under Victoria's spell more than he wanted to admit to himself or anyone else.

What could falling under this one hurt?

Except he was here to record, to keep the list of which guards had treated his brother so terribly. If he didn't do that, he and Victoria wouldn't be able to put the next part of their plan into action.

He raised the fabric to his face, breathing in the sharp, sweet aromas.

The ballerina stopped, waving both arms toward herself, inviting her observers to come closer. Just as he'd done when Victoria held a rosary inside prison walls, Michael leaned in as the steam puffed out around the swirling bits of glass.

The dancer jumped, causing him to gasp and draw the steam deeper into his nose and mouth.

By the time the enchanted toy jumped again, launching herself off the base and onto the table, Michael McDuff sat upright. His hands were folded on the table in front of him and his face was calm and focused.

"Can you hear me, Michael?" Victoria said.

McDuff pulled out a notebook and pen, noticing Jean did the same. Father Hall slipped his rosary through his fingers to the next large bead. McDuff heard the ghostly echo of the prayer in his mind.

Thy will be done...

"I hear you, Victoria."

"Good. Now watch the ballerina, but listen to me at the same time. She will only ever do this dance one time, and only for you."

"Only for me. Is it magic, Victoria?" Like the first time, his speech was more steady and clear than before he breathed in the steam.

"It is magic. Magic that I made only for you. Do your best to stay calm. I need to ask you some questions that won't be pleasant. All of us are here to protect you, so don't be afraid."

"I trust all of you," Michael said, his eyes still on the immobile toy. "And you most of all, Victoria."

McDuff glanced at her, wondering where that came from. Her most of all? Victoria's cheeks were flushed, but she continued to watch Michael.

The dancer bowed low, raising the edges of her long lace skirt out to the side, somehow moving without any gears or cogs. Her clockwork ran on pure and powerful magic now, and all of them were under Victoria's control as much as the ballerina was.

She rose up on one pointed foot again, spinning in the light still flashing from the rotating base.

"I need to know about the guards at Fodelson Prison," Victoria said. "You won't go back there, not any more. We want to catch the ones who treated you badly. We want to make sure they can't do that to anyone else."

"Good! You make *sure.*"

McDuff jumped at his bother's near shout, and Jean and Father Hall did the same.

Victoria didn't move.

"Do you remember the name of the first guard who hurt you, Michael?"

"Gibson," Michael said without hesitation. "Richard Gibson."

McDuff didn't remember to write until he heard the scratch of Jean's pen. He'd been watching the dancer, now leaping a few inches at a time, landing on one foot and continuing her spin.

"And what did Gibson do to you?"

"Gibson broke my ribs. On both sides. The billy club is his favorite. One like you used to carry, Rob."

McDuff nodded, struggling to keep his face neutral. He didn't forget to make notes this time.

"Did another guard hurt you?"

Victoria held out both hands, one to McDuff and one to Father Hall. Jean took the priest's other hand. When McDuff took Victoria's small, cool hand, he was startled by a jolt of heat like a physical touch up his arm and into his chest.

She'd warned all of them that they may feel her drawing from them, using their strength to help her.

He was still surprised at the power he felt.

"Beckits. Russ Beckits. Blue snake crawls on his neck, up in his hair. He…" Michael shook his head without looking away from the pirouetting toy. "He hurt me like a woman. At night, when the others weren't there. He told me he'd stop hitting me if I let him do that one time. But he kept coming back, all the time. He said if I told anyone, he'd kill you, Robbie."

Cold sweat broke out all over McDuff's body, and he had to force his grip on Victoria's hand to relax. Michael might be speaking calmly now, as if he were explaining what he did for a living, but he had to have been terrified in that cell in the dark.

In terrible pain and worse humiliation.

With no way to understand why.

"Okay, Michael." Victoria's voice trembled, and McDuff squeezed her hand a tiny bit. "Did he do that to you the whole time you were there?"

"No. He started after I heard the voices in the walls. Once I stopped doing my work like I was supposed to."

McDuff swallowed convulsively, trying not to throw up. He focused on his free hand, on the vague notes he was making.

He knew he wouldn't need them now. He'd remember these men and their crimes as long as he lived.

He'd remember the part he'd played in why it all happened.

By the time Michael finished naming the guards who'd abused him, Jean had filled two pages front and back with names and notes. Father Hall's face was pale with spots of color on his cheeks, and Victoria's hand was trembling.

McDuff still felt that strange movement of energy between them, but not nearly as strong.

The dancer's movements slowed as well, and they weren't as precise. She landed flat-footed more often than not, even staggering a few times.

She looked disturbingly human in her obvious exhaustion.

"I'm sorry to ask you this when you've been so helpful already," Victoria said. She took in a shuddering breath, and McDuff felt a bit more of his strength pass to her. He wished he could offer all of it. "Can you tell me why you hurt yourself? Your face and your hands?"

Michael looked away from the nearly staggering ballerina for the first time. He stared at his outstretched fingers, then refocused on the toy.

"The voices, the ones in the wall. They told me the guards might leave me alone if I did their work for them. That way I had charge of what happened to me and when." He touched his regrowing hair, traced his fingers down his scarred cheeks. "That worked at first. But then I couldn't seem to stop, even when I wanted to. That's when the surgeons put the jacket on me."

Father Hall let go of Victoria's hand and rested his forehead against his steepled fingers, his rosary twined through. Jean covered her eyes with one hand, but she continued to write. McDuff wasn't the only one would couldn't tolerate one word more.

The dancer walked carefully, painfully, across the table toward her perch. The mirrors had been spinning more slowly for the last several minutes. Now they stopped, sinking back down to form a solid base.

Instead of rising back up to her original upright stance on top, the ballerina curled into a ball in the middle, hands over her miniature face.

"Thank you, Michael," Victoria said. "I can't ask any more questions right now. Do you have anything you need to tell me? Or any of the rest of us?"

"I like it better here. If you helped me get from Fodelson to here, I never got a chance to thank you. I wish I could be outside more, but I'm not afraid of anyone in this place."

"I'm glad, Mike" McDuff said. "We hope to help you more, but right now we're going to make sure those guards don't hurt anyone else. You're very brave to help us with that."

"I can stay brave for all of you," Michael said. He held out his hands, one to Jean and one to McDuff. Even with Victoria's hypnotic toy stilled, perhaps forever, his words remained clear, his voice steady. "Will you pray for me now, Father Hall? For all of us?"

"I would be glad to." McDuff was struck by the priest's voice now, at the sharp and threatening edge. "Today and every day. And I promise I'll do my part to make sure all of these men come to justice."

CHAPTER 41

Victoria made certain she stepped into the church's coach right behind Rob McDuff, for the first time since moving to London truly unconcerned with social expectations of where she should sit in mixed company.

She was more than a little surprised to realize she'd been following them at all, really. Of course, two unmarried women would sit together on the narrow seat. Especially when two unmarried men shared the space with them.

Everybody knew such things, whether they remembered *why* they knew or not.

And every young woman knew she was expected to do what was right.

Rob had obviously expected her to follow those unspoken rules, judging by his raised eyebrows and half smile when she squeezed in beside him. Jean reacted more smoothly. She sat without a word or an obvious glance, then patted the seat next to her for Father Hall. He followed her lead, with only a blush betraying the unusual arrangement.

Even if all three of them had protested loudly, Victoria would have refused to move for decorum or discomfort, even for her mother's often-imagined disgrace.

Every part of her, from her mind to her heart to the bones and muscles inside of her, was exhausted beyond belief. If she didn't have the warmth and support of another human being, one she trusted and had grown to care about more than anyone else alive, she knew she'd collapse.

Maybe not permanently, like the used up husk of a toy dancer huddled in Jean's bag. But her collapse would surely last even past her mother's convalescence.

Michael's voice rang in her ears, her own flashes of light speckled her vision. She couldn't even manage to remove the restrictive fabric around her head and throat like Jean already had.

All Victoria could manage to do was lean against Rob's shoulder, her thigh and hip warm against his.

Even without her conscious effort to draw strength from him, she found his body gave to hers anyway.

"I hope you'll all join me for a meal this afternoon," Father Hall said, his own voice slow and weary. "Whether we speak a word of this today or not, I'd be glad of your company."

"Since I break bread with you more often than not," Jean said, "you know I'll join you. Only rest will help me truly regain my strength after this day, but sustenance will be a good start."

"Victoria?" Rob said, his voice close to her ear cutting through the echoes of his brother's.

So similar, but she'd know the difference with her eyes closed.

Michael's rough and a good bit deeper, perhaps from his hours of screaming not so very long ago. Rob's a pleasant high tenor, his Scottish origins showing in the slight roll of the r in her name.

Rob shifted beside her, and the warmth spread across her tight, knotted shoulders and down her opposite arm.

Most inappropriate, Victoria's mother whispered inside her mind, slithering through Michael's stories of true abuse and violence.

Scandal and disgrace.

"Listen to me." This time she felt warm breath on her cheek, against her ear. She'd never been so close to a man, physically or otherwise. She'd never wanted to until now. "Victoria, I need you to answer. Let us know you're with us."

All she wanted was to move closer and be still and not speak at all.

"I'm here, Rob." He lowered his head so his ear was near her mouth, close enough that she smelled his skin and hair. She wondered if the warmth of her own breath sent matching chills over his flesh. "I don't want to go home. Not yet."

"I think we'll both join you," he said. "Thank you. Thank you for everything today. I can't imagine Victoria could have done this without you."

"I barely managed with you," Victoria said. "Nothing I've ever done before drained me like this."

"Most of it hasn't been in person, from what I gather." Jean had succeeded in removing all the white layers of her habit, leaving her looking more like a severe schoolteacher than a nun. "And only Father Hall among us may have experience with such a litany of horrors."

"Not like this, Jean. What I hear in confession is likely watered down. And the person speaking is the one who committed the sins, not the victim. I'll need my own recovery after this."

"I was shocked to see daylight when we walked out," Rob said. His voice rumbled against Victoria's cheek, now settled against the scratchy blue wool of his uniform. "I would have sworn an oath that it was midnight or later."

"Barely gone noontime," Father Hall said. "We weren't even two hours in there."

"I hope we gained information that will help us." Victoria hadn't noticed Jean carried her notebook gripped tight in one hand. "Michael didn't seem to be affected, but all of us paid the cost for him."

"I can use it," McDuff said. Now his voice coiled tense and venomous like a snake. Victoria's nerves and reflexes cried out that she shouldn't be so near such an angry man, physically touching him and even under his arm, but she was incapable of responding. "And I plan to do just that."

"You're not alone in that, Rob." Father Hall sounded every bit as threatening, again giving her that unheeded urge to withdraw. "I've made no secret how I feel about their *model* prison and the way they run it. I have even less reason to stay quiet now."

"Take care, Father." Jean showed no signs of being afraid of either man, instead focusing on Victoria. "The punishment you create may be your own when you speak honestly about such men."

"Leave that to me," Victoria said. "I nearly had you dismissed simply because I wished it, Father Hall. Jean and Rob as well. Bringing about the same effect, or the opposite, would be just as easy. Once I've regained my strength, of course."

Her head rose gently, moving as Rob's lungs slowly filled, then drifted back down.

He pulled her against his side, only for a second, so briefly the others couldn't possibly have noticed before he relaxed.

Victoria knew he'd explain the bargain they'd just struck without speaking when they were alone together.

She had no doubt that she'd agree with every word.

CHAPTER 42

McDuff struggled to keep up with the conversation over lunch in Father Hall's dining room. Compared to the utterly plain guest room upstairs where he'd dressed and even Jean's more impressive book-filled study across the street, this small space felt far too elaborate to him.

Father Hall said he rarely ate in here himself unless he had special guests. The expensive paintings on the walls, shelves full of gold and silver trinkets, and confusing array of silverware on the delicate lace tablecloth explained why, at least to Rob.

Try as he might to pay attention and participate, words unrelated to the next steps he needed to take didn't want to settle in his mind. Even back in his own normal clothing, not so stiff and formal as his uniform, he still felt like his flesh was shifting, trying to form new and unfamiliar shapes.

Victoria seemed to feel better with the food, though, like the rest of them. She appeared at home and at ease with both the small talk and the expensive surroundings, though McDuff suspected she was faking with the benefit of long practice.

The quieter he got, the more she watched him. Every time her eyes met his, he felt the heat and pressure of her body against his.

The trusting way she rested against his chest when she'd been so weary and vulnerable.

Those thoughts led him to more quiet, lest he say something he'd regret before he stopped speaking.

Not necessarily about the way his body seemed perfectly fitted to Victoria's, though that was a possibility. Just as strong was the chance that he'd blurt out the plan that was taking shape in his mind to deal with Michael's attackers.

Surely such promises of violence were forbidden in the home of a friend, and even more so in a church.

Even though he wasn't particularly looking forward to an evening alone with his increasingly dark and disturbing thoughts, McDuff was relieved when Father Hall offered the church's coach for their trips back home. Victoria didn't bother to hide her own eagerness to join him.

Once they were alone, again sitting across from each other in the coach, McDuff's reluctance to speak drove him to the small talk he so disliked.

"You seem to have regained your strength."

"Better than earlier, at any rate. I fear I shall sleep like the dead this evening. And yourself?"

McDuff tried not to laugh, worried how hard and loud it might sound in the enclosed space.

"I'm glad Michael is doing better now. I feel worse about

how he was treated because of our interference. More determined than ever to set that to rights if I can manage it."

Victoria smiled in a way he hadn't seen from her, or from anyone else outside of a prison or jail.

Not eager, exactly, but not reluctant to face whatever difficult business waited before them. He didn't see the slightest trace of fear.

"I have the strangest feeling you've figured out exactly how to manage that, Inspector."

"Possibly. It will be dangerous, Victoria. To anyone involved, but especially to us."

She shrugged. "Would that be any different, Rob? Since nearly the first day we met? No one alive has ever known more about me and what I can do. You and Father Hall would lose your jobs if any of this came to light, and Jean would certainly see her reputation as a scholar destroyed. Even stripped of his priesthood, Father Hall would say all our souls are in great peril."

"Father Hall is likely right. Much as I want to keep him safe, I need his help for this next bit. I don't think I'd be able to stop him either way. Have you started what you planned with your father?"

"You mean stoking his fears? Helping him think more about dangers far worse than my mother's worries of scandal? I have. He was asking if I traveled alone to do this charity work, or if I always stay in the company of others just last night."

"What of your plans to return to the Caribbean? Where does that stand in all of this?"

She stared at him for a few seconds, then looked out the coach window.

They were just passing by market stalls teeming with people, hoping to afford supplies for their evening meals and get home. People who would never have believed the opulence of the formal dining room inside their shining beacon of a church.

If they did believe, they'd be infuriated.

"The manager of the plantation will be feeling the first whispers of homesickness by now. Opposite the ones I feel. He'll want to return his family to London before another season passes."

McDuff heard his brother saying he wanted to get outside more. Victoria's suggestion that work at that plantation would be hard, but good.

He hadn't felt good about his own work for a few years now.

"That's not all of it," she said. She reached out and took his hand. "If we're to be partners in these next steps, you'll need to share a bit more of your own ideas with me."

McDuff forced his mind away from where it wanted to lead him, deeper into what she might have meant by partners.

"The one person I haven't asked about is your fiancé. I'm not at all familiar with how courtship is properly conducted in this wealthy world of yours. Would it be terribly wrong to go to a play or something like it? Have him walk you home afterward?"

"Not wrong at all. Far more appropriate than these secretive carriage rides with a man I'm *not* engaged to."

He took her other hand and leaned forward. He noticed for the first time that she wasn't wearing her flashing red engagement ring.

"This is where the dangerous part comes in, and the deception. If you're willing, I'd like to speak to your father today. Later this evening would be best so we won't be together. He hasn't seen me since I asked him about your first fiancé, but I'm sure he'll remember me. Luckily your mother's maid and other members of your household have seen Father Hall recently."

"How does Father Hall play into my father's fears for my safety?"

"I don't think we'll need him to do anything, but they know you're working with a priest. He can stand in without getting further involved. We'll just be taking advantage of that good fortune."

"Aren't you afraid I'm manipulating you, Rob? The same way I am my father?"

McDuff let go of her hands, sat back, and smiled, surprised at his own response before he said it.

"Not today I'm not, probably for the first time since we met. I know how tired you are. I feel it in my own bones. I'm not manipulating you, either, for that same reason. If you want, we can each use one of your trust charms and see where the truth lies. Teach Jean how to prepare it so we'll both know the results would ring true."

Victoria did laugh, the light happy sound at odds with the day they'd had.

And the most perfect sound McDuff had heard in all his life.

"For today," she said, "we'll have to decide to trust each other. We'll hold the charm in reserve, shall we? More momentous choices will come our way. If you plan to speak to my father, I'll be certain to refresh the flowers in his study. After I have a bath and a nap."

"As you wish, ma'am. Now let me explain what I have in mind. If you decide I'm a fool for even making such a suggestion, we'll work out another way to go. For all the risk, I believe this will move your plans along quite nicely."

McDuff tapped one foot, gathering his thoughts as carefully as he did with any witness or suspect. He didn't kid himself that Victoria's cooperative mood would last forever, nor that her defenses would stay down after she'd had a good night's rest.

His own wouldn't either.

He had to choose his questions wisely while he could.

"My targets won't be nearly as successful or intelligent as your father's business partners. But we must use every bit of power we possess. Exactly how much can you bend far weaker men to your will?"

CHAPTER 43

Victoria's fantasies of a restful afternoon getting ready for Rob's visit evaporated as soon as she opened the front door. A wave of chattering voices from the formal parlor, just out of sight to her left, hit her exhausted body like a wave.

All velvet and silk and delicate chairs and china, the room was empty except for the most formal and important occasions.

As far as she knew, none had been scheduled today.

She couldn't make it upstairs to her bedroom and work-room or even out to the garden without walking past whatever was going on in there. Even walking around through the side of the yard not blocked by a fence would be tricky, since the sprawling room had windows on all three sides.

Much as she was afraid she wouldn't be able to tolerate socializing, Victoria couldn't quite bring herself to walk all the way around the block to the rear carriage entrance.

She found being a fugitive inside her own home no longer suited her.

Her mother's voice rang out before she took two steps.

"Oh Victoria, thank *goodness* you're home early! Still dressed for your charity work I see, but none of us expect you to stand on ceremony."

The explosion of colors kept Victoria from picking out anyone's faces for a moment.

Every inch of the room was packed, with every hue of the rainbow and many outside of it featured in gowns. She finally managed to spot her mother, glowing in a bright yellow dress in the center of the crowd.

Every one of easily twenty faces now stared at Victoria.

"Do come in and join us," her mother said, her eyes sharper than her tone. "Don't stand and gawk, darling. We'll see plenty of you in more festive clothing in the weeks ahead."

Voices burst out, overwhelming the flood of colors, making Victoria want to cover her ears and run. A few more people stood out now, friends of her mother's, but that didn't explain the sheer number of women.

Or the number of babies and young children adding to the painful noise and motion levels.

She finally recognized women her own age—the ones her mother dearly wanted her to be friends with. The ones Victoria had hardly found a thread of common ground with to begin with.

Even those fragile gossamer fibers shredded as they each married, one after the other.

Her first step forward brought an onslaught of scents that made her head pound. Every variety of exotic perfume mixed with the ordinary aroma of overly warm flesh. The lingering fumes from her mother's latest sloe gin concoction topped off the sensory assault.

"Have I forgotten an occasion?" Victoria said. She hoped the cold sweat drenching her wasn't too obvious.

"The physicians *finally* agreed I could have company." Her mother smiled broad enough to include everyone jammed into the parlor. "Nothing else could help my health more than dear friends. I knew the company of other young women would lift your spirits as well. God bless them all for making time for us on such short notice."

Once Victoria passed the double doorway, she finally spotted three women she could properly call friends. At least what she'd assumed friends were before joining Father Hall's odd society.

They all but huddled in the most secluded corner, and their relieved smiles mirrored her own.

Their marriages and Victoria's attempts to avoid her own had kept them apart more often than not for the past several months.

She likely wouldn't get away with gathering her small group and escaping to the sanctuary of the greenhouse, as she so often had during large parties. But Victoria's nerves calmed at knowing she could join their circle once the social obligations were satisfied.

That delicate calm deserted her almost immediately.

Mrs. Haversham had been busy far beyond the wedding announcement, and she'd kept it even more secret. Victoria spent the next half hour trying to avoid questions about her upcoming happy event.

Those questions turned tame next to unsolicited advice about her honeymoon night with a man she couldn't stand to look at, much less touch. The older women leered more than Bertrand or even her first fiancé did.

She knew it was a mistake, one she might regret, but Victoria swallowed two glasses full of sloe gin in quick succession. The heavy sweetness sank into her middle like a rancid stone, while the alcohol floated her head far beyond her body.

She hoped her good sense and ability to hold her secrets close didn't go with it.

A woman easily her grandmother's age gripped her arm, fingers sinking into the flesh.

"What you must remember is to do your duty to your family first, Victoria." She nodded to herself, towering fluffy white hair shifting with the movement. "And to your new husband, of course. The honeymoon is not for idle adventure, wasting time and money with nothing to show for it. Relax and enjoy your travels, by all means. By the time you return to London, your immediate task will be preparing for motherhood and the end of such frivolity."

Victoria covered her mouth, then wished she'd let the belch of a heavy lunch and recent juniper free after all. Two women her mother's age and three her own nodded at the matron's words.

Only the older ones smiled.

The younger all looked more weary than Victoria felt. Two with babies, one with a toddler held to the side of her swollen belly.

"Thank you, ma'am," Victoria said, stepping back. "How

generous of you to want me to enjoy my *duty* as much as you obviously have."

She turned and headed toward the quiet corner where her three friends still waited, stopping to say hello to every distant acquaintance and complete stranger who insisted on offering their congratulations.

She hoped the flush spreading from her face over her whole body could be passed off as excitement at her upcoming wedding, or at least the gin.

The truth was her mind had played out every lewd scenario the women described, but with Rob McDuff as her willing and ardent partner.

His smooth skin and strong shoulders.

His thick brown hair and musical voice.

After months of wondering how she could possibly tolerate letting men older than her father touch her at all, how she could survive the ordeal night after night, Victoria passed into *needing* Rob to do far more.

Her long day and drinks might explain part of the clenching tension deep inside, a part of her that craved fulfill-ment. Expansion.

But Victoria knew this was no passing trifle.

Jaji had taught her magic to bring about this desire in men, and even in women, as a means of control. A way to shape the world around herself, gain and hold her advantage.

Her beloved nanny also taught her how dangerous those spells were.

The only magic taught with more caution and seriousness was how to end life if she willed it.

Victoria had used the lust spell on her first fiancé without truly understanding its power. She'd been so young when she learned it, and when Jaji died.

Even with all the unintended results in her own life, she couldn't quite feel guilty about the effect on Mr. Abernathy. He'd intended to set her up as little more than a well-dressed brood mare, the same life that drove his first wife to an early grave.

But now that she was drowning in the nearly painful sensation herself, the guilt over so callously using such a young, innocent girl threatened to choke her.

Victoria had trapped Cheryl Mallory as surely as her own mother was scheming to trap her, and without even the benefit of a rich husband and a house of her own.

Nothing but the cold comfort of parents who could only dread the arrival the grandchild soon to be born.

Victoria had never even considered using the death charm, not beyond idle daydreams. Her rising anger at her mother brought the reasons for Jaji's caution against it into sharp focus.

Her three friends stood when Victoria approached, all of them with amused, knowing smiles. Liz Smithfield tall, blonde, and slender, Shelly Richardson short and curvy with curly red hair, and Francis Wellington raven-haired and more than a little pregnant.

"Finally made your escape!" Liz exclaimed.

All three women embraced her, thankfully just like Victoria in using less perfume and powders. Her senses and her mind cried out in relief.

"I ducked when Mother threw the net," Victoria said. She

sat with her back to the swirling mass. "How did she trick you into this?"

"Same with all of us." Liz raised one eyebrow, a quirk far more telling than her smile. She was the only woman Victoria still knew who'd lived on an island near Enceleas when the Havershams did. Time spent in India afterward meant she'd only returned to London two years before. "Your mother sent invitations round to *our* mothers."

"I can't believe she brought out so many since I left here this morning."

"No, sweetheart," Shelly said, patting Victoria's knee. "The invitations arrived three weeks ago."

"I think she meant it to be a sort of bridal shower." Francis shook her head before sipping at her drink. "She was still hoping to recover sooner, not to have your wedding delayed after her illness."

"Three weeks," Victoria whispered. Her head, so recently floating, now plummeted with her heart to the floor. "This was the first I've heard of any of this."

Shelly covered her mouth with one hand, eyes wide and cheeks pale.

"I'm so sorry! It never occurred to me to warn you about… your own party."

"No, don't apologize." Victoria pressed on her stomach with a shaking hand, hoping to stop the twisting inside. Her arousal had soured, crossing that thin line into fury. "I had as much to do with this as I did with the engagement, which is to say nothing at all."

"I thought as much," Liz said. "My parents came back from

their colonial adventures with the same ideas. I didn't elude them as well as you have."

Victoria closed her eyes, struggling against the words and rituals flooding through her mind. With her mother's illness so recently lifted, the spell would be absurdly easy. And the consequences horrifying and everlasting.

She forced herself to speak the first English words she could catch hold of.

"Have you found your marriages tolerable?"

Only one woman smiled: the other two laughed without any trace of humor.

"I'm afraid Shelly here was the only one with any choice in the matter," Liz said, leaning against Francis. "You'll notice she's the one who's smiling."

"Well, it has been." Now a blush climbed up Shelly's delicate throat. "I suppose I was lucky, falling for someone with the right…qualifications."

"Oh, now I feel better about my arrangement," Francis said. "My parents decided Benjamin was eminently qualified." She patted her belly. "I suppose he's proven them right now."

Victoria shuddered, her visions of Rob's passionate caress replaced with nightmares of Bertrand pawing at her. Liz raised her glass of fruity cocktail.

"One must find ways to make our arrangements more tolerable, my dear Victoria." Her laugh this time was throaty and low, not the harsh bark she'd had earlier. "Though we must take care when it comes to the stage Francis exhibits so beautifully."

"Keep your voice down," Francis said, her voice a soft hiss.

"I know better than to land in that sort of trouble. You need to be careful yourself, Liz."

Victoria's mind, still reeling from her mother's elaborate setup, fought to follow the conversation.

"Arrangements? That's the trouble I'm already having. I never would have arranged any of this."

Liz leaned forward, her knees on elbows pose thoroughly unladylike. Victoria remembered it well from their youth running and playing like savages. The effect was scandalous in a grown woman wearing a rather low-cut gown.

"With our *mature* husbands away such long hours at work," Liz said, "sometimes opportunities for entertainment present themselves. Mine drives our carriage. Francis is fond of gardeners, from what I understand."

A breath escaped Victoria, sounding like a cross between a laugh and a groan.

Of course. They'd joked about such things when both Liz and Francis got engaged, though not when Shelly did. She'd missed these three more than she realized, too caught up in trying to avoid a similar fate.

"We're to be discrete and enjoy our lives, then," Victoria said. She hoped the bitterness didn't make it from her throat to her voice. "Or as much as we can manage, anyway."

Liz glanced across the room at her own mother, sitting in the circle around Mrs. Haversham. The old woman who'd lectured Victoria about duty stood behind them, watching the four of them with open suspicion.

Victoria vowed to never fall into the gilded cage her two friends had, no matter the cost or consequence.

"We do the best we can," Liz said. "That makes the times

when we can't far more tolerable. Just take care of yourself, sweetie. Don't let it ruin your life."

"Your first loathsome fiancé disqualified himself quite effectively, didn't he?" Shelly said. "You never know what pleasant surprises the future will bring, Victoria."

CHAPTER 44

McDuff walked slowly toward Victoria's house, wishing he'd had time for the nap she'd planned for this afternoon. Each of the stately mansions were larger than his whole boarding house, and every single one in far better repair.

Stone stood beside brick stood beside lovingly painted wood, with manicured lawns in between. He knew most had gardens in the back, unseen by lower-class sorts such as himself who didn't belong here.

Hours of tracking down witnesses for a recent gang fight hadn't exactly restored his energy, and wouldn't have even when the day wasn't so long and difficult.

The prospect of putting his plan into action cheered him almost as much as seeing Victoria. The guards deserved consequences even more than the gang members did.

A young woman answered his knock, most likely the maid Victoria, Father Hall, and Jean had mentioned. She looked as bad as he felt, as if she'd been on her feet for hours on end.

McDuff sympathized, and he sternly reminded himself not to slip up and call her Mavvie.

"Inspector Rob McDuff here. I'm hoping to speak briefly with Mr. Haversham. We've met before, speaking about another investigation."

"Oh, of course, sir." She nodded, then stepped back. "Please wait and I'll go fetch him."

A general hum of activity he hadn't noticed the last time he was in this house sounded off to the left. Before McDuff could step forward to peek through the double doorway, Victoria stepped out of it.

He tried to stop himself, but he drew back at the sight of her.

Instead of rested and refreshed, she looked more pale and drained than before. She even wore the same dark blue work dress she'd had on under the nun's habit. Now it emphasized the bruised looking circles under her eyes rather than their striking color.

"Inspector McDuff, isn't it?" She smiled and held out her hand, squeezing his painfully tight. "We've met before. Victoria Haversham. My father will be with you in just a moment."

"I hope you're not feeling poorly, Miss Haversham. I understand your mother has been ill."

"She seems to have fully recovered. I envy her that. This has been an incredibly long day here, with a surprise party that's only just ended."

Victoria waved her arm toward the room. McDuff stepped forward to see a huge parlor, larger than the whole house he'd grown up in. He suspected any one of the fine upholstered sofas and chairs—not to mention the paintings and the chandeliers and the discarded clusters of sparkling drinkware—were worth more than that shack back in Glasgow.

The crowd of young men and women cleaning and chatting back and forth to each other in there was every bit as foreign to him.

McDuff knew he'd be afraid to even step into such an overwrought yet elegant space.

He was entirely out of his depths with a woman who'd grown up taking such wealth for granted, every bit as much as he was overmatched by her talent and intelligence.

Before he could say that or anything else, Victoria turned at heavy footsteps behind them.

Mr. Haversham was still dressed in his workday suit, but he'd loosened his tie and collar.

"This is a surprise, Inspector. I hope the news is good?"

"Partly good, sir. Not all of it, I'm afraid."

Mr. Haversham pressed his lips together and nodded once. He touched Victoria's shoulder. His eyes were as concerned as McDuff was trying not to be, at least on the outside.

"I'll speak to Inspector McDuff in my study. Why don't you have a rest, Victoria? The staff can finish cleaning up. I don't want you taking ill like your mother did."

"Very well, Father." She met McDuff's gaze. "I'm afraid I haven't done any of my chores around the house today. But we all must attend to our health."

McDuff watched her walk slowly up the staircase, her steps as slow and heavy as her father's. He wondered if the hidden workroom she often spoke of was up there before what she'd said truly sank in.

No chores, which they obviously had plenty of employees to do?

Or no spells to help ease the way with the delicate conversation ahead?

Despite years of experience in reading people and convincing them do what he wanted, he was again at a disadvantage.

"This way, Inspector. Anything to eat or drink? It seems we have plenty left over."

"I'm fine, sir, thank you. Your daughter says you had a party here today."

"Well, my wife did." Mr. Haversham smiled and shook his head. "She planned it weeks ago as a bridal shower, but with her illness… She did enjoy herself. Not as tired as Victoria is, at least. I'm afraid my daughter is more like me when it comes to social occasions, to her mother's ongoing disappointment."

"I'm not one for large crowds myself."

As soon as McDuff stepped into the far more masculine study, smaller and darker but every bit as expensive, his fears were confirmed. The floral, earthy scent that accompanied every one of the potions and spells Victoria used was absent.

He smelled only rich cigar smoke and the aged leather that covered all of the chairs. A copper vase filled with angular burgundy flowers, both appropriately masculine, sat on the edge of the broad oak desk.

But the blooms were dry and lifeless, with no trace of an aroma.

"What brings you back to our home, Inspector?" Mr. Haversham sat behind his desk with a long sigh. "Has that nasty business with Wilfred Abernathy come to an end?"

"For Mr. Abernathy it has, and for the department. I've found no evidence of wrongdoing besides the obvious terrible judgement. It seems he plans to depart our shores for the United States before the end of the year. Probably for the best."

"More than probably. That will be a fine day, when I never have to worry about seeing a disgrace like that walking our streets. I've heard the Mallory girl has recovered?"

McDuff heard no more trace of sympathy for Cheryl Mallory than he had for Mr. Abernathy. He supposed Mr. Haversham didn't care to see past what he considered a terrible insult to his own daughter.

"She's recovered from her attempt to take her own life, yes. It remains to be seen whether the child will be affected."

Mr. Haversham scowled and waved one hand, brushing aside the matter of a possibly diseased baby born to an unmarried girl.

"He hardly acted alone, did he? Maybe she'll learn a lesson and stop behaving in such a way around engaged men. I'm quite sure it wasn't the first time, not for a girl like that."

McDuff tried to return Mr. Haversham's smile, but he knew he did a poor job. He couldn't honestly smile about such a dreadful situation, and he knew very well the poor girl had not been at fault.

And the man's predatory grin reminded McDuff far too much of the woman who was responsible.

"I'm afraid the real reason for my visit won't be so pleasant," he said. He wished for Victoria's assistance even though he knew the damage she was capable of. And God help him, he wished even more for her company. "I must inform you of problems with the charity your daughter has been volunteering with."

Mr. Haversham's fist barely moved, but the impact against his gleaming desk rang out in a deep thud.

"I knew she'd brought some bloody disease home from that filthy place!"

"No sir, thankfully that doesn't appear to be the case. No one has taken ill there, and they take great care to teach hygiene to—"

"That sort of child won't be helped by something as simple as hand washing, and Victoria knows better than to think so! She wastes her time with this nonsense instead of preparing herself for married life. It's high time I put a stop to her *volunteer* work anyway."

McDuff felt rooted to the spot, too furious to move or even breathe. He wanted to explain, to smash the officious buffoon in the nose, to stand up and go back to his own miserable life and never deal with this sort of people again as long as he lived.

Yet he could barely manage to open his mouth without shouting right back.

"This isn't about the children at all, Mr. Haversham, or the efforts to improve their difficult lives. This is about Miss Haversham's safety. I don't mean from any sort of disease."

A second fist joined the first, and this time everything on the desk rattled in response.

"Are you telling me someone's threatened her? One of these vile gangs destroying our city an inch at a time? That's what you lot at Metropolitan Police ought to be focused on, not wasting time on some wayward girl who got rightly punished for her sins. Nor on the idiot who put her there!"

All at once, McDuff knew what caused this outsized reaction and outburst, one he'd never expected even from such a ruthless businessman.

Mr. Haversham was used to being soothed, calmed, comforted in this space like in no other. He doubted very much that Victoria ever let her influence lapse as she had done today.

Some part of her father sensed the change.

This wasn't the man's true nature any more than the docile parent who allowed his daughter to get so involved with his business and in running her own secretive life.

This was nothing more than an animal reacting to slipping free of its gilded cage at last.

What McDuff didn't know was how to react without making everything worse for Victoria, and for himself.

A knock at the door made both men jump.

"Father?" Victoria opened the door a crack. "I'm so sorry to interrupt. Mother thought you would both like a bit of the sloe gin she served this afternoon. We have plenty, and she's quite proud of her new recipe."

"Of course, please come in," Mr. Haversham said. His voice was still tight, but he'd placed his hands flat instead of clenched into fists. "I believe both of us could use the refreshment."

When she opened the door, McDuff took his own relieved breath.

Victoria carried a wooden tray with three carved crystal glasses full of deep pink liquid, one with floating bits of green. He barely caught the bite of juniper in the air.

The earthy, floral aroma, surely coming from the larger

bowl filled with water and more of those angular burgundy blossoms, set every cell in his body at ease.

"I know you need a rest, young lady," Mr. Haversham said, "but I'm glad of your company and the lovely flowers you work so hard to grow. This room is utterly lifeless without them."

McDuff jumped to his feet to help with the tray, brushing Victoria's fingers with his own. She smiled and took the bowl, letting him have the rest.

"I felt bad for leaving these dead ones on your desk, especially when you have company." She dropped the dry flowers on the tray and refilled the vase. "The cup with muddled mint leaves is for my father, Inspector McDuff. I make sure to keep a good supply going year-round, he loves it so."

Mr. Haversham's broad smile was utterly at odds with his glower and shouting barely a minute before.

The snarling beast soothed and comfortably back in its fragrant cage.

"That I do. Thank you, Victoria. You should probably join us if you can possibly endure it. Inspector McDuff was about to tell me about a serious matter than concerns you."

"Of course." Victoria sat and accepted her cool cup, this time brushing McDuff's fingers with hers. "I hope nothing unpleasant has happened."

McDuff took his chance to reorient himself to his normal role in these situations. The one directing the interview, not scrambling to react.

If Victoria's enchanted water kept him calm as much as it did her father, he could only be grateful.

"I'm sorry to have upset you earlier, Mr. Haversham, and I hate to frighten either of you. This is indeed a serious matter, or I never would have bothered you at home to begin with."

Victoria's father took in a deep breath, then blew it out through his lips.

"Of course, Inspector. I apologize for behaving so terribly. You're only doing your job. I appreciate you taking the time to come all the way out here. What's happening?"

"The director of the charity, Father Sean Michaels, has an additional passion besides helping the young orphans. He also fights to improve conditions of Britain's prisons. He hopes to see more men recover than stay behind bars for a lifetime."

Victoria nodded and looked sad at the same time, playing their game flawlessly.

"He recently counseled a prisoner," McDuff continued, "who confided unspeakable abuse from the guards. Apparently the report Father Michaels sent to the warden resulted in punishment for those guards. Well-deserved given their behavior, but such men don't often respond well to deserved punishment."

"Have you been involved in any of this, Victoria?" Mr. Haversham said. He now looked more worried than angry.

"I knew he worked with prisoners, but I've never been involved. Father Michaels would never expose any of us to such a place."

"No, I suppose he wouldn't." Mr. Haversham rubbed at his chin, then nodded for McDuff to go on.

"Those guards, now unemployed and at loose ends, have been threatening to get even. Not only with Father Michaels, but with anyone associated with him. Employees of the charity have received distressing notes."

"Oh no." Victoria put one hand on her chest, staring at McDuff with her eyes wide. "I hope no one's been harmed."

"No. That's what we're trying to prevent. We have several officers looking for these guards, and we're watching the charity day and night. We're also watching Father Michaels and his employees who request our protection."

Mr. Haversham stretched his fingers out, as if recovering from his earlier fists. He drank the contents of his cup down to the crushed green leaves. McDuff sipped at his, tasting only fruit with no trace of alcohol. No wonder he hadn't smelled gin.

"Victoria, I know you love what you do," Mr. Haversham said. "But I must ask you to take a sabbatical while these men are on the loose. Would you please obey me in this one simple thing if nothing else?"

"Of course I will, Father. How long have the guards been about, Inspector? Have they seen any of us leaving or arriving at the orphanage?"

"I'm afraid they've been watching for a few days now. That's why we're informing everyone who's been there for the past week or so. When I saw your name on the list, I remembered you both helping so much with my other investigation. I wanted to make sure you had access to anything you need."

"What she needs is someone to watch her just like the priest," Mr. Haversham said. "I know better than to expect her to sit at home now that the medical quarantine is lifted. All of us need to get out and about into fresh air. And I certainly don't want that sort of criminal figuring out where our house is."

He stood and turned toward his window, looking out over

the garden. Victoria lowered her head and smiled at McDuff. His heart sped up, and other parts of him responded as well at the stolen moment.

He risked a wink at her before turning back to her father.

"That's wise of you, sir," he said. "I can make suggestions if you don't have anyone in mind or already on staff for this important duty."

Mr. Haversham turned and gripped the back of his chair, fingers sinking into the leather.

"I do have someone in mind. You, Inspector McDuff. You handled that other business discreetly, and you were good enough to make sure we knew about this. I'd like you to make sure Victoria is protected. I believe our physicians will help me make sure her mother doesn't go out alone until this is resolved, just to be safe."

"I'm certainly flattered by your confidence, Mr. Haversham. I'm sorry to say I don't normally do this kind of patrol duty during my working day. It would be difficult to get clearance for that."

"Then hear me out, please. I know it's difficult to be a working man these days with money in short supply. I'd be glad to pay you for this myself, at one and half times your normal salary. No need for clearance that way. I know I can trust you. Someone who can work out of uniform would be better anyway."

McDuff sat back, tapping the arm of his chair, twisting his mouth.

Such a hard decision, after all, and one he'd never made before. He should certainly look concerned.

He reminded himself to drop by the Mallory's home in

Highgate to collect their similar payment now that Mr. Abernathy was removing himself from the scene.

"Is this acceptable to you, Miss Haversham?" he finally said.

"I think I would prefer an inspector over an officer in uniform as well. We must take care in situations like these."

"That's settled, then." Mr. Haversham sat again, his mood greatly improved. "We had excellent security during our entire time in the Caribbean. The unrest never quite reached Enceleas, but trouble on the nearby islands was more than close enough for me. I've often wondered if we shouldn't always do the same in this crime-ridden city."

"I'm glad to be of service," McDuff said. He turned to Victoria. "We'll need to coordinate your schedule and mine as soon as possible, of course."

"We can do that now, if you like. I'll bring my appointment book to the breakfast nook, where you interviewed me before."

Victoria stood and held out one hand to her father. He took it in both of his.

"Thank you, Father. I know the police will resolve this quickly, but I'll feel so much safer with Inspector McDuff watching over me. I'll leave you two to discuss the fee."

CHAPTER 45

Victoria stood close to the window in the round breakfast nook, afraid sitting would put her right to sleep. Her mind's eye, one of the most powerful tools Jaji taught her how to use, overlaid the dying early winter garden with the vibrant riot of life during the height of summer.

She'd been looking at flowers in every shade and shape on the day of that first interview, row upon row of vegetables at their peak, and a greenhouse bursting with tropical abundance.

She'd been sitting across from Rob McDuff, seeing him as nothing more than a casual distraction in her life and her plans.

The difference a few months made was nothing short of staggering.

That was something else her beloved nanny had taught her about, more than her mother or any of her school teachers ever had.

How meeting one person could throw everything into disarray, inside and out, no matter how carefully she tried to protect herself.

She'd stopped just short of warning Victoria to avoid such entanglements.

Jaji's own husband, freely chosen and fully aware of her powers, had been far too vital and dear for her to deny. His death was likely the only thing that could have broken her enough to agree to leave Enceleas and come to London to care for Victoria, leaving her own grown children behind.

Victoria swayed on her feet, more tired than she realized.

She decided she could use one more of the alert charms and remain safe. Too many made her heart pound painfully. She poured the tiny vial into her water glass and swallowed the whole thing.

She was far too disarmed with Rob already.

She couldn't risk a conversation with him in this house without at least being awake.

She sat, waiting for the tingles and chills of the charm taking effect. She should give Rob the other one still hidden in her bodice. He looked nearly asleep on his feet as well.

Or maybe she should draw him a hot bath instead, then climb in tucked up against the front of him. Her well-practiced mind's eye obliged her interest by creating that scenario with disconcerting sensory detail and intensely imagined sensations.

On the heels of her entirely inappropriate thoughts, Victoria started when she heard someone striding down the hall. Not her father's weighty tread or her mother's delicate tiptoe.

Whether from her overly active imagination or from her other means of stimulation, her body and mind were finally alert.

Rob stepped into the doorway, bowing low before her.

"Miss Haversham. I congratulate you on your poise and decorum. And I trust no one is close enough to listen in."

"Thank you, Inspector McDuff. You were equally impressive. I keep this room protected any time I'm in here. Anyone who walks by will be profoundly bored."

"I sometimes miss those days." He sat beside her, but not too close. "Of being bored, I mean. At least once in a while."

Victoria opened her appointment book, bound in rich blue fabric, to be on the safe side. Rob brought out a plainer black version that he carried for his police work.

"It's a lifetime of boredom that kills you," she said. "The heart just doesn't have sense enough to stop beating long after the mind has ceased to function. Did Father Hall actually file a report about these guards?"

"No, he won't need to for our purposes. You can make them target anyone you wish, and the reason will never come to light. I do know he'll be willing. He's said as much more than once. I doubt either one of us would have to convince him if it would help."

Victoria circled the upcoming Saturday on her calendar, then tapped it with her pen. McDuff wrote the same date in his notebook. Enough time for Victoria's letters to arrive and take effect.

"I doubt I'll have to convince Bertrand to take me to a play, either. He and my mother will see it as evidence of my growing affection toward him. How angry are these guards likely to be on the night, Rob?"

He rubbed at the back of his neck, shaking his head.

Victoria wished she could rub his shoulders. The way she sometimes saw her mother do for her father, when they thought no one was watching. She wondered how Rob's face would look as his eyes drifted closed in pleasure.

"Probably more angry than we expect them to be," he said. "I think it's safe to assume that. Whatever happens, we'll need them to forget as much as possible. If they put you and I together with Michael, or Father Hall, we won't be able to keep any of this going."

Victoria wrote St. James Theatre on her calendar, then looked at Rob.

"Memory charms are tricky at best, and that's if I know the person well. Or if I can spend time with them."

"Tricky in being too strong or too weak?"

"That's the difficulty. For someone I can test it on, make adjustments, I can gradually increase the strength to what I need. For my father, for example, or my dear fiancé Bertrand. But the danger of making it too strong is worth the extra time."

McDuff flipped his notebook to a blank page, sketching out a street map. Victoria recognized the neighborhood around the St. James.

"And if it is too strong?" he said. "What would happen to them?"

"They could lose too much of their memory. And they may not recover it. I've never had this happen, probably because I'm so cautious. But my teacher spoke of adults becoming like simple children."

Rob shrugged, mouth turned down, his face hard and cold.

Victoria wasn't sure if she should be worried or impressed.

"I doubt that would make much difference to these men. If given the chance, I'll do the job entire with my baton. But if you're willing, we'll have your magic in reserve."

He circled a narrow street on his map, far away enough from theatre crowds for their purposes, then handed the page to her.

"So we'll handle the matter either way," she said in a low voice. "Magic or muscle."

"Have I frightened you, Victoria?"

She folded the page and slid it into a small pocket inside the cover of her appointment book.

"Not with your plans, no. Nor with your desire for violence. I'd do the same if I were able, after the way they abused Michael."

"But I've frightened you all the same."

Victoria's heart pounded, but not from the charm she'd used on herself.

"Yes, but not for the reason you probably suspect. I'm likely to be far too honest if I tell you why, but I won't deny it. Have I frightened you?"

Rob laughed softly. His hand twitched toward hers on the table, and she wished he would finish his impulse, caution be damned.

Take her hand, take her mouth, take whatever he could reach while her defenses and his were nonexistent.

Once those walls were back in place—solid and hardened

from years of enforcement and the near miss between them—bringing them back down again would be far harder.

"Was there a trust charm in the drinks you and I had?" Rob said. "Or in the flowers?"

"Neither. I didn't particularly want you to trust my father. The flowers kept everyone calm, but our drinks didn't even have gin. Only an elixir for alertness. I'm afraid it's wearing off."

"I doubt anything could keep me alert for much longer," he said. "Well, here's my trust charm. You haven't frightened me, not exactly. The thought of not seeing you or talking to you certainly has. I never expected to feel that way about anyone in my life. The worst part is I am frightened of what you may decide to do, yet I want to be here anyway."

Victoria tried to smile, but she stood and looked out the window to hide her face. Exactly as her father often did.

She was newly worried about what she might decide to do, what she already had done.

Angry as she was at her mother, making her so desperately ill on impulse wasn't something Victoria was proud of.

Knowing Cheryl Mallory nearly succeeded in killing herself, then seeing Michael McDuff's scarred face that very morning fractured something inside of Victoria.

Part of her single-minded focus and resolve had shattered, the pieces too small and lost to rebuild.

That fracture may have been exactly what let Rob McDuff gain access to her mind, and her heart. And made her hope she truly had access to his.

"I'm sorry, Victoria." Rob finally did take her hand. "I've been far too honest myself now."

Victoria leaned down and kissed his cheek, then sat beside him. He touched his face with a slow smile.

"We both have. Once we've rested and gotten through our next task at hand, you and I can continue this conversation. If we're successful, we may actually have options between us to consider."

CHAPTER 46

Victoria's magic rarely began outside of her hidden workroom, away from her tools, supplies, and her most powerful ingredients. Today, though, she started with her mother's stationery supplies.

At the opposite end of the house from her father's dark den, Victoria's mother kept a bright, airy room for the management of the household and her extensive social calendar. The wallpaper was yellow and pale blue, the overstuffed furniture delicate and feminine, upholstered to match the paper. Even the pale hardwood floor was covered with the most cheery, light, floral rugs she'd been able to find.

The social schedule had been less full of late with her illness, but Mrs. Haversham wouldn't tolerate a reduction in her activities for long.

Certainly not with a rescheduled wedding to plan.

Victoria's spirits lifted as they usually did in this space, despite her own dislike of a busy social life. The sunlight, open feeling, and bright colors reminded her of the house she'd loved so as a young girl.

The one she felt closer to reclaiming than ever before.

The deepest sleep she'd had in weeks left her fully recovered from the terribly long day that moved from prison to a party to dramatic meetings with two men.

As expected, she did feel more in control of her feelings about Rob McDuff. But instead of feeling embarrassed or shocked by her words and his, Victoria looked forward to seeing him again.

The next few days would be stressful, even fearful, but knowing she had a chance for a different future at the end kept her moving forward.

The stacks of personalized stationery for every member of the family as well as the household wouldn't do for this sort of task. Even the slight risk of the wrong person seeing these letters was too great.

Victoria shifted those aside until she found plain white paper and envelopes. Still heavy and easy to write on, as was everything her mother may need to use. But not traceable back to this house.

Back in her workroom, bookcase pushed back into place, Victoria laid out everything she needed. Her own black ink, prepared a few days ago and ready to receive her wishes. A small glass atomizer filled with shifting confusion, at least to those who were meant to read the letters she would write.

The effect would be even stronger if the letters fell into the wrong hands.

A pair of midnight-black gloves, rich and thick with Victoria's magic. She rarely revealed herself so openly, since they would function like a beacon to anyone who knew what they were looking for.

In this case, she needed to draw weak-minded men who were compelled to seek her out, even if they were unaware of the compulsion.

The list of the guards Michael had mentioned. She and Rob had decided on the two to target for the theatre night out with Bertrand, choosing the worst offenders of the lot. The danger to Victoria and Rob, and even to Bertrand, was great enough with two. That would be more than enough to serve their purposes.

The others would share a different letter, and face a different fate.

One last letter would go to her father's manager on Enceleas. His doubts about the post would continue to increase, along with the compulsion to keep his feelings from Mr. Haversham. This wasn't a problem Victoria intended to give her father a chance to solve with bribes or bullying.

Victoria sat still and closed her eyes, calling for focus for the task ahead of her. Instead of drifting to the center of awareness, silent and clear, her fingers drifted to her lips.

She still felt Rob's cheek, warm and scratchy with stubble so late in the day.

She still felt his hand in hers, his arm round her shoulders.

The exact shape and taste and color of the strength he'd given so freely.

Well-rested and awake or not, her mind and heart were still playing distracting games with her. That wasn't tolerable with such serious and difficult rituals.

She turned and focused on the painting of her father's plantation, the one that covered her wall safe.

She imagined the warm air on the broad veranda, made for sleeping on fragrant evenings. The cool, breezy house, built long and low. The chorus of insects all day and night, so different from the constant noise of human activity close to a large city.

Victoria saw herself walking the land, secure and confident that she'd never have to leave there again. Not unless she wished it.

"Jaji," she whispered, calling on the strongest, deepest power she knew. "Hear me now. My love is deep, and my need is strong. Help me focus on what I must do now. Tomorrow is soon enough for the troubles of the future to arrive."

Her finally clearing mind reminded her she had no guarantees Rob would want to make the trip to the Caribbean with her, nor that he'd be able to.

She believed he would be a good partner there, in every sense of the word. But until she secured her own freedom, she couldn't depend upon the choices of another.

That had led her from one unwanted fiancé to another, and now to a wedding her mother was determined to plan without Victoria's participation.

She hoped she and Rob would have the opportunity to find out what sort of partners they'd make. And Victoria knew she must put her own work and her own needs first to give them the chance.

She turned her full attention to the work at hand.

CHAPTER 47

Two DAYS before the prison guards, and Victoria's fiancé, were to meet their fates, McDuff woke hours before his normal time. The streets outside were still quiet, but he knew staring up into the darkness would do him no good.

Dwelling alone with his thoughts and his worries would only do him harm.

He dressed and went downstairs as quietly as he could.

The boarding house residents worked all hours of the day and night, so a man leaving before the sun was up wouldn't raise an alarm. Wandering around in the common room trying to find some way to distract himself would be sure to annoy someone, though.

A few minutes' consideration gave McDuff a destination, if not a clear reason.

The walk alone through empty streets helped his mind settle.

Despite thousands of people all around him, McDuff saw

no one. The scent of coal fires in houses paled beside the full reek and roar of the industrial workday soon to begin, leaving the air brisk and relatively clean. Only his own footsteps broke the quiet, leaving him alone with his thoughts after all.

At least the movement provided a bit of distraction.

Victoria assured him the letters had already been sent, and surely read by now. The plan was in motion, no matter what misgivings he had. She still expected to move forward.

Even he had to admit the plan was solid. Except where it wasn't.

So many variables, so many things out of his control.

The guards' level of anger and willingness to act on it in public. Crowds of people interfering, though he thought the fairly isolated location he'd chosen would help. Victoria's reaction once she was in real danger, and even more so her finance's.

Even her most impressive magic couldn't predict what other human beings would do.

McDuff headed toward Father Hall's church, certain that's where he'd be even so early in the morning. This was the day he helped feed the less fortunate at a charity not far away. The priest had pointed out the low windowless brick building as they'd walked toward their own lunches or dinners, but they'd never gone inside.

McDuff wasn't certain, but he thought Father Hall told him Thursdays were for men who'd been released from various jails and prisons. No one was turned away as long as the food lasted, but putting out the call to these men in particular let them know they'd be welcomed openly. No one would shun or scorn them here.

No other destination could have been more perfect.

The men in line outside the charity were the first people McDuff saw. They were strangely quiet for such a large group, standing with their heads down. Their ages ranged from pitifully young, no more than teenagers, through a distressing group who should have been in their working prime, to frail old men leaning on canes or each other. Most had tattered and dirty coats or more than one shirt to protect against the early morning chill, but a few shivered in worn summer weight clothing.

From his own knowledge of how the city worked and did not work, McDuff knew they had nowhere else to turn for something as simple as a meal to start their long, desperate days. As simple and humble as his own life was compared to men like Victoria's father or either of her fiancés, he struggled with guilt as he passed the long queue.

The doubts and worries responsible for his restless nights surged forward at that thought.

Victoria was accustomed to a lifestyle McDuff could never provide for her on his own.

And even if she provided the money and opportunities, assuming his pride could tolerate that, he wasn't sure if he'd ever be comfortable moving in the circles she did so effortlessly.

He passed the four open front doors, two with that long line going inside, two with slightly more hopeful men walking out. McDuff was betting a door around the side or back would be easier than trying to barge through that sad group.

Despite his harsh, angry words to Jean, words he'd regretted constantly and that she'd refused to let him apologize for, McDuff wasn't much more confident about his ability to adjust to life in the wilds of the Caribbean. Being born and raised in one teeming industrial city and living in another ever since gave him a typical urban arrogance.

He suspected most of his city-dwelling skills would be useless in such a distant and strange land.

And all of this assumed he would get through the next few days, and that he'd have an invitation to accept or decline.

Three nuns stood outside the back corner of the building, their faces red and sweaty. All wore the full habit Jean and Victoria mimicked, and steam drifted out of the open door. He wondered how they even breathed inside the broiling kitchen.

"Good morning," he said. "I was hoping to speak to Father Hall if he's inside? I'm Rob McDuff, a friend of his."

The shortest woman, clearly the oldest of the three with lines on her face and white hairs in her dark eyebrows, looked McDuff up and down.

"Father Hall is busy serving needy members of our community, sir. If you wish to speak to him, you'll have to join in his labors."

"I…of course. I'd be glad to, Sister. I don't know how to cook, but I'm sure I can do something to be of help."

She pursed her lips while the younger two women tried not to smirk. McDuff had a feeling he'd walked into an unseen trap, or at least a predictable reaction.

"God's ways are indeed mysterious, Mr. McDuff. It's a grand day when a shiftless grown man learns how to feed himself at last."

She waved one hand dismissively toward the door. Her

grim smile made it clear she expected him to skulk away and never pass this way again.

Instead he grinned in return.

"Then I'll be sure to pass the blessings of my knowledge along to my fellow police officers, ma'am, so we may all mend our shiftless ways. Good day."

Stepping through into the kitchen felt like hitting a solid wall of warm water.

McDuff removed his coat and hat before he'd taken five steps. Everyone tending to vast pots wore the same black as the nuns, with only a few bare male heads in the crowd. Not wanting to encounter another nun for the moment, McDuff found a teenaged boy to point him toward Father Hall.

At first leaving the kitchen for the much cooler dining room felt like a relief. Then the aromas of long-unwashed male bodies seeped into McDuff's awareness.

Two long tables stood in front of him, with a line of men and women ladling soup from more of those huge pots. Several more tables took up the rest of the space, every one crowded with men.

A few talked in low voices, but most of them only stared straight ahead and ate from large white bowls. A familiar voice spoke from beside him.

"Inspector McDuff, what a nice surprise!" Sister Amelia, the one who'd helped transform Victoria and Jean into nuns, held an empty near-cauldron in her arms. "Father Hall will be delighted! He's down there at the start of the line."

She was gone before McDuff could reply, vanished into the sweltering kitchen. He spotted Father Hall's blond head close to the far wall. He alternated between touching the men's hands or heads, closing his eyes and speaking a few words, and handing out spoons and napkins.

McDuff wondered how the priest could stand the smell of some of the men, even more so their filthy hats or hair, before a wave of terrible guilt drowned the thought.

"Inspector McDuff! So good to see you!" Father Hall grinned and waved him over. "What brings you out so early this glorious morning?"

The priest stepped sideways, opening up a space between himself and the sturdy nun handing out clean bowls. McDuff stepped forward just as a man easily twice his age stopped in front of him. The man's outstretched hands were gnarled and twisted, grime caked into every wrinkle. McDuff placed a spoon and scrap of napkin into his palms as gently as he could.

The man nodded his thanks and moved along.

Six other lines split out from the two coming in the door, each headed toward a similar arrangement of clergy and church members serving food as fast as they could.

"Couldn't sleep this morning, Father. I remembered you saying you were here most days. Thought you could use what little help I can offer."

"We can always use more help, Rob, though policeman already serve the city. I'm certainly glad of your company."

Just as in the other lines, some men approached the priest for his counsel and blessing, others went straight to the food. Father Hall nodded and smiled either way, offering words of welcome.

"Is everyone here from your church, Father?"

"Oh no, we don't have nearly this many. Our parish is smaller than most to begin with. We all work together to build up the Church as a whole as well as supporting our local communities. Always more need than support, everywhere you go."

"A fact many residents of this city choose to ignore, as with so many other things."

Father Hall spoke to several men in a row then, leaving McDuff to concentrate on each as they passed in front of him. Having to focus on so many sad and beaten faces was preferable to inside his own head yet again.

Neither imagining the fat and wealthy men he'd interviewed over the past few months standing in line waiting for a rare hot meal nor wondering how they'd tolerate serving that meal improved his mood.

Knowing he'd never stood here and offered this simple service to his fellow man before only made it worse.

"Let's step outside and chat for a bit, Rob."

McDuff glanced at Father Hall, surprised to see another priest taking his place in the receiving line. One of the young nuns who'd met him outside the back door smiled as she waited to step forward into his own place.

"You've been out here for nearly two hours," Father Hall said. "The sun's rising. You must get to your own work soon."

The line still stretched out both doors, but the men waiting were noticeably older now. Anyone who could still look for day work had already departed.

McDuff followed his friend out through the dining area this time. Father Hall stopped repeatedly, accepting gratitude and offering comfort. Several men reached out to McDuff, shaking his hand. He returned their thanks, noticing he didn't mind touching them so much after all.

"I appreciate you working this morning," Father Hall said. The two walked away from the line, passing the corner where McDuff had entered what felt like hours ago. "I have a feeling that's not what you came down here for, but we and the men thank you."

"I've never done anything like that before. I don't know why. My mother certainly took help when it was offered after my father died, so I should have offered the same. I'm not much better than the usual clueless man with work and a full belly."

"Did you know the Havershams have been among our most generous donors lately? Ever since Victoria first visited my church. Her father believes he's giving in care of Father Sean Michaels, of course, but the end result is the same."

The cool air across McDuff's skin helped cool his guilt as much as his time in the hot building. This morning seemed designed to test his assumptions about himself as much as the ones he made about everyone else.

"I didn't know that. I suppose there are many ways to help others. I thought I should see what your real charity work is like, but I didn't expect to learn quite this much."

"My real charity work? As opposed to what?"

"The fake one Victoria claims. Reforming prisons. Helping orphaned children so they don't end up there. Teaching them to read and write, how to take care of themselves."

Father Hall nodded, smiling a little.

"These aren't children, though many of them were orphans. Many more have spent time in prison or jail. But taking care of them, once in a while helping them take care of themselves, is the most rewarding work I've ever done."

The two men walked in silence for several minutes before Father Hall spoke again. Residents of the brick row houses they passed were stirring now, moving around and starting their days. Many greeted the priest as they passed.

"Am I going to hear your confession at last, Rob?"

"My confession? You've been party to my many sins over the past couple of months, Father. Or at least you've known about them."

"I have. And I know your motives are generally good ones. People usually come to confession *after* they feel they've sinned, of course. Did you know many come before they do?"

There was no point trying to hide or pretend. Father Hall, and that meant Jean as well, probably hadn't guessed the specifics of what he and Victoria had planned.

But they were easily smart enough to realize the time was fast approaching.

"I hadn't heard that," McDuff said. "But I remember seeing attendance at church going up at odd times back in Glasgow. I eventually realized that was a clue some kind of gang fight was about to happen. I'd imagine men going off to war do exactly the same thing."

"Yes. So that brings me back to you seeking me out nearly in the middle of the night. We had a terribly difficult visit with your brother barely a week ago, then we haven't seen either you or Victoria much since. The two of you have every right to keep your plans to yourselves, of course. But that doesn't keep me from worrying about my friends."

Father Hall stopped and leaned against a brick wall overlooking a small park. The trees were bare and the grass brown, but it was still a pleasant break from pavement and brick.

"I hadn't thought about anything besides getting away from my thoughts for a while," McDuff said. "But you're not wrong. I'm worried about the future no matter how I think about it. I don't see an easy time ahead no matter how far I look. I'm not sure my actions have been right. Or good. I don't see that changing going forward."

"It's hard to be forgiven for sins you haven't committed yet. Some would argue it's harder still to be forgiven when you know you're going to sin before you act. Do you believe whatever you and Victoria are about to do is necessary?"

"I do. Neither of us can see another way."

"Then consider whether you can live with the consequences of whatever happens, Rob. Such matters are best thought through before acting, though few people really do."

McDuff closed his eyes, surprised at heat and pressure welling up from his belly.

With all his worry about how he and Victoria would adjust if things went well, he hadn't given enough though to the alternative.

"If need be, will you do what you can to watch over Michael?" he said. "Jean and Victoria have several of her enchanted letters ready to send, to influence his treatment. In case the worst—"

Father Hall grabbed McDuff's arm.

"If things can go that badly wrong, then reconsider, man! Make sure you understand what you're risking."

McDuff smiled and covered the priest's cold hand with his own.

"I do understand, Father. I'll do the best I can. Will you do the best you can by my brother?"

Father Hall crossed his arms and looked away for several seconds. When he met McDuff's gaze again, tears stood in his eyes.

"You know I will, Rob." He put his hand on McDuff's shoulder, more gently this time. "Peace be with you. Please be careful, my friend."

CHAPTER 48

Inside the model prison of Fodelson, routine was everything.

The very habits and schedules Michael McDuff had disrupted with his misbehavior—and his screams—kept prisoners, guards, and administrators calm and able to fulfill their duties. As was usually the case when a troublesome prisoner was dealt with, disturbances all through the population nearly disappeared.

For a time.

As summer gave way to autumn, one of the guards received an ordinary letter.

Richard Gibson had stood watch outside the door when a priest came to comfort Michael McDuff, accompanied by his officious policeman brother and two troublesome nuns.

The letter could be nothing more than a solicitation for charity, same as he'd seen countless times.

Or perhaps it was a notice of payment due.

Gibson wasn't quite sure in the end, and the letter inside wasn't addressed to him anyway.

Some street in central London, looked like a place he'd never been to. He slipped it into his pocket, reminding himself to pass it along when he saw the right person.

His ideas of who that would be were vague, but he was certain he'd know when he saw him.

All was well, and Gibson finally recognized the correct recipient later that same day.

Once he passed the letter along, though, he started to feel out of sorts.

Not ill, nor even especially tired or overworked.

He did feel that way sometimes, but not now.

Gibson felt on edge.

Uneasy.

That woman had no cause to report him to his supervisor, and now he had a black mark on his permanent record because of her.

That damned letter, the one he'd thrown into the boiler fire, said one more violation and he'd be out on the street.

Never the most calm of men, now Gibson moved closer to a hair's breadth away from true fury.

The second guard, Russ Beckits, was relieved to see the letter once he read the contents.

Of course he'd forgotten to pay that bill, and he would send it in as soon as he got home that night.

Or was it a notice for that fight he meant to bet on?

No matter, he was glad to have that sorted out in his mind.

That letter, though, that wasn't actually meant for him. He'd misread the address and greeting at the top, after all.

He'd never lived in central London, had no reason to expect he would.

Beckits slipped it into his pocket, reminding himself to pass it along to the right person as soon as he had the chance.

That chance walked by in the grand main hallway barely an hour later, and Beckits was relieved to have that nagging chore behind him.

For the rest of the long evening, Beckits rubbed the back of his neck, trying to soothe the knots of tension building underneath his prickly skin.

A black mark on his permanent record, all because of some troublesome woman.

Good thing he'd burned that letter.

If things got worse, maybe he'd say he never knew about her complaint in the first place.

It he ever saw her again, though, perhaps out on the streets on London, he wouldn't miss his chance to get even.

The letter continued to make its rounds, as did all the guards.

CHAPTER 49

Just as Victoria expected and dreaded, Bertrand leapt at the idea of taking her to the theatre, as did her mother. Her father pulled her aside the day before to make sure Inspector McDuff would be close by at all times.

Once she solemnly reassured him that Inspector McDuff had kept all of his arrangements with her, he approved of the idea as well.

It was, after all, her first actual date with her soon-to-be husband.

Excitement was to be expected.

Mrs. Haversham picked out a sapphire blue gown to accent Victoria's eyes, with a lower-cut front than she was used to. With so much of her energy directed toward much darker matters, Victoria agreed without argument. Sparkling accents for her hair, fingers, and a large gemstone necklace soon followed.

Victoria wondered with a certain amount of dread if her

mother planned this much drama and preparation for her actual wedding day as everyone in the household fussed over her.

And she hoped none of her mother's jewelry was lost in the confusion—and violence—of the night.

Her own far more important preparations took place with considerably less attention and drama. Concealed and free from her mother's attentions, Victoria assembled her tools. And her defenses.

A clear, cold mind being foremost among them.

Victoria had long resisted her mother's pressure to change to a bag that matched her gown on formal occasions, insisting upon her own black opera bag. She'd designed the bag herself, working with a London artisan who was willing to keep to her odd specifications without question.

The typical elaborate beadwork and wide metal opening looked like every other bag seen at fashionable events all over London, even if a bit darker than most with all black accents. A thick black chain allowed her to drape the bag over her neck and shoulder to keep both hands free.

Unconventional, but not alarming.

Inside, though, hidden airtight pockets lined every available inch.

Each closed with a different clasp that she knew by touch.

A few of the larger beads concealed tiny hiding places that held whatever Victoria might need. On most occasions, she filled the spaces with items meant to bring about honesty, increase her influence, or mute the memories of anyone she encountered.

On this night, only the destruction of memory remained in her arsenal, but not what she normally carried.

A protection spell in the room and held over her nose and mouth by a white cotton scarf tied round her head, Victoria prepared herself.

Several blue silk handkerchiefs went into one pocket, with the potential to erase days of recollection if the recipient breathed deeply enough.

She hoped no more than a brief inhalation would be necessary, completely under her control. That brief touch would allow Victoria to fill the memory void with whatever she wished, as long as her suggestions stayed close to reality.

She hoped to avoid testing her resolve to force a much longer exposure, leaving a void most likely to be filled with madness.

Another section held three rough, scratchy red handkerchiefs, each capable of causing even strong and brutal men horrible pain that lingered and intensified with time. She treated the coarse fabric with resin from a curious vine—native to Enceleas but growing in her greenhouse. The result was a slightly gummy feel to the touch. But once the resin was exposed to saliva or secretions from the eyes or nose, it adhered itself in place quite nicely.

A few seconds' exposure caused burning of the eyes, nose, and mouth. That effect traveled to the throat, and Victoria suspected the lungs would be next for enduring agony. She'd never yet had to employ it for that long.

The most dreadful and delicate magic she possessed would accompany her outside her workroom and her imagination for the first time.

A single black vial wrapped in matching lace fabric, concealed behind the largest black stone on the front of her bag. Lace made specifically for her from soft fibers that absorbed and dispersed liquid immediately.

If she broke the glass cylinder, smaller and shorter than her smallest finger, the liquid-soaked fabric would make anyone who breathed or touched it violently ill.

If Victoria remained silent, the person would suffer great intestinal and respiratory discomfort for several days.

If Victoria said the words, secretive and irreversible, and if her will matched their terrible intent, the human life in her hands and under her control would stop.

Her beloved Jaji only admitted to using the full strength of this magic one time: to avenge the murder of her dear husband.

Each square, even the black lace, carried a spell to make it glow its color in low light. Even in chaos and danger, she would know which cloth she touched and looked at, and exactly how to deploy it.

The only jewelry Victoria wore of her own, not borrowed from her mother, was her fiery red engagement ring.

Bertrand would be right to notice if she didn't, of course. The liquid she'd soaked it in for the past few days would make him want to follow any command she gave.

Thus prepared, Victoria submitted herself to her mother and half the household transforming her into someone she barely recognized.

Elaborate hair, carefully embellished features, revealing gown, with bare arms and what felt like her entire décolletage exposed. A light wrap of the same silky midnight blue fabric embroidered with silver thread didn't grant her modesty so much as it drew attention to her lack of it.

She wondered if McDuff would be able to pick her out of a crowd.

The gloves she pulled on last, solid black and elbow length, ensured she would be recognized when it counted most.

CHAPTER 50

The pub was rowdy and crowded, far busier than McDuff would have chosen for himself. This wasn't the genteel theatre crowd a few blocks away, dressed impeccably and enjoying an elegant evening.

This was pure working-class London. Long gleaming bar, thick smoke, shouted conversations.

Mostly men, though a few women plied their own age-old trade, seeking coin not yet spent on beer or stronger drink. Dock workers, construction crews, street cleaners.

This crowd was intent on playing as hard as they worked, and they weren't any more afraid to get hurt here than during broad daylight.

McDuff only waited about thirty minutes before the men he was waiting for burst through the door. They'd shed their uniforms for street clothes just as he'd done, letting all of them blend into the scrum.

While he barely touched his own beer, they downed several shots of whiskey and gin while they ate.

As was usually the case in men with grievously wounded pride, they made no attempt to keep their outrage to themselves.

Despite his anxiety about the steps already in motion, McDuff was fascinated by them.

Neither of them seemed to remember or understand why they were so angry. A woman was involved, as in so many cases just like this. And whatever she'd done was vastly unfair to both of them.

The more they drank and the louder they got, the more disturbing their plans of revenge.

From frightening this unnamed but troublesome woman, to roughing her up, to having their way with her, to not caring whether she lived or died when they were through. Such talk wasn't quite enough to arrest them, certainly not when they never mentioned anyone by name.

Talk was more than enough to change McDuff's own plans, though.

His mood followed a similar trajectory to the men, absent wanting to have his way with them. At least not sexually.

If he were a bit too free and loose with his club and with his fists, the result of these two no longer walking the streets would be worth the fallout.

And if he could do the job without Victoria having to participate, so much the better. He barely spared a thought for her fiancé except to hope a reasonably intelligent man would stay out of the way.

Not long before McDuff would have had to escort the men out himself—both far out of hand even for such a rough establishment—they seemed to pick up on his worry about the time.

They stood, loudly condemning everything they'd been served as worth less than the trashy wench who'd served them.

The girl stepped back, finally in tears from the constant abuse. The guards roared laughter in her face, then turned toward the door.

Neither made any move to pay what would surely amount to a week's wages for the barmaid with all the booze they'd put away.

The burly man behind the bar moved after them, length of pipe in hand.

McDuff stepped forward before he could get to the door.

"I'll cover what they owe," he said, hand on the man's bulging chest. The bartender was easily a foot taller and solid muscle. "They're wanted for far worse. Been tracking 'em for Metropolitan Police for weeks now."

He glared down at McDuff, jaws visibly clenching under his thick sideburns.

"Deserve t'have their brains bashed in, what little they got."

"They certainly do. They'll get that and more once they're on the inside. You have my word, sir."

McDuff held out a handful of coins Victoria had insisted he take just in case of situations like this, worth far more than everyone at the bar could have poured down their throats.

Neither of them wanted to go through the preparation and anxiety leading up to this night again, and neither wanted the guards arrested and out of reach.

The brute stared at the money, then back at McDuff.

"Don't need bribes." He dug out two coins, then jerked his chin at the girl trying to clear the mess the guards had left behind through her tears. "Covers their drink. Make it right with her, then go do your bloody job."

McDuff nodded, urgency to keep up with the guards setting in again. He knew they'd want to stay in the area for a while longer, but even Victoria's strongest magic wouldn't last all night.

"Sorry for their rudeness, miss," he said, touching the girl's shoulder. She held out her hand when he did, then brought her other up to catch the coins.

"This is far too much, sir!"

"Take mine out as well. And the rest is for your trouble, and your quiet about this unfortunate incident."

As soon as he opened the door, McDuff knew he needn't have worried.

He could hear the two men not far away. They'd moved on from complaining about the meal they'd just enjoyed, returning to the nameless woman and her unfair treatment of them.

They stood several yards away, visible in the way the crowd parted around them, leaving them a wide berth.

McDuff took up position leaning against a cold brick wall at the intersection between this street and the one they'd need to turn down.

His mind obsessively ticked over the next steps and all the possible outcomes he could imagine. He despised being in the middle of so many people with unknown risks and uncontrollable actions.

Far more things could go wrong than right.

The stream of people wasn't quite thin enough for McDuff to be comfortable, but their target a couple of blocks away should be more deserted. He and the guards still had several minutes until the madness of his and Victoria's plan would fully swing into motion.

Before all of them were caught up in the clockwork of fate, moving gears and cogs pulling them forward into the unknown.

CHAPTER 51

Victoria's worst fears about an evening spent alone with Bertrand didn't materialize, at least not at first.

Unlike during dinners with her family or with his, he was quiet and respectful. If she hadn't spent those long, uncomfortable hours with him in the past, she might have assumed he was too shy or awkward to speak.

And if she hadn't added a spray of minuscule dark blue flowers to her hair, a bouquet steeped with a deep desire for companionable silence. That charm had served Victoria well on many occasions with not only the men her parents were determined to pair her with, but with her parents and their friends and anyone else who tended to pry.

She'd never tried it with Bertrand before, as anyone who knew him would be deeply suspicious if he stopped pontificating for any length of time.

Having the spell work perfectly was satisfying, and a boost to her confidence on a difficult evening.

He'd arrived promptly, not as disturbed by the entire Haversham household gathering to watch as Victoria was. Bertrand's hair and black suit were better arranged than they normally were, and his condescending manner seemed to have vanished before such a large audience.

His private coach was far more elaborate than the Haversham's, painted dark red with black trim and gleaming brass accents. Even the interior was plush, with richly upholstered seats, floor, and ceiling that matched the outside.

Victoria's strongest response was relief that she wouldn't be required to sit as close to her publicly known fiancé as she sat with Rob McDuff in the much smaller church coach.

Bertrand's reserved silence continued throughout the three acts of the play, leaving Victoria free to make herself increasingly nervous and tense. She smelled her own anxious sweat with the heat of the theatre concentrated in their nearly enclosed box.

She ran her fingers over the beads on her bag, not so very different from Father Hall and his rosary after all.

So many things could go wrong before they ever got to the narrow street between two more stylish and populous areas.

Though he'd cooperated by being quiet and undemanding all evening, Bertrand could refuse to walk with her. The unsettled, whirling state of Victoria's mind could leave her unable to focus enough to defend herself.

A large crowd could follow along, making the plan impossible to carry out safely.

Even if everything went perfectly, one or all of them could be seriously hurt.

But the potential reward of such a risky course of action was too great to resist.

Her father already spoke more highly of Rob than she'd ever thought possible for a working-class man. Mr. Haversham's worries about her safety continued their gradual upward climb. That natural desire of any father, to see his child safe, would play beautifully into Victoria's hands if she remained cautious and wise over the next few hours.

A future with a man she believed she could care for, one she wouldn't dread spending even one evening with, resettled in a land she loved more than her own life, was so close she could taste it.

Victoria remained in her velvet-lined seat for several seconds after everyone around her stood, so lost in thoughts and fears and possibilities that she didn't notice the play was over. She'd barely noticed it started. The motion when Bertrand offered his hand to help her to her feet broke through at last.

She wished she hadn't removed the protection of her gloves when his damp palm enclosed hers.

When the applause died down, he leaned down close to her ear. His breath wasn't warm and soft, dancing over her flesh like Rob's had. When Bertrand tried to whisper, Victoria struggled not to recoil from the sharp hiss and droplets of moisture.

"I certainly hope you enjoyed the performance, my dear. I'm afraid the pleasure of your company distracted me a bit from the actors on stage."

Victoria glanced down from their box, at the thick red velvet curtains barely twenty feet away. Unless Bertrand was as preoccupied as she was, he would have been hard pressed to find anything else to look at besides the stage.

"Sorry to have made you miss the play, Bertrand. It was delightful."

He smiled and shook his head, and Victoria saw a flash of the young man he once was in the low light.

Not so soft and worn, with a network of lines around his eyes and the remains of hair optimistically brushed over his head. Perhaps not nearly as certain of his own superiority.

Maybe the way his first wife had seen him decades ago.

His heavy hand on her waist jerked her back to reality.

"Not nearly as delightful as the scent of your hair, Victoria. This evening spent so close by your side has me looking forward to the future like I haven't done in many years."

The old man was back with her, not some imagined ghost of his past. The old man who expected to be entitled to her body, her privacy, her very life as he was so many other things.

She patted her hair, hoping the movement would stir up the last bit of potency in her flowers.

"This evening has me looking forward to a good supper," she said, winking to keep him encouraged. "I've heard of a wonderful new restaurant a few blocks away."

Bertrand compressed his lips and shook his head. That heavy hand moved possessively to her lower back as they followed the crowd down the stairs.

"The best restaurants in the city are on this very street, and my favorite has a table waiting for us. That will be more suitable."

Victoria turned, lowering her chin with a smile of her own. Steeling herself, she held up her left hand. Bertrand's kiss was as wet and sloppy as she'd feared.

And his nose nearly touched her engagement ring.

"I'd so love to try something new," she said, her voice low and throaty. "And the walk will be so…stimulating for both of us."

He tilted his head, staring at her long enough that she was afraid it hadn't worked. Before she could reach inside her bag, he shrugged.

"We have been sitting for a long while, and it's rather warm in here. In this case if no other, your desire is my command. Which direction is this restaurant you want to try, my dear?"

"I'll show you. I've heard it's an unforgettable experience."

Victoria pulled the black gloves on and all the way up to her elbows, then settled the wrap around her waist and across her forearms and hands to cover them for now. Even in the darkest alley in the world, anyone who glanced her way would be drawn irresistibly toward them.

Whatever was drawn her way, she had to be ready.

CHAPTER 52

Before he even saw people dressed for the theatre walk by, leaving several performances that let out around the same time, McDuff moved away from his temporary station.

He settled in the narrow street where possibility felt thick and heavy around him, hidden in deep shadows, leaning against another rough and badly mortared brick building.

He didn't have to watch in either direction to know all the players would soon appear before him. The only questions left to answer now would have to wait until the action started.

The sensation that told him to move, and now to wait, wasn't much different from the instinct that made him a good policeman and inspector.

A great one more often than he realized.

An odd tingle in his belly, moving to a catch in his gut. This was deeper, more full, pleasant rather than unnerving most of the time.

McDuff was a willing and conscious participant in this

case, but he was no less Victoria's creature than the two guards were.

The two guards who were now turning off the busy bar and restaurant street onto the quiet one where he waited.

He heard their footsteps without the roar of conversation to drown them out. His mind finally calmed, leaving him with the cool detachment he so often found in the middle of a crime scene.

McDuff slipped his club out of his belt—the curved wooden handle worn to fit his palm perfectly—then took off the long coat that covered it. He needed to be able to move freely, and cold wouldn't matter in a few short minutes.

The men walked slowly, still talking to each other but much more quietly. Outraged and drunk or not, they responded to the gathered focus and concentration even as it drew them forward.

For a clear, painfully sharp second, McDuff considered taking everything into his own hands.

He could still take the men by surprise, get them subdued and arrested, then get himself and them away from here before Victoria ever arrived. Two dangerous men would be off the street, at least for a little while, and neither he nor she would be in physical danger.

And the first move he made before Victoria was close enough to tempt them would send them running the other way, right back into that crowd.

That would leave them unpunished and nearly impossible to reach.

McDuff would linger in the same dull and monotonous life, but now more than halfway in love with a woman he could never have. Michael would still be in prison, though they called it an asylum now.

Victoria would still be promised to a man more than twice her age, soon to be married against her will.

When McDuff took a deep breath in an attempt to clear his mind again, he noticed another difference between the busy street and where he stood now. He didn't smell the stink of tobacco, sweat, and too much perfume.

He caught a faint whiff of Victoria's magic.

He turned to see her unmistakable silhouette as she and a much larger figure left the busier street on the opposite end of the alley.

Even from a couple of blocks away, McDuff saw the possessive way the man rested his hand on Victoria's back. He also saw she carried her glittering black bag with both hands. She'd told him some of what would be inside, but he doubted he knew all of it.

He understood he would rarely know everything where she was concerned.

The two men and the apparently happy couple would reach McDuff's waiting place at the same time, as he'd already known they would.

The time for endless preparation and waiting was finally over.

CHAPTER 53

VICTORIA FORCED her body to relax and shift as she walked, not wanting Bertrand to notice her building tension.

Their shadows loomed far ahead of them with every step they took away from the brighter, more crowded street and into the shadows. On the far end of this gloomy passage, perhaps three blocks away, another busy thoroughfare beckoned, full of coaches and pedestrians.

She knew in her bones her life would not be the same when she emerged from the tunnel of darkness ahead.

Bertrand paid her growing anxiety no heed, and he seemed unaware of the threat of their surroundings.

Tall buildings crowded close together with less than fifteen feet between them, and with no shops or eateries, no one bothered with expensive light.

The effects of her quieting charm had not only worn off, but he seemed to be trying to make up for his silence earlier in the evening.

"With our time so limited, we need to make arrangements for our honeymoon travel as soon as possible. The most important thing will be spending time together, of course, but we should enjoy the adventure. Where would you most like to go, my dear?"

Victoria opened her mouth to say Enceleas before she caught herself. She slipped her hand into her bag and opened the pouch with the red handkerchiefs full of agony inside.

They weren't meant for her fiancé, but she wouldn't refuse to use them on him if needed.

"A girlhood friend of mine spent time in India. She and her family loved the culture and the people there. I enjoyed my family's years in the Caribbean, and I hear Africa is lovely."

Bertrand shuddered, the effect comical on a man his age.

Victoria didn't laugh.

"I'll never understand why people willingly choose to leave civilization for those savage lands." He grimaced, perhaps remembering one of the few things he knew about his future wife. "Your family was different, with your father needing to secure his property and his business there. He brought you back to England as soon as he possibly could, the better for all of you."

"Some might feel that way."

Victoria's feigned interest in the conversation vanished at movement at the other end of the alley. She couldn't see anyone with her eyes still adjusting from the brighter street they'd left, but a more solid shadow had definitely crossed from one side to the other.

Rob wouldn't be so obvious, not with the two of them visible by now.

He would surely be in the middle, in place long before this moment.

"Some might feel?" Bertrand shook his head and made several of the same *tisk* noises Victoria so loathed in her mother. As if snapping his tongue against his front teeth would miraculously bring her to reason at last. "My dear, when you've traveled a bit more and have a more solid view of the rest of the world as compared to England, you'll understand the advantages we have here. I'll be most solicitous in your education in such matters."

Victoria was surprised by a smile breaking across her own face, and by excitement cutting through the churning nervousness in her belly.

The education that brought her to this moment, to this chance to finally control her own destiny, would have been quite the shock to her pompous companion.

She slipped her bag over her neck and shoulder, letting it settle against her stomach, then let the wrap fall forward to uncover her gloves. The glittering fabric would have to fall as it would, unless she needed it in her own defense.

"I'm certain you would, Bertrand."

She touched his cheek, bringing her ring up close to his nose again. Even through her gloves, the need to obey her commands should last longer than the flowers in her hair.

"Right now, I need you to stay back, keep quiet, and carefully consider your own safety. And let me tend to mine."

She strode forward, moving away from his hand, his planned domination, and his oh-so-generous offer of a proper education.

Victoria walked forward into her future without looking back.

CHAPTER 54

McDuff closed his eyes, leaving his ears, nose, and other senses to track the movement toward him from both sides. He breathed in until his stomach and ribs ached, then released the air as slowly as he could.

The traces of conversation to his left and right stopped when he opened his eyes again.

Neither pair were trying to hide, but they'd noticed each other.

Victoria increased her pace, moving away from a sputtering Bertrand.

A slurred shout rang out to McDuff's right.

"Where in hell you think you're going, sweet little miss?"

That was Gibson, the one who'd greeted the four of them the first time they used a spell on Michael.

The one who'd broken Michael's ribs.

The guards moved faster now too, Gibson pushing the other from behind.

"Wait," McDuff whispered. "Wait until they're closer."

He couldn't see what Victoria was doing in the darkness, but he trusted her to have her own weapons ready.

McDuff wished he'd ignored his own caution against bringing a knife, or even a handgun.

"Hey, here's that same fancy troublemaker!"

The second guard, Beckits, sounded more happy than angry. McDuff knew that meant the situation was far worse than they'd planned for. "Come to write us up again, have you?"

"We're only walking through," Victoria said, her voice clear and steady. "I haven't written anything, sir."

Her black gloves lived up to their promise as even McDuff was irresistibly drawn to them.

Faint as an afterimage on his closed eyes, but unmistakable to all of his senses.

"Thought you could end our bloody careers and walk free!"

One guard grabbed the other, both skidding to a halt.

Victoria kept walking.

"Be quiet Victoria!" Bertrand shouted, finally trying to catch up with her. "We must not get involved!"

"She was bloody well involved when she spread those bloody lies about us!"

That was Beckits, the guard who'd sodomized Michael. His voice was forever seared into McDuff's brain.

Beckits broke free, leaving Gibson stumbling to catch up.

"That gibbering idiot got what he deserved, and plenty of it! I dare say he quite enjoyed himself once he got himself able to stretch out a bit."

McDuff's jaws ached from clenched teeth, his hand and wrist from gripping the club.

He had to hold himself steady.

Wait.

Wait.

"Please, good sirs!" Bertrand tried to grab Victoria's arm, but she jerked away. "You've made a terrible mistake. We'll give you whatever you want, just let us be on our way."

"Then leave this filthy piece of trash to us, old bugger. Maybe then *you* won't get hurt!"

"I expect you might like it yourself, from the looks of ya!"

The two men broke into a run, making up the distance Victoria had gained while they hesitated.

A handful of men had gathered at the end of the alley closest to the bar.

This had to be decided without that kind of interference, at least not until they were ready.

McDuff stepped forward.

CHAPTER 55

Victoria stripped off her gloves and drew out two of the gummy red cloths, her eyes on the guards now running toward her.

She heard every step and its echo, felt the pull of the air across the fabric in her hands.

Her own heartbeat sounded out time in her ears and throat.

Bertrand's voice behind her faded into the background, no more important than the bricks in the buildings on either side.

He was only here to serve one purpose: to look bad in the eyes of her father.

The man who was here to look good in contrast stepped out of the shadows to her right just as the first guard lunged toward her.

The other guard turned at the solid *thwack* of Rob's club meeting the man's skull.

Too late.

Victoria darted forward, lifting her skirt to free her legs.

She tried to run around him, but he snaked out one arm and caught her waist. They spun with their momentum, barely managing to stay upright.

The guard squeezed hard enough to force the air from her lungs, even through her corset.

"Can't get by me that easy, you worthless strumpet." He blocked Victoria's arm when she tried to raise it, then gripped her wrist hard enough to bring tears to her eyes. "See if you like what that bastard got."

Victoria swung her left fist as hard as she could, employing her engagement ring yet again when the lump connected solidly with the guard's ear.

He bellowed and pushed her down hard on the cobblestones. Pain shot through her entire spine from her tailbone.

Before she could protect her face, he kicked.

The heavy boot caught Victoria under her chin, driving her flat.

He stood over her with his fist raised.

Words twisted through horrific ringing in her head.

"Right on your back where you'll be when you scream your last. One move and you lose every last one of those pretty teeth."

He started to step toward Rob and the other guard, where sickening thuds continued without slowing.

A scream blasted through the gong in Victoria's skull.

The echo of her own frustration.

The mourning wails of Jaji.

The keening of an endless line of unknown, powerless women.

She curled into a ball, twisting her arms and legs through the guard's.

He fell heavily to the cobblestones, air shrieking from his lungs.

Gasping at the pain in her wrenched limbs, Victoria struggled to her feet. Before he could catch his breath, she landed hard with both knees on his upper back.

She covered his nose and mouth with the red fabric, yanking his head back with her fingers laced together.

The guard gasped, then his whole body went rigid as he gasped again.

The next noise he made was an agonized scream muffled through cloth and fingers.

He bucked and twisted, trying to bite her fingers, but Victoria shifted with him.

The only move she was willing to make before the monster lost consciousness was to slip her death charm out of her bag, still bouncing against her belly.

Rob had his man down with the first swing, but he hadn't slowed his attack even as Victoria struggled.

The club crashed into flesh and bone over and over again.

"Rob! Slow down!"

He glanced over, then charged toward her.

Bertrand screamed from behind.

"Victoria!"

A searing line ripped under her right arm, deadening sensation and her grip.

The hand holding the knife free to push, the guard finally jerked hard enough to send her spilling to the street beside him.

Rob savaged the guard before he could move, adding his own furious roar to the night.

A sharp pain under Victoria's arms made her cry out.

Bertrand was trying to drag her away.

"That man…" he said, gasping for air. "That man will… he'll kill us all!"

Victoria twisted, trying to slip out of his grip.

"Let me go! That man is on my side! Let me go, now!"

He only sank his fingers in deeper and continued to pull.

Her numb and useless right hand had dropped the handkerchief she used on the guard, the palm of her hand now matching the scarlet color. Victoria swung her left hand blindly up, hoping to contact Bertrand's face with the remaining cloth.

His shout joined the echoing cacophony when her palm hit his mouth, her fingers sinking into his eyes.

Victoria scrambled to her feet, leaving her fiancé writhing on the stones, the fabric holding the agony firmly in place.

Rob stood between the two guards, breathing hard.

He still held his club, but he wasn't moving.

Neither were the men at his feet.

She was more than a little afraid of startling him.

"Rob," she said in a low voice. "Turn round."

He did jump, but he turned without raising his arm.

Victoria finally heard footfalls of several people coming toward them.

"My god, your arm." He dropped the club and crossed the distance between them. "I saw him raise the knife but I wasn't bloody fast enough. Let's get you out of here."

"No, just wait. It doesn't even hurt yet. We have to finish this. You're bleeding too, Rob."

He scowled, then reached up to his cheek. A line of red, nearly black in the dim light, spread from his cheekbone down to his jaw.

"Bastard got me. Never even felt it."

He lifted Victoria's arm, and she finally felt her own wound. It still didn't hurt, not yet.

But she felt the edges of the flesh slipping with the movement, along with a woozy hint of the agony to come

"I have to make sure Bertrand doesn't remember. You know that. Otherwise he could ruin everything. Go talk to that lot, tell them how the guards attacked us."

He looked over his shoulder at the group circling the two on the ground, then back at Victoria.

"Fast as you can. You're losing a lot of blood."

Victoria turned to Bertrand, still on the cobblestones himself. He couldn't manage to drag the cloth aside, and his moans increased with every breath.

She reached into her bag, clumsy with her left hand, then knelt beside him.

"Bertrand, listen to me. Everything is fine. You'll feel better soon." Victoria peeled the red cloth away, then held one of the silken blue handkerchiefs close to his nose and mouth. "You don't know what happened. It was all a blur, then you woke up on the ground. You know someone besides me was here, and he saved both of us. But you'll never be able to keep his name or his face from sliding out of your mind. Now tell me."

His eyes, huge and wild, as red and watering as his nose from Victoria's painful magic drawn deep into his sinuses, throat, and lungs, finally focused on her.

She felt a flash of pity.

"Don't…know what happened. Woke up. On the ground."
He grabbed at her wrist. "Are you hurt?"

"One of them had a knife." She moved the fabric a bit closer to his mouth. "We were so fortunate, Bertrand. My guard saved all of us. Now tell me."

Bertrand rolled his head to the side, to where Rob stood talking to several men.

"Burning, my whole *head* is on fire. Guard. That man, he stopped them. Your guard saved all of us from the knife."

"Close enough. Can you stand?"

He got slowly to his feet, stopping to cough several times.

She hoped he wasn't having an actual heart attack to go with the pain that had to be settling into his chest.

"Good. Now go tell those men the same thing, Bertrand. Your safety depends on it, as does mine." She relented long enough to pat his shoulder, the only remotely affectionate touch she'd ever offered him. "You've done everything perfectly."

CHAPTER 56

Rob turned to face the crowd of men gathering around the unmoving guards. Their angry and suspicious voices kept him in a painful state of high alert.

That only increased when one of them picked up his bloody club. Young, probably not yet out of his teens, eyes and mouth twisted and furious.

"You the one that did this, then? Beat these men near to death with a policeman's billy club?"

"*My* club." Rob stepped forward, but the boy waved the club in a wild slash, nearly hitting another of the curious bystanders. "Private security guard. These men attacked the two behind me."

The group's eyes followed when he waved toward Victoria and Bertrand, but the one with the club remained unconvinced.

"Someone paid you to act like a common thug? More like you plan to rob all four of them once our backs are turned."

"Settle down, boy," one of the older men said. "Once you've had your first shave, maybe you'll have some sense to go with it." The rest of the group grunted and chuckled.

"Look, they've hurt the young woman," Rob said. "The gentleman almost as badly. I've just done my job and stopped them when they wouldn't listen to reason."

"Had a knife," a shaky voice said from behind McDuff. He turned to see Bertrand and Victoria. "Those thugs, they had a knife. Him, her guard. Saved all of us."

Victoria staggered a bit, clutching her bloody arm close to her chest.

McDuff hoped she was acting, but he wasn't so sure. The bleeding hadn't slowed.

The boy started to speak again, but another man stepped up behind him and plucked the club from his hand.

"Be quiet, damn fool. Can't you see how badly she's bleeding? We should thank this guard fellow and let him get her to hospital. In fact, best you run right now and wave down a carriage."

He handed the club to McDuff and pushed the boy aside. The youngster sputtered but didn't speak.

"Thank you," Victoria said. Her voice was faint, but her eyes clear when she met McDuff's gaze. "I'm afraid we do need help. But Bertrand has his coach back at the theatre."

Bertrand shook himself, then coughed several times.

"Young man, you can fetch that." He held out a card in a shaking hand. "Red and black, one of the few left beside the St. James at this hour. Give this card to my driver, send him here right away."

As the boy took the card, a handful of coins appeared in Bertrand's other hand.

The boy glared at McDuff before he snatched them and sprinted off.

"I'll fetch the police," the older man who'd first interrupted the boy said. "Should have been here by now."

Victoria stepped forward this time, shaking her head.

"No, please, let us handle this. My father would panic at the result of our rare chance to enjoy an evening out. He already believes I'm in terrible danger at all times in London." She touched Bertrand's arm. "I'm afraid the scandal would only cause my fiancé real harm."

The old man eyed the guards, still unmoving in pools of their own blood. He looked at Bertrand, doubt clear on his face.

"Sir, the boy was right about this being a policeman's club," McDuff said. "The truth is I am with the police. Sometimes we must take on extra work to make ends meet. We're nothing more than workingmen ourselves in the end, just like you. I'd lose both my jobs the second something like this got out. Then I'd be done for."

Nods and general mutters of agreement moved through the group, and most of them headed back the way they'd come.

"Right, then." The old man stepped forward and shook McDuff's hand. "Young lady, your father should rest easy with this man watching over you. The rest of us should, too."

He turned and walked away without a glance toward Victoria's fiancé. She moved to his side.

"Bertrand, perhaps you should meet your coach. They may need help navigating down this narrow street."

"I'd know your name, sir," he said to McDuff. "Victoria's safety is always foremost in my mind, and you've seen to it admirably in the face of these animals."

"It's best if I don't share that, if you please. My main job would be on the line if it got out I was here tonight. But you can rest assured I'll take care of these men now. Miss Haversham shouldn't walk any more than she has to with so much blood loss."

Bertrand glanced at her arm, not quite managing to hide a grimace of disgust, then turned on his heel and followed the boy.

"Are they dead?" Victoria whispered.

McDuff leaned forward, hands on his knees, overcome with trembling now that everyone was at last gone.

"They may be. If they're not, they may wish they were. Let me see to them, Victoria."

"Then *do* so," she nearly hissed. "As it stands now, I won't have much time to change things if need be."

He raised up at the sharp sound in her voice, a whisper of anger floating through his exhausted mind and body.

No.

She was right.

Assuming either of the guards were capable of remembering anything, Victoria had to make sure those memories were under control.

He would probably do well to let her charm his own mind as well. At least to take the edge of his rage. And his fear of giving in to that mad drive again now that he'd let it take him over so entirely.

He squatted beside Gibson, the one he'd taken on first. The

man's face was fairly untouched, with only a swelling eye to show for his struggle.

Several lumps on his head, and a deep depression near the back of his skull, told the true story.

The man breathed, but that would likely be all he ever did.

And probably not for long.

"He lives," McDuff said. "Or at least his body still functions."

He emptied the man's pockets—not much more than a few coins and a tattered wallet—and pulled off his shoes. That part of the prison guard's uniform was too expensive and well-made to believe on a street thug.

Beckits looked far worse when McDuff kicked him onto his back. He'd smashed his nose and mouth against the cobblestones when he fell, leaving several of his teeth cracked and jagged.

Most of the damage McDuff's club had done was to his ribs and back. His pockets were as spare as Gibson's had been.

Thankfully for Victoria's face, and possibly her neck, he'd been wearing lighter, well worn shoes. Not worth worrying about.

"He'll wake. No telling what he'll remember, or when."

He took Victoria's offered left hand and stood beside her.

"That birthmark on his neck," she said quietly. "Michael mentioned it. The blue snake. I wish he'd bled more to cover it. Perhaps one of us should *slice* it off with his own bloody knife."

She pushed at her attacker back to face down with her foot. Street filth didn't quite hide the unsettling shape twisting up into his hair.

"Beckits." McDuff said. "The one who…"

"I remember." She squeezed his hand, then let go to fumble with the front of her bag. "Will you help me, Rob? I need something out of here, under the large jewel."

"Don't you have the memory charms inside your bag?"

"That's where the memory charms are, yes. I need something else. Just push down and twist to your right. It's hinged, so it won't fall off."

Cold moved through McDuff's body, freezing his hand and his mind.

"Tell me what it is. I don't want you further caught up in this."

Victoria laughed, further chilling his blood.

"*Further* caught up? You beat one man nearly to death, so much that finishing the job would be a blessing. Only a tiny bit less than he beat your brother. And now you want me to spare the one who did worse, and promised so loudly to do worse to me?"

McDuff stared at Gibson, knowing the memory of his beating and the aftermath would never dull in his mind. Not without her help.

"I shouldn't have done that. Lost control. That's exactly what they did to Michael. Them and a dozen other guards and policemen before them. Exactly the same as me."

Victoria grabbed his chin, turning his face toward hers. The cut on his cheek sang out in protest.

"No! Listen to me, Rob! You're not the same. These monsters earned this and a hundred times worse! Do you really believe Beckits here would never attack another prisoner? Or that he wouldn't attack an innocent woman he happened to encounter alone? Let me stop him from hurting anyone else, and from hurting us! Look away if you must, but let *me* protect *you* this time."

McDuff squeezed his eyes closed, every swing and crushing blow playing through his mind.

He hadn't been out of control, not really. These two men had simply borne the brunt of years of fury and frustration.

Not only at everyone who'd ever beaten his brother, but at Michael himself.

No matter how hard he'd tried to save his little brother, Michael always threw himself back into the muck.

He either didn't understand or he didn't care what damage that did to McDuff's life, any more than to his own.

He'd never been able to get back at the ones who used Michael, the ones who attacked him and pushed him into disaster. And he would never be able to make his brother understand what he and Victoria had done tonight.

The first chance McDuff ever had to try to even the dreadful score.

They needed to finish the job, no matter what it cost either of them.

When he opened his eyes, she held a white handkerchief out toward him.

"I'm sorry, Rob. This hasn't been easy for either of us. Hold this over your nose and mouth and let it help calm you."

McDuff took the strangely cool cloth, but first did as Victoria said, holding his hand under the black stone when it fell forward. She caught his wrist before he could reach inside.

"No, this is delicate work. I'll explain it later if you like, but our time grows short."

Hooves clocked on the stones, still at the end of the street but growing closer.

He watched Victoria draw something black out of the hidden compartment, one he'd never heard about or suspected, then kneel beside Beckits.

McDuff took her advice, covered his face with the kerchief, and turned away.

CHAPTER 57

Victoria sank to the cold stones, settling back on her heels. She was more lightheaded and dizzy than she wanted to admit. The slice across her forearm had settled into a dull ache as long as she didn't move it, and the bleeding seemed to have stopped.

She wasn't willing to turn her arm over and expose the wound to make sure.

She focused on the man in front of her.

Beckits.

One of Michael's worst tormentors, and surely the demon of many other prisoners' nightmares, and likely many outside Fodelson Prison as well. His nose was pushed to one side, and that and his distorted mouth were bloodier than she was.

Air still oozed in and out, for as long as she cared to let it.

With pain from her arm and almost everywhere else, distraction of the approaching carriage, and slow spin of her head, Victoria called on the only thing that could steady her to perform the work ahead.

Her mind's eye, the true center of her power, remained sharp and clear.

None of the magic, whether spells or potions, would function without the inner vision of her desire.

Jaji had repeated the phrase constantly, and Victoria knew the words to be truth.

What your mind can see your life will be.

She held the lace-wrapped vial, the same color as a death shroud, awkwardly in her left hand. Her fingers cradled the fragile glass with her thumb poised to break it. She wouldn't have been able to reach her white cotton square soaked with calm and protection with one hand, even if she did have enough time.

She was thankful Rob had taken one to keep himself safe.

She'd have to keep her distance and cover herself the best she could.

Her vision held this same man in this same space, but with no air bubbling through his ruined nose and mouth. She saw his flesh turning cold as the cobblestones digging into her knees, blue as her filthy sapphire gown.

Words flooded through the lingering gong sound of her head, words both terrible and precise.

Jaji warned her about using these words even as she taught them. How crossing a line as bright and sharp as this one made crossing every other line possible.

Even those she may have chosen never to cross.

Bertrand bellowed her name, still nearly a block away but unmistakable.

This action, ending the bad life of a worse man, gave Victoria a chance to avoid the line of murdering her husband after days, months, years of misery. And opened the door to a future she would actually look forward to for the first time since her father dragged her back to this dank island.

Victoria held the vial close enough that she felt the hot breath of the man she was about to murder stirring against her fingers.

The vial broke with a barely audible snap.

She pressed the lacy square in place and leaned back.

Victoria covered her nose and mouth with her wounded arm, whimpering at the fresh gouts of pain and blood.

Words darker than the fabric, more elemental than the blood, poured forth against her skin.

The vision grew more weighty and real, overtaking the world in front of her eyes.

A wet, heavy chill, as if cold water poured into her heart, moved into Victoria's chest.

She continued to speak, bringing the death at her hands to life.

The chill spread to her ribs, then down her back.

She shivered hard enough to make her voice tremble, but her voice did not stop.

The man's chest hitched, and his head twisted to one side. Victoria shifted with him, holding what remained of the liquid in place.

Her whole body shivered now, teeth chattering as her fingers and toes went numb.

A last breath rattled out of the guard's chest, and he moved no more.

Victoria dropped the black bundle into her bag and clicked it closed, willing herself to remember to dispose of it carefully.

The traces of potency would be weak with the magic directed so firmly, but it was best to take care.

The shivering was far worse, her bones vibrating like a tuning fork. Jaji had warned her casting this dread magic was not easy, that it drained the practitioner like no other. And she hadn't protected herself with her white cloth at all.

Victoria wasn't sure if she was feeling that or the blood drained from her arm.

Either way her vision darkened, leaving a narrow tunnel. She looked for Rob, but he'd walked forward to meet Bertrand's carriage.

They were only a few feet away, still moving toward her.

"Rob?"

The tunnel closed as she fell.

CHAPTER 58

McDuff sat on a bench more uncomfortable than Father Hall's church pews, elbows on his knees, aching forehead in his hands. Sharp odors of cleaners stung his nose, a sure sign they were in a private hospital rather than one of the poor public institutions.

Bertrand's name, and likely his money, smoothed the way with Victoria still unconscious and unable to direct her own care.

Bertrand paced in front of McDuff, as he had since they first arrived. Each click-scrape, click-scrape seemed to tug at another of McDuff's frayed nerves, but he didn't move.

If he'd had to take Victoria to the places he knew, or could afford, she'd likely die of an infection if blood loss didn't kill her. Here, in a clean, modern, royal hospital, she had a good chance of coming back out of the room across the hall without a sheet over her face.

Late as the hour was, McDuff wished he could speak to

Father Hall or to Jean. He was afraid to use the hospital's telephone, worried they'd insist on making the trip to wait by his side.

If Victoria's father walked in and saw the two of them after McDuff's tales of charity work leading to danger, the already taut situation would likely explode into more violence.

He desperately needed their advice on what to say to Mr. Haversham when he did arrive to find his daughter in surgery. Worry for Victoria kept him from making sense of the words flooding through his mind, but McDuff had to get some sort of rational explanation together.

He was supposed to protect her, as a man, a police officer, and as her paid guard.

He'd failed to keep her safe, though he had kept her from the far worse harm the men intended.

The harm they intended because Victoria made them focus their rage on her, with McDuff's participation.

He sat back, wincing when his hand caught the stitches in his cheek. That hadn't taken long since he'd refused the ether, not wanting to chance being unconscious or groggy if Victoria needed him. Salts of cocaine numbed the wound well enough.

McDuff had had more than one wound stitched in facilities where he wouldn't have trusted the anesthesia in any case. Hazard of his occupation, certainly when he was still on routine patrol.

At least the light dose of morphine they'd given him dulled the aches in his shoulders and back.

The door at the end of the hall swung open hard enough to hit the wall, and Mr. Haversham stormed in. He'd clearly been dressed for the evening, with thin sleeping pants visible under his long wool coat.

Clenched fists and a red face gave McDuff a hint of his mood.

"What the hell happened, Bertrand?" he shouted, stopping in front of McDuff. "Inspector?"

"My apologies, Edward," Bertrand said. "She's in the best of hands, finest care in the city."

"I don't want your bloody apologies! She shouldn't be in hospital at all! What I want from you is an explanation!"

Victoria's fiancé stood with his head down, hands twisting together in front of him, as if he were a boy rather than nearly the same age as Mr. Haversham.

"Two men, out of nowhere. One had a knife. I don't... I don't know what happened. I think one of them knocked me out. This man, her guard, truly heroic. He saved all of us."

Bertrand sat, leaving McDuff to stand and face a father's rage.

"Where the hell were you, McDuff? I paid you to protect her!"

"You're right, sir, and I'm sorry. There were two of them, as Mr. Robbins says. Once I moved to protect her, or to try, one attacked me, the other Victoria. I dealt with them as quickly and as firmly as I could."

Mr. Haversham let out a harsh sigh, settling his fists on his hips.

"Where are they now? These monsters who attacked my daughter?"

"In a morgue, somewhere in London," Bertrand said. He leaned his head against the white tiled wall, staring up at the ceiling. His face was nearly pale enough to let him blend in. "Your guard here disposed of them in the best possible manner."

"The best manner would be hanging," Mr. Haversham said, but his voice was no longer echoing in the corridor. He leaned toward McDuff, looming over him. "Just tell me they suffered. Tell me their journey to hell was not an easy one."

"It was not an easy journey, sir." McDuff shook his head slowly, fleshy impacts echoing through his mind along with ragged screams. "They're better off never waking, and the city is better as well."

"Do anything to help, Bertrand?" Now Mr. Haversham loomed over the sitting man, arms crossed. "Anything at all? Or did you leave my daughter to fend for herself against such beasts?"

Bertrand opened his mouth several times, but no words ever made it out. He finally bowed his head in silence. Mr. Haversham muttered under his breath, but McDuff caught it.

Worthless coward.

"The messenger said her arm was cut?" Victoria's father said to McDuff, ignoring Bertrand. "Was there more?"

"She lost a good bit of blood, sir. I believe she passed out from that, and probably from the fright. The doctor said once the surgery on her arm is over, she should recover fully."

Mr. Haversham put his arm around McDuff's shoulders, walking them away from the still silent Mr. Robbins.

"Will there be any investigation of this, Rob? With two men dead?"

"I don't know, sir, to be honest. That all depends on what's reported, I suppose. We left them where they were once I realized they were dead. I called in an anonymous report once we arrived here."

Mr. Haversham nodded.

"Does anyone else know you did this?"

"No, sir, not anyone who knows who we are. Victoria thought you'd want this kept quiet, so I did what I could. A few men came to see what was happening, but they didn't get my name. Neither did Mr. Robbins. They left before we did. Mr. Robbins was with Victoria and the surgeon when I called the police. City of London Police, not Metropolitan like me. They didn't have much on them in the way of identification, but I'll dump that in the river later."

Victoria's father stopped, crossing his arms again, his brow deeply furrowed.

He glanced back at Bertrand, still unmoving on his bench.

"You kept her safe when her so-called fiancé couldn't manage, and I'm eternally grateful to you for that. I don't want you to get into trouble. If they find out about this, about you being in my employ, things won't go well for you, will they?"

McDuff thought being found out for two dead men would cause him significantly more problems than a bit of under the table pay, but he'd learned well from Victoria.

Take the advantage when he had it, particularly in a terrible situation.

"Things might not go well, no. I knew that was possible when I got involved, though. I'm not trying to hide from the consequences of my actions."

"Well, that's noble of you and all." Mr. Haversham once again put his arm around Rob's shoulders. "We all must do that at some point in our lives. But in this case, perhaps I can make the way a bit easier for you if problems arise. That's only the very least I can do in exchange for my daughter still living and breathing."

The door to the surgery opened, and the relieved smile on the surgeon's face along with the fresh blood on his white apron let all the strength out of McDuff's knees.

He didn't quite clutch at Victoria's father for support, but it was a near thing.

"I appreciate that, sir," he said. "If you still want me to, I'll do everything in my power to make sure she stays that way."

CHAPTER 59

The Haversham's dining room table looked vast and abandoned when set only for three people. The length of polished oak seemed to go on for miles, as if the end were invisible in the distance. A white cloth meant for a much smaller table draped one end, as bland and nondescript as the silent meal taking place.

Victoria picked at yet another heavy dinner, evidence of her mother's determination to stuff her back to good health.

Beef had never been her favorite, and it was far less so after two weeks of hardly anything else.

Her dreadful weakness had finally lifted after she convinced her parents to let her venture out to the greenhouse. The fresh herbs and vegetables that she consumed in front of them had been nearly as effective as the healing potions she made for herself in her workroom.

Either way, by the time the cut on her arm had nearly

healed and the horrifying bruise under her chin faded, Victoria felt herself much recovered and healthier.

Not to full strength by any means, but not fit only for languishing in bed, either.

Rob McDuff had visited several times, in the guise of stopping by to keep her father informed of various matters he had business interests in. That falsehood hadn't kept Rob from speaking to Victoria every chance he got, even under her mother's strict supervision.

Both of her parents were clearly growing fond of the inspector, a development Victoria was determined to encourage.

Even with his occasional company, and the renewed closeness with her three rebellious girlhood friends, Victoria longed for the company of Jean and Father Hall. She knew they were sending the letters she'd prepared to influence Michael's treatment, and Rob assured her that his brother was still improving.

More than anything, she simply missed their Odd Society.

"You simply *must* eat more, Victoria," her mother said, tapping the plate with her knife. "That's the best thing to build your blood back up."

"I have been eating, Mother. I only have so much room inside me. All this beef is making me feel worse, not better."

Mrs. Haversham drew breath to reply, but her husband held up his hand.

"Please don't quarrel with Victoria, dear. It may be for the best that she's eaten lightly this evening. I'm afraid I have news that won't make either of you happy."

Victoria's head swam nearly as badly as the night of the attack.

Half her mind was in this very room several months ago, with the table fully set for a grand dinner party that never seemed to happen. Her father spoke then of the end of her engagement to Wilfred Abernathy, the result of the horrible trap Victoria had set herself.

No one had died from those efforts, though the poor girl Cheryl had come close.

"I'm afraid Bertrand Robbins has admitted he wouldn't make a suitable husband for you." Her father caught her mother's hand in mid flutter. "And I was relieved that he came to that decision for himself. I wasn't looking forward to making it for him."

"He's just *abandoned* her then?" Mrs. Haversham said, more angry than sad this time around. "As though she'd done something wrong, something to deserve such treatment?"

"That's not my thinking," her father said, leaning back and lacing his fingers over his belly. "I can't speak for what he believes, since he sent a note round rather than facing me himself."

Victoria gasped before she could help herself. She hadn't imagined such a cowardly act, not even from a man she'd gone to great pains to portray that way.

Now her mother did cry, but they were angry tears.

"A *note*. That weakling never deserved you." She grasped Victoria's hand. "He's handled this every bit as badly as he did that night."

"Thank God Inspector McDuff was there," Victoria said. She stared at the half-eaten steak on her plate, but she felt the words strike home with both of her parents. "I might not have been here to lose yet another fiancé if not for him."

"None of that nonsense," her father said. "Not about you losing anything. Rob McDuff is most certainly not nonsense. He saved your life and Bertrand's too, for whatever that's worth."

"He hasn't come to trouble, has he?" Victoria's mother said, blotting tears from her cheeks. "Over that awful business?"

"No one has put him together with the worst of it, no. He's come to some grief for lagging behind on other investigations, or that's what he'll admit to me. I'm going to speak to whoever I must to sort all of this out next week."

Rob had told Victoria everything was fine more than once, but she didn't believe a word of it. She hadn't used a trust charm on him yet, not since they'd both decided to hold off on that until larger choices were before them.

But she was sorely tempted.

If her father lived up to his normal pattern, as most people tended to do, speaking meant he would pay whatever it took to get the trouble to disappear. Victoria would still need to move carefully, but the time had come to lead her father to a far better solution than another in a seemingly endless line of aged fiancés.

"Well, I certainly feel safer when Mr. McDuff is around," she said, allowing herself a faint smile. "Almost like when I was a child far from this dangerous city."

"We all may have been safer then." Mr. Haversham toyed with the scant remains of his own meal. "I believe the plantation was in better hands then, too. This current man, he seems to have more than half his mind back here in England."

"I'd never want to live there year round again," Victoria's

mother said. "But it was lovely not having these dreadful wet winters."

"Warm weather and honest work certainly did keep everyone's strength up." Victoria's father stared into the distance for several seconds, then shook himself. "A conversation for another time, perhaps. I think we've all eaten enough to bring out the pudding."

CHAPTER 60

McDuff tried to square his memories of standing in a young girl's bedroom in Mayfair months ago with what he faced now.

Gone were the pink frills, the hearts and silliness of youth. The walls were stripped down to bare white, with no sign of paintings or other decorations besides a large map of the world. Even her collection of books that had so impressed McDuff on his first visit had disappeared.

The bed and desk were similarly plain, as if he stood in his brother's room at the asylum instead of in a wealthy home. Or his own dull room at the boarding house.

Gone also was the girl who'd inhabited this space before her sad story came to McDuff's attention. He'd never met her outside of that lonely hospital room where she struggled to recover from her own poisoned hand.

But he knew what the girl who lived in that once cheerful world would have been like.

Cheryl sat at the desk, shadowed eyes downcast, hands on her swollen belly. Her blond hair hung flat and lifeless past her shoulders. McDuff wondered when she'd last managed to wash it.

Her pale, sunken cheeks were covered in spots. Her shapeless brown dress only emphasized her pregnancy, and not in a flattering manner.

He hadn't come here to console a heartbroken girl, and he was starting to regret ever passing this way again. Cheryl's father owed McDuff a considerable sum of money, one he would need if the next phase of Victoria's plan worked.

He hadn't expected to be met at the door by only a servant, then summoned up to this depressing bedroom.

No amount of money was worth being witness to the desperation Cheryl was disappearing into.

"Miss Mallory," McDuff said softly, trying not to startle her. "Cheryl?"

She took a deep breath and looked up at him. Her eyes met his like a physical blow.

"I'm sorry, sir, what was your name again?"

"I'm Rob McDuff. I was assigned to your case when you had your...your troubles."

She drew back with the most painful laughter Rob had ever heard, like stones grating over glass.

"Troubles. That's a lovely way to put it. Whatever did your investigation reveal, Mr. McDuff?"

Trying to fight back his own twisted laughter, McDuff sat on a bare wooden chair against the opposite wall.

"Only that you were caught in an unfortunate situation.

One that was not your fault. I'm sorry to have intruded into your life at all."

"My life is hardly worth intruding upon." She patted her belly, but she wasn't smiling. "Though I'm certainly going to have an intruder before much longer. I wonder if you ever spoke to the woman. The one Mr. Abernathy was engaged to before."

"I…yes, I've spoken to her. As part of the investigation."

Cheryl nodded, her pale lips twisted.

"I'm sure she was as glad to participate in that as I was. I hope she's recovered better than I have?"

McDuff raised his eyebrows and shook his head, his ability to keep his features neutral overwhelmed. Nothing he said or did could make this better.

All he could hope for was not making it worse.

"She's well as far as I know."

"Has she married another? None of this was her fault, so I hope she's found happiness."

He managed to smile a little.

"I don't believe she wanted to marry, then or now. I'd imagine if she does, it will be on her own terms."

"We should all be able to make those choices, shouldn't we?" Cheryl's eyes showed the first sparks of life since McDuff walked in. "To marry or not, and who? I fear those doors are all closed for me now, but it would be horrible to be forced against one's will."

"That would be horrible, miss. We never know when doors may open or close, as long as we draw breath. Can I do anything for you, Cheryl?"

She closed her eyes, then looked at the wall behind McDuff.

At the map of the world.

"The only thing anyone could do for me would be to get me away from here. There's no life for me, no future. Not in this house with my parents. Not in London with what everyone knows about me. What they think they know about me is even worse. Can you do that, Rob McDuff? Get me away from this living hell?"

McDuff stared at her, afraid of the direction his thoughts were taking.

He might not be able to do any such thing. But he knew someone who likely could.

Someone who might even welcome the opportunity to ease the grief of her past sins with someone she'd sinned against.

"I don't know that I can, but don't give up hope. Can you promise me you won't do that?"

She regarded him for a long moment.

"I can't give up what I don't have, can I?"

McDuff still saw that spark in her eyes.

CHAPTER 61

Thousands of miles away, on a small plantation island in the Caribbean Lesser Antilles, the custodian of a substantial sugar operation retrieved the post from his family's weekly deliveries.

The load was larger than usual with the holidays approaching, and with his wife determined to keep every English tradition alive that she possibly could.

He was far more concerned about letters from his employer than having the perfect Christmas pudding in such a warm climate with no possibility of cold, much less snow.

He paid the young driver, wondering as always at how the natives were happy with so little.

What would have been a pittance back in London seemed like a princely sum here, even for a hard day's labor.

The boy turned toward his sizable boat anchored nearby, no doubt borrowed from another plantation not far away, and whistled as he headed to his next delivery.

The letter he'd been waiting for sat right on top, and his hands shook as he opened it.

Things seemed to be going so well here with his work, his wife, and his son and daughter. At least until he received these letters from England.

Trouble built like tropical storm clouds on the horizon.

Trouble that could only get worse if he continued to pretend it didn't exist.

He walked as he read, at first. His mind filled with those dark, threatening clouds, swirling and shot through with lightning.

Organizing into the dread hurricane.

The other mail slipped out of his hands, landing in a puff of dust on the road.

Worse than he thought, all of it.

Nothing he did seemed to change or slow the problems, and now all was perilously close to spinning out of control.

He would soon have no choice but to return his family to England before it was too late.

Hours later, his wife hummed Christmas carols to herself as she unpacked her first batch of supplies for the holiday.

She'd gone overboard, certainly, with enough to cook and bake for far more than her precious small family so far from home. So far from the great crowds she longed to bring happiness and joy to.

Perhaps she would invite all the plantation employees round for Christmas, though it wouldn't be the same.

With the shelves, pantry, and larder full to bursting with food and ingredients no one without their own connections to England would understand, she gathered up her correspondence. She never received as much as her husband, and she was quite glad of that.

He'd been so worried and grim of late. None of his family and none of their success in this paradise could lift his spirits.

She hoped a fine, traditional English holiday would be a start.

By the time she finished the second paragraph of a handwritten letter on fine, heavy paper, she could no longer remember who it had come from.

And she couldn't see the address through her tears.

Her dear, dear, family, or maybe one of her life long friends she missed so desperately. She was no longer certain through the grief befouling her mind.

Homesickness ripped through her mind, her belly, her heart, with the fierce power of the terrifying lightning storms in this dry and distant place.

She'd tried, oh how she'd tried to make a happy and good home for herself and her family here.

The isolation from the troubles stirring uneasily through the Caribbean had somehow soured, concentrated, solidified into isolation from the world she knew, her very self.

All of that paled beside the far too many lives back in England that had fallen apart without her.

It broke her heart to think, but they would have to return home before it was too late.

CHAPTER 62

Metropolitan Police headquarters swarmed with police officers, in uniform and out, making it nearly impossible to find an empty office or space anywhere.

Another bomb plot, this more successful than the one that swept Michael McDuff up years ago, had every officer in all of London on high alert. As was usually the case in the early frantic days of a coordinated attack, no one yet understood what was happening, and everyone felt the need to take some kind of action anyway.

That disorder and near-chaos was the only reason McDuff felt relatively safe making what he hoped would be an anonymous, unnoticed appearance.

He passed through the crowds with his head down, not making eye contact with anyone. The few people he recognized were too preoccupied to pay him any mind.

Just another warm body doing his job, nothing to see here. He despised the violence and lives lost, especially with his memories of his brother's brief trial and harsh sentence brought back to mind.

But McDuff had to admit to himself that the latest disaster for the city was a welcome distraction for him.

He'd already spoken to the few men he needed to, sharing what he'd learned over the last few busy weeks. Digging into new cases had been a much-needed break from worry about Victoria's recovery and whatever would follow.

McDuff found himself enjoying the work more than he had in a long while once he stopped pretending to go so slowly.

He'd even found a couple of occasions to use Victoria's trust charms to great effect.

The last stop would be with his chief inspector's office, filing the final report on Cheryl Mallory's case. The legal aspects—those he was willing to pursue—had all been finalized.

With Wilfred Abernathy on his passage to America and Mr. Mallory's payment made, McDuff wanted to bring the whole depressing matter to a close.

He doubted he'd be able to put Cheryl's shadowy half-existence out of his mind anytime soon. Especially not that faint spark of life when she mentioned escape, the same escape her unwilling partner had so recently made.

But that wasn't a matter to concern Metropolitan with, in any case.

He stepped into the office as quietly as he could, the first time he'd ever bothered with such caution.

Normally McDuff and every other officer would do anything but try to sneak a successfully resolved case past all attention. Proving to themselves and everyone else how damn good they were brought them up from the ranks of patrolmen to begin with.

Making sure the people who really mattered continued to remember that talent was how they stayed there.

The department secretary spoke without looking up from her own furious writing.

"New or completed?"

"Completed."

Mrs. Warren took the file, held it for a few seconds until she finished, then focused on the name on the jacket.

"Mallory." She stared at McDuff, eyes squinted under her dark red fringe of hair. He'd thought Mrs. Warren was angry the first few times he'd filed a case. Now he knew she was calling on her frighteningly accurate memory. "Girl out in Mayfair, tried to kill herself. Turn up anything?"

"Nothing more than we all thought when it first came in. Bad choices, bigger regrets. One of them off to America, the rest as pathetically typical as you'd imagine."

Mrs. Warren slipped the last bit of paperwork required to get the entanglement with Victoria's first fiancé out of his life onto the desk. McDuff wrote as fast as he could.

"Meanwhile we have good men like you wasting time with this," she said, "while bombs wait to go off all over the city."

"One down, anyway." McDuff slid the papers back to her, already making his escape in his mind. "Take care."

He had his hand on the office door when a voice rang out from the inner room.

The room every inspector worked so hard to avoid.

"McDuff? Bring that case and step in here, please."

Mrs. Warren flashed him a tight smile, then spoke in a low voice.

"Speaking of bombs. You take care too, Inspector."

He managed to keep his groan under his breath, tempted to turn the handle and keep on walking. If the secretary hadn't been there to hear Chief Inspector Wells and his abrupt summons, McDuff would have done just that.

He rolled his eyes as he took back the case file, doing his level best to look only annoyed rather than startled to his bones.

The chief's office was an uncomfortably neat contrast to the crowded disorder in the rest of the department. His ancient wooden desk was as scarred and battered as anyone else's surely was, but his was the only one cleared enough to reveal the damage. Bookshelves were dusted and orderly. Even the heavy brass ashtray gleamed under the ever-present smoldering cigar.

"Good morning, sir," McDuff said, standing in the doorway.

"Sit down." Chief Wells held his hand out without looking up, knowing further instructions wouldn't be necessary. McDuff gave him the file and sat in what had to be the only chair in the station that didn't creak. "Finally wrapped this one up, I see."

"Yes sir. Sad business, but not a complicated one."

Wells grunted, flipping through the file. McDuff knew he'd seen most of the progress reports as he'd tendered them.

The chief taking the time to look like he was reading wasn't a good sign.

"Mr. Mallory says you stopped by earlier this week." Chief

Wells closed the folder and sat back. "He wasn't as satisfied with the results as you seem to be."

McDuff took a breath before responding.

The pompous old ass and his satisfaction should be the least of anyone's concerns. Mallory had handed over the payment with only a little grumbling.

"I'm sorry to hear that, Chief Wells. There's nothing satisfying about this case. With Mr. Abernathy on a boat as we speak, I'm not sure what more we can do for him."

"Not a bloody thing. He wanted to complain, and I said I'd speak to you. Now we've spoken." Chief Wells pushed the file across the desk. McDuff took it, afraid to hope this strange interview was over. Wells steepled his fingers under his chin. "Your brother got transferred, right?"

"He, ah, he did, sir. To an asylum outside the city. A couple of months ago."

"Doing better out there?"

Fire bubbled up at the base of McDuff's throat, as if he'd had too much to drink the night before. But he hadn't touched a drop since Victoria got hurt.

"He seems to be. I think the isolation caused him trouble, but he's recovering now. That's hard on many of the prisoners."

"It can be," Chief Wells said. "Your brother was fine for several years, though. Odd that he had trouble after so long."

"I suppose it is."

"You been out there since he left? To Fodelson?"

McDuff clenched his fist, digging his nails into his palms where the chief wouldn't see.

He understood exactly why so many witnesses ended up

breaking, demanding to know why they were asked so many pointless questions.

He knew the game far too well to make the same mistake no matter how badly he wanted to.

"I haven't, sir. Not much reason once Michael left."

Chief Wells nodded and sat back.

"I had lunch with an old friend yesterday, over at City of London. Chance to get caught up, see if we can help each other out with strange cases. Seems a couple of Fodelson's guards went missing about three weeks ago."

"How'd that end up with City of London, sir? That prison is well outside their district. Ours as well."

"Well, it took a little while to put together. A couple of dead men showed up in their morgue, badly beaten, not much on them. Everyone thought it was just another random gang brawl."

McDuff nodded, his face stone. He wished he'd already put on his scarf against the cold drizzle outside, or even that he was wearing his old high-collared patrol uniform.

The pounding of his heart was surely visible in his exposed neck.

"Once Fodelson administration started asking questions, they eventually got round to the city's alarming number of poor unclaimed souls. Those two were long-buried, of course, but people at the morgue are as caught up in this mania of cataloging and saving every damn thing as the rest of us."

"Did they find a match?"

Wells tilted his head forward and to the side, a strange sort of nod.

"Much as they could after the bodies were worked over

about the head and rotted in that morgue overnight. It seems one of the guards had an odd birthmark, down one side of his neck and up into his hair."

McDuff chewed the inside of his cheeks to keep from blurting it out. He remembered the mark, as well as he remembered Victoria saying they should slice it off when the man lay helpless before them.

The blue snake.

"Lucky break then," he said, keeping his lips close together. He was afraid Wells would see the blood.

"Enough to match them up, sure. Not much more than that. All of us have sent men to that place, McDuff. You're the only one I know with a family connection."

McDuff shrugged.

"I didn't really speak to anyone more than in passing, sir. Once Michael left, I never thought much about it again."

"Warden Higgins remembered you," Chief Wells said, his lined and scarred face as blank as McDuff hoped his own was. "From the transfer day. I understand your brother needed medical attention when he arrived at the asylum."

"He did, yes sir. The last few weeks at Fodelson got rougher than we knew about until that morning." McDuff let a trace of anger slip into his voice. "He couldn't tell me who did it, though I very much wanted to know. Have they said one of these dead guards was involved?"

Chief Wells was still long enough for McDuff to wonder about confessions from beyond the paupers' unmarked mass grave.

"They haven't said anything like that, no. Just thought it

was worth bringing up. Good work on the Mallory case. No real way to win there."

"Thank you, sir." McDuff got to his feet, gripping the folder with both hands. "Good day."

"How's the cheek, McDuff?"

This time he had no way to hide his reaction, and no excuse to turn away.

The blood leaving his face would only make his own scar stand out more.

"Healing well, sir. The woman who runs my boarding house says it makes me look more handsome. I think she's losing her eyesight."

The chief grunted, staring unmoving into McDuff's eyes.

"I think you may be right. Good day."

CHAPTER 63

VICTORIA BREATHED deep of countless old books, well-seasoned leather, and a lingering trace of ceremonial incense. She hadn't realized how dear that unusual combination of smells had become to her until she spent nearly a month away from it.

Jean's study was in its usual state of causal disarray, with books, papers, and writing instruments scattered over each of the tables. Victoria's gift of a bottle of the Haversham Plantation rum stood unopened in the middle. She knew from many hours working alongside the Frenchwoman that not one single thing was actually out of place.

Jean claimed being able to see everything at once allowed her mind the freedom it needed.

The scholar herself—wearing her usual black pants and a man's shirt in green rather than white—sat quietly in her oversized leather throne rather than bustling around muttering. Victoria felt as if she'd brought one of her companionable silence charms into action, but she wore neither her engage-ment ring nor her nosegay on her favorite blue cotton work dress.

The welcome back into their Odd Society was simply going far more smoothly than her initial entry, even before they shared the rum around.

"I'm quite sure it will be rude to ask," Jean finally said when she finished her tea, "but may I see your scar? I believe it's easier to get things like this out of the way instead of pretending not to look."

Victoria laughed, already unbuttoning her sleeve. She'd been wearing dresses that fastened at the wrist for that very reason, so no one would catch a glimpse of her injury by acci-dent while it was still so vivid.

She was comfortable enough with the story itself after plenty of repetitions. She was also bored with telling it.

"It's not as exciting as it was before the stitches came out." She rolled the loose sleeve up carefully. "I looked like I'd been put together by an extremely meticulous seamstress."

Jean held her wrist gently, turning to one side, then the other.

"All those stitches keep you from having a horrid scar, though. The surgeon did a fine job, Victoria. You're lucky to have found a good hospital."

"Bertrand found it. I was unconscious, and I think Rob was frantic by that point. I'm thankful the numbness is finally going away."

Jean returned to her chair with a fresh cup of tea.

"Rob was still frantic when he arrived here a couple of days later. He wouldn't tell us much, except to repeat endlessly that you would be fine. And that the two guards would not."

"No, they weren't fine."

The silence played out again, this time not so companionable.

"You know the charms you taught me too well," Jean said. "I can't exactly use them on you to get the truth of what happened."

Victoria tried to keep her discomfort to herself, but she knew Jean saw right through her and just about anyone else. She didn't agree with Rob's insistence on keeping the secret indefinitely.

She thought it was time to share the whole story with their friends now that everything was over and done with.

"I'm truly sorry to say this, Jean, but perhaps we can talk when Rob gets here. At this point he has the most to lose. I'm sure that's why he's so secretive."

Jean scowled. "He told us everything is in the clear for both of you now. Has he told you differently?"

"He's told me and my father the same," Victoria said. "And no, I don't believe him either."

Father Hall opened the door, his arms full of books and packages, then turned to kick it closed.

"Victoria! What a delight to see you here again!"

Jean jumped up to catch everything he dumped on the sofa as he gathered Victoria in a huge hug.

"You look wonderful!" He sat beside Victoria on the cushion Jean had cleared, still holding one of her hands. "How did you convince your parents to let you venture out again, and with a bottle of what I suspect is your father's excellent rum?"

"That was more Rob than me, the venturing out part. He explained how all threats of violence against the charity stopped the night we were attacked. Seems we broke the cycle and exposed those dreadful men as the ringleaders. Once I suggested to my father that I should bring a sample of the finest gift we possessed, he was only too glad to share."

"We certainly thank you for both," Father Hall said. "Where is Rob this afternoon? Wasn't he going to meet us here, Jean?"

"Should have been here half an hour ago." Jean checked the black mantle clock to make sure before she sat. "That's not like him. Has he told you otherwise, Victoria?"

"I was expecting him too."

An undefined, gnawing worry attached itself to Victoria more and more where Rob was concerned, especially when it came to his work. She knew they'd done everything they could to keep their activities secret, and the aftermath.

Keeping anything from a building full of policeman might be the worst sort of fool's errand.

They all jumped when the door opened again, then closed more gently than Father Hall had managed. Rob walked in at last.

Once they all got a good look at him, Victoria knew she wasn't the only one who was not relieved. Victoria barely managed to keep herself from crossing the room to him.

Rob's face was deathly pale, the healing cut on his cheek purple and livid. Perhaps reading her mind, or her feelings,

Father Hall moved to one of the chairs. Rob sat beside Victoria without a word.

"What's happened?" Victoria said.

When he didn't speak, she took his freezing cold hand. Rob turned toward her, his eyes moving more slowly than his body.

"I don't know. Not yet. Maybe nothing."

His words were slurred, his Scottish accent unusually strong, but Victoria didn't smell a trace of whiskey or anything else. She leaned down, trying to get him to focus on her. She then wished he wouldn't.

His eyes were icier than his hand.

"Chief Wells found out about the missing guards. The bodies at the morgue. Michael getting transferred, even the way he was treated."

"That's not enough." Victoria pulled his hand closer. "They can't put that together with us."

"Bodies at the morgue?" Father Hall said. "You mean those guards?"

Rob grunted, turning to the priest.

"There's so much we haven't told you and Jean, and the reasons are still sound. More than ever now. If this is going as badly wrong as it feels like to me, you'll want to be as far away from me as you can get."

"Now just you wait, Rob." Jean's hands clenched into fists on her knees. "Don't tell me what I want or do not want to know. Or who I want to spend my time with. You need to tell us what's happening. We may be able to help."

He shook his head, a horrible smile on his face.

"Help with what? If the Chief Inspector of Metropolitan Police and the Superintendent of City of London Police have already put me together with two dead prison guards, there's nothing anyone can do to help. Not unless you want to get to work sending me out to join Michael."

"But why would they even think it was you?" Victoria said, hating the wail in her voice. "No one knew who you were, or that you were even there. I know my father hasn't said a word, and neither have I."

"You didn't have to, sweetheart." Victoria's racing heart leapt at the word, at the way he touched her face when he said it. "He mentioned my new beauty mark, along with Beckits and his blue snake. The timing couldn't be more obvious."

Father Hall's voice held the command that made rowdy children and rebellious adults alike bend to his will.

"Listen to me, *both* of you. We're your friends, Rob, and we're going to help you if we can. But until we understand the whole episode, we might just make things worse."

"Now that would be a neat trick," Rob said. His voice was a bit more clear, but he still looked shocked. "I want to make it absolutely clear that I'll deny knowing the two of you if I must. It would break my heart, but I'll do it. I'm afraid it's too late to deny Victoria now that her father has nearly adopted me."

Jean slammed her flask down on one of the few clear spaces on the table.

"Adopted? I tire of these guessing games, Inspector. I suggest you build up your courage however you must. And then both of you start talking."

CHAPTER 64

By the time McDuff, and Victoria, finished filling in all the details of their nightmare evening, Jean's flask was long since spent. So were two more pots of tea, a pot of bitter coffee, and half a bottle full of rum he recognized as the Haversham brand.

McDuff was too afraid to look any of them in the eye. He'd spent a lifetime not knowing more about himself than he had to, or at least he told himself that.

Now Father Hall and Jean joined Victoria on the list who knew him all too well; three more than he would have believed a few short months ago.

The only positive was he and Victoria abandoning the fiction about their feelings for each other. She curled up against his side on the floral silk-covered sofa in Jean's study, not caring who saw.

Her warmth against him and under his arm was the only thing keeping his mind from spinning out of control.

"If he knows so much," Father Hall said, "why didn't he just tell you that? Or arrest you on the spot?"

"All I can tell you is why I would behave that way myself," McDuff said. "One, if I was still putting the trap together, but I wanted to make sure I had the right target in my sights. Two, if I had a much larger target in mind, but I needed the smaller one under my control to get there."

"And three?" Jean stared at him with one eyebrow raised. "You have more to say, and I can't imagine why you hesitate after the last hour of confession."

"It's not something I even would have considered before the last few months opened my eyes." Rob surprised himself and everyone else by laughing. "Three, if I wanted my target to understand exactly how much I knew so I could use it against him for some other kind of gain."

"What would he have to gain from you?" Victoria said. "From us?"

"From us is exactly what I'm worried about. I don't have a damn thing he could gain, not unless he wants me to do the same kind of off-the-records work for him. But if he knows how caught up I am with you and your family, he might have quite a bit of gain in mind."

"But do you believe he could be that kind of man, Rob?" Father Hall said. "There are corrupt leaders in every kind of work known to man. But I've never heard tales about Chief Inspector Wells. Is he that talented, to hide his true nature from so many?"

Rob swallowed the last foul dregs of his coffee, barely tempered by more cream than he usually took. Wonder about Chief Wells' true nature had hounded him on the endless walk from the station to the church, changing perspectives with every step he took.

"I don't believe he is that kind of man. But I wouldn't have believed the last few months of myself, either, even before I added murder to my accomplishments. Would you of yourselves? Honestly?"

Only Victoria looked into his eyes, and hers were more guarded than he expected. Father Hall and Jean both stared into the fire for a long while.

Victoria was first to speak.

"I'd done terrible things, whether I realized it at the time or not. But I still wouldn't have believed how I've gotten caught up in all of your lives. In Michael's life. In so many things. Bad as this sounds, even the murder was an attempt to make something better."

"I thought I was here for a straightforward research visit," Jean said, smiling. "Not expecting to learn more about the rich magic of another land in the middle of London. I would not trade knowing any of you. This has gone far beyond what even I could have imagined."

Father Hall stared a bit longer, and his voice was soft when he finally answered.

"I sound like a great fool admitting this, Jean. But I barely believed a word of what you told me when you first arrived. I expected you to stay out your year, cause a refreshing bit of much-needed scandal, and then leave us to our routine little lives here. You've all opened my eyes to a larger world, and I love each of you for that."

Tears burned Rob's eyes, yet another unbelievable development.

He might have last cried when his father passed away.

"I wouldn't trade knowing any of you, either," he said. "Though it may have gotten me into a mess I may not be able to get out of."

"Well, thank goodness that's settled," Jean said. "With everyone's feelings sorted, may we focus on what we may do to stop this slow-moving disaster?"

"I only know Chief Wells by reputation," Father Hall said. "Do we have any other connections who may be able to help?"

"My father would be glad to," Victoria said. McDuff realized he looked more surprised than he thought when she scowled. "He said as much last week."

"What exactly did he say?"

"Both of my parents were worried about you getting into trouble. He said he'd speak to whomever he needed to. To sort all of this out. That usually means money to him."

McDuff couldn't stop the groan this time.

"You don't think your father actually tried to *bribe* Chief Wells, do you? Not when he was already wondering about the two missing guards?"

"And your injury," Jean said. "Stumbling upon the truth or not, that may indeed have created the wrong impression for our purposes."

"I'm sure he…" Victoria's eyes were wide, her face terribly pale. "He only meant to help."

"How certain are you, Victoria?" McDuff said, trying to keep his voice calm. "Can you find out without your parents getting suspicious?"

"I'm so sorry, Rob," she said, tears in her lovely eyes. "I'm sure he would have acted by now. He doesn't hesitate when he puts his mind to a thing. My father may have put a target right on your back."

McDuff sat back, relieved and disappointed when Victoria moved away from him. Now so much of what Chief Wells said made sense. What'd he'd put together.

Father Hall echoed the thought.

"Do you think he could have worked that much out?"

"He's in charge of the best inspectors in the city," McDuff said. "Present company definitely excluded at the moment. He didn't get to that position by not being good at the job himself. I'd be surprised if he hasn't worked out a hell of a lot more than that."

Victoria leaned forward, covering her face with her hands. McDuff hesitated, only for a second, but long enough to feel like a coward. He touched her back.

"If this does have to do with your father, that's not your fault. I've been around him enough to know he makes his own decisions. At least on things you're not purposely influencing."

"I didn't influence anything here," she said, her voice muffled. "Not in a good way, anyway. I've barely been keeping up with the simplest calming potions in his office."

"You don't mean while you were convalescing from a great deal of blood loss?" Jean said. Victoria and everyone sat up at her angry tone. "That was your one and only responsibility, Victoria. I'd argue it still is, pale as you are."

Father Hall held up both hands. "Turning on each other won't solve the problem. We'll figure something out. I hesitate to bring this up, but it's a bit late for me to start refusing to get involved now. Is there someone else who could be charged with this crime? Someone who would be deserving and believable?"

"Only every single person I've arrested over the last several years," McDuff said. "But why would anyone else target these specific guards who were known to my brother? That's a question Wells won't fail to ask, along with finding yet another connection back to me."

"Michael mentioned more than two guards," Victoria said. "All they've had so far is one letter to pass along, to identify each other and set the path between them. They're not obviously connected to anyone but Michael. But if the worst abuse was never reported, this is even less likely to have been."

"With everything you've just told us," Jean said, "I have no choice but to ask what you'd planned for these other guards. Nothing so direct or deadly, I hope?"

CHAPTER 65

THE SILENCE RELIEVED Victoria's growing distress from so many loud voices, but it only emphasized the ringing in her ears.

The company of her friends, the soothing comfort of Jean's study, even the solid warmth of Rob against her no longer drowned out the aching discomfort in her muscles and bones. Her mother had fretted and worried that she was trying to do too much too soon by spending the day out.

Victoria could no longer deny that was true.

Jean's pointed question wasn't going to go away if she pretended to ignore it, and she wasn't quite willing to admit to her growing weariness. The shock of finding out Rob was likely heading into serious trouble only made everything worse.

"We hadn't made specific plans yet," she said. "That was for after we got through the first part."

"The first part that was none too easy on either of you." This time Father Hall was doing the scolding, and far more gently. "I would rarely dare speak for Jean, but in this case I feel confident saying we want to help."

"So we're back to who may have the influence to attend to Rob's problem," Jean said. "I've been here for a few months, nowhere near long enough to know how the power in this strange city functions. Certainly not outside Father Hall's understanding of the religious structure."

"Wait. We can't lose sight of what we were trying to do in the first place," Rob said. Victoria was glad to take his hand when he offered it. "The whole thing was to help Victoria, or to stop her at first. But those men were there, and those men are dead, because of how they treated my brother. Michael is better off now, but I'm not willing to leave him in an asylum forever if I can possibly help it."

"Religion can only do so much there, I'm afraid," Father Hall said. "The Church could appeal for mercy, though the Anglican Church has considerably more power in England. Certainly more political sway. Catholicism hasn't been legal here for all that long."

"I'm sorry to have to say this," Victoria said, squeezing Rob's hand. "No one is going to listen to pleas for mercy for anyone involved in a bombing right now. Not when they haven't even rounded up all of the suspects for this latest one."

"Religion might help with some things," Rob said. Victoria was startled to see his eyes again unfocused, his voice distant and airy. "But what we'll need here is a more worldly power. Political, business, and most of all where they intersect."

"That's not easy with our little group." Father Hall shook his head. "Our Odd Society may be powerful, but not in their sort of world."

"Easier than you think." Rob turned to Victoria. "And more powerful. Your father has more than a few friends in the Anglican Church, and business partners everywhere else. I remember seeing more than one politician in his circles, as well."

Victoria wasn't sure whether to be more alarmed or impressed.

"When did you see this? Don't tell me he's shared all this with you over the past month."

"A lot longer than a month ago. Remember the first day we met, when I spoke to both of you about Cheryl Mallory? He let me take every one of his cards with me for my investigation. That was a huge part of how I saw what you were doing. I caught how the patterns overlapped."

"What patterns? I wasn't exactly obvious, Rob."

"No, you didn't make it easy. What I noticed was those clockwork toys you use. The only way that finally made sense was putting them together with your father's contacts. You know them better than I ever could. Now that he's decided to help me—"

"He set your own chief on your trail!" Victoria cried.

"That's not what he was *trying* to do, though. He was trying to help me, and your mother wants that too. Don't you see? That's where their desire is now, much sooner than any of us expected. They want to keep me out of trouble, partly because he believes I keep you safe. This will be a much easier push than what you managed on your own."

"This does make sense," Jean said. She plucked one of her notebooks out of the general disarray and started writing. "The big challenge was turning their desires to match yours. Now all that's left is to direct those desires."

Victoria rubbed her burning eyes, wishing she could have a long sleep before she had to think about this. Even better would be returning to how easily and clearly her mind worked before the attack.

She was losing patience with her recuperation, and she was terribly afraid Rob was running out of time.

"What we have to find," she said, "is the link between my father and the asylum. Someone with the power to do what we need. I still don't see how this will help you avoid a murder charge, Rob."

"We can't pretend that's not happening," Father Hall said. "What you've told us so far is more than enough to have me worried. I don't like to see true criminals treated the way they are in that wretched prison or any other. I don't want to see a good man in that same pit."

Victoria's heart broke along with Rob's voice.

"A good man? I did murder one of those guards with my own hands, even if his heart didn't realize his brain was gone for a few minutes."

"And I murdered the other," Victoria said. "We were in agreement that it was the right thing before that night. Am I the only one who still believes that?"

The silence stretched out long enough to bring her own doubts and fears surging back, nearly silencing the desperate search inside her mind for a way out.

"Perhaps my vast catalog of sins makes me the least qualified to judge," Jean said. She clutched her notebook over her chest, looking more vulnerable than Victoria had ever seen her.

"Or perhaps most qualified. In any case, we're better off without men like that drawing breath at all, much less in a position to harm the vulnerable."

"I can't disagree," Father Hall said. "And I don't care about any earthly qualifications to judge. That's reserved for the One whose mind we can never know. What we must know right now is who holds this magical combination of religious, business, and political power to help Michael and Rob."

"And what it would take to get them on our side," Rob said.

Victoria gasped, everything in her mind and body seeming to freeze solid. How could she have missed it?

She shook off Rob's solicitous concern and everyone else's before irritation could set in.

"No, I'm perfectly fine, though I feel like my mind is finally waking up," she said. Everyone looked puzzled at her smile, which only made it broader. "We have the answer right in front of us. We only need to find the right means of delivery. And the right targets."

"You know how I respect and admire the way your mind works," Jean said. She once again held her notebook ready for writing. "But I haven't a clue what you could be talking about."

Victoria stood and crossed the room to the overcrowded bookshelves closest to the front door. They were filled with books of an astounding variety of sizes, bindings, and colors, mostly the dry and scholarly works Jean was here to investigate. She reached down to pull out a dusty, heavy tome even the Frenchwoman hadn't opened until they needed a reliable hiding place.

Records of construction for the building she was standing in.

She brought out a large envelope, shocking and new against the yellowed and musty pages. Inside were the letters she and Jean had prepared for Michael's recovery, before Victoria's own wounds brought their efforts on his behalf to a near halt.

"We talked a long time ago about using my talents to help more than Michael." She dropped the envelope on the low table in front of the sofa. "The first day we all met in your office, Father Hall, when we were all very much on our guard. We discussed altruistic reasons, to be sure, and that can still be the case as far as most people know. But I see no reason why we can't use this to help more than the residents of the asylum."

Jean's eyes lit before she leaned over her writing.

Rob and Father Hall still stared at her.

"What medical administrator wouldn't be thrilled with the ability to comfort and soothe all who suffer along with Michael?" Victoria said. "What politician tasked with justifying funding for the asylum wouldn't be pleased with proof of success and reduced cost at the same time? What compassionate clergyman would turn down the improvement in the tragic lives of those poor souls?"

Both men's expressions shifted from confusion to tentative hope.

"And an astute businessman…" Rob said with the first smile she'd seen from him all afternoon.

"Like my father. Or in the unlikely event that he refuses to see such a wonderful opportunity, any number of my own associates I've carefully and secretly cultivated over the last few years. My father would be by far best in this case."

"Exactly like your father, my dear Miss Haversham," Rob continued. "One who's keen to help with my problems, and with my brother's once he knows a modified version of them. I suspect he'd be exactly the one to make the connections we need with very little influence or direction from us."

"And who will bring him this brilliant idea?" Father Hall said. His smile was nearly as big as Victoria's. "Miss Jean Apréndia, with the always kind and generous Father Michaels by her side?"

"He trusts no one more than Victoria." Jean didn't look up from her writing. "He's growing fond of you, Rob, but he's brought his daughter into his business for a long time now. In a culture full of fathers who would never imagine such a thing. Is he aware of what treasures you cultivate in that stunning greenhouse of yours?"

"He knows I have herbs and medicinal plants out there. He's even aware of when I use them on him from time to time. What will help us here is his respect for business secrets."

"You mean the secrets he's trying to get me to track down?" Rob said, shaking his head. "That's what he's been having me report to him about. Any investigations of his rivals."

"And even more so of his partners I'm quite sure. That shows you how much he respects that information, Rob. Otherwise he wouldn't be so determined to get it."

"This has brightened you up quite a bit, Victoria." Jean stopped writing and focused more intently than Victoria wanted. "But you're obviously still exhausted. I hope you plan to wait a few more days before you do this. Even with your talents and Rob's charm, your father isn't going to be easy to convince."

"A week to put our version of reality together?" Rob said. "Though if you're depending on my natural charm, it will take a lot longer than that."

"Is that long enough for you to land in jail yourself?" Father Hall said.

"I doubt it. Investigations generally don't move that quickly. Five days then, this coming weekend."

"Fair enough," Jean said. "Now I need to ask you a harder question, Victoria. You may want privacy."

Victoria did consider if for a few seconds. But she wanted the counsel and comfort of her friends more than she feared the question.

Another of the remarkable changes Rob had asked about.
She nodded.

"I've heard more than one practitioner talk about how certain types of spells drain them more than others. I've experienced it a bit myself, mostly with trying to counter your magic in the beginning. What did you experience when you ended the guard's life?"

Victoria shuddered before she could stop herself. The clammy, foul dread hadn't lingered once she woke in the hospital after the attack. But she remembered the way it had settled into her chest as the man breathed his last.

"I don't know if this was from blood loss or from the magic," she said. "Rob thought the fright may have been part of it, too. I felt cold, down in my heart. Lingering, awful cold. It was gone when I woke."

"Truly gone?" Father Hall said. "I've never encountered it

myself, but some priests have spoken of physical effects of certain spiritual battles. I believe a lot more of it than I would have six months ago."

"I remember it." Victoria rubbed at her chest. "But I don't feel it there anymore."

"Did your teacher ever speak of such things?" Jean said. "When using magic that powerful? You've gone in entirely new directions and beyond what you learned, as the best students must, but Father Hall is right. The drain upon your vitality is a common thread reported with all such activities."

Victoria resisted the urge to open the envelope she'd retrieved, to touch the letters with her bare hands and draw on the calming essence they held. As much as she'd shared and revealed with the three people in this room, she'd barely spoken of Jaji at all.

For the first time, she wondered if her teacher had used a spell to back up her repeated admonitions to keep their work together secret.

"One of my teacher's cautions with this particular spell was how the effects went both ways. She warned me that this power was not to be used frequently or without good reason." Victoria took a slow, deep breath, determined to push through an odd constriction in her throat. Her voice came out louder than she intended. "She said anyone who used this spell routinely would pay the price, in this life and the next. I always thought she meant in a legal or religious sense. I may have been wrong about that."

Jean continued to stare at Victoria. The scholar's expression wasn't angry or threatening, only her normal direct evaluation.

Still, Victoria found herself returning to old curiosity of what Jean may have learned in her travels that she herself had not.

Did Jean have an exotic and unsuspected ability to see right through into Victoria's heart and mind, learned in New Orleans or South America or India?

Or worse, was she simply able to see through the layers of Victoria's clothing, to the nearly black spot just above her left hip?

The spot that looked like a normal bruise at first, and for a week or so after the attack. Before it contracted and darkened into an irregular smudge, as if she'd gotten a bit of soot from the fire on her skin. The stain wasn't painful, as long as Victoria left it alone.

It also wouldn't wash off.

Was it a marker of her taking another person's life simply because she willed it?

"Then you must take care when using magic in the future," Jean finally said, returning to writing in her notebook. "And there's even more reason not to use that spell unless you truly have no other choice. If you have any difficulties you didn't have before, you must stop and let me know so we can work out what to do. Agreed?"

"Agreed. I'll start now by admitting I've probably done as much as I should for today."

CHAPTER 66

Instead of Mavvie like McDuff expected, or Mr. Haversham like he feared, Victoria opened the door.

The week of planning had done wonders for more than his nervousness about getting into a business deal with a master. Victoria had regained nearly all of her color and vitality, and her recovered heath was stunning in the same pale-yellow gown she'd worn the day they first met.

"Inspector McDuff. What a pleasure to see you, and right on time as usual."

"Miss Haversham. You look lovely this evening."

He followed her, expecting to turn right toward her father's study and this momentous meeting. She caught his arm and stepped into the parlor where the not-quite bridal shower had been held.

"Are you ready for your debut as a cutthroat London businessman?" she said, her blue eyes sparkling.

"Not at all, mainly because I'll never be one. I'm utterly

unqualified for negotiating with either you or your father. With the two of you, I don't stand a chance."

"Fair enough. I'll be on your side to even things up considerably." She held out a white fabric square, already neatly folded. "Put this in your highest pocket, closest to your nose."

McDuff slipped the cloth into a hidden pocket in his jacket, breathing in the sweet, vegetal aroma. He'd helped Victoria, Jean, and Father Hall prepare the herbs and flowers to soak these in a few days before.

"The protection charm we made," he said.

"Yes. You'll smell the flowers and charms in my father's office, the documents I give him, everything. You might even feel the effects. But you won't respond to them. And you'll have proof that what I taught you how to make actually works."

"The nuns would be delighted to see me finally learning to cook," McDuff said, then smiled at Victoria's confused expression. "I'll explain on a calmer day."

"I'll look forward to that calmer day." Victoria held his hand for a second, squeezing tight before she let go. "You'll do perfectly well."

He lunged forward and caught her hand again before she escaped into the hallway.

"Wait, Victoria. I may need your help with that. With… calm. Getting calm and keeping myself that way."

She stepped closer to him and pulled them both around the open door and out of sight of anyone passing by in the hall. Her worried, confused look only made him feel worse.

"I'm sorry, I'm not making sense. I don't really know how to say any of this. Can you create memory charms of different strengths? Not one as strong as you used on

Bertrand, Mr. Robbins. It wouldn't do for me to forget what I'm capable of."

"What's happening, Rob? Tell me what you mean by calm."

He lowered his gaze, concentrating on the way she held both of his hands now. Not that far removed from a simple handshake, not really.

But somehow so much more intimate.

"I mean finding a way to deal with my anger, now that I've set it free. That night, in the alley, I'd never let myself get that out of control before. I think I suspected it would lead me into trouble. Into the sort of things I saw too often as a child, and even more as a policeman. More and more, I… I can't seem to keep that night from intruding into my mind."

Victoria waited until he looked into her eyes again.

"You're talking about blunting the anger itself more than the memory. Unless I'm mistaken, what you fear is not being able to keep that side of yourself at bay. Having it take over when you don't want it to."

McDuff managed one word that took all of his breath with it.

"Yes."

She closed her eyes for a second, then brought his hands together and held them to her lips. The sensation chased the strength from his legs, on top of making it even harder to draw air back into his body.

"I can help you, Rob. But you'll have to trust me a great deal for me to do so. You'll need to think carefully about that." He started to speak, with no idea what was going to come out of his mouth, but she shook her head. "Don't answer now. We both need all of our concentration to talk to my father. We'll get through this one step at a time. I promise."

She let go of his hands, but her grip on his heart and mind held deeper and stronger than before.

Much as he wanted to argue, to keep her there in the hidden corner with him, McDuff watched her collect a stack of papers he hadn't noticed on one of the fine chairs in the sitting room. He had no real choice but following her to the dark, masculine study he'd come to know so well.

Mr. Haversham answered Victoria's quick knock, but he didn't stand when the two of them walked in. A large pipe sat on a dish in front of him, the white bowl end carved to look like a hand holding an open flower. The lingering tobacco scent drowned out the aromas of the bowl of fresh flowers on his desk.

The smell reminded McDuff far too much of Chief Wells: not the confidence boost he needed at that moment. He hadn't seen his superior all week, but the silence was anything but reassuring.

"Ah, Victoria. Inspector McDuff." Mr. Haversham sounded tired, but not unfriendly. "I'd forgotten about our meeting this evening."

"I do hope you have time to see us, Father," Victoria said. She sat in one of the leather chairs in front of his desk as if he'd actually invited her to. "This won't take long, but it is important."

"Of course. Please sit, Inspector." He closed the ledger he'd been looking at and took the papers Victoria handed to him. "If I fail to make time for my family, I'm a failure at life itself."

"We won't take up too much of your time, sir," McDuff

said. He glanced at the copy of the same papers Victoria gave him. "I believe it will be worth it."

"Victoria tells me you have a family matter we may be able to help with."

"Partly, yes. We may be able to do a great deal more." McDuff closed his eyes, bowing his head slightly to breathe in the scent from his jacket. He wished the soothing portion of Victoria's flowers worked instead of being blocked.

"I don't know if Victoria has mentioned my brother to you. Michael is a few years younger than me, which made him far too young to lose his father. I'm afraid he's suffered ever since."

"How so?" Mr. Haversham said. He focused on McDuff rather than on the papers, though that only made McDuff more anxious.

"He's always been drawn to older people, powerful men, probably looking around for a new father. Too easy to manipulate once he's caught up with one. I tried, but I'm afraid I wasn't much of a substitute."

"Inspector McDuff was only a boy himself when their father died," Victoria said. "Not yet thirteen years old. They lost their mother not long after."

McDuff had had his doubts about revealing that painful bit of information about his own life, but he saw the result Victoria predicted playing out in front of him.

Mr. Haversham drew back. His mouth turned down and he shook his head, clearly responding to memories Victoria shared of a cousin losing both parents.

McDuff's confidence grew a tiny bit.

"Never an easy thing," Victoria's father said. "I'm sure you did the best you could, and I commend you for trying. What's his situation now?"

"That searching for someone to look up to led him to people who took advantage of him," McDuff said. "Usually to talk him into things he didn't understand were bad. He's more innocent and trusting than he should be, too, likely to believe someone who pretends to care about him." McDuff hesitated, certain Mr. Haversham would balk at this much of the truth. "Right now he's in an asylum outside of the city, the first real chance he's had to get help instead of getting into more trouble since we moved to London."

"Not a horror like Bedlam used to be?" Mr. Haversham said.

"No sir, not at all. It's newer, one of the best-run ones. He's lucky to be there, really."

Victoria's father leaned back in his chair, both hands flat on his desk. McDuff feared he was about to pound the gleaming surface as he had when they'd brought fake news of the danger to Father Hall's imaginary charity.

Fake danger that led to the all too real danger on that darkened street.

"From what you've said so far," Mr. Haversham said, "your brother has struggled more than you have with tragedy early in your lives. Now he's in improved circumstances. I cannot help but wonder why you're telling me all of this. Why are we here?"

"It's the treatment itself," Victoria said. "I believe I can provide a way to help Michael McDuff, and possibly many others besides."

Mr. Haversham's eyes, at first too suspicious and closed-off for McDuff's taste and comfort, lit along with his face.

"You're certainly shown yourself to be quite gifted with your herbs and potions." Mr. Haversham's voice was deeply proud and affectionate. "If anyone could help these poor souls, it would be you. I'm not sure what I could do to help you, though."

"Victoria brings all the skill and knowledge we need to get started," McDuff said. "And there are certainly more than enough people in need of treatment. What we don't have is the means to make this happen."

"In a way we can control," Victoria said. McDuff was relieved for her to take over now that the business side was firmly in view. "If we simply release this information to the physicians, we'll never be able to adjust and refine the treatment. To improve it over time. And with everything out of our hands, inferior formulations would no doubt crop up."

Now Mr. Haversham nodded, his eyes distant. His keen business sense that entirely escaped McDuff's understanding engaged.

He drew the materials Victoria had given him close and flipped slowly through them.

"So many of these false nostrums and trickery," he said, almost to himself. "Half of them peddled by physicians. Even if there *were* miracle cures, we'd never know through the flood of nonsense." He looked hard at McDuff, then at his daughter. "You know full well how vital it is to maintain control over a precious supply, growing up around plantations and imports. What do you need me to do here? Invest, get you started up?"

Victoria laughed, soft and low in her throat. McDuff knew it was meant to disarm her father, to get him more relaxed and trusting.

That didn't change the deeper, far more inappropriate effect it had on him.

"I would never put such financial concerns above our desire to help others, Father."

McDuff jumped when Mr. Haversham laughed in return, a huge, booming response he'd never suspected the man could produce.

"Of course you would, Victoria! We raised you to be smarter than that, and sent you off to college to make bloody well sure of it. You can't help anyone if you don't support both your business and yourself." He shook his head, but he was smiling. "What you need is connections. Who to talk to, how to bring this up to speed with the most control and the highest quality. And yes, despite your noble wishes, the most profit."

McDuff wondered at the shifting tides he felt in the room, the movement from curiosity to suspicion to excitement. The only thing inside his own mind at the moment was slowly declining anxiety, so the changes had to be coming from Victoria.

The sensation of feeling the difference but not responding to it himself was fascinating, and disorienting.

"Thank you, Father. I knew you would be the one to turn to."

"Have you tested this treatment of yours yet?" Mr. Haversham said to McDuff. "On your brother?"

"I'd only just mentioned it a few days ago," McDuff said. "When Victoria told me about some of the things she's made, especially during her recovery, I knew it would be worth trying."

"A slight adjustment to the sleeping draught I've made for

you would surely work, Father. I believe it would be well worth trying."

"Then try we shall." Mr. Haversham was positively beaming now, the first time McDuff had seen that expression from him. "I'd suggest Dr. Marcus Trent, a colleague of mine at the Royal Hospital. He checked in on you, Victoria, during your recovery. He consults with various institutions about advancements in medicine, including the asylums. I can set up a meeting, deliver correspondence, whatever you're ready to do."

"I'll prepare a letter," Victoria said. "With a copy for you, of course, Father. I expect our dear friends Father Michaels and Miss Appréndia would be happy to assist since they work with prisons along with orphaned children. This will help a great many people, and most importantly Inspector McDuff's brother. He's been such a comfort to us. To me. I do hope we can return the favor."

"If we get Victoria's potions into the water supply, we could put you out of a job, Inspector." Mr. Haversham stood, smiling again. "Everything going well at Scotland Yard? None of us want to see you have trouble over helping our family."

McDuff stood when Victoria did, wishing she would answer for him.

His nervousness over this whole encounter roared back with a vengeance.

"Chief Inspector Wells can be a bit suspicious," he said. "That comes with the job, no avoiding that."

Mr. Haversham nodded, lips pursed beneath his mustache.

"Perhaps we can come up with a better method for smoothing the way for you. We'll need to speak again soon to organize this business a bit more anyway." He clapped McDuff on the shoulder. "No more work tonight, though, for any of us. I insist you join us for dinner, Inspector. No sense going back to a single man's plate so late in the evening."

He charged out of the room without looking back. A few seconds later, McDuff heard him cheerfully informing the staff about their guest.

Victoria giggled, yet another reaction McDuff didn't expect from any of the Havershams.

"I do hope you're ready to be swept up in my father's plans, Rob. He may be slow to turn as the Thames, but he's unstoppable once you set him loose."

CHAPTER 67

The director of the asylum Michael McDuff had settled rather quickly and easily into was pleased to receive the post most days. His assistants kept the useless solicitations and political claptrap down to a minimum, and made certain any offers that might be of benefit made it through.

Especially if the benefit was to him first: the patients or the asylum itself, second.

He was a practical man.

The letter on top hadn't been opened during the usual inspections, which was unusual in itself. Only an address somewhere in east London that he wasn't familiar with.

As soon as his fingertips brushed across the thick, fine paper inside, he didn't care to scold or even ask about how the letter had gotten through.

He was simply glad that it had.

Because as it turned out, this letter held benefit for the

patients, the asylum, and himself, and all of those in potentially great measure. After a quick read-through and a bare minimum of consideration, he put his spectacular plan into motion.

Within days, directors of several asylums across London, throughout England, and even into distant Wales, Scotland, and Ireland held similar information in their hands.

All transcribed in the hand of the director of Michael's asylum.

Each containing a trace of the offer of help, solid business plan, and a bit of magic the first letter had brought to him.

Every single person receiving the letters agreed to tests of the renowned and scientifically proven calming elixir on offer. They were certain they'd heard of Mr. Haversham—the businessman backing the production and sponsoring the product itself.

More importantly, none of them wanted to be the only facility who'd turned down this generous and kind proposal, and six months later to have exactly the same levels of discomfort and mental burdens among their patients as they had before.

Each of them wanted to implement the new formula and the new suggestions as quickly and successfully as possible.

All of their physicians and surgeons and staff who saw the letters agreed immediately.

It never occurred to any of them to verify the source, or write back and require a trial run or tests.

The risk of falling behind and risking continued suffering for the poor souls in their care was far too great.

Had they met in person, all would have agreed the letters carried a sense of purpose and urgency too great to be resisted, or ignored.

CHAPTER 68

OVER THE NEXT FORTNIGHT, Victoria felt as though she'd been caught up in London's great tidal river herself, swept along with the Thames and heading out of England altogether.

Contrived and successful testing with physicians and nurses at Michael's asylum—already accustomed to the will of her magic—quickly led to requests for more of her treatments. Word spread quickly, both naturally and assisted by her own efforts. The need outran the supply she could make by herself.

Before another season passed, demand was certain to pass beyond what she could possibly grow even in the huge greenhouse. She expected to be calling upon her own business network before much longer. Especially her connections in shipping, locally and overseas.

Her larger plan of moving the entire operation to a superior climate well underway, Victoria was delighted to create a miniature plantation in her greenhouse.

Much as she wished she could have The Odd Society openly participating, her girlhood friends were a wonderful alternative.

Gathered around the long, slate table, luxuriating in the warmth and humidity, the four women turned the tedious work into a pleasant ongoing party. Stripping off leaves, extracting seeds, or crushing fruit went unnoticed in good company with good conversation.

"If this is a calming tonic," Francis said, brushing her black hair away from her face with her forearm, "can I use it for the baby?"

"I think you need it for your mother," Liz said. "You told me yourself the baby is calm when she's not around."

"I'm calmer then, too," Francis said. "I've only been *un*-pregnant for a few weeks, and she's already hinting about little brothers and sisters."

"I don't know that I'd use this formula for a baby," Victoria said. She was carefully weighing the various ingredients and sorting them into clear glass bottles. "I can make you something if you like for your son and your mother."

"Tell me you haven't used it on your own mother," Liz said.

"I'll tell you no such thing." Victoria grinned, reaching for the rounded wooden muddler to gently crush the herbs. "Except to say I didn't come up with this formula by accident."

In fact, she'd already refined it more than she'd expected for Rob, taking his trust in her as a commitment to help him as much as she was able. She'd given him a small red coral pendant, not much bigger than his thumbnail, and a soft leather cord long enough to hold it round his neck under his shirt.

Warm and safe against his skin, not far from his heart.

The rounded triangular shapes carved into one side of the pendant matched the spectacular crimson leaves of a flower native to Enceleas, carefully transported and grown in the greenhouse not far from where she sat.

A flower well-suited to binding the will and wishes of another to her own.

Victoria of course included that flower among others in the potion she'd used to soak both the pendant and the cord, much like she'd soaked her opal engagement ring. Along with her wish that Rob wouldn't be controlled by temper or tormented by memories of violence.

She refreshed her will that he remain loyal to her every time they were together, with a quick whispered reminder to the pendant and to herself. A breach she considered minor in an already close partnership that promised to develop into more.

"Have your parents found you another perfect match yet?" Francis said, seeming to read Victoria's thoughts as she often did. "Since you've had your second reprieve?"

"Still want to know how you managed that," Liz said.

"I didn't manage anything but not getting killed." Victoria pushed corks down into each completed mixture, ready for her final whispered preparation once everyone else was gone. "Bertrand took himself out of the picture not long after that night. My father didn't argue with him, though."

"And what about this private guard I've heard of?" Shelly said with her typical warm smile. As the only one who'd chosen her own husband, Shelly could be counted on to catch where

Victoria's heart wanted to be. "Any arguments about him being around?"

"None from me," Victoria said. For once she didn't care that her face was turning red.

"But will he manage to win Mother and Father's approval?" Liz wasn't smiling, but her eyes were sympathetic. "Or would he be willing to fill in the empty spaces left by a less suitable arrangement, so to speak?"

Victoria worked for a moment, not sure how much to reveal of her true feelings without hurting anyone else's.

"I don't know if he's willing to do that," she said. "I do know I'm not."

"Then I hope it works out," Shelly said. "From what you've told us, he wouldn't hesitate to stand by your side."

"She didn't quite answer, though." Francis leaned back in her chair and stretched. "Not about whether her parents approve of this guard fellow."

After all three of them stopped to stare at her, Victoria rolled her eyes.

"They approve or him in general I suppose. That doesn't necessarily mean they approve of him as a husband for me."

"You've already won more than half the battle," Liz said. "Or he has, by saving you when dear old Bertrand couldn't manage. With you as the only child, it's not like you need a wealthy old goat to take care of you, anyway. You might end up with Shelly's fairy tale life after all."

This time Shelly's face turned as red as her hair

The soft squeak of the greenhouse door opening cut through the silence before anyone could respond.

Victoria shivered before she could control the reaction. The burst of cool air from outside couldn't have reached so far into the warm space, and it would be diluted by the rows of taller fruiting bushes by the time it did.

She hadn't set a strong protection boundary here as she always did in her upstairs workroom. Too many people needed to come and go to make it practical, and the space was too large to make a strong enough spell to be effective.

Victoria did set a warning, though, to let her know when people who brought trouble crossed the invisible line.

When her mother walked silently into view, Victoria's chill deepened at the unladylike tense expression on her face.

"I'm sorry to disturb all of you," Mrs. Haversham said. Her voice fell like a shadow, barely audible. "I need to speak with Victoria for a moment. Alone."

The three women no longer smiled, their own faces strained and upset now. Shelly started to get up, motioning for the others to follow her.

"No, please stay," Victoria said. "I'll return in just a moment."

She shook her head when Liz opened her mouth, then joined her mother.

"Walk outside with me, Mother?"

Victoria held her own face as calm as she could, but that inner alarm still sounded. Her mother wasn't upset enough for the news to be about her father, and she knew nothing about Michael.

Victoria's clenching heart told her something had happened to Rob.

"They probably should leave, Victoria." Mrs. Haversham

glanced over her shoulder as they headed toward the house. "Someone is here to speak to you."

"About what? I'm not expecting anyone."

Her mother grabbed her arm as Victoria closed the greenhouse door behind them, releasing the mental energy that maintained the boundary.

The bad thing she was trying to guard against was already happening.

"I wasn't expecting anyone, either. There's a City of London policeman here asking to speak to you, one I don't know. He's asking about Inspector McDuff."

Despite her earlier suspicion, Victoria's body attempted to root her to the spot. She forced her feet to keep moving with barely a stumble, determine to act as normally as she could.

"I'm not sure what any City of London officer would want to ask me about."

Her mother stopped and moved in front of her.

"You know *exactly* what this is about! I told your father we had to stay out of this."

Victoria closed her eyes, clenching her fists.

"You told him no such thing, Mother. You said you hoped Inspector McDuff wouldn't come to trouble, not over what the two of you *paid* him to do. Protecting me, remember?"

Mrs. Haversham looked away.

"Whatever those arrangements were, they were made by your father. Not by me. And the man is waiting. The only way I could imagine for this to be worse would be for him to notice how long it's taking me to fetch you from our own garden."

Victoria leaned close to her mother's ear, her own voice a near growl she barely recognized.

"My father's arrangements, and yours, are exactly what led to whatever mess I'm about to walk into. If either of you had ever even considered what I wanted for my own life, we wouldn't be here!"

Her mother's wide eyes and shocked silence gave Victoria the composure she needed to walk away.

Toward whatever awaited her and Rob inside the house.

CHAPTER 69

Victoria walked into the house as slowly as she reasonably could, wanting the time to calm her breathing and her flushed face and neck. Whatever this was about, the last thing she needed was to rush in looking frightened or upset.

She rolled her sleeves down as she walked through the back hallway, buttoning them at the wrist. Her mother hadn't followed, which helped with settling Victoria's nerves. It didn't help with letting her know where this policeman waited.

Mavvie burst out of the dining room door and answered before Victoria could ask.

"Oh, miss, thank goodness." The girl twisted her hands more than usual, glancing back over her shoulder constantly. "That man wanting to ask me questions, and your mother telling me not to say a word."

Victoria touched Mavvie's knotted fingers, and the restless motion stopped.

"You did well, Mavvie. I'll talk to him now, don't worry. Just tell me where he's waiting."

"Pacing around in the formal room, proud as a peacock. I tried to get him to wait in the dining room or your breakfast room where you like to take company, but he wouldn't have it."

"That's fine," Victoria said. "We won't have to worry about serving him refreshments, then. Would you mind to see if my friends need anything, though? They're out in the greenhouse."

Mavvie's exaggerated sigh and slumping posture showed she knew exactly why Victoria suggested that little chore, and that she appreciated the chance to get away from the house.

Victoria suspected the girl would find Mrs. Haversham still lingering out there once her surprise wore off, and for the same reason.

She only wished sneaking up to her workroom to fetch her tiny bouquet were possible. With him in the formal room, she'd have to face him with no such protections.

Victoria turned the corner to see a tall, thin man walking away from her. His dark blue greatcoat billowed around his frame, along with the fringes of black hair around the back of his head. He'd tossed a battered brown case into one of the absurdly expensive upholstered chairs.

Between that and the street shoes wearing a groove in the plush rug, it was no wonder her mother and Mavvie were upset.

When he turned and she got a good look at his sharp eyes and angular face, Victoria understood why she should be upset as well.

"Miss Haversham?" he said, eyebrows raised. "So kind of you to take time out of your busy day."

He retrieved his case and walked to the sofa furthest from the door. He didn't sit or say anything else, but his hard expression made it clear he didn't expect to ask permission.

"I'm Victoria Haversham." She stood for a few seconds before walking toward him. "And you are?"

"Superintendent Stewart, City of London Police. I understand you're an acquaintance of Inspector Rob McDuff, out of Metropolitan?"

Victoria tried to hide her reaction, but she blinked at the abrupt question. No bother with the niceties from the superintendent, so she'd play along. Even if that didn't include granting him such a lofty title.

She kept quiet until she arranged herself on a chair across from Mr. Stewart.

"I know Inspector McDuff, yes."

"And how did you meet him?"

Victoria smiled, shaking her head a little.

"He was investigating a case that's since been closed, a bit of a personal matter, really. He spoke to me and my father. May I ask why you're here, Mr. Stewart?"

"A personal matter of your former fiancé getting a gullible young girl pregnant," he said, his eyes never leaving Victoria's. "Then leaving for America, I believe."

Victoria scowled, deciding not to hide her annoyance.

"I apologize, but I fail to see what that awful man departing our shores has to do with Inspector McDuff."

Mr. Stewart raised his eyebrows, nearly as fine and delicate as a woman's.

"Perhaps nothing at all. I do find it curious that Inspector McDuff is still involved with your family all these months later. There's no record of any other investigations involving you."

Victoria breathed deeply, sending her fear away to the broad porch of her Caribbean plantation home. She could almost smell the clean, earthy air there instead of the lingering pipe smoke of cheap tobacco around the man across from her.

"You'll have to speak to my father about that. He and Inspector McDuff meet from time to time, but I'm not privy to those arrangements."

Mr. Stewart folded his arms and sat back, the fabric of his coat scratching across the velvet sofa. Victoria wondered how he wasn't broiling in the overly warm house.

"How did those arrangements lead to you ending up in hospital in London, Miss Haversham?"

"I do wish you'd speak to my father, Mr. Stewart. He knows far more of the details of their arrangement."

"That may well be, but right now I'm speaking to you, Miss, about your injuries and how that happened. Your father wasn't there that night, was he? You were in the company of yet another fiancé, though. At least he was your fiancé at the time."

"No, my father wasn't there. I attended a play with my fiancé, yes. Inspector McDuff protected both of us from a couple of street thugs. Thanks to him, I left that hospital with my life."

"Yet two men did not leave that alley with theirs. I wonder if you could tell me more about that?"

"I cannot tell you much, as I was quite frightened and overwhelmed. The two men attacked us. I remember the terrible pain in my arm, then waking up in hospital."

"Yes, I've seen the records. You could have been injured far worse, of course. Lucky thing that fiancé of yours got you to a private hospital, or you might well have lost your arm. Or worse. What I'd like to know more about is how those two men ended up lying dead on the street, then unidentified in the city morgue long enough to get dumped in a paupers grave."

Victoria shook her head, holding her features firm and cold.

"As I keep repeating, Mr. Stewart, you're asking me questions I cannot possibly know the answer to. I barely remember what those criminals looked like alive. And I never saw them dead."

Mr. Stewart nodded slowly, never dropping his gaze from Victoria.

"You do keep repeating that, yes. Well then, I won't give you any more information this afternoon, then." He leaned forward to retrieve his case, then raised his head enough to catch her eye. "I suppose I should say I won't be *asking* you for any more information. I do hope the rest of your day treats you well. Good day, Miss Haversham."

He stood staring down at her. Victoria only returned his stare, making no move to stand or offer to see him out.

He finally shrugged, permitted himself a small, mean smile, and strode out of the room.

CHAPTER 70

Thomas Haversham's business office wasn't nearly as showy or as shabby as some of those McDuff visited during his long ago investigation of Wilfred Abernathy and that poor girl from Mayfair.

Every surface, from the gleaming dark wooden floors to the brighter desks to the walls and cabinets, was spotless and well organized. Everyone who passed by had the same air of being well cared for and prosperous, and each of them were calm and polite. From rushed errand boys to polished secretaries, they all asked if someone was helping him.

Even the middle aged businessmen also there to visit with Mr. Haversham asked after McDuff. If nothing else, pointing out how very out of place he was there.

The whole arrangement felt at odds for a typical wealthy Londoner at first, but he admitted the Haversham household ran much the same way. Even when the errand was unpleasant —or clandestine—he felt well taken care of there.

Despite the solicitous staff, McDuff gripped the chair arms hard enough to make his own arms ache. Fifteen minutes for a meeting with such a busy man was normal procedure for any police officer, and a short wait at that.

But McDuff had never been the subject of an active investigation himself.

He knew Victoria would be furious with a meeting in her father's workplace rather than at home, a meeting so far out of her control. Word of an officer so much senior to himself asking such pointed questions at the Haversham household left McDuff too shocked and horrified to insist on a specific location.

If Victoria's father had any assistance to offer, he needed to know as soon as possible.

"I do apologize." Yet another young woman paused in front of McDuff on her way from one door to another. "He'll be back any minute now. Would you like a cup of tea while you wait?"

"No thank you, ma'am. I've had far too much already today."

The truth was even a sip was too much when all of his nerves and muscles vibrated, threatening to send him bolting out of the chair and hurtling down the busy London street. The dead guards, the ongoing meetings with the Havershams, Michael's abrupt move from prison to asylum had all been fair game to this Superintendent Stewart. Victoria's note had been maddeningly brief, but the details she shared were more than enough.

Superintendent Stewart seemed to know everything about

McDuff except for his friendship with Father Hall and Jean Marchér. At least for now.

He was afraid everything he did or said was already being reported back to his own chief.

If that was true, neither Mr. Haversham's political and financial power or all the magic Victoria possessed would be able to save him.

He resisted a strong urge that seemed to come from every part of him to touch the flattened lump of her pendant against his chest, invisible under his clothing.

Against his bare skin.

He knew she'd enchanted the gleaming red charm, and his mood and thought had been calmer until today.

He suspected the idea of her fingers—and possibly her lips —touching an object that now touched him had a stronger distracting effect.

"Ah, Inspector McDuff," Victoria's father said in a booming voice. He stopped long enough to hand his wet overcoat to a young man wearing an identical dark gray suit before shaking McDuff's hand. "Sorry to have kept you waiting. Weather like this doesn't make travel easier, underground train or not."

"No sir. If you need more time to settle after your trip, I can certainly wait."

Mr. Haversham's mouth compressed, and he glanced around the temporarily empty room.

"I'm afraid time is of the essence, in this and so many other matters. Please join me in my office."

McDuff stood, thankful his trembling knees held him more or less steady, and followed Victoria's father through a wood-paneled door none of the bustling staff had opened. Inside was a near replica of Mr. Haversham's office at home.

The same leather furniture, the same broad desk and shelves full of books and mementos, even the same lingering pipe smoke. McDuff had no doubt the same fine cut-glass tumblers and even finer bottle of rum waited, tucked away out of sight.

The usual bouquet—and Victoria's calming influence— were striking omissions.

"I'm sure Victoria has mentioned that unpleasant business with Superintendent Stewart to you," Mr. Haversham said as he settled behind the desk. "Barging into my home like that, making sure to catch me away. Pressuring my wife and daughter, even badgering our poor Mavvie. The coward still hasn't shown his face here. Probably a good thing I didn't meet him right away."

"I did hear about that, yes sir. I have to apologize for dragging your family into such a mess. That was never my intention."

"Dragging us into a mess? You saved my daughter's life, Inspector, and her useless finance's as well. And if you think back, you'll remember you were there at my request. More of an insistence if I'm honest with myself. In any case, arguing these fine points won't help either of us. What we have to work out now is how to head this man Stewart off."

McDuff pulled out his small notebook and struggled to read his own shaky handwriting.

"That's going to be the real trick, sir. He's not Metropolitan Police. I don't know nearly as many of the men at City of London. I don't know any of them well. And, well, we're not in the same force, but he far outranks me. He's senior to their Chief Inspector."

Mr. Haversham nodded, rubbing at his chin. "In other words, you don't have the leverage we may need. I may be able to help on that side."

"It may not be wise to get more involved with this at all, sir. I've never met Superintendent Stewart, but he's the sort of superior we all know about. The sort we all respect, and fear if we know what's good for us. Relentless and damn good at his job. He won't be a safe man to cross."

"Then we'll simply have to work out a way to solve this problem without appearing to cross him, wouldn't you say? You've proven yourself most capable of such considerations. And I'm quite certain you're aware of Victoria's skill in applying her more subtle touch when needed."

McDuff closed his eyes for a second, recalling Jean the first day they met, talking about a woman using a gentle push rather than a solid blow. He'd supplied more than his share of solid blows that dreadful night, but at the moment he had to admit he was far more afraid of Victoria's gentle push.

"I've grown to appreciate your daughter's many skills, sir. None of what we've accomplished with this calming tonic would be possible without her. Michael has shown vast improvement."

Mr. Haversham smiled, and McDuff would have sworn he actually winked.

"That's a skill of your own that I've learned to pay more attention to, Inspector. Your manner of changing the subject of conversation, and in a way that's easy to miss. We start out talking about you, add in Victoria, and you've turned it all around to your brother."

McDuff knew his face was red as a schoolboy's, and there was nothing he could do about it.

"I'm sorry, sir, I didn't mean to—"

"That wasn't any sort of criticism, Inspector McDuff." Mr. Haversham waved his hand, and his smile lingered. "More that I was wondering if you learned that in your policing work, or if you've picked it up from spending more time with Victoria. The two of you do seem to bring out the best in each other, judging from how well you've been working together."

This time McDuff couldn't help but lower his gaze. He had precious little experience with women, and none at all talking about them with their fathers.

"I'd say I learned how to direct a conversation as a policeman. But Victoria's influence has certainly helped refine my technique." He hazarded a glance up at Mr. Haversham's low chuckle.

"Well said, Inspector. Well said. She does the same for me more often than I'd like to admit. The only weakness I've ever spotted in her business sense is her ideas of shifting her growing operations to the Caribbean. I'm afraid she remembers Enceleas a bit differently than the reality."

"You don't recall it so fondly?"

Mr. Haversham frowned, tilting his head to one side then the other.

"Oh, I wouldn't say it's a bad place, no. The house is quite pleasant, and the weather certainly tops London on a day like this. Fresh air, plenty of honest hard work. But the colonies all over the Caribbean are failing, you see. Despite what that overly energetic young fool Steven Winston seems to think, still obsessed with trying to rebuild his shipping routes there."

He scowled, waving one hand in front of his face as if trying to banish such nonsense from his mind forever.

"The truth is sugar has shifted to Europe with the sugar beets. Tobacco to the American South. Not to mention how much more unruly the local population has become. Even on our remote little island, I'd worry too much for my family's safety. And almost as much over the success of any business venture."

McDuff nodded, pretending he'd heard of similar difficulties, aside from interviewing the befuddled Steven Winston himself what felt like a lifetime ago. The interview that had twined his path with Victoria's.

And pretending his heart didn't ache for Victoria's cherished dream of a home that might not exist for much longer.

"The world adapts and moves on, sir. I'd imagine there are places all over the world that would provide a suitable home for growing operations."

"To be sure, the tropics aren't limited to a tiny chain of islands. I expect we'll all be better off in the long run if I sold Enceleas and focused elsewhere. But now I'm the one who's dragged our conversation off course. I'll make a few inquiries, see who may be able to assist in your unfortunate matter with this superintendent. I promise I'll borrow from you and Victoria and be a good bit more subtle."

He cleared his throat noisily and shifted in his chair. A crystal-clear signal of either guilt or unease. Quite likely both.

An unmistakable flush rose in his cheeks: yet another trait McDuff would have thought him incapable of.

"I'm afraid I might have added to your troubles with your own chief in trying to solve them before. That might have brought this new man down on all our heads. I am sorry about that."

"I… That's quite all right, sir. I appreciate you saying so. And I believe you're correct in that if we all work together, we can solve this problem as well as any other that may come our way."

Mr. Haversham grunted, and his discomfort fell away at once.

"Well said again. Now, I'll get to work and see what can be done. You're a fine addition to the team, Mr. McDuff. I'll speak to you soon."

Rob nodded, smiled, and made his escape.

He walked slowly through the rain back toward…no, he hadn't decided that just yet. So he continued to walk.

He'd somehow missed a shift in how Mr. Haversham regarded him. A transition. Now that he'd noticed, the change was obvious as the threat he'd seen in Chief Wells' eyes. He felt it as clearly as the gentle push Victoria wielded with the bouquets in her father's home office.

For whatever reason—long association, difficult circumstances, or Victoria's influence—Mr. Haversham had moved McDuff out of the "useful public servant" box, and possibly even out of the "useful and in my employ" box as well.

He couldn't imagine a man like that apologizing to someone so far beneath him.

McDuff also couldn't imagine ever standing as an equal to Mr. Haversham, or to Victoria herself.

But he was pleased to stand not quite so far beneath them.

CHAPTER 71

Between the ongoing rain, his chilly rooms at the boarding house, and the clammy undercurrent of worry that accompanied him every hour of every day now, McDuff half suspected he'd never warm up again.

Standing inches away from the roaring fireplace in Jean's study was the closest he'd gotten in days.

Jean herself perched in her usual leather chair, with a thick ivory wool blanket tucked around her. Father Hall had even thrown a heavy brown lap blanket over his long legs.

Both of them added a liberal splash of whiskey to their tea, calling it medicine against the foul weather and endless drafts.

McDuff had refused so far, but not on any sort of newly adopted principle. He suspected Victoria's pendant and potion reduced his dependence on the numbing effects of drink without his will doing the work.

He simply wanted to be clear-headed when he asked his friends for much-needed help.

"You're either going to catch yourself on fire there or drive me insane with watching you brood," Jean said. "Please do sit and tell us what's happening."

Father Hall held up a dark blue blanket and winked.

"I can fetch you another if this doesn't do the job."

McDuff finally managed to smile as he crossed the room and joined Father Hall. The blanket at least kept the fire's warmth from leaving his clothing.

"These last few days have me understanding why Victoria so hates the cold. I'm not sure I'd be cut out for the tropics, but a sunny day would do me a world of good."

He picked up his own tea, still resisting Jean's flask waiting in a cleared spot among all the papers and books on the table.

"The last thing I want to do is draw either of you deeper into my own troubles. And, you're the two I trust most when it comes to certain things."

Jean raised her eyebrows. "More than you trust Victoria?"

"In this case, I'm afraid so. Despite everything that's currently crashing down around me, I'm more concerned for her. I've heard more than one person talking about how the Caribbean seem to be failing. Such matters are far beyond my ken. Besides worrying about Michael, I've never paid much attention to what happens outside my work, much less so far beyond these shores. Have either of you heard anything like that about the colonies?"

"There was unrest a few years back," Father Hall said. "Along with cries for independence. Even with that settling a bit, now the profit and therefore the work is drying up, which keeps unhappiness forever present. I don't understand as much about the business reasons as I'm sure Victoria's father would, but I have heard of much suffering."

Jean nodded. "I saw signs of struggle during my time there, and heard rumblings of growing dissatisfaction. I understand the plantation Victoria loves so is on one island, so perhaps a bit removed from that sort of difficulty. But with the price of sugar collapsing, managing any large operation would likely be more challenge than it's worth."

"That's much like what her father told me," McDuff said. "He's even mentioned selling the island itself, perhaps finding another location for her needs when it comes to the calming potion. I don't think he's said a word to her about that. I certainly haven't. Even if I could wield spells and potions and charms the way she can, I won't be able to soften this blow for her."

"You won't," Jean said. "Not even with her own magic. That's her deepest desire, so influencing her to go against it wouldn't be easy. It may not be possible. I'm sorry, Rob. For her and for you."

"You don't think there's any chance she'd agree to a different path?" Father Hall said. "I can't imagine this country giving up on colonialism altogether. Perhaps somewhere else with an agreeable climate?"

Rob sat forward, staring into his half-empty cup.

"I have no doubt you're both aware of how I feel about Victoria. Even knowing she could easily hold dreadful power over me, in a way it's too late. I'm already powerless when it comes to her. I feel like a shameful coward saying so, but I hope her father can convince her to change course. A change that makes sense for many reasons. I still don't want to be the one to break her heart."

"Some might say cowardice," Jean said. "But I'm not one of them. I don't want to break her heart either, and I'm not the one falling in love with her. Are you aware how worried she is for you right now?"

"I'm certain she has far more important things to be thinking about," Rob said, though he couldn't deny a spark of heat in his belly and heart at the idea. "She's at risk, and so is her father."

Jean shook her head with a sad smile.

"You were moments ago telling us how you worry for her. Yet you bat aside the idea that she may feel the same."

Rob turned away, staring into the fire.

"I wouldn't know what to do with that idea if I could accept it, Jean. Between my father loving his trouble more than us and my mother struggling with him and with Michael, that sort of…*concern* isn't familiar to me."

"You might want to get familiar with it," Father Hall said. He looked more worried than sad. "From Jean and myself, certainly, but much more from Victoria. She sees you as far more than some sort of coworker or guard, you must know that. No one does well when their feelings aren't returned."

McDuff rubbed his eyes until he saw little purple flashes. Even that didn't dull the flood of images that had been crowding into his mind too often lately. Daydreams of far more touch between the two of them than a bit of coral and his increasingly vivid imagination.

Images he didn't have to be Catholic to know were inappropriate here and in the company of a priest.

"Maybe we've already pulled each other into enough trouble," he said. "Everything we try to make things better only yanks us deeper."

"No, not everything," Jean said. Her scowl was enough to make Rob pay attention. "She's bringing real help and comfort to those in asylum, and Michael most of all. You do remember those guards brought their troubles down upon themselves by mistreating him."

"The guards." McDuff rubbed his temples now, glad of the change of subject but now wishing he'd taken a bit of whiskey. "Victoria's letter is still doing its work, and Superintendent Stewart is accelerating his. He's rounded up three…no, five more who've suffered misfortune. Each of them linked to Michael, of course, and to each other."

He lowered his hands to his lap, letting them twist into tight fists that would only get him into worse trouble.

"If Stewart could work out exactly what to charge me with, he would have already. The great coward hasn't even seen fit to speak to me or put himself in my presence. He only torments Victoria, and makes sure word of his ongoing investigations get back to me."

Father Hall drummed his fingers on the arm of the sofa.

"I don't like to bring this up, but not for the reasons you might think. Is this superintendent someone Victoria could influence? Or at least put off the trail somehow?"

McDuff snorted out laughter, and immediately felt bad for being so rude.

"I'm sorry, Father, are you saying you're *not* uncomfortable with suggesting we again use what most in this country would call witchcraft?"

"For all my failings," Father Hall said, raising his head high but smiling, "I do try to avoid hypocrisy. That ship has long since sailed, Rob. My concern is knowing the attempts to put the guards to right helped spring the trap you and possibly Victoria are caught in. Jean and I aren't exactly innocent ourselves. I'm frightened further interference might only make everyone's situation worse."

"Not half as frightened as I am. The results might be unsurprising if Stewart wasn't watching for connections. Two more caught in brawls. One escalating his visits to brothels until he could no longer afford his lodgings. One openly beating prisoners to the point of being reprimanded and fired. The last stealing from prisoners, and eventually from other guards. That one's in hospital himself now, not likely to last out the night."

"We know how these may be connected," Jean said. "And we know that's all a result of escalating their impulses. How could this Stewart possibly put you together will all of that?"

McDuff finally relaxed and sat back against the deep cushions, but not because he was relieved. He'd crossed closer to resignation.

"I don't believe even someone as good as Stewart would have even looked at those things before. Not until he and Chief Wells got suspicious about the two guards who went missing and ended up in a pauper's grave."

Jean uncurled herself, stood, and picked up the flask. She poured a generous bit into McDuff's teacup without asking before she resumed her seat.

"I'll ask directly what Father Hall was dancing around. Making a habit of this sort of attack and escalation makes me uncomfortable as well, for the record. But in this case, each of those guards deserved some sort of consequences for their behavior. Rob, are you willing to consider talking to Victoria about moving against this Stewart? Or your own chief? Not fatally, or even as directly as the guards. Only as a possible diversion?"

McDuff swallowed everything in his cup down in one go and closed his eyes. He wasn't exactly expecting calm or clarity, not with so much piled up against him.

He opened his eyes when he felt the small shift he was after. In the tiny fire in his middle, the unknotting of his muscles. The welcome slowdown in his mind.

"I'll consider it. But that's all. We've all crossed a lot of lines over these past few months together. We need to take care we don't leap over one too many."

CHAPTER 72

Victoria's third floor hideaway no longer approached any sort of comfort or warmth.

The chill of a rainy morning permeated the floor, walls, even the rough wooden table that served as her workbench. A tiny hearth in Jaji's room on the other side of the wall was lit, but precious little of its heat passed through even with the hall door closed and the hidden door propped open.

She kept herself well bundled with a black woolen riding dress, thick stockings under her boots, and a blue wool coat that buttoned up to her neck and fell past her knees. She'd reluctantly pulled a cap that matched the coat over her hair, deciding the sparking tangles later on would be worth it.

A pair of knitted gloves made without fingertips was hardly fashionable, especially since they were a jarring shade of yellow. But they kept her hands warm enough to do what she needed.

Not for her normal delicate work, with clockwork toys or tiny flowers. That was too difficult with the cold, and with her breath fogging up the magnifier. Now she had sheets of paper on the table before her, and a selection of fountain pens alongside.

Unremarkable pens to anyone not sensitive to the magic contained in and around them.

Victoria focused on the painting of her Caribbean house, her plantation paradise on Enceleas. Her mind's eye effortlessly added the spark and sensation of reality. She felt the warm breeze against her skin, heard the rustle of the vines and palms, even smelled the sweet flowers and the salty spray of the sea.

The pull inside—away from the dank, smoke-filled city and toward the life-giving air of tropics—was strong enough to bring tears to her eyes.

She picked up her most reliable pen: with a golden nib and a carved wooden barrel. Jaji had made it especially for her the year she turned ten. Even Victoria didn't understand all the shapes and inscriptions worn dark into the pale wood after so many years of use.

All she knew was this beautiful writing instrument carried her magic strong and true.

The ink inside was pure black, as dark and potent as her opera gloves. Ordinary ink to begin with, enhanced with a touch of rainwater collected on Victoria's previous birthday, along with kohl from Egypt and India

Victoria had used many of these tools to write all the letters she'd sent over the past few months, and to address the boxes containing her clockwork toys. She rarely combined this most powerful ink along with the pen made only for her.

She needed to use every advantage for these documents,

meant to clear the way forward out of a situation that only seemed to get worse.

Superintendent Stewart had visited her twice more, both times when her father was out and only Victoria, her mother, and Mavvie were home. He'd kept up his repetitive, maddening questions, adding a new bit of evidence each time.

He'd also apparently never bothered questioning Rob, or even making himself known.

Bertrand wasn't with her when the guards were killed. Only Rob.

A boy had seen Rob talking to Victoria before and after the beatings, and he was certain more went on while he was sent off to fetch the carriage.

More of the guards who worked with Michael had fallen into difficult situations, while Michael seemed to be thriving. Still a bit simple, perhaps, but much healthier than he'd been in Fodelson Prison.

Wasn't it odd, the way Michael was transferred? The timing of it? Might be the sort of thing that should be reviewed with higher authorities.

That last part had pushed Victoria over the edge of talking endlessly with Rob and her father and Jean and Father Hall, and into taking action herself.

Letting Michael get transferred back into Fodelson—where what had happened to all of those guards was uneasy common knowledge—would be an absolute disaster for him.

Mr. Stewart was right. Michael had improved greatly, along with many others at the asylum who took her calming tonic. Nothing would let him fully recover what he'd lost after so much abuse, to his skull and to his body and mind.

But Victoria would see herself be damned before she'd let him slip back into his desperate state of the day she first met him.

She wrote the address for Mr. Stewart's station in neat, quick strokes at the top of the page. Nothing like her usual expert penmanship, full of both flourish and precision.

This was quick. Decisive. Untroubled by any sense of style or artistic flair.

A faint smile curved her lips when she realized she'd appropriated handwriting much closer to Rob's. Not identical by any means, or likely to draw him into suspicion over what she was writing.

Simply enough to look no-nonsense and masculine.

She might have thought Rob himself rather regimented and dull when they met, and he very well may have been. But the last few weeks had softened her view of him.

Softened his demeanor, too, at least when he was with her.

He noticed the flowers she wore, and the jewelry. How she styled her hair. Not only noticed, but made the effort to tell her so. He'd taken to engaging her mother in conversation whenever he could, and even Mavvie was growing fond of "their own inspector."

She brushed her fingertips across her chest, near to where the pendant would even now be resting against his skin. Hoping in a whisper-quiet corner of her heart that the change in him was his own, and not influenced by her magic.

The idea of Rob withdrawing again, vanishing into rigid and cool Inspector McDuff, upset Victoria nearly as much as the thought of Michael disappearing back into the foul vortex of a model prison.

Rob had helpfully left a few pages of his own reports behind a few days before. They were stacked neatly off to the side, turned upside down so she wouldn't be tempted to copy his handwriting or phrases too closely.

Seeing the general composition, though, the way information was laid out on the pages, was incredibly helpful.

She wasn't sure whether he'd left them on purpose. She hadn't asked him for them or made a point of giving them back.

Victoria had learned long ago to take good fortune when it found her.

Meeting Rob McDuff—and Jean and Father Hall and even Michael—had turned into good fortune indeed.

She meant to return the favors they'd all given her the best she could.

If returning those favors led to a better situation for Rob, Michael, and herself, and Father Hall and Jean if she could manage it, who was she to protest?

With a few whispered words to Jaji, the information and the magic flowed from her mind, through her pen, and onto the paper.

CHAPTER 73

Victoria opened the front door—bundle of documents for Mr. Stewart already created and safely delivered —to check the afternoon post.

Jean had been true to her promise to remove the blocks that kept Victoria's magic so contained. But like so many of her special letters and packages, she carried them to a public postbox a few blocks away as soon as they were ready.

Even with that alternate means, getting her family and everyone who worked for them back into the habit of seeing her with the post was essential and long-overdue. She knew of too many households where the all-powerful man of the house controlled all means of communication.

Knowing how unusual it was for her father to trust her in so many matters didn't mean she could allow such restrictions to gain a foothold here.

When she stepped outside into a foggy, misty break in the

rain, a young woman walked toward her from across the street, purpose clear in her strong but awkward stride.

Awkward because she was several months pregnant.

Victoria's heart sank into the sodden ground under her feet when she realized this wasn't a woman but a girl. A girl she'd only glimpsed in passing months ago before settling on her as the target for her first fiancé's unwanted advances.

Her face was pale and too thin, the blonde hair escaping around the edges of her brown hooded cape duller than the rain could account for. But Victoria saw all too clearly that she'd have been lovely in a state of full health and happiness.

This could only be the unfortunate Cheryl Mallory.

Victoria did her best to hide her near-stagger as she continued her own walk across the smooth gray paving stones, between flowering bushes gone dormant for the season. Cheryl couldn't possibly understand the focus that had been trained on her, or the reasons for the changes in her life.

She could even less suspect who had directed those events with a pair of simple blue boxes that hadn't even been dropped into the Haversham's private postbox. *As she always did with such sensitive items, she'd carried the box for both her first departed fiancé Wilfred Abernathy and Cheryl to a public postbox down the street.*

But then Victoria would have never imagined an inspector from the Metropolitan Police would have put all of those things together. Or that a maddening superintendent from City of London could have linked a savage attack in the theatre district to the deceptively bright and airy corridors of Fodelson Prison.

She unlocked the metal box on the back of the tower of

jagged tan and black stones, slipping the bundle of letters for the next pickup inside. The carriers in this upper-class neighborhood would stop at least eight times during the day, so two more pickups were assured.

And her earlier delivery dispatches to the superintendent were well on their way.

When she stepped around front to open the box for deliveries, the girl stopped beside her.

"Excuse me, ma'am," she said in a low, shaky voice. "I'm terribly sorry to bother you out on the street like this. I wasn't sure what else to do. Are you Victoria Haversham?"

Victoria gathered the envelopes and small packets inside the box and relocked it before she faced the girl. Up close, her pale green eyes were startling and beautiful, and shone with a quick intelligence.

"I am," Victoria said. "May I ask your name, please?"

A flush overtook the unnatural paleness in the girl's cheeks, but she looked anything but rosy with good health. She didn't drop her gaze from Victoria's.

"I'm Cheryl Mallory, ma'am. I'm…I was acquainted with your former fiancé."

Victoria took a slow, deep breath, doing her best not to betray her own discomfort.

"I assume you mean Mr. Abernathy. I'm terribly sorry for what happened to you, Miss Mallory."

Cheryl nodded and bent the tiniest bit, as if she couldn't stop herself from at least sketching a tiny curtsey. Victoria's heart broke for her all over again, and her stomach soured with the part she'd played in the girl's misery.

"Thank you for that, ma'am." Cheryl's voice dropped to a

whisper, barely louder than the cold rain now sprinkling all around them. "But I came round to tell you how sorry *I* am. I know my actions caused you pain, and everything I did was wrong."

Victoria resisted a surprisingly strong urge to drop the post she had clutched to her chest, pull Cheryl into a tight hug, and confess everything.

She settled for holding out one hand.

"Will you come inside, out of this dreadful rain? I'll get us some hot tea so we can talk. Please?"

Cheryl stared at Victoria's hand as if she'd raised it to strike rather than offering it as a gesture of kindness. After everything this child had been through, she might never trust another soul as long as she lived.

Victoria vowed to stand there for all time if need be.

When Cheryl finally took Victoria's hand, the girl's slender fingers were like ice.

"Thank you, ma'am, for your kind and generous offer. Tea would be lovely."

Victoria dropped the post unsorted on the entryway table and insisted on taking Cheryl's wet cloak, then walked her to the round breakfast nook where she'd first met Inspector McDuff. The room was too small to bother laying a fire in the tiny fireplace most days, but Victoria had been planning to take her afternoon tea there overlooking the nearly dormant gardens once she'd finished the post.

"I'll have the fire built up a bit so you can get warm," Victoria said. "Will you take food along with your tea? We can all use a bit of extra when the weather is so dreary."

Cheryl shook her head and opened her mouth to protest, but Victoria touched her shoulder.

"It's no trouble at all, Cheryl. You must take care of yourself."

Lovely pale green eyes filling with tears, Cheryl turned away toward the gardens.

"Only if you're bringing something for yourself already, ma'am. The last thing I'd want is to be any trouble to you after all you've been through."

"It's no trouble," Victoria repeated. "I'll be right back."

By the time Victoria returned with the tea service in her arms and Mavvie hot on her heels ready to stoke the fire (and surely to spy upon the new arrival), Cheryl was just resettling herself in her chair.

The fire danced high and merry, and the room was noticeably warmer.

Victoria turned, effectively blocking the doorway.

"Mavvie, could you please help bring in the rest of our tea? And add extra scones and butter? Mother is out at her own tea this afternoon, isn't she?"

"She is, miss, likely to attend at least three different ones."

"Then there's no need to trouble her about this one. Thank you."

Victoria stood still, refusing to shift to the side and let Mavvie peer at Cheryl. Her curiosity thus curtailed, Mavvie flashed a tiny frown and turned on her heel.

Victoria poured tea for Cheryl and added a healthy serving of sugar and milk before sitting beside her.

"Oh, that will be much too sweet, ma'am."

"That may be, but you need to indulge yourself when you

have the chance. We have more than enough sugar from our own plantation, so now's the perfect time for it. It's a perfect time to call me Victoria as well."

Cheryl took a tiny sip and allowed herself a tiny smile.

"Thank you, Victoria. It's very good."

Victoria stirred a bit of extra sugar into her own tea, wishing for a splash of her father's rum.

"You're welcome to drink all you like," she said. "I don't want to spoil your appetite, so we can wait to talk more until after we eat if you like."

Cheryl shrugged, taking another sip of her tea. She wore a rather plain green dress, primly close around her neck and too loose around her breasts and the swell of her belly. Victoria didn't have to ask to know she either hadn't been given a choice in the garment or didn't care.

"I think being out of my father's house will do wonders for my appetite," she said. She carefully put her teacup on the saucer, and glanced quickly at Victoria. "That and finally speaking to you after months of dreading it, even though I knew I had to."

"How did you find out where I live? I don't mean to be indelicate, but I doubt Mr. Abernathy shared that information with you."

"No, he was rather single-minded during our brief association. You've offered to be careful of me, Victoria. So please do tell me if there are subjects you would rather I avoided."

Victoria shook her head slowly, remembering her revulsion at the thought of Wilfred pawing at her like an animal in heat.

She hoped it hadn't been as horrid for Cheryl in reality as it had been in her own imagination.

"That business is all behind me," Victoria said. "To be rather painfully honest, my father arranged the match without input from me. So I'm afraid I wasn't in love with Mr. Abernathy at all."

Cheryl sighed, absently refilling strainers with loose leaves for herself and for Victoria.

"I fancied myself in love with him. And to be fair, he was perfectly sweet in the beginning. Looking back now, I have no idea what I was thinking. If it weren't for what my mother calls *my shameful consequences*, I'd expect the whole thing would feel more like a dream than something that really happened to me."

Victoria added the same amounts of sugar and milk to Cheryl's cup, and got a small smile in return rather than any sort of protest.

"I didn't know your name at all," Cheryl said in answer to a question Victoria had nearly forgotten asking. "Or where you lived. Not during that time or after. Not until I read about that dreadful attack in the theatre district. I saw your name there."

She ducked her head for a second, then looked back into Victoria's eyes.

"I'm ashamed to tell you this, even though it wasn't me that said it. I put it all together when I overheard my mother gossiping with one of her friends afterward, and they mentioned how you'd had a second engagement turn out badly. Not in a cruel way, because none of this has been at all your fault. They were afraid your association with Wilfred had attached bad fortune to you."

Victoria laughed before she could stop herself, and she was

hugely grateful to Mavvie for stopping outside the door as she always did and dramatically clearing her throat.

When the table was laid with enough scones, preserves, clotted cream, butter, and dainty triangular watercress sandwiches for five people, plus a tray full of cookies and candies and chocolates on the sideboard, Victoria finally spoke.

"I'm terribly sorry to laugh like that, Cheryl. It's just that I've been relieved when both of my engagements were called off."

"You don't wish to ever marry, then?"

Victoria focused on pulling her round scone into two halves, noticing Cheryl copied her every move.

"I might not mind being married someday, no. It's more that I objected to having my father decide which men were suitable for me. It's not as if he has any experience being a young woman, or falling in love with a man. Between him and my mother with their traditional ways, it truly is a wonder I was permitted to go outside this house at all, and certainly to go to college."

Cheryl let out a longer sigh, but she didn't stop slathering one half of her scone with plenty of butter, then the other with clotted cream.

"I had hoped to attend college myself. Both my parents were finally beginning to consider the idea before all of this happened." She paused to rest one hand on her belly before reaching for the strawberry preserves. "They'll never agree to it now. They've taken away my books and everything else in my room. It's more like a prison cell now, which is what my mother believes I deserve."

A hard knot of anger clenched in Victoria's chest, and the

undercurrent of guilt at Cheryl's situation settled in a bit deeper. Imagining such a delicate young girl in the model prison that had so tormented Michael made it worse.

"That's not fair, to take away your books. Or your education. Those things aren't rewards for when we've been good girls, any more than they are for when men have been good boys."

Cheryl raised her pale eyebrows in the middle of biting into one well-loaded scone half. After a reasonable amount of chewing and a sip of tea, she shook her head.

"You sound as if you've come from another world. All I hear about is getting through the next few months, then possibly learning how to be a proper nanny. Maybe a teacher in some kind of dull finishing school rather than anything I'm actually interested in. Since no one in his right mind would agree to marry me, they're convinced I have no other options. They're probably right."

"I do come from another world," Victoria said. "My nanny did, too. We lived in the Caribbean when I was a girl. It was my nanny Jaji who taught me how to be independent and strong. She didn't have…as much control over her own life as she should have. But she wanted to make sure I did. That education even more than my college may have limited my own options more than I realized."

Victoria blinked, amazed she'd said so much, to Cheryl or anyone else. She'd hardly talked about Jaji to Jean or Father Hall, or even Rob.

She bit into her scone, covered with almost as much butter and preserves as Cheryl's. The crumbly, barely sweet bread combined perfectly with the rich butter and tart sweetness of the strawberries.

"My nanny was a bitter, mean thing," Cheryl said. "I'm afraid I will be too. It isn't the life I dreamed of by any means."

"My own life has turned rather strange over the past few months as well. What do you want to do, Cheryl? I don't mean some sort of daydream about turning back time and changing things. That useless game only makes things worse for me. What would you want to do now, if you could choose?"

Scone dispatched with a minimum of crumbs on the tablecloth, Cheryl nibbled on the edge of a triangular sandwich.

"I'd leave England," she said in a strong voice. "There's nothing for me here. A lifetime of raising or teaching other people's children, teaching them things I don't care one whit about. My parents haven't said so out loud, but I expect they'll take my baby away as soon as I manage the birth. *If* I manage the birth. Not to a foundling hospital, mind you, not for someone of our status. They'll find a suitable home, far away from me."

Victoria touched Cheryl's arm again, her heart aching at the thought of losing a child in such a way.

She wasn't sure how she felt about the solid expectation everyone had of her becoming a mother herself. Not after two old men in a row had made it clear that was to be her *only* purpose in life once they had hold of her.

The idea of having a child taken, though, a baby who'd grown inside her own body disappearing to never be seen again. That hurt every part of her.

Sandwich finished, Cheryl hesitated with her hand reaching for another. It was plain as day the poor girl was half-starved. Not only her face was too thin, but her hands as well. All Victoria's difficulties with her parents paled in comparison to those who would watch their daughter fall into this state.

She put two sandwiches on Cheryl's plate, along with a second scone. Cheryl blushed a little, but she did pick up a sandwich.

"Where would you go?" Victoria said. "If you could depart these shores and go anywhere?"

"I'd go *every*where," Cheryl said, her eyes lighting. "Maybe not America, since Wilfred went there. At least not where he went. It's such a vast land. And anywhere else in the wide world. India, Africa, your Caribbean, China. Even France and Germany and Spain and Italy should be far enough from here. Where would you go, Victoria?"

"I'd go back to our Caribbean island. Enceleas. Live in our beautiful house there, change over from all sugar and add many more useful plants I could send back here to England. Take people I care about with me if I could. Most of all, decide my own course in life. That sounds like one thing we have in common, Cheryl. Wanting to be left to live on our own terms."

"If we could only work out how," Cheryl said. She smiled at Victoria, but the excitement had gone from her face.

Victoria reached for a sandwich of her own, unsettled by the turn of her thoughts.

Trying to put herself together with the person who'd sent the enchanted clockwork penguin to this lovely girl only months ago felt impossible. She could get hold of the anger, certainly, and the determination.

But the impulse of lashing out not only at Wilfred, but at

this innocent child, no longer made sense to her. That mindset, that action, seemed to have come from someone as young as Cheryl, maybe younger.

The past few months had aged Victoria more than the past few years somehow.

None of that meant she could walk away from what she'd done here. Not without trying to make it right.

"One never knows the twists and turns our lives may take," she said. "Perhaps things will work out for the better for both of us."

CHAPTER 74

McDuff stood outside Victoria's house longer than he
meant to, still struggling for words or an idea of anything
sensible to say.

He did want to go along with Jean and Father Hall's
suggestion about moving against Stewart. Very much. The idea
of escaping the investigation that had passed from hanging over
his head and well into tightening round his neck was near irresistible.

And he kept coming back to what Jean said about the idea
being uncomfortable.

What worried him was allowing Victoria to solve this
problem—with such help as he could offer—felt less uncomfortable by the minute. The thought of not acting, of simply
letting everything play out along its natural course, sounded
much more difficult.

Which brought McDuff firmly into his fear of the opposite: being too comfortable, too calm about relying on magic to solve all their problems.

Especially since magic had inadvertently created the current set of problems.

Talk about crossing lines figured into his unease as well. Meaning taking another man's life in that case, of course. The biggest, brightest line of all as far as McDuff was concerned, even when he knowingly crossed it.

But the smaller, dimmer lines had an effect, too. He'd seen it far too often as a policeman to pretend ignorance.

Once you allowed yourself to cross the first line you were certain you never would, the next one didn't require nearly so much thought. Unfortunately, he was finding out for himself how that effect got stronger with each crossing.

McDuff shivered, not sure if it was from the path his thoughts were taking or standing out in the chill rain. Either way, he'd put it off long enough for no good reason.

Mavvie answered his knock right away, her smile quick and cheerful.

"Oh, Inspector McDuff. Do come inside. Only Miss Victoria is home at the moment, with a guest for tea. But I'll let her know you've arrived."

She was off before he could protest, and he wasn't sure he would have anyway. He was more curious about who this guest could possibly be without either of her parents home.

He hung his damp coat in the entryway beside a brown cape he didn't recognize and followed Mavvie toward Victoria's breakfast nook. Far enough behind her to give Victoria a chance to send him away, though he very much hoped she wouldn't.

He and Victoria had met in the intimate room several times lately, taking advantage of the privacy she'd created there. Mostly for talking, supposedly about their thriving business venture. More often endlessly discussing the same bloody thing McDuff had come to discuss now.

They'd used the time to get closer, too. Sharing more about their childhoods and lives and feelings, of course. But physically closer as well. Holding hands and sitting scandalously close. More affection than they should share as two unengaged people, and business associates at that.

All intensely pleasant activities that kept McDuff slightly-off balance on top of the other disorientations currently in his life.

A rather massive new one struck when Mavvie stepped out the door and waved him into the breakfast nook.

Victoria sat there with none other than Cheryl Mallory.

And from the looks of the table, they'd been there for a good while enjoying a rich and decadent afternoon tea.

Victoria smiled openly at him, while Cheryl only took a quick glance before looking down at the scone in front of her.

"Will you be taking tea yourself, Inspector McDuff?" Mavvie said. "I'd be happy to fetch a fresh pot, and more food if you like."

"I think I'll find plenty to eat," he said, sitting beside Victoria.

"We have enough tea for now," Victoria said. "I expect it's warm enough with the good fire Cheryl built up for us. Thank you, Mavvie."

When Mavvie disappeared down the hall, Cheryl raised her eyes and studied him. She still looked like she was wasting away despite her growing belly. But today her face had more healthy color.

Even better, her eyes were more curious than hopeless.

"You're the same inspector who came round to my parents' house," she said. "And visited me in hospital. Didn't I read in the paper that a guard was with Miss Victoria that awful night at the theatre? Were you the guard who protected her, Inspector McDuff?"

McDuff shook his head, feeling the room closing in on him like so many other things seemed to be lately. But for some unknown reason, he felt comfortable confirming Cheryl's suspicions. He actually felt glad to have the chance.

"I have spoken to you at your house, yes, and when you were in hospital. I wasn't with Miss Haversham at the theatre that evening. But her father employs me as a guard from time to time. That's why I was on the street nearby that unfortunate night."

"If he hadn't been there," Victoria said, "I probably wouldn't be sitting here right now. I had quite forgotten you two have met."

McDuff watched her, but she didn't seem angry or upset. In fact, she seemed more lighthearted than she had for a while now. She poured tea for him, while Cheryl set a plate with four little sandwiches in front of him, then added a scone for good measure.

"You seem much better than you did last time we spoke, Miss Mallory," he said. "I'm glad of that."

"I feel a bit better," she said. "I'm ever so glad I finally worked up the nerve to come for a visit with Victoria. That being said, I'm sorry to leave so abruptly, but I really should be getting back home before I'm missed."

McDuff stood at once, but Victoria waved him away as she got to her own feet.

"I'll walk Cheryl out, Inspector McDuff. Please enjoy your tea. I'll return in a moment."

He watched them leave, walking nearly shoulder to shoulder, as if they'd known each other for years. He couldn't work out whether to be worried or relieved.

Instead, he resumed his seat and bit into a tiny sandwich, sighing with pleasure at the crunch of fresh, peppery watercress and rich butter.

His disdain at walking into this house for the first time—for the surroundings and everyone who dwelled within—felt like a distant, naïve memory. But an undercurrent of fear stayed with him all the same.

Getting used to such fine food and accommodations and comfort seemed fundamentally unwise. Exposing him to consequences he couldn't yet foresee.

"This is a pleasant surprise," Victoria said, standing beside him with her arm along his shoulders. He couldn't help noticing her warmth after the cold outside, and the way the curve of her hip pressed against him. "What brings you round today?"

McDuff looked up at her, enjoying the flush in her cheeks even as he wondered about it.

"The same reasons I usually come round to see you, Victoria. Business matters on the surface, of course. Personal matters increasingly mixed in. All that to say I'm pleased to see you as always. Should I ask why Cheryl Mallory decided to pay you a visit after all this time?"

Victoria sat beside him, shaking her head but with sad smile.

"She's an unusual girl. One I very much wish I'd gotten to know in a different way and time. She said she felt she should come by and apologize to me for the role she played in ending my first engagement."

McDuff was painfully aware of the impropriety of their situation, with no one else in the house besides Mavvie and perhaps kitchen staff. Not because he'd developed worries about what the upper-class sort might think of him.

Because the sadness, the regret, in Victoria's voice and eyes made him very badly want to hold her close and do his best to comfort her.

"That must have been difficult for you, Victoria."

"I wouldn't say it was pleasant, especially when I first realized who she was and why she was here. Talking to her was pleasant, once I convinced her to come in out of the rain. I'm sad to say I recognize the same sort of quick mind that's caused me trouble in the past. Even more sorry to say I've played a part in making her life that much harder."

"She is clever and curious. I've never forgotten how many books she had in her room the first time I was there. Her parents were lurking outside the door, and I was in a rather foul mood at being dragged out to Mayfair. Long ago when I thought it was a simple and rather personal matter that I shouldn't have to involve myself in."

Victoria shrugged. "You might have been better off then.

Before we formed our Odd Society and all descended into this madness together. She told me today her parents took away all her books. As a punishment."

McDuff scowled, his disgust with the Mallorys flaring anew.

"People like that have so *much* available to them. Limitless money and property and everything else compared to what most of us in this country have to scrape by on. And yet they would choose to deprive their own daughter of the simple comfort of her possessions. Of her books, which weren't simple in the slightest. At a time in her life when reading a book could bring her so much comfort. They think only of themselves."

He caught the slight narrowing in dark blue eyes that flashed anger, and a bare second later realized what he'd said. She spoke before he could attempt to apologize.

"They've apparently decided she won't be allowed to attend college, either. She's to struggle through her pregnancy, half-starved from the looks of her, give the baby up to one of those awful wealthy families, and become nanny or work at a finishing school or some such nonsense."

"I didn't mean to—"

She shook her head and stared out the window toward the wet, dreary gardens. He couldn't help noticing how she twisted a napkin in her lap.

"But it *is* awful, the way I behaved toward Cheryl. Toward Wilfred too, if I'm to be honest with myself about it. Toward you and Jean and Father Hall, and even Bertrand. I won't go as far as the guards, but I could add others to the list."

"You did the best you knew how, as we all do. Right or

wrong. I am sorry for what I said, Victoria. I wasn't thinking. I can't claim good behavior in the beginning, either. I assumed Cheryl enjoyed the games but didn't want the consequences when I first met her family."

Her hands relaxed in her lap, but she still didn't look at him.

"Do you think it's possible to atone for such things, Rob? Our horrible wrongs, or even our sins? Like Father Hall would be so glad to offer us in his confessional? Do you believe we're allowed second chances?"

"I certainly hope so. People have told me for decades I'm not responsible for what happened to Michael. I understand that much of the time. But so many of my choices have been because of him. For him. Sometimes despite him. Perhaps I've been trying to atone for that all these years. My own family's original sin."

Victoria turned to face him, and he couldn't understand her expression.

Not cold, not exactly. Not angry or hurt. But nowhere near warm or welcoming, or even friendly.

The tight, clipped of her words clarified it for him.

"What do you think my family's original sin is, then?"

McDuff lowered his gaze, staring at his half-finished sandwich.

He should apologize again, thank her for the tea, and leave. Whether it was his mood today, the conversation with Jean and Father Hall, or his worries dragging him down, he couldn't seem to say anything right.

Managing to *do* anything right in this moment—or even

the lesser goal of not doing anything wrong—might elude him as well.

"That's not what I meant," he said. "I know it sounded that way, but I don't see you and your family as like the Mallorys at all."

"No? What did you think of us that first day? When you were forced to speak to my father, then to me? Were you in a foul mood from being dragged all the way to Park Lane? Forced to involve yourself with such a trivial, personal matter as a disgraced young fiancé?"

McDuff's jaw clenched every bit as much as if he were standing in front of Chief Wells or even Superintendent Stewart. He didn't quite understand what was happening, but he suspected a wrong step or a wrong word could be just as disastrous here.

"I did not think that, not at all. For one thing, your father was cooperative and helpful rather than breathing down my neck. Insisting I produce the verdict he expected, and making sure I understood he could afford to pay me *handsomely* for doing so. Assuming he could pay me enough to sway my investigation, likely because he believed any working-class sod like me could easily be bought."

Victoria breathed in sharply through her nose.

"And did Mr. Mallory's money accomplish that goal, Inspector McDuff? Did he set the amount high enough to get the outcome he desired? Were you indeed bought?"

McDuff closed his eyes for a second, trying to stop himself before it all got worse.

"Do you really think that of me, Victoria? That I'd so easily be turned to that vile man's favor?"

She frowned, as if she was trying to find a way to stop as well.

She did as poorly as McDuff had.

"I don't know, Inspector. I'd somehow convinced myself you wouldn't accept payment in that way at all. Even though you've certainly arranged matters to my father's favor. Were you turned? Did you accept the money from Mr. Mallory, as you have from my father? Or did you refuse?"

McDuff stood, taking care not to scrape his chair across the rug.

He wouldn't give her the satisfaction of him acting like the coarse fool she seemed to believe he was.

He only wished she hadn't convinced him of it.

"You're right. I have helped your father, and accepted his money. I thought I was helping you as well. And yes, I did accept Mr. Mallory's filthy bounty. You'll be the one to decide whether to believe me or not, but much to his disappointment, I did not arrange things to suit him. He was most displeased with my final report. For all I know, he may have helped convince my chief to send Superintendent Stewart my way for my trouble."

Victoria stood as well, both fists planted on the table in front of her. McDuff suspected she wanted to strike him instead.

Angry as he was with her, he couldn't blame her.

He was every bit as angry at himself.

"That's not what I remember you saying before," she said, too loud. "Wasn't that bit of trouble because of my father's money yet again? When he tried to *help* you, correct? It seems your association with those of us who aren't noble working-class sods doesn't work out well for you."

"Whatever your father's intentions were, his trying to intervene likely did set Stewart on my trail. I was foolish enough to think that was something we could work through together. But you're well on the way to convincing me to reconsider my association with people who aren't my kind. It's certainly not going well today."

McDuff was dismayed to realize he'd nearly shouted that last bit, giving in too much to his tension and emotions. Victoria glared at him, fists clenched at her sides now.

"I said earlier you might have been better off before you ever set foot inside this house. Perhaps I was right. Perhaps we've all intervened in each other's lives quite enough."

"Perhaps you were right then, and even more so now. Good day, Miss Haversham."

McDuff turned on his heel and walked out, thankful beyond measure that Mavvie wasn't hovering in the hallway.

And that he knew his own way out.

He nearly yanked his coat from the hook, too furious to notice whether he slammed the front door or not.

The unpleasant surprise of a full rain did nothing to cool his temper.

He was several streets away before he realized he should have worked to derail the argument rather than helping escalate it. The most basic of his skills in questioning the lowest criminal, much less speaking with someone he cared for.

He hadn't even tried to ask Victoria what was making her so upset, a response that his thoughtless comments about the Mallorys surely didn't merit.

His heart ached at every step taking him further away instead of returning at once and attempting to make things right.

His pride—and not a small amount of shame at taking Mr. Haversham's money to go with the dreadful way he'd just behaved—kept him walking away.

CHAPTER 75

Victoria gripped the edge of the table until her fingers and forearms ached, struggling with a terribly strong urge to destroy everything she could reach.

Throw the teapot and mugs through the window into the gardens. Turn the remaining sandwiches and scone into mush between her fingers. Throw the tablecloth and whatever she could break off the chairs into the fire.

All of it absurd, and so wasteful.

And so much easier than having to spend one more moment thinking about what she had just done.

She managed to relax her grip enough to step back. To sit, and draw in a slow breath. Even to let that breath out without bursting into tears.

Was what Rob said truly all that upsetting?

Or was she reacting to her own horrendous and growing guilt about how she'd treated Cheryl Mallory? Not to mention Rob himself, and her friends?

She could dislike the idea all she wanted, but guilt about how her family used their wealth certainly played its own role.

Realizing the tray of sweets remained untouched, she leaned over enough to retrieve a dark brown square from a chocolate bar, then added a small lavender cookie.

Then shoved her plate away when images of Cheryl's gaunt-cheeked face floated through her mind, followed immediately by memories of near-skeletal men inside Fodelson, swaying children on the streets in rough parts of London, too many suffering across the islands of the Caribbean.

Even on Enceleas.

Victoria had within the hour stuffed herself to an unreasonable degree during the middle of the day, with dinner still to come. Her mother was planning at least three teas, with plenty of food at each.

Could she stand to be as self-centered and oblivious as her mother in this?

Victoria strode down the hall and turned toward the back of the house, picking up one of her father's black oilcloth umbrellas on the way out. The mist had developed into a true downpour that promised to echo her mood.

She hoped surrounding herself with the fruits of labor designed only to help others would soothe her a bit.

The rain pounding on the open umbrella drowned out her laughter that sounded too much like a sob.

Even her project making calming tonics for Michael and so many others confined in asylums were designed to benefit *her*, to create the funding and the excuse to get her back to the Caribbean. Maybe to create plausible reasons to take Rob and Michael and even Jean and Father Hall with her, to create her own Odd Society paradise far away from the judgmental eyes and ears of London.

The kind and caring aspects were nothing but side effects that she also leveraged to her own ends.

Driving Rob away with her misplaced anger and incredibly rude shouting would hardly advance her desires or his.

She saw Rob as a young boy, forced to cope with the death of his father, then his mother not long after. Struggling to help Michael when no one else cared or could.

And she'd taken out her guilt over Cheryl on him, getting far too angry over his words because they cut too close to the truth. She'd taken it out on a man who'd fought for what little he had, over her own misdeeds toward a girl who despite her distress still lived a life of wealth and safety.

Victoria closed the greenhouse door behind her and closed her eyes, drawing in a shaky breath filled with the lively scents of growing things, the sweet perfume of plants fooled into blooming during such a dreadful season. The rain sounded a symphony like a waterfall on distant Enceleas, bringing her so much closer to home in her heart and mind.

"Enough of this, Victoria," she said, opening her eyes and settling her father's umbrella beside the door. "Selfish or not, you *are* helping people. Selfish or not, you aim to help countless numbers more."

She walked along the central aisle of the greenhouse, not focusing on any particular plant. Gray skies overhead let her see only an oasis of muted green, broken by the flashes of color from their citrus trees from Spain and Italy.

The boilers held a pleasant, perfectly balmy temperature that did finally seep away the edges of Victoria's foul mood.

way plantations can operate. I feel the time of these indentured servants from India will be short-lived as well."

Victoria fought the urge to get up and pace rather than facing her father head-on. If she was to have even the slightest chance of saving Enceleas and herself, she mustn't show any weakness.

"I would make a fine plantation manager, you can't deny that. I can pay laborers, much like we do here. And acceptable pay would be lower there. With the demand we have building for these tonics, I can go further and offer generous pay. The houses are all already built, and the patterns and habits of the work established. You speak of how well Jaji knew the island. Well, that's something else I hold in my mind as easily as all these plants. I can't say that about anywhere in Africa or America."

He shook his head and looked to the side, toward where Victoria grew the most potent plants for her magic.

"It would simply be too much, even with your evident skills and knowledge and passion. I know you understand the requirements of importing well enough to grasp this. You simply don't want to."

"No, I *don't* want to, Father. I *won't*. You know how much I love Enceleas. You know how well established it is, how easy it would be to make the small changes for my needs. I've never been happier anywhere else in my life."

He looked into her eyes again. His were sad, but showing no signs of retreat.

"I do know that. I also believe you could be happy in England if you'd stop yourself from constantly planning and expecting to leave here. You may have been born on Enceleas, but you're an Englishwoman first and foremost. That's what runs in your blood, Victoria. *This* land. But you also burn with the colonial fervor, so that's why I mention America and Africa. You could build a home and a business in either place that would far surpass what can be done on that tiny island no one wants to ship to or from anymore. A home that suits you and your modern sensibilities far better than an old plantation house."

"Returning to Enceleas is what this has all been about," she said, waving her hand over the table. "All the study and learning and creating a demand, exactly as you taught me. Even finding people I trust who could help me once I get there. You'll leave me with nothing, Father."

He scowled, but Victoria didn't care.

"I hardly think giving you the means to set up your business after years of letting you *learn* the business is nothing. I don't have to remind you how many people in England and all over the world survive on a mere pittance. You're very intelligent, and better schooled in the ways of the world than many men. Don't let your nostalgia from years past cloud your judgement now."

Victoria got up after all, more willing to move around than she was to shout for the second time today. Or to pound her fists on the table.

"This is the only thing I've been working for. The only thing I've ever wanted to do with my life. I'll assume all the risk, in my own name if you'll permit it. Please, Father. Please don't take this from me."

"I'm quite sorry," he said, at least looking and sounding regretful. "I've thought this over a great deal over the past few the sitting area. Since you're here, though, we can get on with it."

"I assure you I didn't ask your fellows to leave us, any more than I did your fine matron. Curious how they all removed themselves from the scene on their own. In the interest of not blocking them from this lovely sitting area any longer than we must, I'll get right to my point. How does your brother Michael fare after his transfer?"

McDuff flashed a tight smile, reminding himself how this man had been badgering Victoria. Stewart would never let on how much he knew under any circumstances. And he undoubtedly knew more than McDuff imagined possible.

"My brother is much improved. Thank you for asking after him."

Stewart showed no reaction.

"A pity the guards who helped care for your brother at Fodelson Prison haven't fared nearly so well."

"They have had rather a run of bad luck from what I've heard," McDuff said. "After seeing how poorly Michael had been *cared for* at the end of his time there, I can't say I'm sorry about that."

Just as he had with Victoria earlier, McDuff regretted the words the second they left his mouth.

"And were you sorry about the two guards who died in an alley near the theatre district, Inspector? By rather violent hands from all accounts."

Where he'd felt the lingering cold from the day seconds before, McDuff now felt unpleasantly warm. He hoped the superintendent couldn't smell the sweat oozing from his pores.

A powerful urge to meet Stewart where he stood rather than continuing to dance away rose in him anyway.

"I never wish a man in a similar line of work to ours ill, sir. From what I understand, the two of them were involved in assaulting a young woman that night."

Stewart quirked one eyebrow for a second, then smiled. A reaction at last.

"That's correct, a Miss Victoria Haversham. A family you're quite familiar with if my information is correct."

McDuff looked away from Stewart's eyes for the first time, nodding and staring at his own case. Victoria had given him more than one of her trust charms not so very long ago, and he'd used a couple of them to good effect. At the moment, he wished she'd given him something far stronger.

And realized he might not use it if she had.

He'd grown tired of this game.

Either Stewart had him dead to rights or he did not.

Whatever that answer turned out to be, McDuff didn't want to play any longer.

"Yes, Superintendent Stewart. I do know the Havershams. I've worked with Mr. Haversham on a number of private matters. Now, as you said earlier, it would be best if we conducted our business quickly. Why don't you tell me your opinion of what that business might be?"

McDuff couldn't help but feel pleased when Stewart blinked, then narrowed his eyes.

"This business, Inspector McDuff, is determining whether you might have been involved with the beating deaths of those two guards first and foremost. That should be enough, but the

CHAPTER 77

The cold, clear sunrise found Victoria already in her greenhouse, working with a single-minded purpose. Sleep had eluded her despite her own best calming draught and more than one slumber charm Jaji taught her long ago.

She'd grown used to managing worry without staring wide-eyed all night long. The past several months had given her more than enough practice.

The disruptions of guilt and loneliness proved too much for Victoria's skill and determination. Anger at her father kept all her other discomforts tuned up high enough that her whole body ached today.

Besides the scarlet flowers she'd need to refresh Rob's charm, she'd brought out fresh supplies for bending her father's will to her own. Stronger than she normally used, with more intricate spells to keep them safe.

The work of returning her preferred suitor to her side

would be simple indeed compared with diverting her father from the madness of selling Enceleas.

Especially if he'd set his mind long before he'd mentioned it to her last night. That sort of entrenched, long-standing desire could be terribly difficult to alter.

She dreaded to even think of going through with it, but her own mind kept returning to her own business associates built up over the last few years. Unaware of her identity through her enchanted correspondence, but no less willing to work with her on a venture so likely profitable as what she created in this greenhouse.

Between those connections and access to her own substantial supply of money in her safe, Victoria could likely accomplish her goal without involving her father.

And lose all contact with both parents in the process. An outcome she deeply hoped to avoid, even after their attempts at marrying her off.

A long, loud complaint from her stomach made her realize she'd been out here long enough that breakfast would be ready inside, along with fresh tea. The cup she'd made herself hours ago and a slice of yesterday's bread had long since served their purpose and made way for a more substantial meal.

Victoria covered all the various flowers, leaves, roots, and seeds with a bright yellow square of silk, one she'd enchanted many times over many years. Anyone looking toward it wouldn't remember seeing it at all. The only thing they would remember would be a strong desire to remove themselves from the area.

She'd almost reached the greenhouse door when Mavvie

burst in, Father Hall and Jean hard on her heels. Father Hall looked solemn and imposing in his full black cassock, and Jean's severe brown dress made her even more impressive.

"I'm so sorry to disturb you, Miss Victoria," Mavvie said, slipping herself inside and closing the door, "but you have callers. Most insistent that they must see you. They say the matter is urgent and can't wait."

A chill deeper than the rush of air that followed Mavvie gripped Victoria's middle. Her stomach growled at the scents of fresh bread that came along, but none of that mattered now.

Her friends and their frightened expressions couldn't possibly mean anything good.

And Rob was not with them.

"It's perfectly all right, Mavvie. You'll remember we've received both of them before. They wouldn't cause such disruption unless something truly was wrong. Let me see if they need breakfast as badly as I do."

She stepped past Mavvie and opened the door, speaking before the other two could even walk inside.

"So good to see you both. I'm having breakfast brought out, would you care to join me?"

Jean and Father Hall drew back, and their wide-eyed looks would have been amusing under different circumstances. They looked as if the idea of breakfast had never occurred to them in all their lives.

"I'm afraid we must act quickly," Jean said, clutching at the side of her skirt where her pocket would be in trousers. "But we can eat while we talk if you like. We may not have time later on."

Now Victoria's insides felt like nothing more than sluggish, slimy rocks churning about. She doubted she'd manage to swallow a single bite.

Her hands shook as badly as her voice when she turned to Mavvie.

"Would you please have breakfast sent out for all three of us? Do you know if my father has left for the day yet?"

Mavvie nodded and glanced toward the house, clearly ready to be away.

"He has, Miss," she said, her irritation showing in her voice. "Talking about important matters he must attend to, no time for common courtesy. The same as the three of you."

When she'd gone, Victoria reached for Jean's hand.

"What's happened to Rob?"

"He's been arrested, Victoria," Father Hall said, taking her other hand. "This morning at first light. They at least waited until he was on his way to work rather than taking him at home."

They each grabbed one of Victoria's elbows when her knees threatened to spill her to the ground, slowly walking toward her work table.

"How did you…"

"A dear Anglican priest friend of mine attends to prisoners awaiting trial or transfer to prison," he said. "In an ancient, vile jail in of City of London's jurisdiction. They're never kept there long, at least not most of the time. Rob managed to speak to him as soon as he was brought in, then begged him to get word to me."

"Was he hurt?" Victoria said, trying to walk on her own, grateful when they kept supporting her. "I know what happened to Michael when he was arrested."

Jean shook her head.

"Not like Michael, no. I doubt they'd be that brazen with an inspector. But he did… He resisted them, Victoria. He fought them. So he'd been forcibly subdued when he arrived."

Victoria sank into her chair, covering her mouth with her hand.

Of course he'd fought them. Not out of fear, though that certainly played a part.

He'd fought them because she hadn't renewed the charm he'd asked her to make for him. She hadn't maintained the help and protection he depended on her to provide.

"He can't stay there," she said. "He'll keep fighting unless I can help him."

"What do you mean?" Father Hall said. "He doesn't seem the sort, not once you set aside that awful business with those guards. And they'd richly earned their fate."

"That's exactly the trouble," Victoria said. "He asked me to help keep his temper under control after that. To help him forget enough that his memories of that night wouldn't torment him. When I saw him yesterday, I didn't renew the charm. We were… We had a quarrel and he left before I had the chance."

Jean closed her eyes. Her hand seemed to move of its own accord toward the yellow silk covering Victoria's ingredients.

"I'm terribly sorry, Victoria. I was listening to you. I know you've done something to repel me from whatever you have on the table. I was trying to ignore it enough to get past. Terribly rude of me. Quarrels happen, that's understandable. But do you think his temper truly is worse now than it was before?"

Victoria nodded as she pulled the silk aside.

"Please, don't touch anything. These are potent and dangerous. It's likely his temper *would* be worse after being suppressed. That was his fear too, after he indulged it more than he normally would. Which he did at my request and with my participation. We need to get something to him, and we'll send letters or whatever it takes to whoever is holding him. I'll get started right now on the potions, and write the letters this afternoon."

"We won't have much time, Victoria," Father Hall said, and the sound of his voice nearly stopped her heart. "He's being transferred today to await his trial for murder. They're taking him to Fodelson. The same prison Michael came from."

A soft gasp escaped her, and now her heart felt like a great and howling pit in her chest.

"He *can't* go there," she whispered. "They'll know about all the guards, not just the first two, with the way this superintendent has been asking around. They'll know what Rob did. Or what *I* did, but he'll suffer the consequences for it."

"What we all did together," Jean said, her voice sad and low. "That's what likely brought all this on from what Father Hall's friend told us. Superintendent Stewart spoke to Rob at his boarding house last night. The interview didn't go well. So now this Stewart is insisting that Fodelson is where Rob must go."

Victoria realized the essential fact she'd missed a few seconds earlier.

"Murder? They're trying him for *murder*? And he's already being held, surrounded by policemen?"

Father Hall nodded, reaching for his crucifix.

"The situation is desperate for him, yes," he said. "I'm

afraid we'll have a difficult time reaching him now, and much worse once he's moved. If word is out of what Superintendent Stewart suspects him of, things will not go well for him in any prison. That one least of all."

Victoria pushed herself up, bracing against the table with her hands.

"Wait, did your friend mention Rob's chief? Chief Inspector Wells, I believe his name is. This Stewart isn't even with Metropolitan Police."

"I don't remember that name coming up," Jean said. "But we must assume the whole thing has been entered into record, so he may not be able—"

"We'll deal with that when the time comes," Victoria said. "If we can get Chief Wells on our side, that can only help. I sent him a package yesterday that should make that quite a bit easier."

She was surprised to see Father Hall and Jean flash relieved smiles at each other.

"So Rob spoke to you about that yesterday," Father Hall said. "About getting Chief Wells under your influence."

Victoria scowled and shook her head. "No, he didn't mention it at all. He wasn't here very long, to be fair. I had a guest, and then we…then he left soon after. I sent the package on my own before he arrived. But it may help us now."

"Then we must speak to Chief Wells," Father Hall said. "Perhaps I should be the one to do that, in my guise of Father Michaels. As a man of God I should be able to counsel anyone who's been arrested, so I won't draw suspicion. We'll still have a terrible time getting Rob away, assuming we can. We'll have to face those problems when the time comes."

Victoria heard the door open, and two chattering young women walked toward them. She was surprised to feel and hear her stomach demanding food again.

"I have an idea of what to do once we have him away," she said. "It won't be easy, but it may solve several problems at once."

CHAPTER 78

McDuff waited in a stone cell not unlike the one he'd left Michael in all those years ago back in Glasgow, wondering if his fate would equal his brother's at long last.

Damp walls and floor, stench of mildew and human bodies and everything that came out of them, amplified by an open privy pit in the corner. A narrow window so high it barely gave any light and no air at all. A hard bunk that would have hurt his hips and back even before he managed to treat himself to the finest hospitality his fellow policemen had to offer.

He wasn't quite as badly beaten as his brother had been that awful night. Not barely conscious, barely recognizable, and unable to understand what he'd done wrong.

He knew exactly what he'd done wrong, and he had no doubt what awaited him.

The various scrapes and bruises about his hands, face, and torso would seem like a tumble on soft grass once he was transported to Fodelson.

Where Superintendent Stewart had made it quite clear the guards would be eagerly expecting his arrival.

He shifted on the bunk, turning onto his side so he could see the hallway through the bars of his cell.

How many times had he consigned men and not a few women to this fate, convinced it was the only true and just solution? Then walked away without looking back, without a second thought as to how their lives played out.

More than enough to know he'd sealed his own fate the night before, when he made an ass of himself with Stewart.

He reached up carefully, not wanting to twist his aching and possibly cracked ribs. The flat lump of Victoria's charm raised a small spot, barely noticeable against his blood-stained white shirt but clear to his fingertips.

Had her magic stopped working for some reason, letting his temper rage last night and that morning worse than it had ever been?

Or had she quite reasonably cut him off from her protection the day before, when he'd begun his spectacular fall by yelling at her?

No matter.

It was done now.

Maybe they'd give him Michael's old cell for a bit of family tradition.

He slowly pushed himself into a sitting position—more a slumping position against the cold, damp wall—when he heard footsteps coming toward him along the gloomy hallway.

His worries about more than one smack on his skull affecting his vision faded when he finally recognized pale, ghostly faces taking shape. Both men wore the black clothing of priests.

And thanks be to Anglican and Catholic and every other sort of god, one of them was Father Hall.

McDuff tried to stand, but gasped at a particularly sharp pain in his side.

Father Hall rushed forward, holding both hands up and shaking his head.

"No, Rob, don't try to stand. You and I passed the need for such ceremonial nonsense the day we first met."

McDuff eased himself back, pressing one hand against the jagged ache. He now had a sickening headache for his efforts.

"Maybe so, Father. But I'd just as soon have the choice about whether I stand or not rather than my ribs dictating the matter. I believe I've managed to break at least one."

The Anglican priest—a much older man who helped McDuff when he was first brought in—scowled and shook his head as he opened the cell door. His Irish brogue rose and fell thicker than McDuff's Glaswegian.

"That's rich, son, saying you managed to break your own bloody rib. I've spent enough years ministering to the poor souls dragged in looking even worse than you to know how it's truly gone out there."

He stepped aside to let Father Hall pass, with a brief nod between them. Then he stood facing out of the open door while Father Hall settled himself beside McDuff.

"I can't say you're the most pathetic looking prisoner I've seen this year," Father Hall said with a grim smile. "But only because I'm acquainted with your brother. What have you gotten yourself into now, Rob?"

McDuff smiled, ignoring the fresh pull of split lips and bruised cheeks.

"My mother would probably have said I finally got round to following in my father's footsteps. She'd probably have a point, too. I ran my cursed mouth in front of the wrong man, that's all. The worst man I possibly could have. I knew better, and I did it anyway."

"I've never been a believer in predestination, not even for sinners such as ourselves. Are you in urgent need of care?"

An unwise chuckle followed by a pained grunt had McDuff pressing his side again.

"I'm in need of more care than an army of clergy and all the nurses and attendants at Michael's asylum could manage, Father. As for medical care, I believe everything will heal. More slowly than I'd like, but I don't expect I'll need a surgeon."

Father Hall nodded once and glanced back at the other priest, still standing with his back to them. He pulled a tiny bottle out of his pocket: no bigger than his smallest finger joint and full of scarlet liquid.

"First thing I'm supposed to do is give you this. Victoria told me a clever way to let you know what it's for, but I don't want to make you laugh again."

A spark of hope lit up the sadness and regret suffocating McDuff's heart.

"I'll take my chances. Please tell me what she said."

"She said both of you are in desperate need of renewing your charms."

McDuff nodded, closing his hand over the bottle in the middle of his palm.

"She's right about that. I'm glad to know Victoria is willing to help me at all."

Father Hall raised one eyebrow.

"This is only the smallest portion of what's she's done, what she's still doing. Jean as well, but for quite different reasons, of course. We know you're due to be transferred this evening, probably scheduled that way to keep us from finding out. We must act then to have any real chance of getting you away."

"Then how did you find out? About the transfer?"

"My long-standing connections within this building, most of all. Along with my current distribution chores and Victoria's brilliant writing skills, both amplified with her brilliant magic."

He reached into the huge pocket of his cassock again, pulling out several kerchiefs. Red, blue, and white, all folded into tidy squares. Victoria's vivid descriptions of what each would do flooded into his McDuff's mind. Red for hurting, blue for forgetting, white for calming and protecting.

McDuff shivered at the way Father Hall handled the scratchy red fabric filled with agony with no signs of fear or discomfort. He found himself relieved not to see a black-lace-wrapped vial among them, and distressed that he hoped Victoria would carry at least one.

"These are for you," Father Hall said, lowering his voice, "depending on what we may need to do during your transfer. We have the same, along with bottles full in case we can't get close enough for a cloth. I expected she would ask me to make sure you memorized what each one did. She assured me she'd do her best to shout what was needed. And, that you wouldn't need reminding."

"No, I don't need reminding. I know them by touch as well

as color. Probably will as long as I live. But I won't let her endanger herself on my behalf," McDuff said, even as he tucked the squares into his jacket's various pockets, with the red where he could easily reach them. "Nor Jean. I'd stop *you* if I thought you'd listen to me."

Father Hall's eyes flashed with real anger, and his voice carried no small amount of frustration.

"And exactly how do you plan to stop any of us with the shape you're in, and once you're bound and held inside a transport wagon? What you must do now is listen to me, and be prepared to listen to Victoria when the time comes. Agreed?"

McDuff reached up and gingerly touched a throbbing lump on the back of his head. Leaning against the rough wall kept it irritated, but he couldn't manage to sit up straight.

"My own efforts at keeping myself in operating order today haven't worked out well. I'll do whatever any of you tell me. But please, all of you, be careful."

Father Hall gently touched McDuff's arm.

"We will, Rob, I promise you that. So you'll understand what's happening, I've spoken to your chief inspector. With this Superintendent Stewart ordering you held in the City of London and the crime happening here as well, your chief says he can't legally halt the case against you. But I can tell you he's now convinced of your honest efforts to stop Victoria's attackers without hurting them. And of your complete innocence when it comes to the other guards."

"More of Victoria's work, I presume? I'm sorry to say the pain in my thick head is making all of this hard to follow."

Father Hall's lips drew back in a grimace, and he dug into his pocket again.

"I'm terribly sorry, Rob, I was meant to give you this first thing. Victoria's labors did bring your chief round, yes. But Jean contributed a healing and pain relief potion."

This time he brought out three thumb-sized vials full of blue-tinged liquid, nestled into another of the white cotton squares.

"One now." Father Hall worked the cork loose before handing it over. "Keep the rest for later. I'll admit I was worried about all of this being taken if they search you, but Victoria tells me she added something to your charm that will discourage anyone from doing so. Apparently they'll all feel they should trust you."

"If she can manage that, there's nothing in all of England she can't accomplish."

McDuff swallowed the liquid, pleasantly surprised at the sweet flavor and flowery scent. The sensation of his head being as nauseated as his stomach faded, and the various pains throughout his body receded.

He still felt like death dragged over broken glass and stabbed with white-hot pokers. But at least he could think.

Father Hall raised both eyebrows and smiled.

"If Victoria's larger plan comes to fruition, no person on Earth itself would be wise to doubt her in the future. For now, let me tell you what you must do to get through this night. And with any luck, away from London and all this madness afterwards."

CHAPTER 79

With winter-bright sunlight streaming through the windows, Victoria's third-floor workroom was surprisingly comfortable. The fire going in Jaji's bedroom actually managed to beat back the chill without endless rain stirring up the intolerable damp.

She stood in the middle of the crowded space, surveying the various clockwork toys on the shelves that surrounded her. The room was fragrant with the freshly ground components of the strongest suggestive magic she'd ever put together.

A masculine aroma this time, created with her choices of allspice flowers and a touch of cinnamon, but with a sharp pine undertone. Those touches would make the resulting objects more appealing to their targets, but her wish and her will would create the most powerful effect.

All of her minuscule jeweler's tools and her black velvet cloth waited, with her magnifying glasses set beside the rest. One of the colorful earthen jars containing Jaji's ashes—made to fit the curve of Victoria's hand and fired with her tears—sat on her rough wooden worktable.

Several smaller jars brought on the long, sorrowful voyage from Enceleas to England surrounded the larger one. They held soil, sand, and water, all collected by Victoria under Jaji's watchful and loving eyes. Her store of money in the safe with them—with profits from her business adding to them faster than she'd expected—provided a buffer in case different action was required.

Last of all she'd brought glass jars full of herbs, spices, and flowers grown by her own hands in the greenhouse, prepared that same morning.

Everything she needed to create and deploy the most important enchantment of her life thus far.

A life that felt oddly empty compared to where she stood right now.

She could hardly put the self she'd been a few short months ago—barely half a year—together with how she felt on this early winter afternoon. A grouping of the same tiny penguins she'd used that day brought it all back too vividly.

That furious young woman working in the oppressive summer heat, more of a girl, had been seething with resentment. Impulsive. Focused only on changing things to suit her wishes and desires, and damn the consequences for anyone and everyone else.

That girl hadn't cared one whit to destroy a man's reputation badly enough to send him fleeing across the ocean. Or to use an even younger and far more innocent girl to accomplish the task.

Victoria didn't deny for one second her relief at not

currently trying to endure a horrible existence as Mrs. Wilfred Abernathy. Or later as Mrs. Bertrand Robbins. She still believed without reservation that her parents had been wrong to try to force both men and marriages upon her against her will.

All of her self-focus had cracked and started to give way when she first visited Michael McDuff in the dreadful model prison. When she allied herself with Jean and Father Hall to create their Odd Society.

When, much to her surprise, she fell in love with Rob McDuff.

She touched a clockwork ballerina on a polished silver base. One that could never achieve the stunning effect of the mirrored version that could spin all its facets in different direction.

She then reached to her right and picked out two gleaming black clockwork locomotives: one with spring green highlights, the other with sky blue. Each not quite as long as her index finger, and barely an inch tall.

She sat, placing them on the black velvet cloth, and used the tiny pick to remove the rounded smokestack from the front. With the help of her magnifying glasses, she slid the pick inside and pushed to the side. The toy fell into two pieces in her hand.

The perfect miniature gears and rods inside truly were a remarkable feat of design and engineering. Nearly as much as the full-sized versions that carried people all over England, Europe, and even distant America. The rods and pistons would drive, the wheels would turn.

More importantly, the layout provided an empty space

large enough to hold as many of her fingernail-sized muslin bags as she could possibly need, already laid out and waiting. She disassembled the second locomotive and laid it beside the first.

Once Victoria had finished her preparations, the smoke-stacks would carry her fuel to exactly where it needed to go.

Using her silver spoon barely as large as a teardrop, she slipped four scoops of the pink and blue powdery mixture into two of the bags. She slipped the well-worn cork out of the clay jar of Jaji's remains.

Spoonsful of irregular gray ashes faded the powders already in place.

As she performed each precise and careful task, her lips constantly moved with whispered incantations.

A dusting of earth, a sprinkle of sand. A tiny eyedropper meant to refill fountain pens added a single drop of Enceleas water.

Despite the intense focus Victoria depended on for such demanding work, images of Rob kept invading her mind. She saw him as wasted and scarred and confused as Michael, as disfigured as those two guards in the alley.

Imagined his howls of fury disintegrating into cries of pain.

All the while knowing her charm had failed him, that his trust in her had proven disastrous. Getting hauled away beaten and weak because he'd risked his life trying to protect her from an *engagement* of all things.

She caught one of the tears she couldn't seem to stop on her fingertip, transferring the crystalline drop into one muslin bag. One more for the second, and she pulled the single threads that closed them tight.

For the first time, Victoria didn't draw upon this most powerful magic while thinking only of herself.

She tied the tiny bags inside each of the locomotives, close to the smokestack and away from the forest of miniature gears. The pieces went together with faint but solid snaps. Victoria pushed each toy back and forth on the desk, making sure everything still turned as it should.

When the time came, each would turn and move exactly as she willed it.

She held both locomotives in her hands, pressing them gently to her lips as she whispered the last words before she sent the newly created magical objects on their way to do her bidding.

"Jaji. Hear me now. My love is deep…" She swallowed hard, doing her best to fight back too many tears to contain. "My love for you is deep and eternal. And now my love for this man is deep, and my need for this man is strong. Please, help me to protect and save us both."

CHAPTER 80

That afternoon, time stretched and twisted and turned itself into the longest day of Victoria's life. At the same time, she felt each minute and hour racing away from her, fleeing before she could even begin to catch hold of it.

She couldn't possibly get all of her arrangements made in one day. Much as she hated to admit it, she could only manage so much, even with magic.

The best she could do was get enough in motion to have a chance to help Rob, and Jean and possibly Father Hall if they'd agree. Herself in the end if all went well.

She pretended calm when her father arrived home for tea, less than an hour after he should have received her special delivery. Her relief when he mentioned having a meeting here not long after was easy enough to pass off as surprise.

So when the calling card for Mr. Steven Winston arrived, her insistence on delivering it to her father in his office herself surprised no one. They weren't back to the normal comfort between them after their argument the night before, but no one could doubt how much he trusted her when it came to business.

She'd done everything she could to lay the groundwork for him to trust her with so much more.

He sat at his desk, flipping through letters she recognized, though she made sure he never caught that it was all written in her own hand.

"You may wish to join us for this meeting, Victoria," he said, glancing up at her. "This Mr. Winston takes an unusually keen interest in the Caribbean and has done for months now."

"Like I do, you mean?"

He stopped shuffling the papers and looked directly at her, smiling the slightest bit.

"Like you do. This may prove to be a good opportunity for all of us."

Victoria nodded. "I'll get refreshments ready."

She took the chance to scan his shelves, but she didn't see the locomotive. He must have left it at his main office, which was just as well. She'd spelled both toys to make memories of them fleeting and difficult to hold onto, as she always did with paired enchantments. That precaution had served her well until Rob recognized the pattern in several toys scattered across the city.

In any case, neither she nor her father needed the clockwork carrier of her will any longer. Its magic had already been spent.

The rest was up to her.

She arranged the flowers she'd prepared earlier in his wide brass vase, with the multi-petaled burgundy blooms of allspice that he loved so packed in across the top. The flowers carried a spicy chocolate aroma that mixed nicely with the earthy notes she added to the water.

So early in the day wasn't the proper time for sloe gin, no matter how much her father enjoyed it. A hot tea against the brisk wind outside covered curious scents and tastes.

Victoria had barely finished arranging everything on her father's desk when Mavvie knocked softly at the door.

"A Mr. Winston is calling for you, sir. He seems a bit… well, starry-eyed and excited might be the kindest way to put it."

Victoria had been in the process of swaying Mr. Winston into line months ago, when she deliberately turned his attention toward the Caribbean. Right before Rob had brought himself, Jean, and Father Hall into her life and her plans. Mr. Winston's shift toward her interests had proven long lasting from what she'd heard lately.

Victoria's father smiled with barely suppressed enthusiasm of his own. She had no doubt he expected Mr. Winston to solve all his problems at once.

She only hoped both men solved many of hers.

And despite knowing neither she, Jean, or Father Hall could act until after dark, her nerves thrummed with certainty that time to save Rob grew desperately short.

"By all means, show him in," he said, waving Victoria toward one of the chairs in front of his desk. "Perhaps we can send him on his way in an even better state of mind."

Mavvie moved forward to retrieve the tray, exactly as Victoria knew she would. And with it, she took the enchantment that would make her an integral part of Victoria's plans in a splash of milk that appeared quite accidental.

Victoria's father gazed at her quite seriously when they were alone. Almost sadly, as if he regretted the disappointment soon to come.

"You do understand, my dearest Victoria, that I've never had anything but your best interests at heart."

"I know, Father." She smiled and looked at her hands held tightly together in her lap. "I wouldn't be the person I am today without all of your help and guidance. And your protection."

He beamed, apparently considering their squabble of the night before resolved and behind them. She hoped to make the same determination this afternoon and forever more.

Her father stood when Mr. Winston walked in. Victoria resisted her usual insistence on standing as well, shaking his hand, being taken seriously as a businesswoman in her own right. This was a time for observation and subtle direction

Mr. Winston stopped just inside the doorway, nodding so deeply he nearly bowed.

The effect was most impressive with his tall, lanky frame putting him at well over six feet. Slender though he was, he gave no appearance of weakness. His healthy sun-kissed complexion spoke of recent time in a warmer land.

Victoria expected he'd be able to load the heaviest of containers onto his own ships, then sprint to the front to take the wheel himself when it was time to set sail.

His shock of blond hair—sun-bleached lighter than Father Hall's even in winter—was cut short enough to stand up all over his head like a rounded halo. But his sharp green eyes were anything but soft and angelic.

"Mr. Haversham, thank you for meeting me on such short notice. Time is often of the essence in these matters, and I appreciate you for letting me take up a bit of yours. In that spirit, I'll dispense with the pleasantries except to your lovely daughter."

The briefest of nods from Victoria, faintest of agreements from her father, and Mr. Winston was off and running.

"I'm sure you've heard I'm changing course in my business, so to speak, not with the whole thing, but with enough to make a difference and set tongues wagging on at least two continents. Not getting out of America or Africa, no matter what you may have heard. Only making certain I supply the needs of folks still working in the Caribbean. That area was mighty good to a lot of us for generations, not simply going to abandon it when a new fancy snaps its fingers."

Victoria's father had apparently been watching for him to take a breath as intently as she had. He spoke more deliberately than he normally did, as slowly as Mr. Winston's words sped merrily along.

"Understood, Mr. Winston. Great fortunes have been made in that part of the world, great fortunes indeed. A fine foundation for our empire, I must say. The focus has shifted a bit over time. I expect it will continue to do so. I would agree, however, that it makes sense to have all of our options open."

Mr. Winston grinned, looking more like one of the sharks that prowled the warm waters around Enceleas, and probably entirely aware of the resemblance.

"I'm pleased we're in agreement, then. The reason I'm here

today is I'm interested in working with other smart businessmen who have a base in the Caribbean. And men who understand even when times change, it makes good sense to maintain our success and our standards. I know you have a solid sugar plantation, one that's produced well for you and your family for a respectable stretch of time. I'm aware of how that market has changed, though, despite what my competitors might believe. I don't happen to believe the solution is to cut and run and abandon everything we've built. No, I'm convinced the smart money is on making certain our assets can shift right along with the market."

He paused, this time for more than a breath. He was waiting for a sign of how Victoria and her father were thinking. An ideal time for her to play her advantage in the situation.

She took the opportunity to take a long drink of her tea, rightly predicting that both men would follow her lead. Swallowing more than enough to leave themselves susceptible to her wishes.

"A well-developed asset can often be…leveraged," her father said, almost ponderous in his speech. "Turned to a different purpose when conditions and timing are right." He glanced at Victoria. "Or perhaps passed along to someone who has the vision to make that adjustment. And of course, the ability to manage the asset and insure it survives and thrives far into the future. Assets do want managing, Mr. Winston, else they'll fall into disrepair and not benefit anyone."

Mr. Winston drew back, his eyes comically wide. If anything, he spoke even faster.

"I'm afraid we're speaking at cross-purposes, Mr. Haversham, not an efficient use of our time, not at all. I understand you have competent management in place at your Caribbean property. More than competent, from what I've been led to believe."

A fast, hard series of knocks at the door made the two men jump and look that way. Victoria turned as well, but she wasn't the least bit surprised.

Mavvie had only followed her compulsion to check the post on the hour, and a stronger compulsion to make sure Victoria's mother received it right away.

Victoria's mother in turn simply followed an irresistible urge to open an ordinary seeming letter, one Jean had helpfully posted earlier.

The contents alone would have served to alarm both her mother and Mavvie, as deeply as writing the words distressed Victoria. Mrs. Haversham's obsessive need to inform her husband of the letter's contents would overcome any reluctance to interrupt a meeting in progress.

When Victoria's mother opened the door without waiting for an answer—a bold move Victoria was certain had never happened before—her father scowled as he stood.

"I'm terribly sorry, Mr. Winston. I must see to my wife at once. Please excuse me."

Victoria knew an uncomfortable thread of worry twisted through his mind, because she'd placed it there.

Her mother grabbed his arm, pulling him closer and whispering low enough that Victoria could only hear a faint hiss. They both glanced at her, then stepped out into the hall and pulled the door closed.

CHAPTER 81

Before Victoria could take up her role as a diversion while her mother explained the dire situation to her father, Mr. Winston leaned toward her, his eyes sharp and gleaming.

"I must say, Miss Haversham, it was your business in calming tonics that drew my attention to this opportunity. What you're accomplishing here in England's rather challenging climate has been remarkable. With reliable shipping routes and far superior growing conditions, you could build something extraordinary."

"However did you hear about my little enterprise, Mr. Winston? We haven't exactly put the word out to the general public."

As far as she knew, even the people who'd heard of what they were doing associated her work with her father's name. An unfortunate necessity in London society that she could tolerate for her own purposes.

He smiled and nodded once.

"That's how I got myself ahead in *my* business, Miss. Keeping aware of what's happening now, yes, and understanding what's happened in the past. But the most important thing is knowing what's about to happen."

"That's a skill I'd like to cultivate more of for myself. And you're absolutely right. Enceleas would be the ideal location for expanding my operations, if I had a reliable shipping partner."

Her father pushed the door open hard enough that it shuddered in its frame. Victoria caught a brief glimpse of her mother, red-eyed and dabbing at her cheeks before she pulled the door closed.

"Right, Mr. Winston," her father boomed as he hurried to his desk. "We've had a bit of an emergency situation come up. Please forgive me for the interruption."

Mr. Winston stood at once, leaving Victoria wanting to grab his arms and pull him back down again.

"Quite understood, Mr. Haversham. We can certainly reschedule for—"

Her father frowned. "No, you mistake me. Or perhaps I'm not speaking clearly, this is not… It turns out I may very well need your services. With arrangements made today, if at all possible. And if we can conduct other business, that may make this entire procedure go more smoothly."

Victoria held her breath for a second, hoping she did indeed have some idea of what her immediate future held. She drew the peace and comfort of Enceleas around her as closely as she could and still concentrate.

She would need all of her strength to act her emotions without falling too deeply into them.

"May I ask what's happened, Father? Or, perhaps you'd like me to step out."

"This concerns you far too much for me to ask you to leave," he said. "But I must ask you to keep yourself in check. I know very well how sensible and level-headed you are. But some events test all of us to our limits."

Victoria didn't have to act her worry and concern. She nodded.

Instead of speaking to her, her father turned to Mr. Winston.

"All right, Mr. Winston. I'm going to ask you an important question. I want you to answer honestly, and to make certain you can live with the answer for a very long time."

Mr. Winston looked at Victoria, then her father.

"As long as you don't try to force me to answer in a specific way, I'll be honest with you."

"I'm glad to hear that. How closely do you insist on being involved in what cargo is shipped on your vessels?"

Mr. Winston tilted his head sharply.

"Are you asking me if I insist on inspecting every single item that's brought onboard? Or whether I'll turn a blind eye to outright theft?"

Victoria's father rested his hands on his desk, fingers splayed wide.

"I would never ship stolen goods. Never. You can rest assured on that point."

Mr. Winston shrugged. "In that case, I believe we'll be on the level."

"And with that threshold for honesty met between us, will

your shipments and perhaps passengers be maintained in the strictest of confidence?"

"Again I must ask, sir," Mr. Winston said, with the light of challenge in his eyes, "will this be a victim of kidnapping? Or a desperate fugitive wanted for treason on the high seas?"

"Neither of those."

"Well then, with those modest requirements, we should be able to conduct our business successfully, Mr. Haversham."

"One last question, if I may. Can you have a sailing for Enceleas arranged quickly? Within a few days at the most? I assure you your diligent effort in this matter would be well compensated. This speed and discretion would work in your favor in any agreements between us."

"I have a ship loading at this moment to sail for Antigua sometime before the end of the week. That's next door in nautical terms. I can arrange an adjustment in cargo. And in personnel, if need be."

"We may be nearly agreed on our initial business, then." He looked at Victoria, and her breath caught of its own accord at the worry in his eyes. "We've had a rather unfortunate incident involving a…a good friend of the family. A misunderstanding that's gone rather badly over the course of the last few weeks and especially today. I would like to see this friend aboard your ship headed for the Caribbean and away from here."

Victoria gasped, covering her mouth with one hand. Her heart clenched anew at how badly things had indeed gone for Rob that morning. So much of on her behalf, or at least encouraged by her.

Mr. Winston watched her for a few endless seconds before he answered.

"I see how this has affected you all. Once we've come to an agreement on my fee, I'm certain I can help relieve your minds and deliver your *friend* safely to a kinder climate."

He shifted in his chair, sitting straighter, holding his head a touch higher, squaring his shoulders. Clearly feeling the balance of power between himself and Victoria's father shift in his favor.

The two men focusing on each other and letting her operate more openly worked in her favor.

"What I would ask of you, Mr. Haversham, is whether I'll be investigating a new shipping route while on this all-important journey. And how you'll handle the apparent uncertainty about management of your property there."

Victoria's father darted a quick glance at her before focusing on Mr. Winston.

"It's true our manager has expressed interest in returning to England. I was rather hoping you would have someone in mind from your own organization."

"*My* organization?" Mr. Winston flashed a sour smile. "What I have in abundance is men at home on the sea, the sort who barely want their feet to touch solid ground before they're off again. None of them would agree to staying in one place in the Caribbean or anywhere else. In fact, I wager they'd see it as a punishment and react rather badly. Have you no one you can trust to the management of your property there?"

Victoria froze, staring down at her own hands, gathering all of her effort and concentration. Directing both men toward thoughts of her. Playing on her father's knowledge of her: her love of Enceleas, understanding of his business, growing proficiency at her own.

And yes, her obvious closeness with Rob.

For Mr. Winston, she gathered his surprising and useful awareness of her operations in the greenhouse. His apparent interest in helping her own business succeed, along with his own.

"I'm afraid the change in management has caught me rather flatfooted," her father said. "I'll have to conduct a search to find a reliable man for the position. Perhaps our friend will be able to function in that capacity for us while I seek another."

Victoria forced herself to breathe slowly and keep her face calm as she looked up at her father. His brow wrinkled, but not in anger. He knew what he was proposing made no sense. His eyes kept flitting toward her and away again.

She shifted all her efforts toward Mr. Winston.

"Has this person you have in mind taken up a study of the work that running a farming enterprise in the tropics requires?" he said, surprise clear in his voice. "Supplies and labor and cooperation with other islands, not to mention managing everyone who lives and works on Enceleas? Is he known to those who live there? And comfortable with the surroundings and culture?"

Her father crossed his arms on his desk and leaned forward. He pointedly avoided looking at Victoria now.

"These all sound like skills you possess, Mr. Winston. Are you not interested in the chance to possess your own property in the tropics? Where you can have a steady income of your own, a place to retreat to when weather is foul here at home?

Perhaps eventually retire to? Something to hand down to your children?"

Mr. Winston shook his head slowly.

"It seems to me, Mr. Haversham, that you already have someone quite close to you who possesses all of these skills. And who has shown a talent for creating and growing a new business interest from rather humble beginnings. To the point that a lack of opportunities and…shall we say *support* is slowing her down."

He stared boldly into her eyes, and cold certainty gripped her.

Mr. Winston was indeed interested in being on her side. With a possible and disturbing impression of wanting to be *by* her side, as not just a business partner.

Her skin crawled at what she was certain was considering look on her father's face.

While Mr. Winston was nowhere near as loathsome as the first two men he'd paired her with—not to mention far closer to her own age—he was not and would never be her own choice.

Most importantly, and most simply, he was not Rob McDuff.

And yet…

Playing along with this distasteful game might get her into a much better position to help Rob, and eventually arrange matters to suit them both.

"What exactly did you have in mind, Mr. Winston?" she said, raising her chin.

He had the grace to politely incline his head rather than leering at her.

"I suggest we begin by continuing to get acquainted with each other. All three of us, of course. I'll remove this friend of yours far from England with no one the wiser, and take the opportunity to explore Enceleas while I'm there. One or both of you would be most welcome to accompany us on the voyage, with a chaperone acceptable to you both as needed. That way, Miss Haversham, you can get to know how I run my business and how it could work harmoniously with yours in the future."

Victoria kept how very well she knew Mr. Winston's business—and how successfully she'd already manipulated it—to herself.

Keeping her elation at his suggestion of such an elegant solution to so many of her problems to herself proved far more difficult.

"We would definitely have to agree to a traveling companion," her father said, "as I wouldn't be able to make such an extended trip at the moment. I'm not certain what the long-term prospects for the Caribbean will turn out to be, so I make no promises there. But what we've discussed thus far seems reasonable to me. Enceleas has been in my family for generations, but I myself do not know it as well as Victoria does. She's far more interested in continuing our involvement there."

"This is acceptable to me as well," Victoria said. The time for letting these men believe they made all the decisions had passed. "I have two people in mind who would make excellent companions if they're agreeable. My father is correct. I'm not ready to abandon the lovely island of my birth. Mr. Winston, may I ask you to please let us know exactly when you'll be sailing?"

She turned her magical focus to match her desire that Mr. Winston remove himself at once. This meeting had more than served its purpose.

She had vital matters to attend to this evening.

"Of course, Miss," he said, unfolding to his impressive full height. "I'm sure you'll need time for packing and organizing and all. We'll be away for near on four months, possibly longer depending on arrangements in the Caribbean, so prepare yourself for a long absence. Please be aware this is a cargo vessel, powered by the wind rather than steam. Slow and often rough sailing this time of year and for our return. I'm afraid we'll have nothing more than a few staterooms aboard, none of them as fine as what you're used to in first class on a great steamship. You may of course consider my own cabin as your own. I'm never afraid to take my rest among my loyal men."

"That's a most generous offer, Mr. Winston," Victoria said, lowering her eyes as her modesty would dictate. The truth was she much preferred a working ship for this voyage, without the endless social trifles and obligations and general nosiness of a grand crossing. "My companions and I are grateful for the passage and not particular about accommodations."

Victoria's father stood, an odd little half-smile on his face.

"You'll find my daughter is quite the accomplished traveler, Mr. Winston. We all have busy days ahead, so I'll see you out. Victoria, please wait for me so we can discuss our own plans."

Victoria closed her eyes when they left, raising her own teacup laced with calming and clarity herbs, spices, and spells to her lips. She finished the last sweet dregs, then whispered.

"Thank you, Jaji, for clearing the path before me."

She'd walked into this room hoping to secure rescue and

safe passage for Rob, and to slow her father's efforts to sell Enceleas away from her forever. She'd expected to leave to do her best to rescue Rob while still working to secure her own passage to the Caribbean in the near future.

Now both her father and Mr. Winston expected her to prepare for the amusing *horror* of not returning to England for an unimaginable stretch of sixteen weeks.

If things continued to fall her way, she'd happily depart these shores and stay away for as long as she could imagine into the future.

CHAPTER 82

McDuff had no idea how many hours had passed in a haze when he tried to push himself back up into a more or less upright position.

Light still drifted in through the narrow windows, so it shouldn't yet be time for his transfer. The stench of the privy pit and his own foul sweat were certainly stronger than before, or perhaps his battered nose had miraculously opened up a bit.

Despite the hard bunk, he still felt like he'd slept a whole night through and maybe another day on top of it. The rotten, furry taste in his mouth certainly matched sleeping off a particularly rough evening.

But he didn't exactly feel refreshed. And the various wounds and injuries all over his body sang out louder than they had before.

A low murmur of conversation down the hallway reminded him that noise cutting through the quiet had woken him to begin with.

The same Anglican he'd first spoken with earlier came into dim view first, but Father Hall wasn't beside him.

Chief Inspector Wells was.

McDuff held his breath and once again tried to force himself to stand. This time a massive, bone-deep cramp in his left thigh defeated him. An uncomfortably vivid memory of one of the policemen who'd arrested him driving the point of his boot into that muscle explained it.

No one said a word while the priest unlocked the door. Rather than standing guard as he had for Father Hall, he nodded once at McDuff and walked away.

Chief Wells only stared at him for what felt like a long, slow lifetime.

"Didn't quite believe it when I heard," he finally said, still standing in the cell door. "The great Inspector McDuff coming to such a rough, humble spot. I'm not certain I believe it even now I'm looking right at you."

"If it's not true, sir, we're both suffering from the same hallucination."

The chief crossed his arms and leaned against the bars.

"I never liked this business of policemen hiring themselves out as private security. Yours isn't the first case I've seen go wrong. But I like the idea of City of London Police picking up one of my men without the courtesy of letting me know beforehand even less."

"I truly am sorry, sir. I've caused you distress, and I've disgraced the entire department. That was never my intention."

"The hell of it is now that you're here, it's nearly impossible for me to do anything about it if I decided to. Tell me one thing, McDuff. Why the hell did you push at Superintendent

Stewart that way? You had to know who he was, and you more or less drove him to take harsh action."

McDuff closed his eyes, trying to nod without grinding the think lump on the back of his head against the rough stones.

"I knew who he was. I have no excuse, sir. I had a difficult day as we so often do. But I let it affect me and follow me home. I do know better. Same as I knew better this morning when they picked me up."

Chief Wells leaned forward, peering at McDuff's face.

"I can see from here they were none too gentle with you. You're closer to your patrol days than I am, so I won't tell you what generally brings that sort of reaction on. You may have been asking for it, but that doesn't mean it was appropriate for them to follow through. Certainly not with a fellow policeman."

A thin whisper of hope drifted through his belly, but McDuff pushed it away.

"These were my decisions at every turn, sir. I don't blame any one of them for reacting the way they did."

Chief Wells uncrossed his arms and slowly walked over, sitting on the bed like Father Hall had earlier.

"You don't blame any of them, you say?" he said. "Any more than you blamed the prison guards who tormented your brother so?"

"I…I'm not sure how to answer that, sir."

"Then do your best to tell me the truth, McDuff."

McDuff turned away, pretending to examine the cracks and ridges in the wall beside him. Wishing he had any idea what was in the letters Victoria had sent to Chief Wells that very morning.

"There were some, sir, who treated him horribly. Finding out any of them had come to a bitter end wouldn't bother me overmuch."

When he turned back, Chief Wells stared into space himself.

"I wish I'd known how bad it truly was for your brother in there. The report I've lately read describes how his mind was… impaired in some way during his last arrest. Between that and the injuries he brought with him to the asylum, an unpleasant, grim picture takes shape."

"Yes, sir. He's in a better place."

Chief Wells locked gazes with McDuff.

"And you'll be in the worst possible place this evening, won't you? Right into the belly of the beast that nearly destroyed your brother. A beast that harbors even more dangerous suspicions about you than reality holds."

McDuff forced every trace of hope and optimism Father Hall had brought out of his mind. He wouldn't do himself any favors by pretending he wasn't afraid.

"I don't expect my time there will be easy."

"No. Nor will your passage from this jail to Fodelson Prison. The only thing I have to say to you is I regret ever mentioning you to Superintendent Stewart. We draw a line between our two departments for very good reason. I lost sight of that somehow. Lost one of the best inspectors I've ever had as well."

He got to his feet, looking up at the window set high in the wall. The light outside had noticeably faded while they'd been talking.

"Interesting thing. The route from here to Fodelson runs

entirely through Metropolitan Police jurisdiction. This jail marks the edge of City of London's territory. Take care of yourself, McDuff."

He turned and walked out of the cell and down the hallway without a backward glance.

By the time the priest came to ask if McDuff needed anything and lock the cell, he had nearly convinced himself that Chief Wells meant nothing by his words. Only an awkward way to try to offer comfort and as much of an apology as he would ever manage.

Nothing more.

He was likely to live out whatever days he had left in the same hellhole that had nearly destroyed his brother. Paying for his many sins the same way he'd sent others to pay for their own. He'd known that was the risk when he agreed to walk into that alley and wait for Victoria.

But the bright sliver of hope still twisted itself through his heart.

CHAPTER 83

Victoria was surprised to see her mother walk into the office with her father a few minutes after Mr. Winston departed. She could easily count the number of times she'd seen her mother inside this most masculine of spaces.

Not because he forbade it, certainly not with as often as Victoria was welcomed in. Mrs. Haversham had a firm belief that her husband could enjoy full control over this space, since she had unlimited control over every other space in the house and on the grounds.

Or at least it comforted her to believe that.

She sat beside Victoria, blinking back tears and lips trembling.

"I've asked Mavvie to bring fresh tea for all of us," she said. "Unless you'd prefer sloe gin, Victoria? To calm your poor nerves from the dreadful shock."

Victoria let the full extent of her worry for Rob float back toward the surface, in her downcast eyes and sorrowful voice.

"Tea would be best, Mother, thank you. I'm afraid anything stronger would leave me quite useless. Please, tell me what's happened to Inspector McDuff?"

Her father sat with a great sigh, shaking his head.

"It seems our friend has met with great difficulty despite my efforts to protect him. I believe it's our duty to do our best for him now. He was taken into custody this morning, and he was not treated kindly."

Victoria let a few tears slip through, struggling mightily to keep them under control. That slight relaxation of her iron-willed reserve left a frightened cry of worry for him rip through her heart and mind.

Her mother patted her arm and dabbed at her own eyes.

"Then he must be on Mr. Winston's ship and away," Victoria said. "His treatment will not improve if he slips further into the hands of police and prisons and disappears."

Her mother fluttered her hand against her chest.

"He wouldn't end up in a dreadful prison, surely?"

"On two charges of murder?" her father said. "He may at that. Victoria, are you certain you wish to accompany Mr. Winston on this voyage to Enceleas? The only thing I know about him besides his shipping business is his odd choices in shifting his focus over the last few months. And he's clearly interested in you as a match."

This time her mother gripped her arm, and not gently.

"Why would you go to Enceleas, Victoria? And with a man not well known to your father or I? I've heard nothing about such a match."

"I wouldn't be going *with* Mr. Winston," Victoria said. "I'd be going along to accompany Inspector McDuff in this difficult time, as well as to acquaint Mr. Winston with Enceleas and how we may work together in the future with my own business interests."

She touched her mother's fingers with her own, waiting for the painful grip to ease.

"This was divine providence, Mother, don't you see? We were all in the right place to provide help when it was desperately required. Even Mr. Winston stands to benefit from agreeing to help a man he never heard of before today."

Victoria stopped, remembering Rob telling her how he'd seen her clockwork toys all over London, eventually tracing them back to her. Mr. Winston might very well recognize him. He couldn't be anywhere near the gifted investigator Rob was, but he'd managed to find out about her business.

All the more reason for her to get herself onto that ship to keep any suspicions under control.

Her father got up to get himself a glass of rum. For the first time in Victoria's memory, he held up a glass toward them, eyebrows raised in a question. She and her mother shook their heads, both without any trace of surprise from the offer.

"We have many tasks ahead of us before we could even begin to discuss this," he said, "but I don't believe for one second that you're interested in Mr. Winston. Or that you'd be any happier than you were with…those other two. Your traveling with Inspector McDuff, however, might prove to be a far greater temptation."

When he turned with the drink in his hand, he didn't look annoyed or upset like she expected. He only seemed curious.

Her mother surprised her even more, leaving her wishing for a bit of rum of her own after all.

"If I'm to agree to any of this, Victoria, you simply *must* have a traveling companion. One who understands how such things develop. The two of you seem to have grown quite fond of one another. I'm concerned about a great many things when it comes to our inspector, but his dedication to you and keeping you safe is not one of them. It seems reasonable to me that we must all do the same for him now."

Victoria had been working for months now to bring her parents around to accepting Rob, through his example of protecting her and through her own magic. Still, realizing her own unintentional behavior may have done more of the work instead took her aback.

"Yes, well," she said, trying not to babble and certain she was blushing furiously, "I admit I enjoy Inspector…*Mr.* McDuff's company rather more than I did either of my fiancés. I wouldn't want to presume anything more than that right now."

"That's wise of you," her father said. "We still have matters to arrange before anyone boards a ship. There's the challenging problem of his being held in police custody. Let us work to resolve that and discuss the rest on a calmer day. What we must decide right now is how to make sure he even has the option of leaving England."

He sipped his rum, then stopped himself in the act of reaching for his pipe. Victoria herself didn't mind the earthy fragrance of pipe tobacco, but her mother was far more of the Queen's attitude about all forms of smoking. Yet another reason for her to avoid this room.

She recognized her chance to escape at once.

"Victoria, I know you have even more worries than the rest

of us do at the moment. But if you're determined to make this voyage, may I ask who you prefer for your traveling companions? Once that's settled, I would be glad to begin arrangements for packing for the trip."

A twist of dread mixed freely with the churning anxiety in Victoria's belly. Of course she would have to gather her belongings, in very short order, all while making sure Rob was well enough to travel and hidden enough to have the chance.

Add to that the necessity of packing her workroom herself, along with intending to be gone for much longer than several weeks, and the few remaining days before departure felt entirely too short.

"I'd thought of my friends from my charity work," she said, putting the rest out of her already crowded mind. "Miss Appréndia and Father Michaels. They've been such a help to me, and they're more than thankful for your financial support, Father. There are many troubled souls and orphans they could minister to there, and much they could learn."

Her mother raised her eyebrows and gave an approving smile.

"Very well, I find that *most* reassuring. A man of faith and a woman dedicated to helping others. In that case, I'll have your trunks brought out for airing this very evening."

She stood, resting her hand on Victoria's shoulder.

"We'll do everything we can for him."

When she closed the door on the way out, Victoria turned to see her father pouring a touch more rum into his own glass, then preparing a glass for her. He'd never even offered to do such a thing before.

She accepted it and waited for him to sit across from her.

"This may seem an odd time to mention this," he said, "but I must say how much you've grown and matured over these last few months. I would have hesitated to even discuss the idea of your going off to Enceleas alone a year ago. Much less with a young man you're clearly affectionate toward, though he's certainly been a great help to our entire family. I can only assume the difficulty of your two engagements pushed you out of the sheltered life you've known."

He sipped his rum and sighed deeply.

"And for that difficulty, I'm the one to blame. Such arrangements were already a bit old-fashioned by the time you were in college, I know. I suppose times have changed even more in recent years. The truth is you'll be the one to inherit such wealth as I possess, and you're creating a healthy business of your own. You won't need anyone's financial help. Your mother and I have discussed this a great deal, and it's more important to us that you be happy."

Victoria took the chance to take her own drink, not worrying about pretending she'd never tasted it before. The line of heat tracing from her mouth and all the way into her stomach steadied her.

Something fundamental had shifted between her and her father without her notice, perhaps after their argument the night before.

Perhaps the idea of possibly seeing Rob lost to all of them, over actions he'd taken *for* all of them.

Or, perhaps her father was telling the truth. The last few months had matured her. Shifted her needs and desires.

The next several weeks only promised to accelerate that process greatly.

"I appreciate that, Father, I truly do. It has certainly been a year like no other in my life."

"If you're lucky, my dear, each year will bring you that sense of adventure. I hope with nowhere near the same level of strain. Now, we must see to Mr. McDuff's safe delivery." He brought out the letter than had so alarmed both him and Victoria's mother. "I shall petition this Superintendent Stewart at once in hopes he can be made to see reason. Otherwise, we'll engage my barristers and judges to bring this nonsense to an end."

Victoria finished her rum, not sharing her own thoughts on the matter. Her father likely could manage to save Rob from a trial and possible death sentence.

But too much potential damage waited for him within the walls of Fodelson Prison.

Even one night was far too much risk.

The vital work of her evening—stopping any of that before it ever started—would begin once she was away from here.

CHAPTER 84

McDuff waited as long as he could, but not long after the light finally faded from his cell windows, he swallowed the second of Jean's healing tonics. His discomfort again receded, and the fresh taste cut through the rancid gunk in his mouth.

Unfortunately far more traces remained than before.

The catch in his ribs had only grown worse, to the point that he suspected at least one was more than cracked. And an ache lower on his side along with a decidedly bloody tinge when he managed to relieve himself in the privy pit worried him even more.

None of that boded well for his ability to participate or even move himself from one place to the other if Victoria's daring rescue and escape actually happened.

Not that he should even be hoping for such a thing, not with the risk it would put her and his friends under.

But the past few months had given him a habit of hoping.

Of thinking things would get better for him as opposed to staying in the same dull rut. A dangerous habit, indeed.

Even more uncomfortable was knowing how much he depended on others to get him through the next few hours. He'd spent a lifetime working very hard to make sure that was never the case. Now his only choice was accepting a new reality.

A faint light moving along the thick darkness of the hallway turned out to be the jail priest with a lantern.

"Mr. McDuff, they're nearly ready for your transfer. Is there anything I can do for you?"

"You can forgive me before I ask, Father, but I've forgotten your name. I'd like to know it since you've been so kind to me."

The priest smiled, all at once looking twenty years younger.

"I'm Arthur Ryerson, and there's nothing to forgive. You've had a difficult day. I shouldn't like to make promises I'm in no position to keep, but I've known Father Hall for a long while now. He cares a great deal for you, and he'll do his very best to make sure you're treated well."

Father Ryerson put the lantern on the floor and sat beside McDuff, bracing one arm around him.

"Please tell me if I'm hurting you," he said.

McDuff tried not to, but he gasped and cried out at the gentle lift.

"It's not you, Father Ryerson. There aren't many parts of me that don't hurt at the moment. I appreciate your help."

After an increasingly painful few minutes and with an embarrassing amount of assistance, he finally stood upright, holding on to the cell's bars to keep himself that way.

"You should have seen a surgeon," Father Ryerson said, retrieving his lantern. "Anyone should when they're brought in so badly beaten. The lot that arrested you can be counted on for such abuses every time. And a policeman yourself at that. But I'm not the one to make those decisions here."

McDuff checked his pocket, making sure Victoria's folded squares were still safely tucked inside. He'd pulled out her charm earlier and coated it with the scarlet liquid as best he could before settling it against his skin. The tiny bottle joined the larger empties down the privy pit.

"I gave them every reason and excuse they needed to act the way they did, Father. And I'm hardly an innocent myself."

"Innocent or not, you deserved better. Are you able to walk?"

McDuff steeled himself for a recurrence of the agonizing cramp in his leg and took a few shuffling steps forward, still holding the bars. The muscles threatened, along with most everywhere else in his body.

But he could move under his own power.

Slowly.

"I wouldn't mind you staying close by," he said. "I think I can make do if you have the patience for it."

Father Ryerson stepped into the hallway, holding the lantern high to provide more light.

"I'm sure Father Hall could tell you how this work builds patience, especially in a place like this. I'll stay by your side as long as I'm able. In case I don't have another chance to tell you so when our ride is over, I wish you well, Mr. McDuff."

McDuff smiled, wondering how long since someone called him that rather than Officer or Inspector. No matter what happened over the next few hours or days or years if he was lucky enough to have that long, those days were behind him now.

"Thank you for your kindness, Father Ryerson. I wish the best for you as well."

They made their slow and unsteady way down the hall and out of the jail, and McDuff went to face his uncertain future.

CHAPTER 85

Victoria did her best to hold herself still that evening, waiting outside beside the towering post box in the front garden. The street had been quiet since she watched the family carriage roll away, taking her father off to an unusual late supper away from home.

Nothing more than the streetlights trying their best to banish shadows that grew thicker of their own accord.

After her parents' startling pronouncements about her feelings toward Rob—and even more startling lack of immediate disapproval of him—her mother complained of a headache. Likely brought on by supervising the retrieval and airing out of Victoria's trunks and bags.

That was certainly possible, with the way luggage grew musty in storage. A more likely explanation was Victoria's gentle suggestion through words and magic that they should both make an early evening after a challenging day.

A similar suggestion that her father join friends of his

rather than dining alone was just as quickly taken and acted upon.

Victoria once again carried a bag full of everything she might need, or she hoped she'd gathered enough supplies. This wasn't her dainty opera bag, but a great sturdy thing over a foot tall and nearly twice that width.

When she caught herself wishing for a stiff-sided case like Rob carried, she had a terrible time getting herself calm and steady enough to arrange everything within.

A heavy black woolen cloak kept her warm enough now, and should keep her concealed enough when the time came.

Jean was bringing not only her healing charms—which she lately showed more skill with than Victoria had—but she was also stockpiling as many medical supplies as she could find. Rob might be injured badly enough to need treatment at hospital.

And yet, that much exposure might prove too dangerous.

For better or worse, Father Hall had experience treating minor injuries or seeing them treated from his work with needy men.

And Father Hall's carriage should have already been here, had to arrive before Victoria's nervousness twisted her into a useless state.

She tried to draw her house on Enceleas to her mind's eye, to draw upon the soothing calm it always held.

Instead, she saw the rainy, foggy street from yesterday as clearly as if she'd gone back in time.

Victoria even glanced up at the faint stars overhead, expecting the vivid scene in her mind to spring to life. Her mind's eye saw Cheryl Mallory crossing the street with her awkward but determined gait. Cheryl eating as if her life depended on it, which it probably did. Her life and the babe she carried.

Cheryl saying she'd go anywhere but England if she had the option.

The option to help a young girl in distress—especially since Victoria had caused the distress—made a great deal of sense if she could arrange it in time.

The vision faded at the sound of hooves on cobbles. Father Hall's coach arriving at last. The first time she'd be inside without Rob either across from her or pressed close by her side.

A change that did not bear thinking about. She needed all her composure and concentration.

She climbed into the cramped interior before anyone could step out to help her. A small lantern inside revealed the worried faces of her friends.

Jean wore her usual trousers with a dark shirt and a man's jacket, and Father Hall's normal cassock seemed to disappear in the dim light.

"Everything arranged, Victoria?" Jean said. She had her own black medical bag at her feet.

"Arranged better than I ever expected. If we all make it through this night, we'll have passage to Enceleas by the end of the week. Mr. Winston seems to have an idea it will be a courtship voyage, which I didn't expect until he nearly said as much."

Jean shook her head, muttering in rapid French under her breath before raising her voice.

"I do hope your father hasn't already promised you to him."

Victoria smiled, surprised the expression came to her so easily on such a night.

"You may find this as hard to believe as I do, but both he and my mother seem to have had a change of heart. They both insist I have traveling companions, to be sure. Because they expect any courtship taking place will be between myself and Rob."

Father Hall nodded and smiled himself.

"That's a bit of diligent effort on both your parts that's paying off at last, likely in more ways than you realize. I'd imagine Rob made a good impression to go along with your magic."

"As he often does," Victoria said. "Until the last twenty-four hours, anyway. We'll still be ahead of the transfer, won't we?"

"According to Father Ryerson, we should have a good twenty minutes to get prepared. Chief Inspector Wells confirmed the route as well. Turns out he doesn't appreciate one of his inspectors getting arrested, beaten, and charged with murder before anyone bothered to mention it to him."

"He is aware of the role *he* played in this disaster?" Jean said. "Asking this superintendent to harass Victoria and eventually Rob?"

"He understands," Father Hall said. "When I spoke to him, he'd only just been informed. I'm not afraid to admit he was angry enough to frighten me."

"Our best result would be for Superintendent Stewart to underestimate how angry all of us are," Victoria said, staring out the window onto the deserted streets. "I only hope none of them expect trouble along the way. I still wish we could simply block their coach with ours, break one of their wheels, and be done with it."

"That's where the possibility of them expecting trouble comes in," Jean said. "Even with the one lowly prisoner, if this superintendent is angry enough, there may be several guards on board."

"Father Ryerson tells me that would be most unusual," Father Hall said. "Since dangerous criminals are always shackled, he generally takes this ride with them alone so they feel free with their confessions. Rob is in no condition to be violent. But I agree. We can't take chances that might get him treated even worse, or further injured in the struggle. Not that I want any of us to be hurt if we can possibly avoid it."

The rest of the drive passed in silence, with all of them likely reviewing their plan and their roles. Victoria certainly did, doing her best to spot anything that could go wrong. Jean and Father Hall each checked to make sure they could retrieve the charmed vials and kerchiefs Victoria had given them, in shirt and trouser and cassock pockets.

She'd done her best with a dress made with pockets on the sides for vials, and more than one of the fabric squares concealed quite inappropriately in her bodice.

She couldn't help wishing Rob could help them plan. Even with the challenges they'd had back in the alley with the guards, he'd kept much worse from going wrong with his understanding of how wicked men behaved. He'd likely understand his fellow policemen even better.

The neighborhood where the driver finally slowed was more shops than houses, selling more working class goods rather than the fancy and expensive items available near Mayfair and Park Lane.

Sturdy work clothes, kitchenwares to withstand long and constant use. More durable canvas and woolen fabrics instead of delicate laces and silks. Row upon row of brick and wooden buildings crowded close along the curving street, the rising and falling land creating shadows deeper than Victoria was used to navigating.

She wasn't familiar enough with the area to know when they were getting close, but she felt the carriage slow, and her heartbeat speed up in return.

Father Hall sat forward, examining their surroundings before he nodded to himself and crouched beside the door.

"Here's where we'll wait for the police carriage to come by. The driver will go to the next side street and turn to keep himself and the carriage out of sight."

He touched Jean's hand, then Victoria's, and crossed himself.

"Take care, and God be with you."

CHAPTER 86

McDuff opened his mouth for a careful breath as soon as he and Father Ryerson stepped outside the hulking red brick jail. The coal smoke and fresh, chilly air after the dank reek inside was worth the stab in his ribs.

A massive gray coach waited under the lamplight, with two huge horses already stamping their feet with impatience to be off. Theirs was the only noise that broke the eerie silence of the city around them.

Two City of London policemen in their full blue round-hatted regalia stood beside the coach's closed door. Neither was known to McDuff, and both refused to meet his gaze. He was deeply grateful they weren't the much older and far more brutish men who'd so vigorously arrested him that morning.

Father Ryerson walked them forward, one arm still supporting McDuff round his waist. The policemen nodded once at the priest before one of them reached up and opened the coach door.

Superintendent Stewart stepped out, balding head gleaming in the light, a slithery smile on his angular face. His black greatcoat billowed around him like a shroud.

Father Ryerson squeezed McDuff hard enough that he couldn't fight back a grunt of pain.

"Mr. McDuff," Stewart said, standing to the side and waving one arm toward the door. "Seems only fair that I should accompany a fellow policeman on such a momentous journey. Especially since I'm the one responsible for sending you."

"Sir?" Father Ryerson said, frustration clear in his voice. "I'm not sure I understand. Mr. McDuff needs to speak to me alone, as all prisoners have the right to do."

"Nothing to worry yourself about, Father," Stewart said. "You'll still have your traditional honor of attending to the condemned man along the way. I realized I simply wouldn't be able to rest unless I accorded our former inspector the respect he's earned."

McDuff shook his head. "It's quite all right, Father Ryerson. My sins are well enough known. I reckon I'll accept this honor for the occasion."

He pressed his free hand to his ribs, then slid it down into his jacket pocket. The scarlet cloth felt faintly sticky under his fingers.

In his half-crippled state, trying such a move against Stewart was almost certain suicide. The man was undoubtedly armed with a club, possibly even a Webley revolver as some night patrollers were these days. But McDuff couldn't take the chance that Victoria, Jean, and Father Hall were actually planning some sort of foolhardy rescue of him.

He'd rush gladly to his own death if he could prevent harm from coming to any of them.

Victoria most of all.

He and Father Ryerson took the last of their painfully erratic walk. When they drew even with Stewart, Father Ryerson spoke sharply.

"*No, Mr. McDuff.*"

Rob withdrew his hand from his pocket—where he had indeed wound the rough fabric through his fingers—instead reaching up to brace himself against the carriage door.

"I'm sorry, Father?" he said.

"Only that I'll steady you up that step. I'll not have you fall right here in front of the jail on my watch."

Stewart laughed, the sour sound of it curdling the air.

"Oh no, we mustn't let the prisoner come to any sort of harm while he's in our care. Of course I can't possibly speak for the guards at Fodelson Prison, since they're outside of my control or influence. Please, take all the time you need. We're well ahead of schedule."

One of the officers stepped forward, silvery handcuffs in one hand, nearly identical leg irons in the other.

"He can barely walk, sir," Father Ryerson said, his words tight and clipped. "Is this truly necessary?"

Stewart stared at him for several seconds, then turned to McDuff. Who refused to give him the satisfaction of showing discomfort on his face or in his stance.

"I suppose we can dispense with the leg irons, though I doubt they'll give him the same courtesy at the other end of his road. He gets the cuffs."

When the officer tossed the leg irons into the front of the

carriage and moved closer, Father Ryerson all but snarled at him.

"You'll do that when he's inside."

Without waiting for a reaction, Father Ryerson helped McDuff step up, taking almost all of his weight. The strain on his deeply bruised thigh and twist to his side and everywhere else still took McDuff's breath, but he didn't make a sound.

Four small lanterns showed an interior more sparse than even the church's coach. The floors, walls, and benches were bare wood painted blue, with thick iron rings set in several spots. The surfaces looked clean, and the sharp vinegar smell of recent cleaning lingered. He didn't want to think about what may have been spilled there to need scrubbing away.

As soon as McDuff settled as comfortably as he could, the officer laid the cold half-loop of metal around one of his wrists. He slid the loop into the flat lock, squeezing until it was too tight for McDuff to pull his hand back through. As if he had the strength for such a feat.

While he repeated the operation with the second loop attached by a single chain link, McDuff stared at him. In the end, the policeman looked up, holding the gaze for a long moment.

He shook his head the tiniest bit before climbing out of the carriage.

Now that he had the handcuffs on his own wrists for the first time—preventing him from moving his hands more than a couple of inches apart—McDuff could no longer pretend the dreadful weight was only because of the steel.

Superintendent Stewart wasted no time getting in and sitting across from McDuff and Father Ryerson.

"There now. That should take care of you, the state you're in. We'll enjoy our ride in comfort compared to having you in leg irons as well and chained to your seat."

"Your generosity is truly magnificent," McDuff said, now focusing his stare on Stewart.

"You must understand I had no intention of hauling you in for murder," he said, crossing his arms as the coach jerked into motion. "Only doing a favor for an old friend. We're all under much harsher scrutiny these days, and a few of us damn well should be. Like those men you removed from the population, for a very good example. But as far as I'm concerned, the sort of thing you did isn't an issue unless you make a habit of it. Especially if you do so in City of London territory."

He shook his head, and his features took on a downward, sorrowful cast.

"Where you crossed the line, Mr. McDuff, was pushing me last night as if I was no more than a politician or a nanny sent to inconvenience you. Acting as if you were not accountable to me or any other sort of law. That I cannot allow to stand."

McDuff shrugged, carefully. "And now I'll take my reward for making Fodelson Prison, City of London, and the whole of England a better place."

Father Ryerson shook his head, obviously not liking the turn of the conversation.

"I'm fine, Father," McDuff said. "I've had my say, but rest assured Superintendent Stewart here will make certain he has his last word."

Stewart inclined his head.

"Indeed I will, Mr. McDuff. I believe it will be the guards at Fodelson who will speak last and loudest. If you survive there long enough, which I doubt, the hangman's noose will put an end to you and all your flippant words."

CHAPTER 87

JEAN WAS UP and out of Father Hall's still-moving carriage the second he opened the door. Victoria wished yet again she'd had time to procure trousers of her own or borrowed them from somewhere as she gathered her skirts and followed. At least her dress was smooth, tough cotton, with no fiddly bits to get caught on rough edges.

The carriage kept its same crawling speed, with the driver half-turned in his seat to make sure they were safely on the ground. As soon as Father Hall stepped out and pushed the door closed, the driver sped the horses back up to a steady pace and away.

They'd stepped out into a cozy and humble shop district, in the midst of a collection of clothing establishments. The silence was as thick as the sulfurous aroma of coal smoke gathering in the air, and the cobblestones shone as if they'd been carefully polished.

The faint street lights revealed tailors, shoemakers,

milliners. Everything one could need for daily life that didn't involve a never-ending stream of exclusive teas and parties and corsets that crushed a woman's lungs half to death.

All the things Victoria missed wearing from her childhood on Enceleas, and hoped to wear for the rest of her life.

She and Jean hurried to the side of the street, hiding their bags in a deeply shadowed area in front of a cobbler's shop that specialized in heavy work boots. Father Hall concealed himself in a dim spot on the other side.

No sooner had the church's coach faded away when a renewed jangle and clop of an approaching carriage took its place.

"They're early," Victoria said, reaching into her bag. She pulled out a slim knife and harness she hadn't wanted to wear or secure in the moving carriage.

"If that's them at all," Jean said. "Does Father Hall know you've brought a knife?"

Victoria shook her head as she strapped the harness around her forearm, over the healed scar one of Michael's guards had given her to remember him by. With the black leather, it shouldn't be visible against the underside of her arm. Her cloak would conceal it completely.

"I haven't mentioned it to him, no. I hope I don't need to use it. But after my last experience with such things, I had no desire to rely on my usual gentle methods."

Jean shook her head, pulling out a short, wicked-looking blade she'd somehow hidden under her belt.

"A woman who can kill with a spell isn't limited to gentle methods," she said. "Any more than an intelligent woman is unwilling to prepare for whatever might happen." She slipped the knife back into place, staring down the direction they'd come from. "I don't like that they're early."

"No. And they may be counting on that keeping any interference off balance."

Jean's coat nicely concealed slender hips and girlish breasts, and her short curly hair wouldn't draw a second glance.

"Are you ready to play your role, Monsieur Marchér?" Victoria said.

Jean smiled, her excitement plain even in the darkness.

"*Oui*, mademoiselle. My apologies in advance if our performance causes you harm. These cobbles look none too soft."

The coach swung into view, with two policemen seated high at the front, their rounded hats unmistakable with the metallic accents catching the light. Victoria saw no signs of other guards, but she had no way to know how many might be riding inside with Rob.

The way they'd devised to find out—and to possibly *draw* them out—felt more dangerous than walking into the darkened theatre district alley with two furious drunken men on her trail.

Jean gripped her upper arm, and Victoria wondered if her friend could feel how much her body trembled and thrummed. They needed to time this perfectly.

When the coach was about fifteen yards away, Jean yanked Victoria forward, nearly dragging her off her feet.

"Vile strumpet!" Jean yelled, her voice guttural and deep, her harsh Cockney accent near perfect. "I'll not put up with the likes of you n'more!"

Any further shouts were drowned out by the high shrill of the horses' startled protest and the clatter of the carriage coming to a stop. Victoria didn't have to pretend to cower away from the huge heads rising and falling so close to her own.

"You'll have to move along!" one of the policeman called, his hands firmly on the long leather reins. "Stop blocking the road here."

Jean turned the two of them toward the carriage, raising her chin and standing tall.

"Take 'er with you, then, get her off me hands! Won't have 'er dragging round me house no more."

The second policeman stood, fisted hands on his hips.

"I don't bloody care what sort of domestic squabble you've gotten yourselves into. We're not on patrol tonight. Step aside and let us complete our official business, or we'll run you both in."

"Please do run me in!" Victoria cried, pulling away from Jean as hard as she dared. "To jail if you must. He won't see *reason* when he's like this!"

Jean pulled her closer to the horses, then pushed her to the street. One of the great beasts blew through its nose and stepped backward, making the harness jingle.

"Here now, that's quite enough." The officer who wasn't driving climbed down, drawing out his club. "We don't have time for this nonsense, but don't assume that means I'll put up with it."

From Victoria's spot curled up on the cold cobbles, surrounded by the thick scent of horse, she saw Father Hall step into the street. He moved through the shadows as if he was made of them, stalking alongside the coach from behind.

"Don't much care what *you* got time for," Jean said, swaggering up to the policeman. Victoria didn't have to see to know she already held one of the glass vials full of excruciating pain in her hand. "Think you got what it takes t'stop me, come on and take your chances."

A muffled shout followed by the loud smash of the coach's door flying open drew everyone's attention, just in time to see Father Hall stagger back and land sprawling on the cobbles. Rather than pressing her advantage as the policeman turned away, Jean dragged Victoria away from the stomping hooves.

The coach shifted as a balding man in a swirling black greatcoat stepped out to loom over Father Hall lying dazed on the street.

Superintendent Stewart.

"Having a problem out here, are we?" he said, moving to stand with his feet on either side of Father Hall's body. He drew his club out slowly enough to make certain everyone saw the light gleaming off the shiny black paint. "All cleverly staged distractions aside, I say this man trying to interfere with police business is more than a trivial distraction."

Victoria got to her feet and inched toward the policeman standing with his back to her, drawing out one of the red kerchiefs.

A man dressed like Father Hall launched himself out of the coach, yelling in a heavy Irish accent.

"Can you not see he's a man of God?"

Stewart swung his club up, but stopped short of impacting the priest's face.

"What I see, Father Ryerson, is two men hiding behind the *cloak* of the church. With you the only man who could have shared the schedule for our prisoner transfer tonight. And strangely enough, these two louts and our prisoner's visitor from this afternoon have intercepted us. Care to explain yourself?"

Father Hall shifted on the ground, moving his legs and grabbing at his chest. His body twisted with horrible, wrenching coughs.

Jean stepped closer to the coach, working her way around the opposite side from the group of men.

Victoria's heart pounded so hard her vision pulsed with dark spots as she shadowed the policeman in front of her.

Was Rob not in the coach at all?

Or was he hurt so badly he couldn't even cry out?

Father Ryerson tried to push the club aside, only to have Stewart shove him back against the open coach door with the length of wood at his neck. The pressure distorted the Father's voice, but he still managed a shout.

"Let me tend to him, man! You can't mean to let him choke to death on the street!"

"Haul him into the coach, then. I'm sure they can find space for him. Likely you too, once we encourage him to confess."

The driver set the handbrake and climbed down on the same side where Father Hall still struggled to draw breath.

The officer closest to Victoria turned and noticed Jean, now crouched near the back of the coach.

He lifted his own club and walked toward her.

Victoria followed, agony in hand.

She heard Father Ryerson bellow into the night.

"I'll confess my sins to God the Father, *never* to the likes of you!"

Victoria darted forward.

Slapping the cloth over the policeman's face, hard enough to stagger him.

She ran toward Jean before he drew breath to shriek.

The coach rocked on its springs, and an ear-splitting scream from within.

Victoria and Jean rounded the corner.

Rob McDuff threw himself at Father Ryerson and Stewart, tumbling all of them nearly on top of Father Hall.

A deafening shot rang out, sending the horses into a frenzy.

CHAPTER 88

McDuff lay stunned, face against the freezing cold cobblestones.

Chest and legs on something warm and soft.

Arms wrenched and miserable underneath his body.

He had no idea where the gunshot had come from.

And couldn't do a damn things about it even if he did.

Not when he was more than half-convinced he'd be better off if the unknown shooter's bullet had found him and put him out of his misery at last.

He felt the body below him twist, then move away, leaving him to lurch against the hard stones.

At least they were cool against his feverish hot flesh and now the rest of his body.

Even if they seemed to be preventing him from ever drawing a breath again.

Shouting trickled through the ringing in his ears, voices he couldn't keep track of.

Someone grabbed his shoulder and wrenched him onto his back.

Forcing his mouth into a silent scream.

"Rob! Look at me!"

McDuff opened his mouth again, dragging in enough breath to finally put sound to the countless white-hot flares of pain all over his body.

The jagged moan came nowhere near doing it justice.

This time hands touched his face.

Hands too soft and gentle to belong to Father Ryerson or even Father Hall.

He forced his eyes open at last.

Victoria.

Victoria knelt beside him, tears streaming down her cheeks, landing on his skin.

"What the hell did you do?" she cried, stroking his forehead.

This time his voice came out raspy and week.

"I think…I must have thrown myself…out of the coach. Stewart, where is he?"

Victoria glanced at something beyond McDuff's head. When she looked back, her eyes were hard.

"Senseless on the street behind you. With any luck, he won't recover. Can you sit up?"

Father Ryerson moved into view than on his other side. His chin, cheek, and forehead were scraped down one side, purpling into a bruise underneath.

"I'm sorry, Father," McDuff said. "Your face."

"Nonsense, Mr. McDuff. You did the only thing you could, though you probably shouldn't have with the shape you're in. Support under his back, Miss."

McDuff was panting by the time they had him upright and propped against the coach's wheel. Other sounds seeped in then as he tried to understand what he was seeing. Several policemen seemed to be turning people away as soon as they tried to gather around the strange tableau.

Father Hall sat cross-legged not far away, with Jean crouched in front of him. Jean looking very much like a man, wearing a man's jacket that flared over her trousers.

One of the policemen who'd been driving the coach knelt beside Superintendent Stewart, who was indeed flat on his back and muttering.

The other officer squatted nearby, holding his face in his hands and coughing. His visible skin was bright red.

"Can you help him, Victoria?" McDuff said, keeping enough of his wits about him to not say more. "The policeman?"

She scowled at him.

"And leave you here suffering?"

He reached for her hand, only then realizing he was still handcuffed.

"You can come back to me. I dearly *hope* you come back to me. But ease him first."

She stood without another word, drawing a white cloth in one hand and a blue one in the other.

McDuff nearly went senseless himself when Chief Inspector Wells walked up beside him.

"Chief Wells, sir? I don't understand."

Wells leaned down with his hands on his knees, peering at McDuff the same way he had back in the jail cell. Then he squatted himself. Father Ryerson touched McDuff's shoulder and walked toward Father Hall.

"Once I saw you hurl yourself toward the superintendent," Chief Wells said, "I knew it was time to step in."

"It was you that fired a gun."

Wells pulled a black Webley revolver with custom wooden grips from his pocket.

"Seemed a reasonable move with all hell breaking loose."

McDuff watched Victoria talking to the red-faced officer, helping him hold the white cloth to his nose and mouth.

"But why were you here at all, sir?"

Wells looked toward Superintendent Stewart, finally attempting to sit up, but without anyone's assistance.

"You crossed the line, McDuff. More than one. But my *old friend* there went to the extreme when he repeatedly interrogated a young woman within Metropolitan Police boundaries without clearing it with me first. The same young woman who has rather effectively staged your rescue, if I'm not mistaken. Stewart crossed lines even more so with arresting you for murder. Then in case I might not be angry enough, he let his specially-chosen thugs beat you worse than a common criminal. So, I decided letting them haul you away to Fodelson was a line *I* wouldn't allow *them* to cross."

McDuff barely managed to whisper a question he was frightened to ask.

"What does that mean for me, sir?"

"I expect it means you'll have to get yourself out of his sight. Take the opportunity she's given you. And keep yourself away. Whether I like it or not, if you stay in London or anywhere nearby, I won't be able to protect you. If you stay after I've told you not to, or try to return, I won't make any attempt to do so."

Victoria now held the silky blue kerchief close to the policeman's face, and she seemed to be whispering into his ear. McDuff had no doubt she and Jean had more than enough of those silk squares with them and ready to go.

"I can do that, sir. Thank you, and I truly am sorry."

Wells shook his head.

"That's not necessary, McDuff. Thank me by getting yourself away from here. I assume your brother will go with you."

"That's the plan."

"Good. Now let's get you on your feet."

McDuff turned, trying to grab the coach door with both hands, and drew in a sharp breath through his teeth.

"Why he bothered with cuffs with you in such a state," Chief Wells said quietly before he raised his voice to a shout. "Get the keys here, now!"

The policeman who'd been watching Superintendent Stewart attempt to haul himself upright was beside McDuff in a flash, and had the heavy steel loops off a few seconds later.

"Before we haul you upright and cause you more damage in the process," Chief Wells said, "what's hurting you?"

McDuff tried not to laugh, pressing his hand against his battered ribcage.

"It would be quicker to say what isn't hurting, sir. But the worst is my ribs at the moment. I'm afraid one must be broken."

Chief Wells reached down and pushed McDuff's hand harder against his ribs.

"Putting pressure on it helps?"

"Yes sir. There if nowhere else."

"Then it's likely not broken. Probably still hurt like the devil for a while, can't do much about that. My men and I will keep the crowd at bay until you leave. You have my word none of us will speak of any of this. And no need to call me sir, McDuff. You don't work for me or for Metropolitan Police any longer. Understood?"

That quiet pronouncement somehow rang louder in McDuff's head than all of Stewart's threats of Fodelson, or even the harsh reality of spending the day in the disgusting jail.

The pang of regret twisting through him bit deeper than he could have imagined.

"Understood. I'll be out of sight as soon as we're away from here. And out of reach shortly after."

Chief Wells and the policeman who'd removed the cuffs had McDuff more or less upright with less discomfort than he expected, though he couldn't say he felt stable on his feet. He still managed to walk to Victoria's side just as the City of London policeman she'd been speaking to stood, shaking his head.

The young man's eyes seemed to slide over McDuff's face without registering him at all.

"He has no idea what happened here," Victoria said, watching the policeman tend to the nervous horses. "They were en route to Fodelson to retrieve a prisoner to be released, but they were recalled to the jail instead. He can't see your face or mine, much less hold us in his mind. Quite suggestible, really."

"Young men too often are, especially when faced with a beautiful woman. Can we do the same to the other officer? And to Stewart?"

She turned to face him, a slow smile curving her lovely mouth.

Seeing that sweet expression, being the one to draw it out of her, meant more to McDuff than drawing his own next breath.

"The other policeman will be easy enough. We may have to work with less…delicacy when it comes to Superintendent Stewart."

"I have no objections to that. Is Father Hall all right?"

He staggered when he tried to turn, and he couldn't pretend he minded when Victoria slipped her arm around his waist to steady him. Father Hall still sat, but he was alert enough to speak to Jean and Father Ryerson.

Chief Inspector Wells and the Metropolitan policemen with him stood at a distance on either end of the street. They indeed kept the crowd from gathering, not watching the scene playing out around McDuff at all.

"Our friend Stewart landed rather a vicious kick to his chest, and he knocked his head on the cobbles. I imagine he'll be sore for a few days. Probably not as much as you will."

McDuff eased his arm round her shoulders, pleased that she didn't pull away.

"I hope he won't suffer near that much. And you, Victoria? Are you hurt?"

She laughed in that low, seductive manner that would have weakened his knees if they'd had enough strength to allow for it.

"Contrary to all my expectations for this long, long day, I'm perfectly fine. I may even recover from the shock of hearing of your arrest first thing this morning. And you, Mr. McDuff? Tell me how you are, and don't *dare* lie to me."

He shifted to bring them face to face and brushed back a loose curl of her hair.

"Standing here with you, free of that prison coach and handcuffs and Stewart's dubious mercies? It may take me longer than I'd like, but I'll mend. I'd love to be away from here, so I can learn whether Father Hall's fanciful tales of departing England for a friendlier climate have any basis in reality."

"Then let's get you off to the side and out of the way," Victoria said, with a bigger, more joyful smile. "Somewhere you can lean so you won't fall down. Jean and I will adjust the recollections of our two remaining witnesses as needed. Then I'll enlighten you as to the adventures in your near future. Assuming you don't have more interesting plans."

Rob smiled himself, leaning closer, and grateful when she lifted herself to meet him.

"I wouldn't miss any adventure that includes you, no matter how it may risk my life and limb."

Despite his bruised and battered state, her lips against his own carried the promise of paradise.

CHAPTER 89

Every time she visited with Rob, Victoria was amazed that time passing only seemed to make the bruising on his face more horrifying. The unseen injuries to his back and ribs and even his legs could only look worse. She did her best to accept his reassurances that he continued to feel better each time he saw her.

On the third day after his arrest and nighttime liberation, they gathered for an afternoon visit with Cheryl Mallory, Jean, and Father Hall in the residence across from the church.

The residence that had become Rob's temporary home until they could set out for Enceleas at the week's end. Between his dreadful struggles to walk up stairs and the fact that Superintendent Stewart had already been to Rob's boarding house, it only made sense.

Even after modifying Stewart's memory as much as they dared, neither Victoria or Jean felt confident he wouldn't recover the target he'd pursued so recently. All the magic either of them knew could only do so much to turn a person against their own will.

Father Hall had paid the lease current and gathered Rob's small collection of belongings, while explaining to a distraught Mrs. Richards that her favorite tenant wouldn't be returning. He'd taken great pains to convince her that she hadn't sent Rob to condemnation by allowing "that horrible vulture of a policeman" into her boarding house.

Victoria had initially been heartbroken and confused by Rob's quiet tears when he pulled out Michael's clothing. His explanation of keeping them all those years while never expecting Michael to need them again made perfect, painful sense.

Now Michael's clothes were packed away with Rob's, all awaiting departure for the Caribbean. Victoria's enchanted letters along with her father's most generous donations ensured Michael's timely release. He'd been an entirely pleasant patient at the asylum, after all, as had many others. Thanks in part to Victoria's tonics, now supplied to that facility at a deep discount.

Assurances of continued treatment by Father Sean Michaels and Dr. Jean Apréndia—along with shared information about any breakthroughs—soothed any worries of Michael McDuff's future.

Victoria hadn't yet begun the most difficult packing job of all, one she'd been pleasantly surprised to have Jean's eager offer of assistance with. Her secret workroom in her father's house would soon stand nearly empty, and spelled to be even more forgettable once she departed.

The only thing she meant to leave inside was a portion of

her collected money once all the jewelry from her fiancés sold for a healthy amount. She had no intention of returning to London with need of any sort of financial support. But having a fair reserve set aside—for herself or anyone who might someday need it—seemed prudent and wise.

She sat with Rob in Jean's study, once again unusually tidy. As it had been when Victoria used her influence to get Jean dismissed—then reinstated—to her research post in London. The same bishop who nearly sacked Father Hall had been charmed into agreeing to his rather abrupt transfer to Enceleas as well.

Correspondence with Cheryl's parents had worked too quickly for Victoria's taste, but she was relieved all the same. And Cheryl's buoyant spirits when they'd shared the news with her earlier proved infectious.

Not even dread for a winter ocean voyage could stand up to her youthful enthusiasm, and her deep and obvious relief. The Odd Society had expanded by one, with promise of another on the way.

Rob turned to her, one eyebrow raised in the spectacular arrangements of black and purple and red and yellow all over his face.

She admitted to herself and not yet to anyone else how much she enjoyed the loose-fitting cotton shirts he wore for his recovery, to save his ribs and back from the twist and strain of typical suits. Almost like one of her own nightgowns, and surely as scandalous as Jean's trousers outside this building.

The sapphire blue one he wore today suited him particularly well.

Victoria could just see the leather cord round his neck. Still holding her charm against his own anger nestled to his skin.

"I don't want you to imagine I'm complaining," he said, "but I am curious why Jean and Father Hall were both so eager to leave us alone and entirely unchaperoned just now."

Victoria gently kissed his cheek, then pulled two clear glass vials out of her pocket. Each full of slightly viscous colorless liquid topped off with a rough cork stopper. She dropped one into his upturned hand and closed his fingers around it.

"These, my dear Rob, are promises we made to each other a long time ago. Riding together in Father Hall's coach, making plans that turned out to be far more complicated than either of us could have imagined. Though perhaps we should have."

He held the vial between his thumb and forefinger, examining it against the light of the fire.

"The honesty charm. Are you asking me to tell you the truth? Or suggesting I ask it of you?"

"Either, if you like. Or both. Jean prepared these, not me. So we can both trust how well they work."

Rob turned his attention to her, and the intensity of his gaze warmed her more than the fire did. And in different places.

"So we've arrived at the more serious choices before us," he said. "I can hardly argue, seeing as we're about to set off on my first long sea voyage, and spend at least two months in each other's company."

Victoria laughed, and the way his expression changed from serious to light and happy brought joy to her heart.

"I won't pretend to predict how the voyage will go for you, certainly not this time of year. With luck and all the soothing herbs Jean and I have packed, you won't suffer overly much. But I hope to remain in Enceleas much longer than two months. I hope you'll want to stay there, too."

Rob winked. "What *will* your eager suitor Mr. Winston think of the affection between us?"

She resisted the urge to shove her elbow into his side, though he deserved it for that remark.

"I'll tell you what my parents said yesterday at dinner. My father believes Mr. Winston will be an excellent business partner for him and for me. I think Father is relieved to keep up his supply of good rum more than anything else. He and Mother both suspect the partnership between you and I will be a long and happy one."

He wrapped his fingers around the vial again, then leaned closer to her. As happened every time he kissed her, Victoria wished the heated contact would go further than their lips and the tentative explorations of their tongues.

Rob's smile and sigh when he drew back let her know he felt the same.

"I thank you for the offer, Victoria. And for the promise made and kept. My hope is that's only the beginning of promises fulfilled between us. As for me, I'll take a chance now as I did that day. I say we should each hold these for the future. And promise neither of us will refuse the other's request to use them."

A prickle of fear passed along Victoria's spine, one she immediately decided was a ghost of fiancés best left in her past.

Rob's suggestion made perfect sense from both their perspectives.

In fact, she wished she'd thought of it herself. Sitting beside him now, holding his hand, sharing any sort of activity with him—all of it felt like home to her. More than anything else had since she'd been forced to leave Enceleas behind so long ago.

And now she looked forward to the happy prospect of returning there with Rob by her side.

"That's a promise I'm happy to make, Rob. And one I wouldn't make with anyone but you."

ABOUT KARI

Kari Kilgore's wanderlust and imagination lead her all over the world on grand adventures. Her heart and family bring her home to her native Appalachian Mountains of Virginia. From that solid base and with the help of the ever-changing lens of her imagination, she brings those adventures to life in fiction.

If Kari ever obtains her Victorian greenhouse, she probably won't grow magical plants. At least not out in the open.

Kari writes fantasy, science fiction, romance, mystery, and contemporary fiction, and she's happiest when she surprises herself. She lives with her husband Jason A. Adams, various house critters, and wildlife they're better off not knowing more about.

The Confidential Adventure Club

For Kari's exclusive free After The End stories and deleted scenes, discounts, early pre-sale releases, adorable pet photos, and a whole lot more not available anywhere else, join us in The Club.

Hope to see you there!

www.KariKilgore.com

www.SpiralPublishing.net
www.ConfidentialAdventureClub.com

bookbub.com/authors/kari-kilgore
amazon.com/author/karikilgore
goodreads.com/karikilgore
facebook.com/kari.kilgore.1

ALSO BY KARI KILGORE

I hope you enjoyed *Independent by Means of Magic* as much as I enjoyed writing it. For more adventures with Victoria, McDuff, Jean, and Father Hall, be sure to check out the next title in The Odd Society, *Protected by Means of Magic.* And be on the lookout for more tales in this series!

For tales of fantasy, head over to www.KariKilgore.com/Fantasy. For Steampunk and Gaslamp, including more books about The Odd Society on the way, visit www.KariKilgore.com/Gaslamp. If you enjoy romantic suspense, stop by www.KariKilgore.com/RomanticSuspense.

Be the first to know about release dates and check out my fiction across almost every genre at www.KariKilgore.com.

The Odd Society:

Independent by Means of Magic

Protected by Means of Magic

The Storms of Future Past Series:

Dreaming the Storm

Joining the Storm

Into the Storm

Fighting the Storm

Storms of the Heart: A Storms of Future Past Romance

Storms of Future Past Books One through Four Collection

The Voices through Time Series:

Songs in the Mountain

Secrets in the Land

Sorrows in the Earth

Walking the Ghosts: A Voices through Time Novella

Dispatches from the Galaxy Stories:

Restricted Species

The Becalmed

The Garbage Belt

Plurapod Pathogen

The Changes Cascade

Novels:

Until Death

The Dream Thief

Hand Me Downs

Protecting Her Own

The Coffee Bomb and the Corporate Spy

The Great Gold Record Heist

Novellas:

Legacy of the Land

In the Pines

DNA Never Lies

The Box of Possibilities

Murder at the Fabulous Feline Emporium

Collections:

Fantastic Women: A Dark Fantasy Novella Trio

Fantastic Shorts: Volume 1

Fantastic Shorts: Volume 2

Dispatches from the Galaxy: A Space Opera Novella Trio

Fantastic Shorts: Volume 3

Escape into Romance: A Collection of Sweet Beginnings

Stepping Out of Reality: Short Spells of Appalachian Magic

Facing Down Extraordinary: A Series of Ordinary Heroes

Hacking Cybercrime: Dana Sanderson Short Mysteries

Investigations Beyond Belief: The Initial Adventures of Deb Powers

Passages in the Real World: Six Stories of Life's Transitions

Fantastic Side Trips: Side Characters Take Center Stage

A Kaleidoscope of Cat Tales

A Tapestry of Holiday Tales: Winter Adventures from the Odds and Endings Bookstore

Aunties Among Us: Five Tales of Fabulous Women

Four-Legged Heroes: When Pets Rescue People

Anthologies with Jason A. Adams:

Near Future Forward

Partners in Romance

Shadows Mountain Deep

Uncommon Holidays: A Different Side of the Season

Partnership in Crime: Six Journeys to Justice